"A great thriller that mixes science and philosophy.
It also evoked memories of the Khumbu region, where I have traveled
and seen the wonders of Everest. The author did a good job
revealing the character of the Nepalese."
Liz Wedderburn PhD
Glasgow University, Faculty of Science

"Give me good speculative fiction, like Harlan Ellison or
The Twilight Zone, any day. I would say *Everest Rising* falls
into this category. Kambic is a damned good writer and
has obviously done his homework."
John Harper, PhD
Pennsylvania Geological Survey, Retired

"*Everest Rising* is a thought-provoking tour-de-force,
packed with a kaleidoscope of brilliant images. Matt Kambic has
produced a modern classic, certain to keep readers on the edge of their seats."
Ken Gormley
New York Times bestselling author and educator

"I admire the devotion to all things environmental
and the clear messages put forth. The characters are well-developed
as are the overlapping complexities about our challenges regarding
technology, profit and human ambition."
Randy Gaul
Co-Creator, Production Designer
Zeke the Odd, the Next Great Maker movie

"Shades of *Jurassic Park*... Matt Kambic combines lean prose, vividly
imagined characters, and a dramatic Himalayan setting to render a story that
is as thought-provoking as it is gripping... you owe yourself this
fast-paced yet philosophically astute read."
Ben Wecht
Forensic science educator and co-author
Cause of Death and Grave Secrets

Everest Rising

Matt Kambic

Everest Rising

Copyright © 2021 by Matthew D. Kambic
All Rights Reserved

This edition published November 2021 by Chalk Hill Publishing
First edition published in 2016 by Science Thrillers Media

No part of this book may be used or reproduced in any manner
without written permission except for brief quotes in articles or reviews.

Everest Rising is a work of fiction. The characters, places, and events are
either the product of the author's imagination or they are used fictitiously.

The right of Matthew D. Kambic to be identified as the author
of this work is asserted.

Chalk Hill Publishing / Raglan New Zealand
ISBN 978-0-473-59502-9

Original cover photography by Rebecca A. Kambic

For more information:
www.mdkambic.com

*For Louetta Jo Anastasia
and Alison Barbara*

AWARDS

BEST FICTION

NEW ZEALAND MOUNTAIN FILM AND BOOK FESTIVAL

HONORABLE MENTION

NORTHERN CALIFORNIA PUBLISHERS & AUTHORS

Chapter One

Nepal

Mount Everest brooded.

At the summit, tattered flags held on in the tearing wind. A few tokens stood fast: a discarded oxygen tank; a scarf trapped under rock; a broken camera frozen in the ice.

Chomolungma, the goddess mother of the universe, preferred to be alone. The humans who had left these markers— so many of them traipsing to this pinnacle as a trophy for the ego— didn't please her.

The mountaintop stirred, the earth convulsed. A low rumble rose, drowning the rip of fluttering nylon. The oxygen tank rolled, disappearing over the edge. The summit flags bowed on their poles, their anchoring pins loosed. With a sullen crack, the rock opened.

The flags fell inward, swallowed.

* * *

John Bateman led four pack-laden men off the slopes. The team had landed early that morning, clambered off the plane, shouldered their gear, and headed north. Climbed just high enough to scout some prospects for their surveying camps. Not a grueling day, but sufficient. Decent enough for a start, Bateman thought. No point beating up everyone's legs. They'd be needing them.

He glanced behind at his New Zealand mates. Edwards still had a kick in his step. Muldoon was flagging. Dawa, their Sherpa guide, brought up the rear. His forehead, strapped to the load on his back, gleamed brown above his bright grin. He looked like he could go all day. Bateman wondered if the Sherpa ever frowned.

Dawa stopped, cupping a hand to his ear. "John-ji, did you hear?"

Bateman stopped. "What?"

"Up there, top of mountain." Dawa pointed.

"What?"

"Did you feel? A shake?"

The hikers halted.

"I didn't feel anything," said Bateman. "It's cold, Dawa. Let's keep it moving. A hot shower beckons."

"Bugger the shower. I want beer and a bed," said Muldoon, hands on hips.

"May be avalanche," said Dawa, shrugging, as they continued down the trail. "You say cold. Not cold, anyway!"

Bateman led them over a ledge, following the track across a field of broken rock. Dawa was right; the snow was soft, Bateman's steps mushy. It was not as cold as predicted, when the mission was blueprinted many months ago.

Edwards caught up to Bateman. "Should be there in less than an hour," he said.

"Did I tell you about the lodge, Eddie? New owners poshed it up," said Bateman.

"I should hope so. No denying we're upscale, right?" said Edwards.

"Original owners cut down trees, screwed up wells, didn't give a fig if anybody griped. Treated the locals like chattel, from what I heard."

"That's stupid," said Edwards.

"Guests woke up choking. Choppered in from Kathmandu without acclimatizing, right? Someone almost died."

"That's a tough sell."

"Then the earthquake. Owners gave up. Japanese, I think. They sold it."

"Now posh-i-fied," said Edwards, passing him on the trail.

"Some high rollers bought it. Hired New York architects. Cupertino engineers. Pressurized it. Oxygen masks if you want them, for a good night's sleep, can you believe it?"

"Guests can't pay the tab if they're dead," said Edwards.

"I'm not that fussy. If the shower is hot, I'll pay the tab," said Bateman.

"For me, a cold stout." Edwards looked back, grinning. "Might order one for you– if you're buyin'."

Bateman's laughter carried up the mountain. He smiled, relishing the thought of being dry, clean, and sated with hot soup and a mug of mead. He liked his team– mostly. Muldoon was a part-time grump, but he had a knack for managing field gear, from nailing down the quirkier aspects of high-altitude radio to keeping gas stoves alight. Edwards was a savvy surveyor and long-time associate. Dawa was Sherpa: an uncomplaining stalwart. He carried heavy things, made tea at dawn, and knew the mountains like the back of his gnarled hands.

The team descended, snow giving way to muddied earth and a well-tramped path. Before long, Bateman looked up to notice bright banners fluttering on silver poles. They walked over a rise and saw their destination: the Everest Vista Lodge. Bateman was grateful the expedition's bean-counters had been coerced to include a stay at this distinctively situated luxury hotel. They made their way under an elaborately carved arbor and entered the complex, navigating past gardens and ponds. It was not spring, but he could picture bright blossoms and flowing water in the well-manicured plots.

"Check it out, Johnny," said Edwards. He gestured at the indoor pool, glistening aqua, though no one seemed to be using it. Glass doors led to an outdoor deck where bar stools, folded sunshades, and silver tables glinted in the sun.

"Spiffy," said Bateman. "Never thought of packing togs." They reached the front doors, tall glass panels hung from rock pylons. Above, great eaves framed the word *Swagatum* chiseled in stone over the entryway. *Welcome* in Nepalese. Bateman hailed his crew. "Don't forget to wipe your feet."

The doors slid open– *whooossh*– venting pressurized air. A Nepalese from the lodge staff greeted them as the men shook the snow and mud from their boots. The staffer circled around behind to urge them inside. The pressurization depended on a closed system. Expensive, Bateman thought. Money was flowing out. The doors shut. *Whooossh.*

"Namaskar, sirs," greeted a bowing concierge. The low chatter of guests filled the lobby, which was replete with hanging ferns, plush couches against floor-to-ceiling windows, a huge fish tank, and a striking wood-hewn doorway to the dining area. Staffers tidied the floor the surveyors had muddied. Bateman walked to the check-in desk.

The Nepalese clerk bounced to attention. "Namaste, sir. Welcome to the Everest Vista Lodge." He bowed.

Bateman bowed in return; he thought the custom lovely. "Namaste. Reservations for four. John Bateman. Joint Nepalese-New Zealand Everest Surveying Commission."

"I have it, sir, thank you. Two nights, two rooms, party of four. Additional nights dependent on your fieldwork." The clerk programmed the electronic key cards, slid each card into a small envelope, and set them on the counter. "Rooms 27 and 28. Second floor. Anyone wish a mask for oxygen?"

"Yes, me," said Muldoon.

"Muldoon. You're kidding me," said Bateman. "Dawa, if he snores, shut off his air."

The clerk reached under the counter and brought out one of the masks. Juggling it awkwardly, he promptly lost his grip. The mask fell, hitting the floor with a clatter. *"Ke garne,"* said the clerk, palms spread. He picked up the mask, did a quick glance left and right, and handed it to Muldoon. Must have a fussy boss, thought Bateman.

"He dropped it," frowned Muldoon. "Nice work." He gave the mask a shake.

"Muldoon. It's hardly broken," said Edwards. "Ever hear of courtesy?"

"You feel that?" asked Dawa.

Bateman looked at him. He had yet to notice any kind of shudder. "Dawa. Again? That tea you drink all day must be spiked with caffeine. You need to cut back."

"Attach the mask to the air flow valve next to your bed," the clerk said. "Please be considerate and make certain the air flow is turned off when you don't require it."

"Let's shower," said Bateman. "So we can mingle with the aristocracy." He started towards the steps, with a last look at the fastidious-looking crowd in the lobby. At a lounge table, a middle-aged woman sat reading the *London Times*. She reached for the cup resting on the table and tipped it, spilling her tea.

"Goodness."

Bateman saw the front desk clerk reach under the counter, probably using a discreet button to hail staff to the lobby. Two showed, almost immediately.

"We will bring more tea. Stay and relax," said one, bowing towards the woman. She nodded back.

Bateman glanced at the fish tank, where exotic species drifted in the hyper-blue water, playing lazy hide and seek behind a plastic mountain and sunken pirate ship. A Statue of Liberty sat on its base with a tiny plastic figure of Charlton Heston. The water stirred. As Bateman watched, the Statue of Liberty tumbled, falling gently on its face.

Eugene, Oregon | United States

James Von Kamburg expected what was coming. That didn't make it easier. He heard his wife call to him. He heard the bathroom door close. A half minute later she walked into the room.

Maggie had auburn hair, dark jade eyes and a physique, James thought in more peaceable moments, that made him wish he could paint, with an undraped Maggie posing under pale light. But she was the artist. He was the geologist. And Chair, Department of Geophysics and Earth Sciences, the University of Oregon.

Painter and scientist shared the space. An easel with unpainted canvas was propped near a north-facing window. Maggie's taboret held a smattering of brushes, tubes, a jar of thinner, and gessoed panels. James sat before a large computer display at an oversized oak desk. Hidden under stacked exams, the wood surface was barely visible. In one corner, a ceramic sculpture of Mount St. Helens rose above the sea of paper.

James looked at the screen, but couldn't focus. He glanced at his wife, who stared at the floor, sliding her foot over the hardwood, heel to toe. The pregnancy test indicator hung from her fingers.

"It's negative," she stated.

James leaned across his desk, re-organizing the piles of student exams.

"Did you hear what I said?"

"Yes, I heard," he said.

"So…?"

"So." James turned. "All that hard work and you're still not pregnant."

Maggie pitched the indicator into the trash. "Thanks for understanding."

"Maggie."

"You can't take one afternoon to see a doctor."

James took off his glasses. "Nature will do its job, if we let it."

She picked up a small brush, dipped it into red paint, and jabbed at her canvas. "Nature's doing a job. On my biological clock. A year we've been at this. If you call this trying."

"Okay. I'll chuck everything and run out to see the fertility doctor. Dedicate my life to the study of making babies." James swiveled back and shoved at the exams.

Maggie walked over, brandishing the paint. "That was uncalled for. You haven't spent two hours finding out if you're fertile. See if this is all a waste of time."

James held back. They were escalating again. He took a breath. "Not to be technical, but didn't we try last night, right on schedule?"

"This isn't about a schedule." She dropped the brush into thinner. "Stop making it worse."

"Look. You keep conjuring up this rosy picture of bouncing babies while I'm watching fluorocarbons chew up the ozone layer. Just for starters. You want our children to grow up in this nightmare?"

She glared at him. "It's the apocalypse. The world's ending. Why bother." Her hands went to her neck, pushing at the roots of her hair. "The world doesn't roll over and play dead just because things aren't perfect. It's ridiculous."

Same discussion, different week. He couldn't find anything else to say.

"Breathable air and drinkable water– ridiculous? You think the future's shiny and bright." James reached across his desk and slid the monitor towards him. "The Earth's got its own ticking clock."

Maggie exhaled and walked to the window. A light rain drizzled grey down the glass.

Bzzzz.

Someone at the door. James walked over and placed a hand on Maggie's shoulder. "Bringing kids into this mess is not smart. It might actually be irresponsible. You don't want to see that. But it's true."

Bzzzz.

"And we don't dislike each other as much as this feels like," he said.

Bzzzz. The slight, half-second smile Maggie managed made him feel better. Neither knew this odd territory, being so far apart on such an important issue. Maggie retreated to a small coffee table and picked up a magazine. She dropped cross-legged onto the rug. James opened the door to see a UPS delivery driver.

"Yes?"

"Priority lettergram for Dr. James Von Kamburg."

"That's me."

"Sign here."

James signed, closed the door, tore open the lettergram, and picked up his glasses. "It's from Jared Griffon."

Maggie set the magazine on her lap and looked up at him, her eyes suddenly warming.

"What…?" asked James. Mentioning an old flame's name was not supposed to enable a surge of *happy.*

"Just weird. Had a dream Jared was in. A few nights ago."

"You're kidding," he said. "No you're not." He read out the letter. *"Dear Dr. Von Kamburg: Your research into the frontiers of geology and earth science is internationally renowned. We would be honored if you could join us at a media event, to take place at the corporate headquarters of Earthyield Incorporated, Vancouver, BC, where we will announce and elucidate a significant breakthrough in mineral resource synthesis. Et cetera, sincerely, Jared F. Griffon, C-E-O."*

"CEO. Rich, and about to be famous," Maggie said.

"Elucidate. That's Griffon. Preening." James leaned back in his chair. "Civil of him to invite me. I'm sure he hasn't forgotten I wasn't that fond of him." He looked over at his wife. "You were," he said.

"I gave him up for somebody else."

James nodded. "You did." He picked up the lettergram, scratching at the return address. "I saved you from a horrible fate. You could have ended up in wet, cold, Canada."

Bourn Institute of Seismic Research | Geneva, Switzerland

It was after midnight. Xavier Frauz, robed in a smoking jacket, warm socks and slippers, stepped softly down the spiral stairwell that connected his upstairs apartment with the research facility below. The director of the Bourn Institute flipped a switch. The newly installed LEDs faded on overhead. A cold, pale light illuminated the spacious lab area.

"Loathsome."

He switched the LEDs off, navigated to his desk by the dim glow of the security lights, and turned on a small lamp. The warm incandescent threw shadows across the wide room.

"Melodious."

Seismic sensors located around the world fed data to the Bourn Institute. An alert light had flashed on in his apartment, indicating that *significant data* were incoming. The night crew would normally get this, but he'd given everyone an extra few days off after the new year. He knew there were other organizations that would get the feed. The world's alert system was nothing if not watchful. He was checking from curiosity as much as responsibility.

Like the brass alarm clock he wound punctiliously every night, Frauz had shepherded much of his original research equipment into the modern world. He vowed to continue using it as long as it didn't "muck things up." He had connected the server-based telemetry to a paper printer, and as long as the ink held, he'd be able to see the data without powering on an electronic display. He rued the day when perfectly hale equipment, such as those precious few still-in-operation paper-fed seismographs, would be retired for more digital contrivances. He was doing his part to hold that day off. He smiled at the t*ick, tock, tack* of the venerable machine. *Music, that.* Though it might need a smidgen of lubricant.

Frauz shuffled over to a worktable, gently slid a few beakers out of the way, and felt around the top of a glass-paneled cabinet. "Drat." He moved to another table and groped behind a stack of reference manuals, and found what he was looking for. He tossed the tobacco pipe lightly in the air, clutched it as it fell, then gave it an affectionate shake. "That's better."

He struck a match and lit the pipe, the amber glow reflecting off his face. He was in his early fifties, with silver-black hair and a goatee. His nose was sharp, his eyes creased under their lids, his beard a tidy triangle of razored hairs.

His cheeks expanded as he savored the Red Burley blend, crowned with a deliberated exhale. He studied the feed, then tore off the paper. He grasped a lever and gently slid it to *Stop*. With a soft clatter the telemetry puttered, then ceased. He patted the machine, took a moment to burnish the metal with his sleeve, then sat and peered at the paper. Smoke from his pipe wandered into the hazy dimness.

"A disturbance in the Mohorovicic Discontinuity."

He leaned back and sent out a few distended smoke rings, holding the telemetry close. The Mohorovicic Discontinuity was the theoretical transition area between the Earth's crust and its mantle. It was a long way down and only barely discernible to measuring technologies. He rose and walked to a large freestanding relief globe of the Earth. He set his hand on the round surface and gave it a spin, abruptly stopping it at Asia. He ran his finger over the continent, alternately reviewing the paper and studying the globe.

"Somewhere under China, maybe, sixty to seventy kilometers." He looked at the paper again. "752 degrees centigrade. Has to be igneous, but should be hotter. No record of anything equivalent, that I recall."

On the globe, his fingers traced greater Asia, with Nepal in the center. The Himalayan terrain stood out in shadowy relief. A smoke ring from his pipe floated in, impacting and dispersing on Mt. Everest.

"Hmm. Might need another wad of Red."

Chapter Two

Earthyield Inc. | Vancouver, British Columbia

The Earthyield corporate park gleamed. James noted the finessed architecture and open, airy walkways, seeing his prize student's proclivities poured out as solid realities that shone in the sun. He remembered how Griffon clothed himself on road trips to the sun-blasted Dakota Badlands. His outfit was black jeans, designer-label outerwear, and never a hat, hard or otherwise. No bad hair days for Jared. He should have been a male model. As it was, he belied his own image as a pretty boy: hardworking, shrewd, and capable of flashing wild, interesting ideas with startling regularity. James had barely certified the diploma when Griffon disappeared into a sea of beckoning corporate offers.

Maggie and Jared: there was a story. James only got to know Maggie at the end of that relationship. She spoke well enough of Jared, but didn't say much. He didn't pry. Very occasionally, and quite uselessly he knew, he cultivated a suspicion that she had caught James on the rebound, as it was known. Yet he and Maggie had never been discontented. Until now.

He remembered the distraction of her presence, seated in the back of the left-most row in his classroom. Just the hair was enough. But he'd maintained his respectful, professorial, academic distance. The Earth

Science department's solar system orrery was mounted on a stand in that corner. At times she nudged her desk behind the dangling planets. Probably sketching.

She was a bright student, though she struggled with math. James asked another student in the same class if he might tutor her in calculus. Two quizzes later, she and the classmate, Jared Griffon, were companioned. A casual query from James about her friendship with Griffon was met with a curt– yet somehow not unfriendly– digression. Then, the following semester, the convenient accident of bumping into her outside the faculty lounge. Did James have a moment? She wanted to ask him about geology as a major. She was thinking of switching. The calculus class was daunting. They conferred briefly, professor and student, next to the water cooler.

By the end, he'd learned, in an aside about the challenges of math, that Jared's tutoring had not worked out. In fact, *they* had not worked out. Several Starbucks later, she and James had exchanged more than e-mail addresses.

From that point, their relationship had metamorphosed along the lines of a wonderful dream. Almost magically, really, James would remember, despite his genetically dismissive disposition towards unquantifiable phenomenon.

They burned the midnight oil, bright selves drawn together into a mutually generated flame of passion, and romance, and– unquantifiable as it was– love. They stayed after hours and researched her thesis. She dropped geology and changed her major to studio arts. He gave her a ring cast in neodymium and, when she said yes, shook off the notion of a half-life. They agreed it was a frothy amalgamation. The best kind of alchemy. Good years crystallized.

Things in the present were not that kind of fine. Sex, though no less physically satisfying (he would say) had taken on a clinical air. Pillow talk was ovulation and sperm health. Half asleep on sterile-feeling sheets, he labored through tormented dreams of new human life. His progeny would have to make a go of it on a planet that was gagging, near to choking. Progeny that might never arrive if he was infertile. Crisis for the marriage. Watershed for the world.

The planet was in the throes of suffering. The long-term effects of hosting humanity were taking her down, fume by contrail, run-off by overload, consumption by decimation. His own research felt more and more desperate. A year spent chasing the ultimately futile idea that the ocean's sediment might be a practical carbon sink. More recently a distressing discovery that the agricultural byproducts of biofuel production were starting to look as nasty as burnt coal. Solar might be the ticket, but the energy corporations were pit bulls, slavering teeth dug deep into fossil fuels. Then there were the red herrings. Last week, the Navy had announced that they'd soon be making fuel from seawater, with no greenhouse gas asterisk. In the fine print: 23,000 gallons of seawater to produce one gallon of fuel. No real answers in sight.

He, not only his wife, yearned to watch his own kids frolic with fireflies on overgrown front lawns, cavort in curbside rivers after a summer rain, and be lulled to sleep by his off-key lullabies. And why not more "greened-up" Von Kamburgs in the world, for heaven's sake?

It was asking too much. Bring them in and watch them suffer through the blistered future humanity was scripting. What kind of offer was that? Still, he loved Maggie. Whatever *love* meant– and he at least had useful inklings. There should be, would be, a way through. Elusive formulas, in marriage and profession, stalked his psyche.

So. Why *was* he in Vancouver?

Hoping, and also doubting, that Griffon's new take on synthesis could cut into the carbon fuels' ecotastrophe. Both he and Griffon understood that synthetic fuels could be engineered to discharge alternate, less harmful by-products than fossil fuels. Emissions might be lowered significantly, if Griffon was somewhere on the right track.

The sun went behind clouds. The colorful plaza took on a pallid cast.

James put a hand against the small of his back and thought of Maggie. Their issue with kids, they needed to find a way through, to dialog it into a workable place. The space between them was getting precarious. *Fate—would you mind intervening?* As long as fate landed on his side.

Carrying his flight bag, he made his way inside and approached the front desk, where a woman rose to greet him.

"Dr. Von Kamburg?"

James nodded.

"I'm Jill Collins. I'll take you to Jared's office. He's looking forward to seeing you."

"Thank you."

The elevator took them to an upper floor atrium. Collins opened a large, metal-sheened door and leaned in. "James Von Kamburg is here."

James walked in. Jared Griffon stood beside what James thought was an awful-looking desk. The granite face went straight to the floor, merging with the gloss of stone they walked on, like a monolith. Griffon's jet-black hair was coiffed to match. His face had changed, though, the callow student not there. He looks like a salesman, thought James.

Standing off to one side was a striking young woman, trim and meticulously fitted into black jeans. Her dark hair flashed blue highlights as she tracked the new visitor.

Griffon extended his hand to shake. "Professor Von Kamburg."

"Jared Griffon. You remind me of a student I once had." Griffon smiled and they shook hands with gusto.

"James, this is Leslie Finch, our executive VP." James and Finch shook.

"Leslie. Nice to meet you."

"Nice to meet you, doctor," she said, cocking her chin. "Would you like something to drink? Coffee, tea, water?"

"Coffee, thanks. Extra cream."

"Sugar?" asked Finch.

James shook his head. She had a nice mouth, and he stared a fraction too long appreciating it. She left the office as James settled himself into a plush chair. "It's been a while," he said. "That said, you still look like the student."

"I tell my staff I was a disciple of the century's most notorious rock doctor. Succeeded in spite of it," said Griffon.

James laughed. "We had some earnest discussions about synthesis."

"We did. You scribbled your maxim on a piece of scrap tin. I still have it. The tin *and* the scar."

"Ahh, right. How embarrassing. I shoved it at you and cut your knee. Did I apologize? It was all in a good cause."

Griffon, with no small sleight of hand, brought the tin out from somewhere under his desk. He held it out for James to read: *The increase in the internal energy of a system is equal to the amount of energy added to the system by matter flowing in and by heating, minus the amount lost by matter flowing out and in the form of work done by the system.*

"I believe we've addressed this, you and I, in a series of letters to editors. Wasn't technically new, or mine, Jared. I applied the Carnot cycle to synthetics in a definitive tome. Then got it journaled in four-color."

"You took basic enthalpy and used it to kill synthesis. Synthesis eats up your power and spits out a little pile of nothing. Your maxim made that the bottom line."

"Unless you skip some fundamental canon. You bending time and space? That would be news."

James managed an earnest smile. This annoyingly self-assured former student was sounding cocky. If Griffon had beaten this thing, he'd somehow hurdled Von Kamburg's maxim. It had been published and accorded the mantle of sound and authenticated science. James had been lauded across the discipline. He'd earned it, too, working to eliminate false starts in the climate war. Perhaps he was also getting cozy with his reputation as point man in the pursuit of Earth's greened-up future. There'd be academic blowback if it unraveled. But blowback was an acceptable footnote to the paradigm shift that could happen if Griffon was onto something big. Something that would make a difference.

Griffon was speaking.

"What was that again?" asked James.

"The press conference. Bells and whistles in two hours."

Finch returned with a steaming cup of coffee. "It's hot," she said. "Be careful."

"Thanks." James set it down on the small table next to him.

"Leslie and I have another idea we want to discuss with you, James," said Griffon. "We want you to join us."

James folded his hands under his beard.

"We've put together a new lab. New *kind* of lab, actually," Griffon continued.

"We think you should be running it," said Finch.

James laughed and looked at both of them. "I don't want to see it. Maggie won't leave Oregon."

"Your wife," said Finch. James nodded.

"I have prior experience with the Von Kamburg clan," said Griffon. "Maggie and I took classes together. Magnetic Fields and Basics of the Lithosphere, both taught by this man. How is she?" Griffon didn't wait for James to answer, turning to Finch. "Maggie and I were almost at the altar when the good professor peeked up from his books and forgot about his plate tectonics."

"At the altar?" said James. "You saw a few bad movies together and got thrown out of some study halls."

Griffon laughed. Finch frowned. James smiled, and took a sip of the coffee. This slightly disquieting bit of mutual history might be a sticking point. Maybe not, James thought, stealing a glance at Finch. Still, with matters of the heart it was hard to read anyone. Including, too often, yourself.

"Tell her I said hello. Tell her about sunny Vancouver," Griffon said.

"I'm not telling her a thing until I hear bells and see whistles," said James. "Or is it the other way around?"

* * *

Media types and other invitees packed themselves into the presentation hall, forcing some to stand along the rear wall. James had found a seat up in the back row, his preferred place at these things, where escape was quick and you didn't have to small talk. Pads and pens were handed out as gifts, each embossed with the slick little slate blue Earthyield logo. The pen refused to yield its slate blue ink; James was making circles on the slate blue-tinted notepaper to no avail.

He relished the small failure of the pen. It was envy. Not an unreasonable reaction to Griffon's success. But envy was mixed with pride; here was a successful student from a successful program that he'd administered. With the mentoring came a strange suffering. His graduates were a kind of offspring and he did a poor job of not caring about how each was using their talents. Owned their philosophies too readily. Didn't manage to coerce enough of them into seeing things through his greened spectacles.

At the front of the auditorium, resting atop a long curved table and shimmering under the glow of arc lamps, was a row of seven silver pellets. Two giant display screens appeared from slots in the ceiling and hummed their way into position. Griffon and Finch entered. Each lifted a microphone from its stand.

"Thank you for coming. Welcome to Earthyield," said Griffon. Then he waited a beat.

James could see Griffon gauging his audience. He half-expected canned applause to rise up out of hidden speakers. Or at least a glorious corporate musical anthem. Artificial orchestration designed to manipulate the all-too-ready human heart. It annoyed him that it could inspire.

Griffon pushed a button on the remote held in his palm. The display monitors lit up, flashing images of underground mining, gushing oil wells, and deep-cut quarries. In scenes and bar graphs a rush of data on worldwide industrial trends spun past. James was reminded how clichéd business videos had become.

Griffon spoke. "The home planet, taxed by the sheer abundance of humanity, requires more and more energy, demands more and more resources, and, as it stands, is not legislated in a way that might curb this risked-filled overreach. Mother Earth is our solitary home in space. We should strive to remind ourselves, both as stewards and guests, that our welcome here is conditional. In order to compensate, as a way of bringing balance, we've been focusing our efforts on a singular vision: to introduce synthetic alternatives that will take the place of the Earth's irreplaceable and diminishing natural resources."

James thought that particular screed was a bit over-the-top, politically speaking. Then again, Griffon was never one to be less than direct. To be fair, James would have agreed with his fundamental premise. Maybe the boy had found a higher calling after all.

"The vision is realized," said Leslie Finch. The room darkened. The music came up, loud. Preceded by copious lens flares, the Earthyield logo spawned into view. Finch's recorded voice narrated.

"Iron. One of nature's fundamental building blocks. Imagine taking an ounce of iron ore, extracting the pure iron, and replicating it to a thousand times its initial mass." The screens threw up charts forecasting world iron use and ore extractions, plus mining areas and remaining veins. The Finch narration continued.

"Coal. A fossil fuel that still provides a vast percentage of the world's energy needs. Imagine producing a synthetic coal that burns cleaner and requires no underground or mountaintop mining." Accompanying imagery gushed forth. "Magnesium. Aluminum. Platinum. Imagine a virtually endless supply of these minerals, produced synthetically.

Imagine the tremendous reduction in the cost of extracting, smelting, and delivering them. Imagine it happening now–" A pause. "Because it has."

The carbon-arc lamps pivoted to shine their light onto Griffon. "I'm proud to announce our Earthyield team has succeeded in accurately replicating virtually every major mineral known to science," he said.

A dramatic pause.

"We call it Synthium replication. S-y-n-t-h-i-u-m."

Another pause.

"The process is clean. It uses only water, oxygen, a small amount of the mineral one wishes to replicate, and a substitute mineral, such as abundant, inexpensive silicon, purified from silica sand, to provide the mass. There are few undesirable byproducts. And Synthium chambers can be built on site wherever they are needed." The monitors spelled out *Synthium*. The crowd stirred. James, in the back row, chewed on his pen, grinding plastic in his mouth.

"Synthium is a proprietary process, a new science, whose mechanisms and chemistries will remain undisclosed. Its benefits we're eager to share with the world," said Griffon.

A correspondent seated near James rose. "What about synthesizing gold?" he asked.

Someone else called out. "And diamonds?" A loud murmuring coursed through the auditorium.

Finch answered. "Yesterday, we invited select representatives from the world's governments to inspect and suggest regulation for our production warehouses. Precious gem and precious metal replication is not our goal. And won't be legal. We're not out to undermine the economy that will grow our business."

Griffon lifted a golf-ball-sized aluminum pellet from the table. He held it high. It gleamed under the arcs, the crowd craning necks for a better look. Two staff people brought out silver cartons and set them at either end of the front tables. Small, handsomely fabricated boxes were taken from the cartons and stacked.

"Each registered attendee will be given a sample produced in our Synthium forges, one of these aluminum pellets. At the end of the presentation, come to the front and find the silver box with your name on it. There's also a USB stick. You and your science editors can do a thorough exam. We'll be waiting to hear if you've experienced a metal this pure, in this form."

Another pause. "Our website has just been updated. Anything you can't find on the USB, you should be able to find there."

Griffon paused yet again. *He does know how to bask,* thought James.

"Now," Griffon said, "we're happy to take your questions."

A few listeners raised their hands, but forthcoming questions were drowned out as more and more attendees hustled to the podium to claim their boxes. Not wanting to miss out, the entire audience soon followed suit. The presentation was effectively concluded, short as it was.

Griffon and Finch were soon engaged with a scrum of media people. James shouldered his way forward to get near enough to Finch, then tapped her shoulder.

"Leslie– hey– congratulations."

She turned, nodding her acknowledgment.

"I need to see that lab," he said.

"There's a mountain of non-disclosures to sign," she said, turning back to the reporters.

Hmmm. Nice friendly cold shoulder there. He ducked away from the carbon-arc lamps and slipped out into the hall. A crop of skeptical media mavens was hard at their smart phones, forwarding the grand scope of Griffon's as-yet-to-be-proven vision.

The mad scramble of his home life and endless work responsibilities suddenly diminished. *Synthium. Could it be real?* The laws of physics were immutable. Conservation of energy was a lock Earthyield couldn't bypass. Yet he couldn't shake wondering exactly what Griffon had stumbled on.

He'd take the sample pellet back to Oregon. Somehow he'd make time to figure it out.

* * *

Griffon and Finch took the private elevator up to Griffon's office. Finch carried a small object she had wrapped haphazardly in white tissue. He'll want this, she thought. Then me.

They exited the elevator. Finch pressed a button on the wall. With a weighted *thunk* hidden electromagnets secured the entryways. In the office, a wall-mounted display monitored the crowd lingering in clamorous packs in the auditorium.

"They are buzzing," said Griffon.

"Come here," said Finch. She drew Griffon's arm around her and leaned in to find his mouth. They kissed, deep and long. Griffon pushed her away and looked at her. Smiling, he returned his eyes to the display. Finch tapped the object she carried against his sternum. "I got you something,"

Griffon leaned against his desk and took the gift. The tissue fell away to reveal a crystal globe. Set inside was the Earthyield logo cast in what looked like gold. Griffon held it up. "Feels good. I'm very partial to gold. Real gold, to be precise."

"Real gold? Precisely what is my salary?" said Finch.

They laughed. Griffon turned to watch the display again. He waved the globe in the air. "Von Kamburg's got to be stoked."

"We don't need him." She slid a hand behind his neck and tickled at the nape. "It's his wife you want hanging around."

"Don't be stupid. He might be able to crack it. The mystery at the center."

The monitor showed two media people jousting with each other, apparently arguing about the feasibility of Earthyield's claims. Griffon ran his hand down Finch's back and whispered in her ear.

"You're jealous. Forget him. Forget her. This is a moment to cherish." He pulled her to him, tongue and lips. They stumbled against the desk and she wriggled to free his tie. The globe rolled along the granite surface, stopping near the edge. They fumbled at each other's buttons and fell into Griffon's leather chair. Abruptly, the intercom chimed with two soft beeps. It was Jill Collins.

"Mr. Griffon, your visitor has arrived."

Griffon reached for the intercom with one free arm. "Five minutes." He switched off the intercom, extricated himself out from under Finch and stood, straightening his tie and jacket. He looked at Finch. "Fix your hair."

Finch let her chin drop to the surface of the desk, her lips pursed. The last few moments hadn't gone exactly as she'd hoped. This should be easy territory. Today was still good, though, in other ways. She rose to brush back any wrinkles in her clothing.

"Be extra nice to the gentleman. He's come a long way to see us," said Griffon. He pressed the *talk* button. "Collins. Send him in."

The door opened, revealing the folded, brown hands of a Buddhist monk, who stepped into the room. He wore a traditional crimson robe and open sandals. A pendant of polished bone hung from his neck. His dark Nepalese skin was creased with fine wrinkles, save for the smooth roundness of his shaven head. He bowed deeply.

"Welcome, Abbot Gaia," said Griffon.

"Namaste," replied the abbot

Chapter Three

Slopes of Mt. Everest

A plume of wind-driven mist spilled from the summit of the tallest mountain in the world. Down, down, thousands of feet, where the high amphitheatres ran out into vast, open bowls of cold beauty, a light snow was falling. On these snow-blanketed lower flanks, icicles dangled like fine crystal from the top of hanging cornices. Tiny globes of water fell from the tips of the icicles. The snow shouldn't have been, but was, melting.

There was a subtle, distinct shake. Some of the icicles broke and fell away, shattering like brittle glass and disappearing into shadows. In a few spots, tiny green shoots pushed their way up through the white crust, like newborns blinking in a first light.

*   *   *

The New Zealand surveying team was bivouacked at 17,000 feet– 5,181 meters– above sea level. Bateman preferred the use of "feet" as a unit of length. It added something regal to Everest's height: 29,035 *feet* vs. a mere 8,850 *meters.* Either way, he and his team were now at elevation, perched at a spot that wouldn't end up under an ocean even if the most

23

extreme climate change zealots were proven right and all of Antarctica's ice melted into water. His mountain climbing days behind him, it felt good to be standing where he was.

They had set up on a hillock a kilometer from Everest base camp. From this distance, the camp looked like a shanty-town, with collapsed and abandoned tents, cardboard and plastic debris, and trodden paths crisscrossing to small heaps of climbers' and trekkers' versions of landfills. But no people.

This was January, and the site was deserted, with climbing season months away. It was part of the reason for the time frame of their surveying mission. They preferred to work without the circus of base camp expeditions and Everest-gawking trekkers. The lower elevations still drew travelers throughout the year, but the mountain was left alone. Day temperatures were cold, but comfortable with plenty of sun. The nights were a different story, but his team would stay warm thanks to the tents Muldoon had requisitioned.

Bateman let his eyes travel up the astonishing ramparts to the summit of Everest. The juxtaposition of human junk with the magnificence of the mountain disturbed him. He shook his head, almost wanting to kneel, and thought about coming back someday to help remove these markers of humanity. If Everest could talk, she'd be saying *clean up after yourselves, for God's sake.*

A short field away was the sloped flat where the earthquake's deadliest avalanche had struck, killing climbers, trekkers, and Sherpa. Along with a propensity to generate rubbish, men bore a madness for tempting nature out here where control was a pretense. Nevertheless, he mourned the dead, and tipped the visor on his hood.

Enough reverie. Lifting his dark goggles, he looked down and tapped his boot. Rock, flat and solid.

This spot should work.

A good base for the equipment. From here the team could draw an accurate bead on Everest's summit. Every decade or so, the world's highest peak warranted a new survey. Science, and the world, liked to keep a meticulous watch over geology's highest showcase. Growing in millimeters from natural processes, shrinking from rock fall, or static, Everest's condition was news. Which is why they were here, though not quite exclusively.

He'd been asked also, in an oddly circumspect manner, to field-test a new piece of tech called the modal interferometer. It had been shipped to Kathmandu where they picked it up, primping in its dry-ice housing. It bore glass tubes, weighed too much, and had no display interface. Ridiculous for field tech. Newly designed equipment should be small, light, fast, consume less power and offer some novel advantage. This was an analog throwback. But the commission was insistent and Bateman was instructed to run a battery of trials after the surveying was complete.

A light wind grazed his cheekbones. As Dawa had noted, it was, oddly, not as cold as they'd prepared for. Everest shared latitudes with Tampa Bay, Florida, but the high elevation in the Khumbu meant one had to plan for anything and expect it to be freezing. Their expectation was not met. The January pre-monsoon season should have been colder. The men layered their clothing, insulating their body heat with goose down and hi-tech synthetics, protecting their faces under hoods and their hands inside gloves. Today, Bateman noted, all of them had unzipped their jackets and removed hats. Rivulets of chilled water slushed under their boots.

He came off the small rise and joined the team.

Edwards and Muldoon were fiddling with the switches on the mobile satellite dish. The dish was hard-wired to the theodolite, which was used to confirm elevation vectors. The theodolite looked like an over-wrought telescope, Bateman always thought, with its rotating twin-axis mounts and tripod base. With a bit of brass dressing, it could have passed for steam punk.

Dawa heated water over a portable stove, cupping his hands around the flame and tapping his foot. Bateman heard him softly humming. He walked over.

"It's warm. What happened to winter, Dawa?" Bateman said. "You have anything besides tea? What about juice? In the packs?"

"Juice in the food bin. Orange or cranberry. Sugar will rot your teeth. Tea is better. Or chips." Dawa smiled, and took a small bag from his pocket. He ripped off the top and slid a potato chip into his mouth. "The chips of potato," he said. Bateman was tickled by the Sherpa's affection for potato chips. Martin's brand potato chips, to be exact. *Made in Pennsylvania and a blessed land it must be,* he would tell Bateman, who had brought along a carton to augment their canned meals.

"You better ration those, Dawa," said Bateman, smiling back.

Muldoon wandered over. "D'ya have more?" Dawa shook his head. "Quit hiding them," said Muldoon, rummaging through the food bin. He located a cardboard box near the bottom and dragged it out.

"You crush them," said Dawa, standing.

Muldoon smirked, then ripped the box open. He pulled out a bag and dropped the box in the food bin. Dawa pulled the box back out, hugging it to his chest.

"Ike, show some manners, will you?" said Bateman.

Muldoon smirked again. Bateman shook his head; Muldoon could be so petty. He thought about saying something more authoritative, then decided against it, for now. He walked over to Edwards, who was peering intently at a small LED monitor. Edwards pressed his head against the theodolite's eyepiece, then looked again at the LED.

"This theodolite is cockeyed. Or I am." Edwards leaned back, rubbing both eyes. "Can't bloody be," he said. "Keeps saying the same thing."

"What's up, Eddie?" asked Bateman.

"Bloody hell. The mountain is bigger. I'm not sayin' it can't be a goof. It's either the theodolite, or I'm not calibrating correctly. This is not some slight margin for error we're talking about. I'm getting 8,872 meters. Could it be something with the satellite link? Are we connecting to bad telemetry?"

Muldoon came over. "We have a good lock on a good feed. You can check it yourself, boss," he said, gesturing to Bateman.

Bateman studied the read-outs, occasionally fussing with dials and switches. "Everything's online. Feed's clear." He moved to the theodolite, adjusted a few calipers and squinted through the eyepiece.

"Perhaps she wants to give us boot, as you say. Weary of *bideshi* crawling over her," Dawa said. "We give to Chomolungma our respect," he finished quietly. Bateman noted the Sherpa making a subtle bow toward the mountain.

"Choma– *what?*" asked Edwards.

"Chomolungma. The Sherpa name for Everest," said Bateman. "Eddie, calibrate this thing again. This doesn't make sense. Don't tell me about faulty tech. If we traveled five thousand miles with bad equipment, someone will catch it hot." He studied the surrounding peaks. "Take a reading from Lhotse."

"Good idea, Johnny. If Lhotse's reading is skewed we'll know it's the tech."

"Got to be something we're doing on the ground, though. The GPS data from the satellite can't be corrupt. Never happens," said Bateman. He turned to Muldoon. "Ike. Haul out the cospec. Connect the geodimeter. Pick up your trash." Muldoon looked slightly taken aback. Bateman pointed to the empty chip bag wafting away in the slight breeze.

Edwards slowly rotated the theodolite's lens, then squinted into the eyepiece. Bateman appreciated Edward's work ethic. He watched Edwards take a breath and hold it as he took additional readings from Mt. Everest's neighboring giant, Lohtse. Edwards planted his feet to get a solid stance as he focused on his summit target.

What happened next seemed both strange and somehow not. A single leafy shoot broke the snow's surface, unfurling its miniature fronds across the tip of Edwards's boot. Edwards shifted his weight and, with a step, unknowingly crushed the shoot.

Namche Bazar, Nepal | 20 miles southwest of Mt. Everest

Sherpani physician Maya Danheela stepped into the daylight, out through the door of the hut where she had just assisted with the delivery of female triplets. It would usually be cold, but the winter was playing tricks this year. She ran a cloth across her forehead. The slight wind felt good on her neck.

Three Buddhist monks, hoisting cloth bags, each sack brimming with vegetables and fruits, ambled up the dirt lane before her. *Three monks to pray for three newly-arrived souls,* she thought.

Maya liked the bustle here in Namche. Her western friends would call it a *vibe.* Namche Bazar was built into a steep mountainside, a strenuous two-week hike from Kathmandu, the only option for those who couldn't afford or didn't want to pay the high price for the flight to Syangboche. The village was on the trekking route to Everest's base camp and also the path that led to the Everest Vista Lodge. The lanes crowded up daily, locals jostling with the visitors who traveled here from everywhere on the planet.

Namche was primitive and modern, isolated and connected at the same time. Populated originally because it was a rare stretch of land that wasn't vertical, the town was pleasantly warm for much of the year, with soils that could be cultivated into crops for the Nepalese who had been here for centuries, and their animals. Soon after the region was identified as home to the tallest summit on Earth, and the mad mountaineering had taken hold, the outside world conspired to provide every amenity money might be spent on. Internet cafes, lodging, restaurants, outdoor gear stores, even a DVD rental shop. Currency flowed, cultures fused, a hospital was built and doctors were hired to staff it. Including Maya, who grew up here.

She liked to browse on Google Earth, and noted that from above Namche looked like brown and red dominoes that had fallen in a curling half-circle. And yes, Maya thought with a quiet laugh, she knew about Google and dominoes. East was become West.

Maya heard the newborns crying in chorus. She re-entered the hut to finish her tasks. The mother of the triplets watched as Maya gently washed the babies. The Sherpa family gathered around, grinning and chattering.

"Ma tapainlai bholi herna aunchu. Aramle basnus," said Maya. "I will be back tomorrow to see how you are doing. Rest."

In thanks, the mother reached out to grasp Maya's hand. Maya stroked the mother's arm, shouldered her pack, picked up her walking staff– hand-painted with red swirls, yellow flowers, and purple stars– and stooped out from under the low doorway. Squealing and baying blended with the infants' crying. A gaggle of children came racing around a corner, coursing past Maya. The last child did a full spin and stopped, panting.

"Maya come! See!"

Maya followed them to the back of the hut. A large sow wallowed in its pen, surrounded by twenty or so baby piglets. A few of the children made an effort to keep some distance, but their circle closed in on the animals. The older children clasped hands to create a barrier around the sow. Maya shook her head.

"Have you ever seen so many? Look at them, Maya!"

Maya stooped to pet one of the squealing piglets. The mother snorted an opinion. Maya caught the stare of its lidded eyes and stepped back. "Don't get close. Give mama some space to be with her babies." More children hurtled past, chasing a young boar up a dirt alley.

Maya stood to leave and looked skyward. Behind and above the racket of life in the village, Mt. Everest rose, white and seeming serene against the brilliant blue.

* * *

Passang would write a book. Or a blog, if they wouldn't publish his book. He found it amusing to ponder everything during the ten busy hours he waited on tables. Everything and anything that would take his mind from his duties. And, most especially, the boss. *You are wanting drama; this lodge has the drama.*

First chapter: *Everest Vista lovely place for guest. For employee, not so much. Low wage for staff helps make profit. Profit nice. Investors smile. But boss not smile. Boss is riddle. Guests a riddle, too. Guests pay lots and like to be spoiled. More rich, less happy. 'Bring me this. Get me that. Hurry up!'*

Maybe a book was too much work. A blog would be better.

Blog post: *Less hurry in morning. Not so good at noon when lunch crowds come. Today, trekking company bring many hungry walkers. Boss tell us good service mean big tip. Some people okay. Some people just air that is hot. Big tip pretty rare. Mostly Passang find leftover food, sitting there, with one sloppy bite to ruin it.*

There was a bang and swoosh and scurrying feet. The kitchen doors swung open, pushed by a large calloused hand with ugly rings on several fingers. It was the big boss, the overfed one, the dreadful Clarence Gault. Passang knew he was about to be lectured again, as Gault parked in the doorway, blocking a dish-laden busboy and a waiter with a tray full of steaming prawns. Prawns! *My favorite.*

"Don't make these people wait," said Gault, leaning his red face into Passang's. "They've come thousands of miles and paid big money. If a man wants the breakfast menu give him the goddamn breakfast menu!"

"Yes, Mr. Gault. I am apologize."

"You want this job? Are you taking the language classes? Learn the language, for God's sake." Without waiting for Passang's reply, and with a forceful push of the swinging doors, Gault marched back to the dining area, scattering several busboys.

Passang understood that Gault saw himself as a great mentor, feeding Western wisdom to the ignorant masses. He recalled one of Gault's oft-repeated mantras: "Don't give people a reason to be grumpy. For example: if you feel anything shake, don't ever say earthquake. Tell them it's trucks loading or the air pressure kicking in or whatever you think of to distract them. Earthquakes make bad impressions!"

There was wisdom, unchained. Passang laughed.

BLOG: *Lodge doing good business, recovering, here where great earthquake shook. Everest Vista built on high hill, not like buildings in valleys. After big earthquake, some villages in valley gone. Just gone. Don't tell guests, boss say. Guests should be happy, never mind quakes; and pampered, never mind behavior.*

Passang grabbed a breakfast menu and hurried into the dining area. He glided up quite smoothly (he thought) to the table of the tourist in question, a man with hair combed in great strands from the side of his head up and over the top in a bid to cover his mottled scalp. *Such a head.*

The man sat with his family, a wife and three bored-looking teens. The tourist is grumpy, thought Passang. I shall call him that: *Grumpy.* Grumpy smacked his lips and turned his head from side to side, like a bobble-head doll Passang had once seen. Passang stood with his back straight (as Gault liked) and offered the menu. He took a deep breath.

"Your breakfast menu, sir."

"About time. Thank you, thank you. Now can you bring me some Evian water before we order? It's listed right here. Evian. See it? Right here." A big finger covered the item.

"Evian water. At once." Passang trotted back to the kitchen. A quick look in the cooler revealed no Evian. He hustled to a storage area at the rear of the kitchen. There sat a cardboard case with empty plastic bottles, including two with Evian labels.

He peered out an interior window near the kitchen's back door, which led into the garage and loading area. A lodge van adorned with the Everest

Vista logo was parked there, its back doors partially open. Inside, Passang spied to his delight, rested several cartons of bottled water. The brand name, which he could just make out, read "Everpure."

BLOG: *I suck in breath. What I was about to do was not a thing of great wisdom.* Passang pushed the back door open, looked right and left, then hurried to the van. No one around to make a hash of his scheme. He opened one of the cartons and pulled out a single bottle. He closed the carton and shoved it under another carton. The missing bottle would not be noticed.

He stopped to take a closer look at the label: '*Everpure* ~ the drinking water sprung from Mount Everest'. What a good falsehood, he thought. Probably from glacier melt. Back in the kitchen, he uncapped an empty Evian bottle, and filled it with the Everpure water. He took a sniff; and hesitated. *A bit of a funny smell. Expensive water tastes different. Can't waste time. Gault and Grumpy are kin, both impatient.*

He re-capped the Evian bottle and hid the Everpure bottle inside his cloak, hanging near the rear exit. An inch of water remained, sloshing around in the plastic. Passang held the Evian bottle high as he bounced through the swinging doors and hurried back to the man. The man was squinting at an empty water glass, rotated in his chubby grip. He maneuvered it against the light shining in from the picture windows.

"Here is your water, sir. Evian water," said Passang. Speed and politeness were always recognized, always rewarded.

"This glass has water spots. You see 'em?" Grumpy grumped. He tilted the glass towards Passang. Passang pulled in his lower lip.

BLOG: *I did best to appear dutiful and remorseful.* Passang uncapped the bottle and began pouring the clear liquid into the held up glass. It looks okay, Passang thought. Clarence Gault will salute me.

"I guess this means you're not getting me a clean glass," said the man. The man's wife lowered her gaze. Passang finished pouring the water into the glass. He re-capped the bottle and stood up straight.

"Thank you," said the wife.

"I am back shortly to take your order," said Passang. He left the table, pausing at a wall near the swinging doorway. The man was holding the glass up and pointing at it. "What a knuckled-head," Passang muttered. He entered the kitchen, went to the back window and saw the lodge van pulling out of the garage. "I shall taste this expensive water."

He removed the cap from the Evian bottle to swig the remainder. And halted. Cheeks gone pale, he sniffed with concern at the bottle's opening. The unusual odor was keen and more pungent with each inhale. Not that it was horribly bad-tasting: it simply wasn't what Passang understood as the typical Westerner's idea of unsullied, contaminant-purged, drinking water. It tasted more like earth.

"Ah no." His sneakered feet motored, spinning past the sinks and stoves and dishwashers and cooks, taking him out again through the swinging doors to the dining room. The show will not be good, he thought. It happened as he watched and he could not prevent it. Grumpy wiped the edge of the glass with a napkin. He lifted the glass to his lips and slurped the water. He gagged, and spat the water out, chubby forearm smearing blubbering mouth. He put the glass down, then knocked it over, spilling the rest on the rug.

"What the hell is this? Sewer water? Managerrrrr!" Grumpy's wife lowered her face. BLOG: *Teenagers hide laugh. See father do this before.* Grumpy stood, spat again, and marched towards the hostess station. BLOG: *Job terminated.*

Passang shook. He'd never felt such a physical wrenching. He shouldered his way back through the swinging doors and found his cloak. He pitched the Evian bottle in the trash, grabbed his wrap, and with trembling fingers lifted his employee time card to swipe out. He felt the shape of the Everpure bottle under his cloak. The time card slipped, fluttering to the floor.

A waitress, Niwa, reached for the card. "Passang, what?"

"I poisoned him." Passang turned, tripping through the room to the rear entrance and out the door.

Blog entry: *blank.*

* * *

Passang raced down a path crisscrossed by gullies, one hand clutching the bottled water. He gulped for air, searching side to side for something that might calm. Dirt, mud, flies. Up another path, down a run of stone stairs. He flinched, nearly tripping when a wild hound bared pink gums. At last he saw it: the Himalayan Trust Hospital, a stone structure set up on a terrace. He reached the front doors, chest heaving.

"No breath," he panted. He opened the glass doors and entered the lobby, where a receptionist waited to receive clinic visitors. Many of the seated patients were visibly pregnant. He hurried past them, down a hallway to a separate nurse's station.

The nurse, Ralla, smiled up at him. She was a cousin of his neighbor. "Passang."

"Is Dr. Maya attending today?" he asked.

"What's wrong?"

"I am cooked."

He saw Ralla wince, then she called down the hall. "Dr. Maya, can you see someone?"

"I am here," came the answer. Ralla pointed. Passang caught his breath, and walked to Maya's door. It was open, the doctor perusing patient records. As if it contained a plague, Passang held the bottle outstretched in his fingers.

"Passang, hello," she smiled. "Shouldn't you be at your job?"

"Dr. Maya, a tourist at the lodge drank this water. Will he die?"

Maya stood, reaching to take the bottle. She sniffed, then pulled her face away. "Ugh. Where did you get this?"

"At the lodge. The tourist wished for Evian but we had none. In the garage, I found a van full with bottles. Spring water– for drinking. The label says. See it, Maya, *Everpure.* Khaane paani."

"It has a smell."

Passang clutched his neck. "I brought it to the tourist and poured it and he drank it. Then he gagged and shouted."

Maya brought the bottle up to her face. "Go back to the lodge. Tell your manager what happened. I will send word if there is a health concern. I don't think–"

"Clarence Gault. My job."

Maya sighed softly, and pushed her chair away from her desk. "It may be time to find other work, Passang."

Passang ran his hand through his hair, glanced over his shoulder.

Maya sniffed at the water again. "I don't know the odor." She picked up a small red-capped plastic vial, uncapped it, and poured some of the Everpure water into it. She walked to the nurse's station.

"Ralla, when will the next flight leave for Kathmandu?"

Last blog entry: *Bad Western curse word.*

Airborne over Oregon

James held the silver orb with his forefingers. He was on the flight home, a short breather he could use to ponder Synthium. He looked at his notes, scribed in green felt pen on a yellow legal pad.

Griffon would never have gone public with such fanfare unless manufacturing sustainability was guaranteed. There was no point in over-selling Synthium. It worked or it didn't. Still, the mystery confounded. Unless Earthyield had come up with some unconventional purification angle, it could not be a chemical process.

James had jotted down a phrase from the website.

The process is amazingly clean. It uses only water, oxygen, a small amount of the mineral one wishes to replicate, and a substitute mineral, such as silicon, purified from silica sand, to provide the mass. There are few undesirable byproducts.

They must have walked into something everyone had missed. What about a nuclear catalyst? The large hadron collider at CERN was hot on the trail of a new particle. Had Griffon found it?

James squirmed in his seat.

Hold it. *Yes.* The Synthium catalyst was probably a *transuranic*– an element artificially generated inside a fission reactor or particle accelerator. Griffon must've cross-bred some mixture of found nature with his own mutant chemistry. Messing around with God-stuff.

Okay. *What else?* What about a complementary bilateral atomic reaction present from creation? *Never registered. Underneath instrumentality. Earth's core might produce that, with ongoing radioactive decay.* Had Griffon somehow tapped it? Found a way to make it fizz when combined with some transuranic he'd test-tubed into existence? James would bet on it. *Something like the Higgs boson.*

If that was the case, Griffon's catalyst had the potential to scramble the molecular structure of everything on, under, or in the earth. Higgs turned out to be harmless but this– the Synthium catalyst– spewing alpha particles at a transuranic level, could be paradigm-shattering. If it wasn't controlled what would prevent it from catalyzing anything and everything? Fundamental stable compounds that life depended on might be altered.

Hold it. *No.* He was being an alarmist. The transuranic theory was more like science fiction. Plus, there's no way Griffon could have kept such a discovery under wraps. The catalyst would be showing up at the Bourn Institute, at CERN, and other places. If Griffon were merely exploiting a previously unknown catalyst he'd have no ability to maintain ownership. The man had invented it.

James was simply envious, again. He set his notes down and put his head in his hands. Griffon earned this through sweat and toil in his lab. He was certainly capable. Messing around inside a molecular, atomic, and chemical spectrum, you can conjure up all sorts of surprises.

In the end, and most importantly lest he forget, the potential to make up ground in the climate change wars trumped a wounded ego. And remained a principled reason to cheer every move his famous student pulled off.

Still. Did it have to be Griffon?

Southwest of Everest

From shelter, the monk herder was much further than he wanted. *I'm not cold. I'm warm, walking. But too far, too far. I want to get back. Find the beast before dark.*

The horizon flared orange, the mountains radiant in the glow from the last of the setting sun. Falling snow swirled in the air and melted on his face. The monk, dressed in a worn cloak, hobbled about in the uneven mud. From where he stood, he could no longer make out the low rock wall that marked the border of the monastery's grazing lands. The other side of that pasture was already a haul from the monastery. *Find the beast.*

The herd should be in the shelter by now, their grazing finished for the day. But one yak was missing, its tracks wandering across the muck and up the rock-riddled slope. It had meandered out, as the yaks sometimes managed to do, searching for the proverbial greener grass. It was winter; there wasn't much of anything growing and some of the bolder beasts took it upon themselves to find something better than dried silage. *This is well beyond where the grasses grow. Why would Balloosh stray like this?*

Under the robe, sweat rolled down the monk's skin. He grappled at the cord around his waist, loosening it. He wiped his brow and pulled at the cloth, struggling to extract his arms from the sleeves. Free, he bundled the cloak into a ball and shoved it into a burlap sack. He sat down and gulped at the night air. He cupped his hands around his mouth.

"Balloosh. Ballooooosh!" His cries returned as echoes out of the gray. "You devil."

The monk rose on sore feet and took a few cautious steps. Odd, he thought; berry bushes were blossoming, through a scree of broken stone and ice. He peered more closely. A number of the berries were not only nearly ripe (very early this season) but picked over, chewed, and half-eaten. Balloosh had wandered up the hillside chasing fresh fruits. *Can't blame it, accursed beast.*

The mountainside loomed abruptly, a steep rock wall, patched with frozen snow. Sporadic beds of the same berry bush sprouted from the face. Balloosh can't climb this wall, he thought. But the yak's hoof prints continued, picking a way up and around.

"Ballooooooosh! Come out you hairy mass. I want to go home." The monk followed the tracks, sometimes on hands and knees. He stopped again to cup his hands around his mouth and yell. And saw something.

He squinted to focus. Something above him. A structure. He tucked his hands into his underarms to quell a shiver. Up the slope, several meters ahead, he glimpsed what appeared to be a tower of metal. The fog and fading light prevented a clear view. He could only see the top; the base of the thing must have been set back near the edge of a flat. A dark, menacing thing, it rose as a bizarre spectral shape out of place on the mountain. It looked like the poles he had seen lining the streets in Kathmandu, with their mess of wires and broken lights. Now one of these poles was looming like a bad dream above his pastures. He would use the house axe and chop its roots.

"Arooghhh." The bellow of his yak broke the stillness. The beast stepped its way fastidiously over boulders scattered not far below the tower. The monk knew that the yak liked these berries. Here, she had them all to herself. Casting sidelong glances at the tower, the monk scrambled towards the animal. The ditches were wet and handholds scarce. His sandals were muddy and the ground slimy.

"Come here, ass." The yak let out another bellow, followed by a prolonged low octave burp. The monk reached the animal and took firm hold of the rope attached to its neck collar. The man and the animal, more reluctantly, moved down the slopes away from the tower. The monk turned for a final sighting of the odd metal structure, which had no place here and shouldn't be here and neither should the berries be here and last of all his yak shouldn't.

"Ah, no!" A missed step. He felt his ankle fold and he crumpled, landing on his bottom in the wet sludge. He rocked and groaned, holding his ankle with one hand and gripping the yak tether with the other.

"It hurts, it hurts." He bit his tongue to hold the curse words he had learned from his uncle. The initial stab of pain subsided as he took long gulps of air. He leaned over to rub the flesh swelling above his sandaled foot. He put a hand on the yak, its nostrils sniffing at the end of its long neck, broad teeth slathered with purple.

"Balloosh. You will be ornamental. Stuffed for the walls." The yak licked his face. *A good yak.* The sweet disgust of its breath and the sandpaper lick of its tongue, nature had given. The yak was innocent. The monk pulled himself up, mounted the yak gingerly, and prompted it to take slow steps down the mountainside.

* * *

Mr. Grace watched the herder and yak shuffle away, shapeless forms floating on nimble hooves. If he calculated correctly, the monk was now distant enough that he wouldn't be able to see them, three figures materializing out of the murk. Cloaked in dark outerwear, with masks and headgear, their faces were as featureless as the gloom around them.

The monk wanted his warm home, and with the night closing, he would hurry to get there. Still, Mr. Grace was concerned by how far afield they had come, man and stock. It could develop into a problem. For now, it was a one-off event he guessed would not raise alarms. His men were not spotted. A strange tower imagined by one monk herder– if he saw it at all– would be interpreted as an invention of an over-wrought imagination. Gault's drilling station could remain in place. But as a precaution, they would stand down for the night.

"He tripped over his own robe," said Yates.

"He saw the tower," said Spencer.

"That herder doesn't have a clue what he saw. How could he?" said Yates.

"Lower your voices," said Mr. Grace. "The monk didn't spot us in the mist." He crouched near the tower base and using a spanner, began loosening bolts. "We will do something if it becomes necessary."

"What do you mean *do something?*" asked Yates.

He looked at them, facemask rimed in ice. "Take it down."

Chapter Four

Eugene, Oregon | United States

James watched as Maggie studied the job description. Her hands looked clammy as they turned the pages.

She and James sat on the back steps, jackets and hats on to insulate against the damp winds blowing from the north. The property behind their yard transitioned into a wooded lot, where thickets of trees hid the clutter of a new four-lane being built on the other side. Under a somber roof of overcast sky, the grass looked more grey than green. Dead leaves rustled against the bottom step, gathering, then scattering in the gusts.

"It's a lot of money," said James. He stood and put his hands in his pockets. "For me it's more about what they're doing to reverse the pillaging. I'd be in the thick of the battle instead of hanging around the sidelines. You know the false leads I've chased in the last three years."

Maggie tugged off her woolen cap, pulled her hair to the top of her head, and replaced the hat over the tangle of auburn. "Yeah. I do know," she said. "It's a good offer. I know you'd like to do more for… Mother Earth. On the con side, we have Jared Griffon as your boss, we have goodbye house, goodbye Eugene, we have a bigger workload for you. Really, a mess."

James walked towards the trees. Brown shadows, black branches, and out beyond them, bright snatches of dirty orange and greasy white where road-making machinery was parked for the weekend. Oregon overflowed with striking scenery. Man had a way of mucking up the picture.

Maggie raised her voice against the gusting wind. "The gallery pieces are starting to sell. I have the show in April. Seventeen acrylics."

He walked back. "Keep painting. I love your painting." He looked out at the yellow skies. "The university might agree to a sabbatical. Jared might consider a consulting role. I could get up there a couple months and you can hold the fort here. You paint and I check things out."

"You could," said Maggie, puckering as if to spit.

"They're on to a big thing, but something's missing. Ingredient or formula or understanding, I'm not sure exactly what. Something that makes the model unsustainable. They have bucks, they have backing. The laboratory alone is a piece of work. I didn't see much, but the glimpses I had certainly made an impression." He had a recollection of Leslie Finch and the blue highlights glinting off her hair, as if she was in that impeccably clean research lab working under smart illumination and immersed in clinical secrets. "The samples are spot-on amazing. I was anticipating a pivotal flaw. Part of me was hoping that, to be honest. Green messiah complex."

He expected her smile. No smile.

She fiddled with a bootlace and cradled her heel. "I need to get these fixed if we ever hike somewhere."

"I had to sign non-disclosures and didn't really get the full picture," he said. "I'll say this: if Synthium is everything Jared says it is we might pull greenhouse gas emissions down to pre-nineties levels."

"Why does he need you?"

"To dissect the catalyst at the center of the reaction. At some elemental level, he doesn't know what he's generating. It's like making Coke without knowing the recipe."

She planted both heels in the dirt and stood up. "I don't want to go."

"So that's it," said James. "We have a thing we used to care about called compromise. Are you done, is this wrapped, or should I wait for some sign that you'll at least talk about it?"

"I don't want you to go. There's the discussion, okay?" She walked towards the edge of their property, where the neighbor's house was hidden behind a copse of hemlocks. James watched her, then walked up the back steps to their kitchen and reached for the door handle.

"Jim." She walked towards him. "I'm being unfair. Let's find fair."

A siren wailed briefly. The wind fluttered through bare branches. They sat down on the steps again, hips touching through the denim.

"Let's do this," he said. "I'll call Jared and tell him I need time to make a decision. Then I'll make an appointment to see the doc in the next two weeks. If my fertility is the issue we'll see what we can do about it. Once we know something, we can see if you want to head north. So thing one won't decide thing two. Thing one will be... thing one."

She looked down and brought her hand to her brow. "That's all I've been asking for."

Geophysics-Earth Sciences Department
University of Oregon | Eugene, Oregon

On the third floor of the University of Oregon's Department of Geophysics and Earth Sciences, thin-walled lab rooms and bleached-white corridors surrounded a large, round open area affectionately known as "the quarry." James had spent a fair segment of his academic life here. It was a second home where he could operate in autonomy, without a second thought. Students and graduate assistants busied themselves at the lab tables, pushed up against the outer walls, where coffee spills were as evident as rock samples. In the middle was the quarry's semi-famous circular table. Scarred with stains and divots, it spoke to steady use and good yields. *Nights rocking at the round table.* Yet, he was beginning to feel as though both the place and he could use a new coat of paint.

James and his department co-chair Basil Frew had just arrived. Basil, beanpole lanky with a wisp of a beard and tousled brown hair, was the youngest tenured professor at the University. His only pair of blue jeans, possibly his only pair of pants, sported a Greenpeace patch over a back pocket. He was busily flipping through pages of a stapled document. *My left-leaning right-hand man,* James murmured to himself.

They'd been joined by an earth science professor from Nepal, Dr. Tensing Spa. Spa wore a rumpled tweed jacket, looked out quizzically through bent wire-rim glasses, and took short steps in purple sneakers as he circled the table.

In a small vial, Spa carried a sample of liquid. It was water, apparently a commercial brand called Everpure, acquired by a Dr. Danheela, a physician in rural Nepal, and forwarded to Kathmandu. After a series of tests that mystified its reviewing team of hydrologists, the sample was forwarded to the University of Oregon, hand-delivered by Dr. Spa.

"Dr. Spa," said James, "your report says the water shows traces of mantle. The Earth's mantle is one hundred and seventy miles down. How can you know?"

"It's speculation. Nothing wrong with speculation."

"We need proof," said James. "Does it resemble anything you recognize? Maybe a composite congealed from deeper sources by normal processes?"

Spa continued his saunter around the table. "We tested it thoroughly. First for medical reasons. The water came from a river that is used reliably by the villages of the Khumbu, where it originates. The doctor forwarded it because a man had ingested a small portion and reacted. There was concern for his well-being."

"And?"

"And it smelled funny."

"And?"

"We identified no particular biohazard from the initial dissection. The funny smell bothered someone in the lab at Kathmandu. The electron microscope suggested the presence of kimberlite nodules. Olivine and pyroxene-based. You know of them, I'm sure. Thrown up from ancient volcanoes. As close as we have come to getting mantle to study. Then we did mass spectrometry. The sample registered more, rather than less, unusual specifications."

Spa halted and handed the vial to James. James brought it up to his face and shook it. "Huh," was all he could manage.

"This is a mutation, for lack of a better word," said Spa. "A diffuse peridotite granularity formed from igneous and metamorphic material. We can't identify the chemistry. The Kathmandu facilities have not fully recovered since the earthquake. We thought it best to forward the sample here, where your equipment is maximized."

"I don't know that I'd call it maximized," said Frew, with a wry smile.

"Mantle rock," said James.

Spa continued. "It's dissolved into microscopic crystals, one might say, that aren't technically solid. They're manifesting pliable and permeable. Maintaining characteristics that would be common under the enormous pressures at depth. At the surface this should be solid. It's very mystifying to witness. You'll have to see it for yourselves. I still don't believe it. I understand the requirement for proof."

James looked over at Frew.

"We are also getting traces, possibly, of ringwoodite and ferropericlase," said Spa.

James looked at Frew again, who raised his eyebrows. These minerals were very deep and very rare. James began dragging out maps, charts and diagrams from slots built in below the table surface. Geology department staffers and students began to gather. Spa slid the large color maps about until he found a map showing the Khumbu region of Nepal. He placed his finger on a rectangle representing the Everest Vista Lodge.

"It's right here." Spa seemed to react to the gathering of geologists. He spoke louder. "Today at noon, a report came in from the Bourn Institute in Switzerland. They've been tracking magnetic and gravitational anomalies over the last several weeks. They think a break has occurred in the Mohorovicic– where the mantle meets the crust. Directly beneath Everest." He held up the vial. "This water sample comes from a source not far from Everest. We think it may carry trace elements from the mantle."

"Dr. Spa," said James in a lowered voice, as he looked around at the wide-eyed gathering. "Let's kill the drama until we have more of what we like to call *facts.*"

Spa tapped the vial against the map on the area delineating Everest's summit, then crossed his arms looking slightly offended. "Is accepting not the beginning of knowing? One must sometimes– how do you say it– take a leap."

"Substance, facts, data," said James. "It's a major subduction zone. The South Tibetan Detachment. We should start from there."

Frew lifted his eyes from the report. "But, VK. Volcanic activity is also a legitimate assumption. Spa's readings don't say it. Never seen this."

"What is VK?" asked Spa.

"Basil's abbreviation for me," said James.

Spa looked briefly over the rim of his glasses, then continued. "Seismic activity, the water sample, the Mohorovicic report from Bourn. When the planets align you pay attention. I'm to brief representatives of His Majesty's Government in Nepal later today."

James's office manager entered, carrying a typed message. James noted the unusual urgency in her voice. "Professor Von Kamburg, this just came in. It's from a New Zealand crew. They're in Nepal surveying Mt. Everest."

James read the message to himself and looked up to see that everyone else was expecting to hear it.

"The message is from Dr. John Bateman. His team is on Everest conducting a survey with state-of-the-practice technology. They're commissioned to produce the most precise-ever readings of the height of the mountain."

He paused to catch his breath.

"We are on-site surveying Mt. Everest, based out of the Everest Vista Lodge. We've completed several excursions and established line-of-site and GPS triangulation of the mountain. 29,035 ft. is the internationally recognized height from the survey done in 1999."

James paused for another breath and continued reading.

"Mount Everest is rising. Our team confirmed a reading of 29,106.7 ft. A gain of 71.7 ft. in elevation. Our team is standing by and will continuing monitoring the situation. We expect a more comprehensive mobilization of resources should begin as soon as possible. Please let us know your plans. At this time in our estimation and with the technology we have on hand we do not anticipate a significant geological event is pending. We can tell you we are very surprised. Yours, John Bateman."

James looked up at the faces around him. They looked as bewildered as he. Spa squinted out through his lenses and nodded.

The office manager spoke up again. "There's also stuff happening at the seismograph that I was told you should see."

The three men headed down a hallway to a separate lab office. Lettering on the glass doorway read backwards: *'HpargomsieS'*. Someone had taped a scrawled note below: *'Seise This!'* The equipment inside, though all too typical of the department, Frew would intone, was 'well-loved', if reasonably functional.

Other geology department staff were crowded around the seismograph, which clattered away, scribbling disturbed-looking lines. Frew tore a section from its print-out and held it up for James. "More wild stuff," he said. "Ever seen S-waves like this? Pretty bizarro, VK."

"What are the Swiss getting?" asked James.

Frew fetched another report and held it at arm's length, like a scroll. "Magnetic field insanity. The surveyors must be freaking."

"Any possibility of a volcano?" asked a staffer.

"There's no evidence. Inland volcanoes are rare in Asia. They're rare everywhere," said James. "My inclination is we're seeing accelerated orogeny: mountain-building. Tectonic stuff that would be unprecedented." He exhaled and looked at Spa, then Frew. "Basil, let's go to your office. I want to make a few calls and you can do a couple searches."

They marched to Frew's crammed office. Spa turned to James. "His Majesty's Government has commissioned a task force to study this strange confluence of occurrences. The news of the mountain's elevation readings only adds to the need. The Right Honourable President Ram asked me to find a qualified individual to organize and lead an expedition to Everest. The person best suited for the task at hand. I informed the President I had found him. We wish to see if you agree." He removed his glasses. "You."

James pointed at his own chest.

Spa nodded. "Are you willing?"

"What's he thinking– your President? Is there a plan?"

"President Ram does not believe these occurrences represent a threat. He believes it is a public relations opportunity and a possible occasion for international funding to flow into Nepal. He is my relative-in-law, you should realize, thrice removed; the President of Nepal, that is."

Frew laughed.

"Do not take his Majesty the President for a stooge," said Spa. "He can have you put in a jail cell for many years."

Frew rolled his eyes. "You can tell your royal bro-in-law we won't be lining his pockets anytime soon. Tell him we're in academia. That ought to get a laugh."

James folded his hands. "I'm very busy here, Tensing. I'm at the start of a semester, I've got research I'm responsible for. As chair, I can't pack up at a moment's notice. I'll help, but there's no way I can be on-site. And just to be clear, you are not going to get money. You are going to spend money. A lot to equip and send a team."

Spa sat. "I regret this and apologize. I was instructed to deliver the funding concept at the outset of the conversation. In honesty, I recommended against it. He is sometimes..." Spa didn't finished. "Is there an office where I can obtain privacy?"

"Follow me," said James.

*   *   *

James folded himself into the passenger's seat of Frew's rusted VW Beetle, a vehicle so stickered it was hard to see the paint. *Grateful for the Dead, Choose Choice,* and *Flog U* were just a few of the notable exhortations. The car sputtered away from the curb, Frew bellowing merrily, "...we're splittin' Eugene, baby, and goin' to Kat-man-dooo..."

"We're not going to Kathmandu," said James, as they made time through the back streets of Eugene.

"But we are," said Frew. He spun the wheel, rolling onto the tree-lined lane where the Von Kamburgs resided.

"Look, Basil. I don't know if he's Spa's brother-in-law or not, but coming up with a quarter million in cold cash, that quick, strikes me–"

"–as fiscally improbable, I know," said Frew. "Then Spa name-dropped Senator Bennington." Frew grinned at him. "Do you believe he and Bennington have ties to the same committees? Unceasing wonders never cease."

"We won't have much time to dig up people. The Geological Survey's running some names for me. Oh, I forgot to tell you, the UN checked in. Somebody over there is mobilizing a list: equipment, air services, ground transport, lodging."

"I'm gonna be famous on YouTube, live-streaming from base camp."

"No you're not." James looked across at his beaming cohort. Hard not to like the guy. Or kid. "If Spa has a million I've gotta bite. As long as I get the portion for climate R&D that he offered. You saw him sign the document."

"Gosh damn, VK. You and climate change are bedfellows. Is Maggie jealous?"

James leaned back to rest his head against the seat. A slight ache coiled up behind his eyes and he shut them. "No media contact, you got that?" James said. "It's tricky with Everest straddling China and Nepal. Washington wants at least one Chinese geologist. You need to get on that."

"I will make it happen."

The VW pulled up to the Von Kamburg home. "Call me, not the *New York Times,*" said James, snatching his briefcase from the back. He stepped back as the car pulled away, tailpipe belching blue. Frew drove off, tinny honks sounding from his tinny horn, "...Kat-man-dooo... that's where we're goin' to..."

James walked in the front door. Maggie was sitting at the computer, the light from the big screen playing off her lovely hair.

She looked over her shoulder. "Hello, hub."

He moved behind her and crouched, telescoping his arms around her waist. Thin fabric covered her breasts, sheer against her warm skin. He wove his hands between the buttons of her shirt and set his face against her back.

"Mmmm," she murmured. An uncomplicated yearning bloomed in him, that they could simply fuse. After a moment, he leaned around to kiss her. She reached around to touch his face. "Soft beard for an old relic."

He pulled her up. "Want an apple?"

In the dimly lit kitchen, they took seats at the small table. Newspapers, a vase of dried flowers, scratch paper and pencils were scattered on it. In the middle was a bowl of apples. "I might have to go to Nepal."

"What's going on?"

"Mount Everest is rising."

"What does that mean?"

"A surveying team is there from New Zealand. They confirmed it. It's higher than it's supposed to be. Maybe a glitch in the equipment. Or data interpreted incorrectly."

"They asked for you?"

"His Royal Highness did. He's Nepal's head guy– their version of President. Mostly because of Tensing Spa, the professor from Kathmandu. He's worked with Charles Bennington, the Virginia Senator. Washington, China, India and New Zealand are involved also. Everest is complicated when it comes to politics; the ridgelines delineate national borders. We were told China won't sanction any false steps that could be seen as military."

"Is it safe?"

"Probably, mostly, maybe." He ran a hand through his hair. "They want a team. Earth science people. Figure out what's happening. Don't know how long it will take."

She looked down and then up. "What about the offer from Jared?"

"He's waiting for me to get back to him. If I go to Everest, I won't be able to tell him why or where I'll be. At least yet." Maggie took an apple from the bowl and cradled it. She scratched at the peel. Apple juice trickled down her arm, like long amber tears. "It's not a sure thing," he said. "Getting very probable though." James reached to wipe the juice from Maggie's arm. "You can come," he said.

Maggie looked up, her eyes moist.

"We don't have to be apart," said James. Maggie waved the apple in front of her mouth and took a bite.

"I'll get us some decent lodging. White sheets, low light, your body, my body. Who knows."

She rolled her chair away from the table and stared at the ceiling.

"Crazy life. Someone should be accountable."

"It'll get crazier," he said.

She picked up a pencil and shoved it in and out of the apple, then threw the fruit in the trashcan. "I'll be in the way."

"You won't be in the way."

"I don't want to be so far apart." She managed a tepid smile and looked up. "I could paint."

"We'll get to the fertility doctor as soon as we get back. I haven't forgotten," said James. He smiled. "Hey. A scenery change might do more than any doctor. Something in the Nepalese water, you know?" The smile moved into her eyes. James studied her forehead, the curve of her cheekbones, her lips. The quiet bloom of understanding that rested in the center of who they were— or had been— had a foothold, again.

She wielded the sharp pencil point in front of his face. "Nepal."

She led James into the studio and sat down at his computer. She browsed back through a number of websites until she found the one she wanted. She punched in a user name and password. She typed in "Earthyield."

"This site reviews and rates companies for job seekers. Of course they won't let you see anything useful till they get your credit card. I was debating whether to pay the fee to check out Earthyield. I yielded." She turned and smiled at him, amused at her own humor.

She clicked the link for *Global Assets*. A list appeared. "There isn't much. There was this." She scrolled down through offices and holdings in Vancouver, Brazil and Africa until she reached Nepal. "Check it out." She rested her finger lightly against the screen.

Khumjung, Nepal. Everest Vista Lodge. Luxury Resort Hotel, 18 Miles from Mount Everest. Owned and managed by Earthyield, Inc.

* * *

Accompanied by a low frequency *whoosh*, Leslie Finch entered through the private door at the back of Jared Griffon's office. The entryway was built into the paneling, its seams not visible. It slid closed with another *whoosh*.

"You're late," he said, without looking up from his desk.

His jacket hung from a brass coat rack; she could enjoy the shape of his torso jockeying for attention under the crisply laundered shirt. The tie was wrong, though. He should have been wearing one of the three she'd bought him over the weekend. *Jerk.*

"I'm not late." She wore the company slate blue, in a tight-fitting exercise suit, and carried an open bottle of Everpure water. A wet towel swaddled her neck. She dropped into the chair next to Griffon, draped her arm around his back and took a slow swig of the water. She felt healthy and ready for a moment of quality. A helping of French-style carnality would make an excellent starter. Sushi from the Meteor Café as a chaser. Then the main course: a formal media release about her newly laddered professional station in life.

"I thought you were joining me, anyway," she said. "Get that body up out of that chair. Get that body some ex-er-cise."

Griffon cracked his neck and turned. He gestured at the bottle. "You think our water flows from a spigot, Leslie. That's the last time I want to see you drinking Everpure."

"You think I drink this stuff? I use the bottle, Jared." Truth was, she was managing a long-standing, curious attraction to the liquid. The strange pull revisited her in the last few months and she'd used her admin privileges to liberate a number of bottles. Regardless, she didn't want Jared getting pissed over some minor infraction. She pulled at the zipper on her top, exposing more of her bare neck.

"This morning I got a message from Gault," said Griffon. "The Nepalese have a sample of Everpure. The government's health offices. They want to know where the source is, who bottles it, where it's sold."

Finch rolled her chair away from Griffon. "Unbelievable. That kid waiter. He had a run-in with a customer. Gault terminated him. He nabbed a half-bottle somehow and served it in the restaurant. It all blew over, is what I heard."

"Who told Gault to dismiss the waiter?"

"Gault did it on his own. I got the report. Why would he need our permission?"

"Without knowing what the kid did?"

"He said he spilled it in a ditch. He lied. Punk," said Finch.

"Now it's in Kathmandu. Careless. Sloppy. Stupid."

Finch ran a hand through her hair. "Gault told me once the Nepalese were incapable of lying or stealing. Like our head monk buddy, pure as the driven snow."

Griffon let out a controlled exhale. Finch pulled the zipper up. When Jared wasn't put off his mission by the promise of her flesh, there was a problem.

"You and Gault drew up the security protocols. Are they implemented? Or sitting in Gault's desk? What kind of security do you use with the vans?" He stood up, walked to a bookshelf, and took down a personnel ledger. "You approved Gault's hiring."

"This isn't fair. You vetted him too. It's a tough position to fill. Someone willing to live at thirteen thousand feet and train locals to operate a five-star lodging. Make sure they're good at gilding the storyline while they keep the tech operation going on the side, under the radar." Finch caught herself. She didn't like where this was going. Reading the riot act to Griffon wouldn't get her off the hook. "What about the cover? We draw water from the river? Kathmandu has our permit. Let's get Gault to—"

"No. Leslie. We've just launched. You think we can risk this kind of indiscretion, now? After the buzz we've uncorked? No. You go to Nepal. You leave tonight with the abbot. The tickets are bought. You secure the operation. You keep a tight leash on Gault till we find his replacement."

"Jared…"

"Work to get us off the Nepalese government's radar. Set something up to convince them the water sample is a fluke. Whatever you and Gault devise."

"Jared. Tomorrow's media interviews. The networks will be here."

"Virgil and I can handle those."

Finch leaned her head back to stare at the ceiling.

"And Leslie." Griffon swiveled in his chair to face her. "You *do* understand this water source– and its continuing availability– is critical to everything we've done. And everything we will do in the future. I would come over myself, if not for this opening phase. I'm entrusting you to make it right. I want you to assure me that Gaia will be courted, supplicated, made happy. I'd like to see *your* face a bit happier. He's an observant man. Don't botch it."

Finch rose with her water bottle, snapped the towel from her neck, and took an indignant swig of Everpure. She turned her back to Griffon and got herself to the hidden door, which opened and swallowed her. As the door closed, she mouthed the word *bastard*, in case Jared couldn't read her mind.

* * *

Abbot Gaia rested in a plush chair in the lobby of Earthyield headquarters. The crisp Vancouver air, carried in when the doors opened, refreshed like the winds sent forth by Chomolungma. Nonetheless, it was grey and ugly here. He looked forward to his return to the monastery. He also fretted; he disliked flying and petitioned regularly that should he be reanimated after death it might take place before the advent of flight.

It was placid in the moment. Security staff sat idly behind the reception desk, eyes glued to their laptops. Waiting with him, the limousine driver peered out into the quiet night. An elevator bell chimed and doors opened to reveal Finch, carrying a small flight bag. An assistant carried Finch's heavier baggage. Finch stopped in front of Gaia.

"Ready?" she asked.

He rose and bowed. "Namaste, Madame Finch."

"It's a long flight, abbot," she replied without a bow. She gestured to her assistant. "Let's go."

The assistant went through the doors, followed by Finch, Gaia, and their driver. Finch walked briskly across the concrete terrace. Her baggage-lugging assistant fell behind, along with the driver. Gaia kept the rapid pace, his sandaled feet lean and his stride strong. He could tell Finch was irked.

"We have a flight to catch," said Finch.

"Not my favorite activity."

"Worried? You can pray, then. You're a holy man, right?"

"I pray for our safe travels." Gaia noticed Finch's assistant falter with the heavy bags. The limo driver stopped to help. Finch walked on.

"What's holy about making money?" she said. "Isn't that why you're here, to make sure it keeps flowing, like the water from your holy spring?" He remained silent. She picked up her gait, taking a moment to look back at him. "Don't pray for me."

Chapter Five

Everest Vista Lodge, Nepal

The evening stars blinked on, emerging out of the firmament from behind the flags above the lodge. A night bird cried mournfully somewhere in the distance. Max liked it. The nightly drive under the open sky, the pale, enormous mountain walls rising to touch the shooting stars. Damn, he wished he could scribble a poem. Write home about it.

His van idled in the lodge's back driveway. A hemp cloth bag was tied to its roof rack. Dressed in coveralls, he and Flick checked that the rear panel doors were locked, and got in. The motor coughed to life. The van left the driveway and rattled onto the dirt road. His tires kicked up stones and pitched unevenly over the dirt and rock. Patches of snow smeared the landscape. In the gleam of headlights small prayer stones lined a curve in the road, strange grey orbs reflecting in the headlamps.

"We should liberate some of those," said Flick, gesturing at the front windshield.

"They're worthless," said Max. The van reached a bridge over a deep cutting. Max slowed to a crawl. There were no side rails and the drop looked fatal. At this hour, the road should be empty. Still, safer to ease along. Max maneuvered the vehicle to the center of the road and drove cautiously across. Nearly to the other side, he stopped.

"You see that?"

A snow leopard crept out from under the bridge, a grey-white specter in the gloom. Clenched in its incisors was the carcass of a tahr. The leopard's eyes gleamed green as it surveyed for danger before dragging the carcass out from under the bridge and down a dark hollow. Red-stained slush marked its path.

"Would not want to walk this on foot," said Flick.

"Can you smell the blood?" Max said.

"Yeah."

Max nodded and motored the van off the bridge. Over a close rise, the spires of the Thyzenboche Monastery appeared, the Milky Way luminous in the sky behind. The monastery's subdued eaves and porticos were set off with elaborately-carved but, to Max's eye at least, bleak ornamentation. A mix of carnival and nightmare, he thought, with faded pink and green sculpted animals and sun-faded banners flapping against stone. He only saw it at night, of course. *Have to get up here in the daytime. Maybe I'll change my tune.*

The van drove up to its front gates then veered left. The vehicle followed the low wall to a back courtyard entryway, honoring the Buddhist convention of passing with the building on the right. The van stopped and the engine idled. Max gave two short taps on the horn.

The monastery gates swung open. The van's headlights dimmed. It turned and backed in slowly beneath an overhanging bower. The van stopped and Max cut the motor. A few oil torches were lit, accenting the gleam of vines growing luxuriantly along the sculpted stone fountain set in a corner of the courtyard. From it, spring water flowed, glinting like orange wine in the torches' light, as it gathered in a small gilded pool. From a door fronting the courtyard monks now exited, brown-robed figures moving in a solemn line. Each cradled a wooden urn, its lid fastened with clamps.

Max and Flick got out and greeted the monks. Flick climbed onto the van's roof and opened the hemp bag. Inside were scarves, fashioned from stock-grade silks and garishly colored with crimson, vermilion, and ruby dyes. Max presented a crimson scarf to a monk who stood forward. The monk accepted it and bowed. Max knew him as Red Scarf; he received a scarf with each visit, validating each transaction. Flick opened the back of the van, filled with empty urns. The monks proceeded with ceremony, removing the empty urns from the metal rack welded into the rear cabin, then carefully loading the full ones. Max watched a moment, then handed a small cloth bag to Red Scarf. Stirred by movement, the jangle of metal against metal, the bag revealed its content of coinage.

"That's it, Red Scarf," said Max.

The last full urn was placed in the back of the van. Its doors were closed and locked. Max and Flick bowed again, got in the van, and departed through the gate.

Max pictured what would happen next. Once they were sure the van was long gone, the monks would walk back to the fountain, carrying the empty urns. Each would kneel before it, and set their urn under the flow. They would stare, transfixed, watching the water as it poured forth, a clear shadowless liquid that shimmered under the night skies, stolen from the deeps. Damn, maybe he *was* a poet.

* * *

Dr. Maya, gulping chilly night air, climbed the road towards the monastery. She had been contacted to treat an injured monk. Busy with births throughout the villages, she'd had to wait until now, but was looking forward to this visit, her first inside the venerated Thyzenboche premises.

She wore her backpack and wielded her hand-painted staff, swatting at pebbles and thwacking at the tough grasses that grew near the road. She heard a motorized vehicle approaching and stepped into the shadows. An Earthyield van rattled into view. The van passed and continued down the hill. *A late hour for the monks to accept visitors.*

She reached the monastery. Red Scarf answered the bell's gong. They each bowed.

"Namaste," said Maya.

"Namaste," said Red Scarf. "Doctor Maya?"

"Yes."

"Please enter."

Flickering oil lamps lit the monastery's wide entryway and daubed soft, shifting shadows down its long hall. Her pupils slowly dilating in the muted chambers, Maya discovered the dulled colors on the outside of the ancient structure belied its interior. Rich hues of red, yellow, and blue melded with a myriad of others, following contours, wrapping around window portals and framing the wide carpets. Buddhist iconography bedizened every spare surface. Silk fell from hidden hooks and light flared from quiet nooks. The glimmer from brass handles and copper vessels shone out in warm, reflected shards. It was a beatific sanctuary of calming beauty and it filled her with gladness.

"Welcome to Thyzenboche, physician. I am known as Red Scarf. I extend the greetings of my brothers and Abbot Gaia. He is away. He will return soon from a long journey. I will take you to our brother the herder."

They reached a doorway covered with a curtain. Red Scarf pulled the cloth back to reveal the monk resting on a cot. The resting monk's loosely bandaged right foot was raised, supported by a stack of worn books. Photographs torn from magazines and nailed haphazardly to a wall showed yaks and other animals, along with sketches done crudely in charcoal. The monk herder looked up and bowed, awkwardly, from his supine position.

"Brother herder, this is physician Maya," said Red Scarf. "She will attend to your ankle."

Maya crouched beside the cot and placed her hands on the bandaged foot. Red Scarf departed the room.

"Aaahh, Maya," the herder began, "I fell on the rocky slopes. Balloosh. She's my yak. A tricky one. Always causing fits. She wandered last night. Far from the herd and her pastures. Aaahh, the berries are growing higher this year."

Maya began undoing the bandage. "Can you move your foot up and down?"

With a grimace the herder wiggled his foot. Maya placed both hands under the swelled ankle and noted the warm, taut tenderness of the joint. She couldn't locate a fracture. That was a relief.

"There is a tower above the pasture slopes, physician. Where I found Balloosh. A black tower of metal, high in the cliffs. I stumbled looking! I was afraid. You would be, yes? Aaaah, Balloosh was not. She's a devil." The herder seemed embarrassed he had used the term 'devil' and pulled his shoulders in. Maya gently pulled off the remainder of the bandage and reached into her backpack for an ankle brace.

"Where is the tower?"

"Chodak will take you there. My brother. He has a torch and batteries."

Maya smiled. She unrolled the reinforced cloth brace and secured it around the herder's ankle. "Not tonight. Tell me how you get to the tower."

"I will draw a map," said the herder. "I can draw. See my wall of art?" He gestured up at the sketches.

"You do that tomorrow. Rest. You need a healthy ankle to chase down Balloosh. It's sprained, not broken. Stay off it for a few days. Please wear the brace."

The herder rustled for his drawing materials.

"Have a peaceful evening. Namaste," said Maya. She folded her hands, bowed, and rose. The herder penciled rectangles on his page.

"This will be a good map," she heard him say, as she swung back the curtain and stepped into the hallway. Red Scarf was waiting.

"How is our brother?" he asked.

"A bad sprain. Insist he keep the brace on. He shouldn't walk on it more than needed in the first few days. Be sure he rests and keeps the leg raised. That will help the swelling." Maya and Red Scarf proceeded to the entrance of the monastery. "Please send for me when the abbot returns," said Maya.

South of Mt. Everest

Through a sputtering radio transmission Bateman received word their operation was "halted until further notice." Their camp sat on a level perch, steep slopes above and below. What snow remained was mushy and melting. Wearing light windbreakers, they packed tents, boxed up the radio, and bungeed their packs.

"I'd like to meet the bastard who said these were easy to fold," said Edwards, grappling with one of the tents. Edwards crumpled it into a sack and tossed it to Muldoon, who promptly tossed it to Dawa.

"You lazy, Muldoon," said Dawa.

Edwards turned to Bateman. "You still think we should be standing down?"

"Feeling a bit risky," said Bateman. "I keep feeling little shakes. Or at least think I do. We're not in a rush. Nothing wrong with stepping away to wait for more information." Bateman remembered the odd growth he'd seen wriggling up over Edwards's boot. Flattened when Edwards stepped on it, there wasn't much to recover, and the others hadn't placed much credence in his insistence the thing was more than unusual.

"I don't know. If we've got a Mount St. Helens happening, there's no way it's coming in the next fortnight. Every alarm sensor in the world would be chirping," said Edwards.

"Look at the bright side, Eddie. We can sit poolside at the Everest Vista. Till the American-led unit gets here. Like the cavalry."

"That'll be bloody nice. Some Yank'll march in and steal our glory." He looked up at Bateman with a big grin. Bateman was fairly sure they'd harbor no ill feelings about the recess.

Edwards crouched to pick up the radio antenna and began cocooning it in bubble-wrap. "I'm thinking we should–"

In a thrash of noise, a plant-like growth, its trunk thick as a forearm and shoots unfurling like uncoiled springs, nosed up through the snow, knocking Edwards down over the slope, and pitching Bateman to his knees. Wriggling and shaking like a bizarre vertical snake, the growth burgeoned upward until an almost full-size tree stood before them, its fresh leaves glistening in the sun. With a terrible last shudder, it stopped moving.

Bateman pulled himself up. A trail marked Edwards's slide down the snow slope. Dawa dropped his pack and tore into its contents, pulling out a piton and cord. He pounded the piton into a rocky surface, roped up, and launched himself over the slope. Bateman watched him rappel to Edwards who lay against a ledge of broken stone. The shattered radio had spilled from his pack. Bateman could see blood, but not much. Dawa brushed snow from Edwards's face. Edwards groaned, and folded over, pulling his knees to his chest.

Dawa attached a fixed rope to Edwards's waist-belt. Good move, thought Bateman. At the least, in the event of a slip, Dawa would go with him and arrest their slide with his ice axe. Though in the warming snowfields, it was hard to predict if the axe would hold.

"Are you okay, Ed-ji? Can you move?" Dawa asked.

"My shoulder..." moaned Edwards.

Dawa called up the mountain to the others. "His shoulder is hurt. Help me bring him up!"

As Bateman prepped ropes for an abseil to join Dawa, he took a last look at the bizarre tree, flinching each time it twitched, a staccato mutation of movement happening in front of his unbelieving eyes.

The Himalayas near Everest

The twin-engine Otter aircraft had lulled James to sleep with its powerful, encouraging thrum. He woke when Maggie gently whispered in his ear.

"The Himalayas."

He yawned and glanced through the window. White peaks gathered below. Further off, battlement upon battlement rose, rolling to the far horizon. A few of the peaks soared above the rest. *Maybe one of those is Everest.* James realized he had been holding a breath, and exhaled.

It had been an exhausting two days of hurry-up prep. Spa's royal brother-in-law had come through. After insinuating that Nepal was looking– with the handy excuse of an international emergency– to hustle the world's coffers, he'd orchestrated a promissory note for a quarter million in US dollars. James had bit. Had to bite, really. Cash for climate.

The data stream from Everest had gotten more improbable by the hour. The United Nations had gotten into the act, along with other sovereignties. All weighed in with a promise of support. The earthquakes that had struck Nepal a few years ago legitimized the pervasive anxiety. Those, for all their tragic loss of life, had been "normal" seismic occurrences. What James's team was tasked to explore was a deeper geophysical incongruity. It was hard to get his academic psyche around the fact that there was no antecedent. Nothing that would say, "It's most likely one of these."

He found himself mulling the situation from a neutral middle: the event was unprecedented, but in his gut he could imagine several reasonable scenarios. An unusual shift in a deep tectonic and one or two misfires in data-gathering. A perfect storm of misinformation and honest mistake coupled with Everest's status in the public's consciousness.

James sat across the aisle from Maggie. The "recruitment-mandatory" Chinese scientist Me Ming sat behind, across from the Bourn Institute's Xavier Frauz. Basil Frew sat in front across from volcanologist Dan McPhee. Tensing Spa had been scratched because of arthritic knees.

The ride was getting bumpy. Unusually bumpy, James began to think. He leaned forward to say a word to McPhee, who had been to the Himalayas. "I gather this is the plane you want to be flying in when you're over the mountains."

"That's a fact. Twin Otter. Landed at Lukla once on a single engine. Eight people and two pigs," said McPhee. McPhee was reared in the Snowdonia highlands of Wales and acclaimed for his mountain climbing. He had summited two 8000-meter peaks, though not Everest. With his ash-brown mustache and veneer of ruddy vigor he might have been Von Kamburg's cousin. James was cautioned to keep McPhee on a short leash; the man was keen to bag Everest.

Me Ming was onboard courtesy of China's government. He was a top researcher in the mission-critical discipline of geomorphology, the study of earth's topographic and bathymetric features. James had noted in the recruitment dossier (indicating Ming was to be a compulsory selection) that Ming often took pains to demean rival opinions in science papers he had authored. There was hearsay he was related to a ranked officer in China's military. A small man with black, short-cropped hair, he wore a yellow jacket adorned with some sort of manga logo. He had spoken less than twenty words to James since they were introduced at the airport in Delhi.

Xavier Frauz was somewhat older than the rest of the team. He was spry, very engaged, and, James thought from their brief dialogs, spot-on brilliant. Director of the Bourn Institute, he'd had the closest thing to a free pass when the short list was prepared.

The assembled unit was deemed the Mount Everest Allied Discovery team. MEAD, for short. First told, James thought someone was kidding. Turned out they– *they* being the powers-that-be who funded the trip– needed something quick and dirty as an "acronymic naming convention" (ANC). So MEAD was formalized and now enshrined in the team's international permits and rush-printed photo ID's. D-U-M-B, was what he thought.

Well. It was good to have Maggie here. He reached across the aisle to squeeze her hand. Frauz was loading tobacco into his pipe. Probably not a good idea.

"What do you think of these mountains, Mr. McPhee?" Frauz asked.

"Beautiful. Like a sea. Ripe for scalin'," answered McPhee.

"The cool part is," said Frew, "now you don't have to climb. You stand still, in a couple hours you're higher, without having to take a step."

McPhee laughed, his cheeks going redder. "That's stupid."

Smoking is stupid, thought James. As he observed, Frauz lit a match, set it to his tobacco, and took a deep drag on his pipe. Smoke curled into the cabin. A message light came on over the seats, accompanied by a soft dinging sound. *No Smoking* it flashed.

"What's that mean, do you think?" puffed Frauz, pointing at the sign. The smoke drifted lazily forward and across Maggie's lap. She brought her fingers up to wave delicately in front of her face.

"Talk about pollution," she whispered to James.

"I rather like the smell of good tobacco, me dear. A man thing, I suppose," he whispered back. He called out to Frauz. "Xavier."

Frauz shrugged. "Back in the day, one flew the Clipper to the Danish ports, and one was served a fine chardonnay, and given a spittoon, and no one made a peep," he said.

"One was smoking something they don't allow anymore," said McPhee.

"Not to mention the Clipper hasn't flown since the 1930's, Professor Frauz," said Frew. "If you were digging that scene, we are going to have to have you laminated because you belong in a muse-*ee*-um."

"I believe that pipe should be put away," said Ming. "The pilots—"

The front cockpit door swung open. The co-pilot, a swarthy Nepalese flight engineer, drilled his eyes into Frauz, twisted his thumb downwards, and retreated with a close of the cockpit door. Frauz took a moment to stick his nose in the air, then plunged his thumb into the pipe, snuffing it out.

"Elegant travel in a bygone era," he finished. "We shall never see its like again."

James was grateful Maggie had hidden her disdain. She leaned against the headrest and looked out the cabin window. He saw her hand move to the armrest and her knuckles go white.

Frauz half-stood in his seat, gesturing at the window. "It must be Everest…" he said, hands touching the pane.

"Whoa," said McPhee.

James leaned across Maggie and saw. In a sea of pale, striated mountains, where the sun and clouds and surrounding peaks and valleys created a patchwork of shadow and light, the massive bulk of Everest rose. Wide, high, deep, strong; she shone with a luminescent white glow. Strange clusters of green marked the snowy landscape of her lower flanks. She looked… *what was the word?* Maggie said it.

"Expectant."

"Atmospheric distortion," said Frew, sounding like he disbelieved his own words. A *whomp* of bumps shook the plane. The pilot's voice barked over the intercom.

"Your seatbelts are fastened. We are approaching the Syangboche Airport."

Earthyield Labs, Vancouver, BC

"Dr." Crispin Virgil sat at display terminal B in his slate blue lab coat, wearing a wireless headset, the dark bowl of his straight hair shimmying in concert with the slight movements of his head on his neck. The icon of a spinning clock spun. It spun more. The computer murmured, clicked, and hummed in low frequencies– hints it was thinking. Nothing was happening.

Jared Griffon leaned over his shoulder. A bit close there, Jared, thought Virgil, who had formed a small tech start-up with Griffon and two others. A tech start-up that was now Earthyield. Only Virgil knew if he had finished his PhD. He wasn't saying. Griffon had never bothered to find out. The "doctor" moniker had stuck. No big deal, really.

They were sequestered in Virgil's workshop, one of the few offices Griffon had consented to allow such disarray. It helped that Virgil kept illumination to a minimum. In the techno-gloaming were monitors, calibrators, instrumentalities. Numbers flashing on and off, texts coming and going, warnings and prompts sailing through. This flickering haven was his sanctuary.

Griffon had curtains installed both to hide the mess and ensure Virgil's privacy. The Synthium forges where Earthyield fashioned its empire of synthetics could be glimpsed through glass partitions just beyond the workshop. Workers moved past large sealed chambers. Robotic carts trundled in every direction, crisscrossing like sentient impulses on a ribbon of biochemical interstate. The place was immense and much of it underground, away from prying eyes, clever drones, and nefarious corporate operatives. Griffon's empire.

Virgil knew Earthyield's investors were at the end of a long tether of patient waiting. The assets needed to deliver, or the company debt that had created this shiny empire would sink them. No worry. Synthium was the map to El Dorado. It was all theirs. But mostly Griffon's.

"What's going on with the upgrades, boss?" asked Virgil. "We're wasting time while these processors do their molasses thing. I don't have time to waste. We have stuff to do. You know what the definition of insanity is? Doing the same thing over and over and expecting different results."

"What are you showing me?" asked Griffon.

"It won't load. Pardon while I run some illegal code."

Virgil leaned his thin face in close to the screen, clicking at the mouse in staccato bursts. Abruptly, a series of brightly colored chemical formulas appeared on the monitor: *Legacy Formulas.* There were dates before each formula starting with the year after Griffon had brought the water from Nepal.

"When I hack this software, I'm breaching the agreement with the company who leases it. There's ominous stuff in that fine print. You promise to pay the legal fees if we get sued."

Griffon studied the screen intently.

Virgil hated to be a pain; Griffon had a lot on his plate. At the same time, pestering the head honcho was reassuring. As long as Griffon tolerated his harmless snark, Virgil figured he was safe. Whatever else you thought of Griffon, you had to give it to him for business chops. A long time ago Virgil realized that no matter how fast on the draw he was with code and chemistry and calculations, without a crack operator at the helm of the commercialization ship, he was one more drowning rat. The Earthyield gig had been a good ride. He wanted to continue.

"When you start your own company you'll see what a pain you've been," Griffon said unceremoniously.

Virgil let his shoulders down. Time to be polite. "In the early going, we could only replicate aluminum-silicate feldspars and quartz. Touch and go, remember? At the breakthrough, we began to replicate biogenic mineral resources. Like coal, like dead plants." Virgil clicked the mouse revealing *Current Formulas.* The bottom-most listing under the heading was XPC-77. "Take a look. XPC-77. It's derived from the latest batch of water, came in last week."

The formula built on the screen as Virgil zoomed in. A graphic accompanied the numbers and text and showed what looked to be an amoeba. "It's a single cell amoeba, a living amoeba, we introduced into the XPC-77. Where there was one there are seven. Ta da."

"It's replicating living matter," said Griffon, staring.

"I don't know what you call it. You can call it replication. It's definitely an increase in fertility for this particular brand of amoebae. Our Everpure water has the potential to be the world's most prolific fertility enhancer."

Griffon shook his head. "Incredible," he murmured. "We've got to nail the water's chemistry, Virgil. Then we won't need Thyzenboche Monastery or Von Kamburg." Griffon stood up and moved away from the monitor. He put his hands behind his head and cracked his neck. "It's replicating organic matter. What is in this stuff?"

Dr. Virgil grinned like a Cheshire cat. "Money, boss. Your fourth quarter projections are going off the charts."

Griffon walked to the window and pulled the curtains to one side. The Synthium chambers gleamed. He rubbed his hand against his brow, eyes cast down. He was tired; Virgil could see it. And thinking. Thinking and fatigued. Spent and energized. *That man needs a nap and a guilty pleasure. Popcorn, or something.*

Griffon spread his palms against the glass. Virgil felt the tension emanating from his head honcho. Something besides corn was about to pop. Griffon swept the curtains back across the glass and leaned over Virgil, steadying himself with one arm on the workstation.

"Find the cure," he said.

"What? What are we curing?" asked Virgil.

"Find a way to stop the process. The biological thing."

"What do you mean, specifically?"

"Our Synthium capability can alter the world's economies, Virgil. It'll take a while, but eventually the reduction in mineral resource extraction and the rest of the things Synthium represents will shake out the status quo and leave Earthyield standing. All good, all great, all off the charts, as you put it." Griffon paused. "But think of this, Virgil. If the new stuff leaks– if this astonishing capacity to propagate escapes the lab, what might happen? Imagine it in the water. Imagine if somebody else gets it and markets it as a fertility drug. Who knows what it'll do. The population might explode. No way to stop it."

Griffon straightened up, maybe less taut. Virgil knew, from way back, as long as Griffon held the power to revise the equation, he usually calmed. Still. The man should be basking, not ruminating on the odd latent effect.

Griffon continued. "The third world's consuming us off the planet. The second world and the first world are right behind."

Virgil looked up at him, eyes as rolling as he dared make them. "You're an alarmist. We've only replicated a microorganism. The stuff may be powerful; who says we have to market fertility? Why not increase crop yields or something noble like that?"

"The Nepalese government has a sample," said Griffon. "We don't own the country. Somebody will find out what the water does and tap it or take control from us. This *will* happen. We have to be ready with the answer."

Virgil felt a knot in his stomach. Griffon had a way of seeing down the road. Not always right but not often wrong.

Griffon leaned, again speaking close. "Stop whatever else you have going. Get Becker and his crew on this. Have Merkle take over the Synthium stream. Find the *cure.*" He loosened his tie and sat. "It's a cause, Virgil, I can go with. If that water spreads, goes viral, the Synthium breakthrough could be useless. We'd have a planet overflowing with people. We'd be dead."

"I'm sad," said Virgil. "I'd call how you're reacting *kneejerk*. But.

You're the boss."

Griffon rose, departed Dr. Virgil's workshop and headed down the hall towards the elevators.

* * *

Griffon walked quickly to his desk, followed by Ms. Collins. She carried a small satchel with her. "Did you get my text, sir? I sent it when you were with Virgil."

"I haven't had time." Griffon pulled out his cell phone and read the text. She set the documents out on his desk.

"These are the sales reports, the news is good," Collins said. "Four more companies have ordered preliminary proposals for Synthium deliverables. They want quotes by the first of next month." She noted him setting his phone down. She smiled and looked at him. It was nice to be the bearer of positive news. "Dr. Von Kamburg's team is staying at our lodge in Nepal. I understand we're considering him for a position with the organization."

Griffon turned to look at her, his eyes gone dark. "Not what I call good news."

"I'm sorry?" said Collins.

"When something critical comes in I have to get it. Right away, no excuses," Griffon snapped. "Call Finch, now."

"I'm sorry."

Griffon scattered paper across his desk. "Von Kamburg in Nepal. Why the hell is *he* there?"

Collins picked up the phone and punched in numbers. "He's leading an international earth science team. Gault sent the news and I forwarded it to your phone, as soon as I got it."

Griffon didn't look at her. "He'll get his nose in everything. He'll connect the dots."

"The phone is ringing," said Collins. She spoke into the phone. "Connect me to Leslie Finch."

* * *

In Nepal, in the well-appointed bathroom of the five-star suite at the Everest Vista Lodge reserved for Earthyield management, ensconced in the contours of the porcelain and chrome Jacuzzi, Leslie Finch spilled tepid water over her booth-tanned skin, then watched it run in rivulets down the contours of her naked form. The room telephone buzzed and flashed: incoming call.

She wasn't about to answer, didn't want to hear Jared's voice. The buzzing and flashing ceased. Next to the phone was the open box from a pregnancy kit. A half-full bottle of Everpure rested nearby.

* * *

Ms. Collins placed her hand over the phone. "She's not answering, sir. Would you like Gault?"

Griffon grabbed the phone. "I'll take care of it." He motioned for her to leave.

* * *

Clarence Gault picked up the phone, grimacing. It was his boss, Jared Griffon. This was not going to be fun.

He was already strung-out with Finch on hand, spouting orders as if she knew what the hell she was ranting about. Griffon, thousands of miles away, had a great knack for checking in at the worst times, firing off stupid directives and fussing over stupid particulars. He wasn't on site and hadn't been for over a year. *Typical yuppiefied CEO.*

"Hello," Gault said.

"Clarence, how are you?"

"Hello, Jared."

"You getting out for your walks? You wanted to get in some hiking. Recover from the holiday goodies."

Gault smirked. "The phone lines are giving us trouble; we should discuss what you want while we have a connection."

"Making a bad day worse, Gault. You know why I'm calling."

"The water in Kathmandu."

"That's part of it," said Griffon.

"Finch is here. She and I are looking at it."

"Why was the Von Kamburg team booked into the lodge?"

"Charlie, our front desk guy, he got word we had to clear rooms for a team. All set-up and paid for by the government of Nepal. There was no red flag from anyone in Vancouver about them lodging here. Finch told me after, that Von Kamburg staying here was probably not good."

"Delegating blame, Gault," said Griffon. There was a pause. Gault could hear him thinking. "Kill the reservations."

"We've been *ordered* to lodge them," said Gault. "An official rep just left. Left the requisition and specifics. I'll read it out." *So you get it, Griffon.* "MEAD team– that's what they're calling Von Kamburg's unit– to be given carte blanche to use lodge facilities as required. The water sample led them here, but it turns out they don't care about the water. It's the mountain, Everest."

"Make some sense, Gault."

Gault held the phone from his ear, raised his middle finger to it, then continued.

"Something going on with Everest. Geological. They want Von Kamburg to take a look."

"Okay. Three critical tasks for you. First, the water sample has to be secured. If it can't be brought back from Kathmandu, then empty or drain it somewhere."

"I'm listening," said Gault.

"Second, I want a lockdown. No more access to the water by anyone not directly involved in the line, from Thyzenboche to Vancouver."

"Okay."

"Third, you disrupt and delay Von Kamburg. Whenever possible. Without raising alarms. Make sure Finch gets the word. Where is Finch? I need to talk to her."

"She locked herself in her suite. Said she needed down time. Said it's a long flight over. Probably taking a bubble bath—"

"Have her call. As soon as possible. Now, give me an idea how you'll handle Kathmandu."

Tactless, the way Griffon cuts you off in the middle of sentence.

"I don't know. Someone might end up in the brig."

Griffon didn't respond.

"We've paid off locals once or twice to get around some low-end community ordinances. I don't have contacts for stuff like this. Frankly, I don't see why we should do it. Von Kamburg is here for the mountain, not the water. We are, quote— *legally bound to assist however we can—* unquote. By decree of His Right Honourable President Ram." Gault paused again to give Griffon space to answer. He didn't. "Are you saying we should ignore this?"

"A smart manager might play for time; send the party elsewhere, make it sound like an honest misinterpretation," said Griffon. "But this is not just a matter of the corporation's welfare, Gault. There's been an unforeseen development. Uncharted territory. We need to secure Everpure from all outside parties. And silence the monks."

"Silence the monks?"

"I don't mean knock them off. For Christ's sake, Gault. *Buy their cooperation.*"

"Well, that's not gonna happen—"

"Gault."

Gault winced. A fresh swarm of static buzzed into his eardrum.

"Get the water locked down. Find Finch."

The phone clicked dead. The plans were ludicrous. Gault wasn't about to break the law so overtly. Go to prison for bottled water? Though he wasn't privy to the innermost workings of Earthyield, Gault understood the company's dependence on the Everpure. He was paid very well to keep everything rolling for Vancouver. But it was high time to get out of the Griffon grinder. He took a pad of paper from his pocket and began jotting notes. He needed to start revisiting some old promises about new employment.

Chapter Six

Leslie Finch, wrapped in a bathrobe of white chambray cotton, looked out from the shadowy overhang of her third floor balcony to the lodge's front driveway. The usually well-kept foliage seemed more unruly, growing up around the flat stone steps that made up the walkways. The snow was all but gone. As she watched, two lodge vans drove up the lane towards the concourse roundabout and parked. Dr. James Von Kamburg emerged from one. Other individuals stepped out of both, including the drivers, who moved to get an extensive cargo of gear onto luggage carts. Their gear and baggage gathered, the team moved towards the lodge's front doors. Finch stepped back and watched until they disappeared beneath her. She walked inside, sliding the glass doors shut.

Finch sat down on the duvet. She held the pregnancy test indicator close to her face. "No way. There's no way."

She set the indicator down and went to a mirror. She brushed at her hair with a hand and leaned closely to rub her teeth with one finger. It was time to greet the entourage and change into the Finch she had been, an hour or so ago.

She opened her luggage bag and rifled through the selections. Stretch, form-fitting, black jeans; nylon and Vibram trekking shoes; field shirts that would tuck in smartly. And the slate blue outerwear. She lifted the

Earthyield jacket out of her bag and held it up in the window's light. Jared Griffon had wanted a signature corporate identity, one that informed employees and sold clients. So the uniform: a ridiculous blight that many of Earthyield's personnel bristled at having to wear even as they signed on the slate blue dotted line. Money moved minds. Broke principles. Cracked common sense on the head like a cold stone against an egg.

She knew it because she'd done all of the above.

She appreciated how it felt to be part of the organization. She had been there since the legendary beginnings. If it culminated as projected, their saga would be etched on brassy plates in lobbies, honoring the feat accomplished by, mostly, Jared. Mostly by Jared, but she'd played her part, also.

Now here she was, in the place where it began. It was in this half of the world that she and Jared had chanced upon a vial of liquid those seeming short years ago. They'd been enjoying a hurriedly planned trip through the Khumbu region of Nepal, each with a personal dream to see the tallest mountain in the world. Fares were cheap after the earthquake. The country was yearning for the tourist dollars that had disappeared in those piles of brown rubble.

They had hiked to Everest's base camp, paid their respects to the ghosts and graves, and stood on top of a minor peak to better drink in the glory of Chomolungma. Dream fulfilled. Selfies posted.

On the hike out they'd taken a night's rest near the monastery. The Buddhist order was quietly welcoming to trekkers who were respectful. Always on the lookout for places to fill their water bottles, Jared and she agreed the monastery's spring-fed water had looked delicious. They held their bottles beneath the flow and took great swigs. To their disappointment it had tasted off. They were about to spill it away. But something about it smote Jared. He wouldn't drink the rest of it, but couldn't stop analyzing the odor. He brought it back to Canada.

She had marched in step with him as he harnessed the chemistries hidden in the Thyzenboche H_2O. Late, exhausting nights, clearing a space in the center of the particleboard so they could confirm that the water was doing what it was doing. Squeezing each other like high-school science fair contestants when the reactions lit up their eyes.

Jared had wanted a bed close by. He co-opted a line item from the initial ration of seed money. Instead of two laser printers, Egyptian linens and a slatted cot were delivered, to conveniently facilitate their robust and very regular physical connecting. A joyful ardor drove Jared in that clinching. He called it edacity. She put her fingers to his lips and said "audacity." It was good, though. They did everything but love.

With Earthyield on a red-hot winning tear it all swirled back into her memory. The fame and the fortune had indeed gilded their journey. All the breathless professional possibilities he represented were fruiting, ripe and edible. It was juicy. *They* were not. Their version of relationship was transitioning. Liquid through solid to vapor. It was so disgustingly modern. All she had to do was *be cool.*

Then again Jared always paid attention when she paid him less. *Be cool.*

Okay, the Lycra-wear idiocy. At first she had been smitten with the look: sleek like a fast car and bold like a force. She had worn them to satisfy her boss. She had strutted proud as part of the group corporate identity. She had taken them off, slowly, for her lover.

She shoved the jacket to the bottom of her bag and got dressed. Then she remembered she was supposed to call him and hadn't. Good, good.

* * *

James, Maggie and the MEAD team were at the front desk when Finch wound her way down the lodge's spiral staircase. At first James could not see a face, only a hand gliding along the curving banister, flesh against chrome. The fingers floated above while the thumb rode and caressed the polished metal. He saw it was Finch and noticed his own hand reaching to retrieve the reading glasses from his shirt pocket. He lowered his gaze and found himself moving a half step from his wife. Finch approached them.

"What are you doing here?" he asked, with a broad grin.

"Professor, I might ask the same of you," said Finch, smiling back.

"Leslie Finch, this is Maggie, my wife, Maggie," James said.

"Mrs. Von Kamburg. Hello."

"Great to meet you," said Maggie.

"Welcome to the Everest Vista," said Finch.

"I must say it's somewhat surprising to see you here," said James. *And somewhat unnerving.* "Leslie was part of the team I met in Vancouver, Maggie. At Earthyield, with Jared. Is he here?"

"No, no..." said Finch.

He tried to catch Maggie's eye, then thought better of it. James guessed Finch might have wanted to say more. He considered the odds against he and Finch finding themselves in the same place again. Earthyield and Everest. And what if Jared had been here? Fate was on the move, layering life with some pretty strange permutations. *That's quite enough for now, thank you, Fate.*

"Well, again, welcome," said Finch. "Our porters can grab your gear if you need assistance."

James noticed Finch taking a moment to scan the faces of the MEAD team. Frauz was at his pipe taking no apparent note of the *No Smoking* signs posted in multiple languages around the lobby. McPhee was by the window gaping at the great peaks splayed out like a glorious mural. Basil Frew was at the fish tank, snaking a long wrist into the water in an attempt to lift Charlton Heston back to upright. Me Ming was at his mobile phone, his below-the-surface scowl at the ready. Ticked off at the lack of network coverage, no doubt. Most content when he's perturbed, thought James.

"God damn them all to hell," Frew intoned in vintage Hestonian mimicry.

"Don't mind him, Leslie. He thinks we're descended from the planet of the apes and heading back that way."

Finch raised her eyebrows though didn't seem to get the reference.

"All of this…" asked James with a sweeping gesture at the surroundings. "More entrepreneurial wizardry by Griffon and company? How will the rest of the world keep up?"

"A few years ago we came over to acquire mineral rights," said Finch. "Small, some half-acre extractions. Then the lodge owners did a terrible thing. They told Jared the hotel was for sale. Everything was cheap after the earthquake. Nice views, but we still owe on the mortgage. It is amazing though, isn't it?"

McPhee wandered back to the group.

"Damn!" he said, shaking his head. James felt it also, the preposterous eminence of the geology in this place. He'd read about the Himalayas and knew the storied history of man's quest to get to the top of the world. It was surreal, all of it. They stood not thirty kilometers from the highest point on Earth.

"The Nepalese brought you over to do a safety inspection on Everest," said Finch.

"It's a developing story. Their government people haven't contacted you?"

"They told us to guarantee several rooms for some high-profile guests. At the expense of canceling and refunding current guests, which unfortunately we've had to do."

"Dang. Forward our apologies."

"They sent a representative also," said Finch. "He told us he couldn't tell us much."

"We were told to keep a lid on everything. We'll do our best to keep you and your staff informed. For the time being, please keep anything I tell you regarding Everest confidential, till I can clear what we're supposed to release. They don't want us to stir up panic."

"What is going on, precisely?"

"The New Zealand surveying crew reported new elevation readings. Unusual, to say the least. Over 8,871 meters. There's seismic and magnetic stuff going on we can't identify. I'm not sure what to think till we can collect our own data, but some of this has been cross-checked and verified. Which is why we're on site."

Finch brought her hands together. Almost as if in prayer, James thought.

He continued. "I'll get in touch with the people who are handling the different State Department release protocols. See what we can do about some additional clearance for our hosts. You have wireless and cell coverage here at the lodge, right?"

"Can be spotty, depending. Let me know if you have problems."

He hauled their luggage off the floor. "There's something in the water also, Leslie," said James. "Chemistry consistent with current theories about composition of the mantle."

"Composition of the mantle is theory. You must have more than that."

The inflection in her voice seemed to infer some assumed confidentiality. As if their brief contact in Vancouver had fashioned a private bond, where state secrets could be shared. He remembered her cold shoulder at the press conference.

"We are operating a five-star lodge here," said Finch.

James scratched at his beard. "We intend to take a good look. Try to forecast a few scenarios based on the data. It doesn't make geological sense but you think twice after you see the mountain from the air."

"Jared promised me a nice getaway. I'll be ticked off if my junket is disrupted by an act of God." Finch paused, smiled at Maggie, and continued. "Let's go over everything tomorrow morning. I'll buy you a coffee."

James felt Maggie set her hand on his arm.

"Please bring your team to dinner this evening, Doctor," said Finch. "Courtesy of the lodge. Seven o'clock?"

"Thanks, Leslie. We're tired but definitely famished." James hoisted his gear over his shoulder and put his arm lightly about Maggie. "We're supposed to meet a doctor; Dr. Danheela, I think it is. Can we get a message to her that we're here?"

"I'll have the front desk take care of it," said Finch.

"Thanks. Oh– and Leslie. We need a place to set up shop. With a clear view of Everest, if possible."

"The pool deck should be good. The mountain is right there."

"What about your guests who swim?"

"The pool's inside, under the dome, closed except for staff. We're refurbishing. I'll let the staff know you'll be using the deck."

"Sounds good."

"There's power out there. We have plug adaptors if you need them. I'll have the tables and umbrellas moved off to the side. We can deploy the awnings and dig up some tarps for cover."

"Any chance we can get inside, under the pool dome?"

"That won't work; it's an expensive makeover, with floor tiles and the like. You'd be moving inside and out, correct? Tracking mud, letting in moisture. We have pressurized containment– a lot of entering and exiting runs into money. Sorry."

"We'll hope the weather isn't inhospitable. See you at dinner."

The Von Kamburgs and the rest of their troupe moved across the lobby to the stairwell and up the steps. James whispered to Maggie on the way up. "Wonder how many trees they cut down to build this place?"

"Finch didn't look anything like your description of her," she replied.

* * *

Maggie was working on her second glass of the local beer, known as *chang*. It was pretty average, but she wanted the alcohol and for some reason the hosts weren't proffering wine.

The MEAD team was seated at a large banquet table in the center of the lodge's restaurant. Gault and Finch had joined them. The long, red-brown oriental carpets kept the floors warm and padded the noise of busy footfalls. She liked the high-backed, meticulously carved teak chairs; they sat you up straight and oozed culture. The panoramic windows revealed the vast scope of the surrounding heights. It was an incubated paradise.

The menu listed ginger and garlic dumplings, a curried chicken dish, and potatoes with bamboo shoots. The room swirled in a dizzying stew of delicious aromas. Speculating on the intriguing culinary options was fun. What wasn't enjoyable was trying to purge the loathsome Finch from her psyche. With some assistance from the beer she had coined Finch perfectly: *the lonesome fish*. Maggie imagined her as the subject of an abstract painting. Finch would be embodied as a black neutron star generating an irresistible gravitational siphon that sucked at the male figures around it. Or Finch as a blackened starfish swimming with the gravitational tides and leading those behind to a great whirlpool. Maggie would have to stock up on black paint.

Finch sat to the right of James, Maggie directly across the table. I should be sitting next to my husband, she thought, even while she could agree the arrangement would help break the ice. Maggie understood Finch was not so vile as she had made her out. It was the current chapter of her and James's existence that complicated things.

Maggie pined for the offspring which by this time should have been running around on the floors of her life. It wasn't just that James balked at helping diagnose their infertility. He wasn't trying hard enough to understand her desire. She needed him to assist proactively. He didn't turn down sex but didn't care if it made babies. She wanted his collaborative heart and needed his body fecund. Their center of gravity was not mutual.

The wine flowed at last, the waiters making rounds with merlot and pinot gris. She'd had enough alcohol. With a long sip she killed off the second glass of the chang. It had done the trick, taken her head to a sweet spot where she could observe with stylized acuity and a veneer of pleasantness.

Outside, through the double-paned glass, a panorama of moonlit terrain. Everest rose implacably. The troposphere's winds surged, shearing at the mountain's crown in a wash of vapor. The skies clouded over. The windows began to take hits from a freezing drizzle. A waiter appeared behind her, smiling gently, holding forth two bottles of wine. She shook her head.

"No. Thank you." Maggie noticed that Ming had not drunk anything alcoholic. He was a small man, probably felt isolated in this gang of Western academics. *He should quaff a glass or two, loosen up, find the sweet spot.* She picked up the menu. Order something exotic, she thought, running her tongue over her lips. *Something you can't get in Oregon.*

Maggie looked up. Someone was approaching their table. A Nepalese woman, but dressed in a more professional-appearing manner than most of the locals Maggie had seen. The woman proceeded tentatively towards their table, stopping to bow.

"Excuse my intrusion. I am Dr. Danheela."

"Sit down, please," Maggie found herself saying, rather out of character for the occasion. But she was glad another woman might join their entourage. She pulled a chair from a table behind them and gestured for Maya to sit next to her, but Maya remained standing.

"I was in the area, treating a member of a New Zealand team. I was told you were here, Dr. Von Kamburg, and that you wished to speak. But I feel it is impolite to interrupt your meal."

"Join us for dinner, doctor," said Finch, indicating to the head waiter.

"Yes," said Gault. "We'd be delighted."

Maya studied the seated party. Finally, she took the seat next to Maggie.

Gault leaned to shake her hand. "You're with the Khunde Hospital, that right? Clarence Gault, I manage the lodge. This is Leslie Finch, a senior officer with the parent company." Finch raised a hand and waved.

"I'm James Von Kamburg. My wife, Margaret," said James, reaching across the table to grasp Maya's hand.

Maya refused the proffered hand and folded her own, bowing. "Namaste. Welcome to Nepal."

"I didn't hear about an injury," said James. "What happened?"

"Shoulder dislocation. It's not serious but requires a sturdy sling."

"Was it John Bateman?"

"Edward Edwards."

"He's alright, then, overall?"

"Yes. Sore, with some scratches."

"I'm glad to hear that. We meant to invite the Kiwis to this dinner. Are they back at the lodge?"

Maya picked up the glass of water the waiter had brought and took a sip. "I didn't meet with them here. The New Zealanders left the lodge, looking for other lodging in Namche. They told me their rooms were cancelled, rather suddenly. Space required for another team of scientists on some important mission." Maya glanced at Gault.

James looked over at Finch, one eyebrow lowered. "I believe the New Zealand team had authorization from the same people who sent us," he said. "On paper, they're part of the Mount Everest Allied Discovery team."

"Did we get that authorization, Clarence?" asked Finch. Maggie saw Gault shift in his seat.

"We'll work something out, Dr. Von Kamburg," said Gault. "The suites the New Zealanders occupied were the only ones large enough to accommodate your team and the amount of gear we were told you would be bringing. I'll look into it."

"Please," said James. Maggie could see he was resisting the urge to shake his head. Surely the Kiwis had informed Gault they were part of the expedition. A grating snafu. Waiters arrived with appetizers. James picked up a fork and poked at one of the samosas. Maggie knew he was mulling his reaction. She thought the evening would be better served with a more positive vibe. She wished she could send him the thought. A little metaphysical prompt.

"These are good," he said.

Maggie smiled to herself. *I'm a closet telepath.*

The rest of the table began tasting the delicacies, nodding agreement. Culinary satisfaction abounded and the hungry crew looked happy to attend to eating. Ming seemed invigorated, consuming four samosas in rapid order, smacking his lips after each swallow. Maggie found him odd, and thought his jacket made him look like a juvenile. Be charitable, she reminded herself. She was glad to see Maya engaged in conversation with Frauz.

The waiters made more rounds. Conversations livened, palates were placated. Maggie saw Finch turn towards James and lean slightly to close the space between. She blocked the peripheral noise and focused. James, occasionally, had a wayward predilection for less-than-considerate behavior, where certain social dynamics were concerned. Good heart, suspect will. Not a trust issue. *Dang, that chang. Stop fretting.* She reconsidered. This was harmless, dutiful, professional intercourse between the two of them. *I'll listen, that's all. And consider a different word; not 'intercourse.'*

"The news about Everest. The fact that your team is here. This is not some minor occurrence," said Finch. "Why wasn't the lodge notified? What about the villages nearby? People deserve notification if there's risk. The village authorities should be advised."

"It's somewhat a political issue, Leslie. The Nepalese are sensitive about their shared border, as is China. Neither wants to give the other any excuse for swarming the mountain. Dr. Ming is already very hyper. It won't take much to set him off. We're fortunate that he can't back-and-forth with his government very easily. To be completely honest, I'd trade him for one Leslie Finch," said James.

Finch puckered her lips, maybe to hide a smile. "Of course."

"Sorry if I sound politically rude. I deplore filling positions based on anything other than merit. A Chinese national was a requirement. I can't blame them." He smiled. "For now, the media have been peppered with smokescreen factoids. While we figure out if any of this should be on the evening news. Bump the hot news about Earthyield's rising stock."

Finch smiled. James continued. Maggie listened.

"Tell me something. Earthyield sent you 7000 miles to check on real estate holdings? Last week Synthium was in the headlines. I would think–"

"It's nothing," she interrupted. "Business is cruel. I'll be back in Vancouver in a few days."

"The lodge can't be your only stake here."

"The lodge is a vanity project. Jared likes the view. The mineral rights are void. We sign in guests and leave the land untouched."

* * *

The silver auger spun frantically, biting into the black rock like a hungry, desperate worm. Mr. Grace appreciated the moment. *You don't often have the opportunity to amalgamate a copious budget with a high-stakes task under formidable and significant circumstances.* This was that. He would have liked to categorize it as cool but really disdained the word.

Dirt spewed from two vents as the auger chewed its way deep and deeper into the ground. A low grinding screech accompanied the strong, pulsing hum of the lithium-fission generator and its bank of solar fuel cells.

His Earthyield employees, Yates and Spencer, concentrated as they operated the high-tech portable drilling derrick. The weather was back to inhospitable tonight. Not just a return of the dank cold but a drizzle of sticky ice pellets. The kind that found their way under your sleeves and down your neck and somehow despite your slate blue poncho needled inside to prick at your ankles.

"Christ, I hate this," Yates moaned.

Though he never used it himself, Mr. Grace liked the coarse language. The undertaking was stimulating. Dangerous and illegal. Swearing, cussing, cursing: he never found the correct way to declaim negatives without feeling like a minion. But it contributed something raw and invigorating that he couldn't bring to these primitive circumstances.

The drizzle picked up, spearing the men with wicked spikes of misery. Mr. Grace attended to the operating station in his noiseless manner. Yates and Spencer worked astride the tower. *Forty feet of risible metal.* Minute remnants of flesh adorned the structure where Yates and Spencer had had to use exposed fingers to manipulate exposed controls.

"Christ." Yates put his hand up to his face, twitching his fingers. "Earthyield is going to pay me a million for each." He shoved his hand back into a glove.

A small hose rose out of the well's pit, anchored to the casing. Yates peered over the edge of a metal guardrail as the auger churned into the earth far beneath them. The opening was about three feet across, widened to accommodate the drill, the water return system, and the laser apparatus. Spencer crouched, knees into his chin. Mr. Grace could see he was hesitant to get close to the shaft.

"The mountain hates little buglets biting it. We're gonna get slapped," Spencer said.

Yates glared at him. "I say we boost the bit speed up."

"You say that every night."

Yates spat. "Power up the laser for good measure. The bit keeps getting clogged. That sticky crap down there. Aren't you sick of spending your nights on this godforsaken slag? Sick of putting this thing up and tearing it down and hiding it before the sun comes up?" He ran a gloved hand along the rim of the casement. "Gault says we can't leave till we hit the Thyzenboche water table. What water table? He doesn't even know if there is a water table. He's a d-i-c-k."

"Shut your trap, Yates. I'm sick of it, too. But if we mess up the drill he'll blow his top," said Spencer.

"I say we boost the bit speed up. 690 meters and still no water. A joke," said Yates.

Mr. Grace rose from the operating station and approached. "Take a breather. I'll tell you a few things."

Spencer and Yates looked at each other. They moved away from the borehole and the three stood in a circle.

"Gault says we have to hit water in the next three days. If we can't, we're ordered to scrap the site and dig somewhere else. Closer to the monastery. I told him it's a poor idea. As functional as the rig was designed, the putting-up and tearing-down has turned problematic. If we have to move the assembly and restart, it will set us back. A long way."

Spencer and Yates liked *some* of what they were hearing, Mr. Grace could tell. He paused. "You can't blame Gault for everything," he said. "The water sample coming under scrutiny in Kathmandu has changed the equation."

"Mr. Grace," said Yates, "Gault doesn't get it. He's at the lodge, not in the field. The rock at depth is impossible to drill through. Plus, we're on a portable unit here for Christ's sake. With three of us. *Three of us.* Trying to work without anyone seeing us. Just moving those batteries is enough to break your back. I say we boost the bit speed up. Rake this rock with laser. Stop screwing around. Get the job done and get the hell out."

"Yeah, and collapse the well," said Spencer. "Then we'll be out of work and not paid for the stuff we *have* done, if you read the fine print."

Mr. Grace stood before them, thinking about the best way to express his dissension without coming off as a miscreant. "The weather's warming up. It's out of synch with the annual temperature averages we anticipated here," he said. "Still, I don't expect we'll see yaks or herders in any numbers. They work by a religious calendar. I don't think the unusual warmth will sanction a rewrite of their doctrines." He paused, thinking. "As a precaution, I want you both to double-check the rig's camouflage at breakdown. Step far enough away that you get a bead on its effectiveness. Before we head back we can thin the fruiting berry plants that might tempt the yaks. On the slope below us."

He turned his back to them and put his hands on his hips. It seemed a dramatic way to preface his decision. "Our night hours shrink. Tearing down every 24 hours strips the support bolts. The rig is stressed. As are we." Mr. Grace turned around to see Yates salivating with anticipation.

"Yeah," bellowed Yates.

"If another herder gets close it's going to create a situation," said Mr. Grace. "I want you both to be ready. There are crevices we can use, up and to the right, behind us."

Yates and Spencer glanced at each other. Mr. Grace walked up to the bore hole, leaned over and peered in.

"Let's proceed," he said, "with the laser. If the drill is damaged we tear down the unit and get to the lodge for a reset. Gault is accountable. We won't make him a scapegoat, but I'll direct Vancouver to talk to him about the manner in which the operation played out." Mr. Grace took out a pocket device and began making calculations. "I'll accelerate the profile."

"What the hell," said Spencer, nodding grimly under his wet hood.

The laser was anchored at the business end of the drill. Never used. Risky. Mr. Grace walked to the operating controls and input new parameters. He did a final flick of his thumb across the touchscreen and stepped back from the derrick. Yates set his nose over the edge of the guardrail. An orange-red glow filtered up the sides of the hole and glimmered on the silvery shaft. The biting sound of the auger grated louder and louder as its speed increased and the laser at its tip chewed into rock.

"Cook the mother! Yeah…!" cried Yates.

With no warning the terrain shifted. The drill moved in its casing. The men pitched forward, off balance, and stumbled. Yates steadied himself against the guardrail over the shaft. Blue warning lights erupted on the tower. There was a disturbing, rising, scraping sound. Yates leaned in, squeezing the rail, to look down the shaft. Another terrain shift pitched him forward, the top half of his body straddling the rail. Mr. Grace could see that Yates's equilibrium was compromised. Yates's surprised face reflected the glow from below as he peered down the shaft. The shiny auger tip– looking like a cannon shell– rose rapidly towards his face and torso. With an ugly *whomp* the casing struck him.

Yates was propelled into the night sky, impaled by the auger tip. His body was thrown up and over the hillside, where it landed, broken, on the rocks far below.

Smoke oozed from the shaft. Spencer cowered in the glare of the tower's ghost blue warning lights, clutching his forearm, chest heaving, trying to breathe. Mr. Grace stood over him, in a kind of shock. For all the episodes he'd been involved with, he'd never been in the front row when a human life ended.

"Are you wounded?" he asked Spencer.

Spencer gulped for air. "Yates is dead. It split him, right down the middle."

"We can't get him. We're shutting down," said Mr. Grace. "Ground is destabilized. The shaft could go."

Spencer stumbled away from the drilling station, holding his face.

Mr. Grace moved to a control console near the tower's base and switched off the warning lights. If the assembly had been bent or lost hydraulic fluid, he'd be unable to collapse and disguise the derrick. He pulled open the toolkit and found the silver power wrench. He unwound eight target bolts, then removed an anchoring pin. He snapped his thumb down on the switch. The tower structure hissed and began a slow pivot downward, secured at the base on a large hinge. The assembly slowed to a stop, the tower parallel to the flat. He tossed a mottled tarp over the structure and pinned its edges with steel weights.

There was a subtle quiver. Time to go.

He turned to follow Spencer, and stopped. From the tube designed to catch and draw the precious water from below, a liquid trickled out, darkening the cement platform that anchored the tower. Blood or water.

A second quiver. He'd find out later.

* * *

The banquet continued at the lodge. James and Finch had pulled their chairs away from the table, the better to face each other. Their conversation waxed, each balancing wine in their giddy grips. James was feeling affable, his constitution nicely marinated by pinot gris.

"Clearly–" Finch paused for a swallow of merlot, "–this was indicated in the lateral dimension of the Archean Plates. Jared says I should publish."

"You did your homework. Have to get you back to Oregon for a lecture. There's a nice honorarium."

"No honorary tenure?"

"You got it," said James, a stupid grin spreading over his face. He should stop. He knew he was lead player in the conveniently ambiguous first act of a moral compromise; a kind of theater, this. But Leslie Finch. She was agreeable. She knew the landscape, she was a savvy geologist and he might be working with her in the near future. She had an interesting mouth, when she spoke. It was all on the up and up, was it not? Just talking. Once he had justified his actions he didn't see a reason to spend unnecessary energy debating the moral quotient. At the same time, he recognized the logic was weak and weak logic was a warning flag the color of Maggie's favorite paint. Bright red.

He took a breath and lowered his head to look at the floor. Maybe a return to the issues of the day would serve. He shook off some of the theater and came up for air. "You know your team, Earthyield, you are doing incredible things. The lodge, though, it doesn't fit. Why turn more tourists loose on an ecosystem like this? You know, the fragile kind. If you don't mind spilling corporate secrets, I'd be keen to know."

"That's the problem, Dr. Von Kamburg, don't you see? Mother Nature's undependable. In the long run, she won't last. Synthetics, James. Synthetics." She flashed her eyes around the table to see who might be listening and lowered her voice. The deep-pitched tonalities beckoned across the short space between them. "I wouldn't wait long to join our party. Jared's giving you a window. You should make your move."

"Are you and Jared…?" James waved with his hand. "Are you…?" He waved the other hand. "You know…?" With another wave, he accidentally bumped her wine glass. A drop or two of merlot splashed onto her black jeans. She made no move. "Crap," said James. "Sorry." He pulled a napkin from the table and held it, staring at her thigh.

Finch leaned in, an earnest timbre in her voice. "Come. We'll work close." She placed her hand on James's knee.

* * *

Maggie had been keeping ear and eye on the inauspicious episode playing out across the table. At the same time, she was trying to pay attention to Maya, who had asked her about her art and James's work. She felt Maya had some special part to play in the coming circumstances. Maggie didn't want to appear rude, but splitting her attention made her feel incapacitated. Maya would think she was ill-mannered and she'd never decipher what Finch and James were babbling about in enough detail to call him out.

She had this much in the bag: her husband was being appropriated. Their own relationship was being temporarily superseded by the stupor of drink and the primal infatuation frothing up like nectar with every Finchian utterance. The whole concoction was ridiculous. Like a bad drink from a franchised bar and grill as sick and accurate as its hyperbolic name. *Oregon Smacker. Oregon Smack Her. Oregon Offal.* God, what was in the chang?

She felt a powerlessness in the audience of this feminine spell, a conjuration she also possessed and had occasion to cast or at least cast about. Finch's right to use it, here and now, was wrong.

At the same time, filling her up in a manner that purged these immediate negatives, she was experiencing a gush of intuition. Over the years this second sight had laid hints and asked for attention. She preferred to wait at its edges for clarity, as the sense of a possible point of no return loomed. *Take a bite of this apple, deary, and you won't be coming back to hang with the normal any time soon.* If she let her mind surrender to it, would there be a window out?

The sensation grew, more fervent than she liked. An important choice loomed. She closed her eyes for a moment, then opened them to see where her focus would go. Her eyes found the window where the white, shadowy mass of the great mountains convened, an ephemeral hulking tribunal.

She surrendered to the intuition, allowing it to crystallize and reveal. The Earth itself was reacting, the feminine Earth, to the largely masculine-enabled chaos since humans– males– had dictated where the future should go. *Dick*-tate struck her as appropriate wording. Crude but suitable. The primary female, Chomolungma, was sentient of the escalating damages wrought by humankind and was taking action against the things that were not going as nature– She– intended. Not going well at all, and in cases storming past the tipping point. Summarized in Maggie's meandering psyche, these premonitions suggested Earth might be prepping to lay a trip on its human guests.

James might be right about not having a baby. That thought pulled her back into the room. Intuition or not, she knew what she wanted.

She was eighteen miles from the highest point on the earth. Practical perspective was daunting. She was not pregnant and had no premonition she could become so. What she wanted was coupled to James. She wanted the love between them, wherever it resided, to generate a human body separate from theirs. Love should do that. She cleared her throat.

Seeming to sense the breech in their private veil, Finch withdrew her hand from James's knee. Then Maya interrupted.

* * *

James felt his dinner churning below, a mix of drink and food and stupidity.

"Thank you for dinner, Madame Finch," said Maya.

"You're welcome. Mem-shasib," said Finch. James witnessed her awkward bow, noticed the blue flashing in her silken hair. He sat up, face flushed. Across the table Me Ming seemed to be rendering a judgmental glance. The intolerant associate from China must have thought James was ignoring his wife and prattling on with the hot young maiden. The guy had nerve. He's nailing me because he saw it happen, thought James. Just because he's right. James looked at Maggie. She turned away.

"Dr. Maya. Thanks for coming. Appreciate your help," James managed.

"It is my privilege," said Maya.

"The, ahhh, mantle water you sent in for testing. Where was the sample drawn from?"

"*You* sent it in?" said Finch, her voice quite truculent, thought James. She stared at Maya.

"It is bottled drinking water from this lodge. It is called Everpure," said Maya.

"This lodge?" asked James, fumbling to manage the alcohol inside him. He looked from Maya to Finch and back again.

"We bottle river water. It's sold outside of Nepal. A niche market," said Finch.

"The Walmarts of Earth Science," James said. The words came out, the thought followed: that should jab a stake through the notion he and Finch might have the coolest of platonic relationships.

"The river is Dudh Khosi. It rises from the glaciers of Everest," continued Maya. "The legitimacy of the product is fair enough by Western standards."

"You'd be surprised what people will pay for a sip of Everest water," said Finch.

"I am never surprised at what the West will pay for labels," said Maya.

Definitely not afraid to speak her mind, thought James.

"It makes sense that the water came from the river. What's the big deal?" asked McPhee.

"Well," said James, picking his way through the conversational minefield, "the water contains unusual chemistries. I assume it was tested for human consumption. Leslie, if you can get us that information. Secondly, the particulate in the Kathmandu sample appears to have come from somewhere very deep. Under the earth. Which is the reason we're here." He took a breath and lifted his pinot. Without a sip he set it down and reached for his glass of water.

"Excuse me; my throat is dry." He stared at the glass, briefly wondering if it could be Everpure.

"We know there's been a discernible shift in the Mohorovicic Discontinuity," offered Frauz, taking advantage of the pause. "Moho, for short." Frauz dipped his bearded chin and looked at James. "A short treatise, for the lay among us?"

James coughed into his water, nodding yes.

"Croatian seismologist found it," said Frauz. "Andrija Mohorovicic. They've tried to drill down to it twice with no results. Project Mohole by the USA, circa 1960. Year I was born by the way. Failed at start. In 1989, the Russians got to 40,000 feet, the deepest hole ever dug. They didn't arrive there either."

Me Ming weighed in, his voice both kinetic and solemn. "A team at our laboratories is developing a radionuclide-powered capsule with a heavy tungsten needle that will self-propel into the Moho Discontinuity. The capsule will explore Earth's interior in the upper mantle."

James was glad to see Ming get off his nationalism soapbox, even for a moment. Ming jumped back on.

"We are not assured you can license this water, Ms. Finch," Ming said. "The water melt may come from the territories of Tibet and there would be a surcharge even if you were approved for the license. You can expect formal requests for information. My government will want to know about the situation and procedures."

James set his water on the table. A busted dinner party was not the ideal start. End it, let everyone get some rest, start fresh tomorrow. "Dr. Maya, we're pretty spent, truth to tell. I'd like to meet with you again. Tomorrow?"

"Day after then I could meet. My office at the clinic. Do you know where it is?"

"I'll find it. We need sleep. Long flights, jet lag, you know, but great food, amazing place." He leaned to speak privately with Finch and caught himself– remembering where the evening had gone. He stood and rested his hands on the back of his chair.

"Leslie, Clarence, please thank the chef and staff for the many courtesies. Just a quick heads-up on our immediate plans: our equipment will arrive at the airstrip tomorrow. We'll get out there and pick it up as soon as we get word. Hoping and planning to set up outside on the pool deck tomorrow. General FYI if you hear aircraft or otherwise unusual sounds above; we've requisitioned flights for photo mapping, including low altitude. If the weather aborts the manned flights, we'll be calling in drones." James looked over at Ming. "They're United States Air Force drones used for civilian operations, such as mapping. The Nepalese government has agreed to their use."

Ming began tapping notes into his smart phone.

"CIA," said Frew.

James wanted to punch Frew. Though he did make the truth sound bitterly hilarious.

"The weather here is what we call mercurial, doctor," said Gault. "Forecasts are useful for major fronts but hour-by-hour you can't much go by them."

"We'll hope it clears," said James. "I'll print our schedule and contact info and get copies to you and Leslie in the morning."

"Thank you, Doctor," said Finch, already sounding a bit more formal to James.

"We'll get a notice out to our guests not to be alarmed if a drone appears at their window," said Gault. Heads turned to see if the lodge manager was serious. James figured he was trying to be funny.

"Man, I'd love to get my hands on a drone," said Frew. "Pepperoni pizza, delivered piping hot to our high-altitude camp. Some start-up in Minnesota droned beer to fishermen out on the frozen lakes there. Brilliant. Till the fuzz spoiled the party."

The party stirred to leave, to accompanying "good evenings."

"See you for coffee, Leslie. 9:00 a.m. work?" Finch nodded. James maneuvered himself behind Maggie's chair so he could pull it out for her. "Thanks again for the warm Everest welcome." That didn't come out quite as he intended.

Finch smiled with closed lips, turned briskly, and left.

McPhee sidled over to Frew. "A stick-in-the-mud she is. We were buzzed for an all-night drone-party, were we not?" Frew nodded. "Where's the elevator?" McPhee asked. They headed out, along with Ming and Frauz.

"Dr. Maya," said Maggie, "please let me know if you have some time in the next few days, to go over some of your customs. I'm a painter, looking for places where I might set up an easel. I don't want to do anything that might upset someone."

Gault motioned for James to step off to one side with him. He lowered his voice. "Wife an artist, huh? I love art." He took a moment to look around. "Listen, you're in charge of this affair. You need to know what went down. The New Zealand crew was sent away because they trashed their suite."

James looked at his feet and casually covered his mouth.

"They were intoxicated," Gault continued. "Supposed to work a stretch of days and come into the lodge for a night. Get some good sleep, food, get a break from winter camping. Then head out again," he said. "Yesterday, at some point– I guess someone radioed up there– they apparently were told to cancel everything. I'm not sure where the word came from. We thought it might have been from your team."

"It didn't," said James.

Gault chuffed out a crude exhale. "The Kiwis broke camp, came down off the mountain, came back to the lodge. They were served beer at the bar. Must have bought more liquor in Namche. It got out of hand. Our guests thought somebody was being strung up. One of their suites had a hole punched in the wall. Someone broke a lamp. Beer spilt, potato chip crumbs mashed into the rug. A mess."

"Not good conduct. Not expected," said James.

"The Sherpa got in on it. The Sherpas are usually mild-mannered. Nearly broke the one guy's nose." Gault took a furtive look left and right. "The kicker was this, Doc. They insisted a tree burst from the snow and knocked a guy down the slope. Edwards, with the dislocated shoulder.

They had photos. I looked at them. Not much to say. A tree in the snow is no miracle around here."

James glanced to see Maggie waiting. He didn't have the energy to hear any more of Gault's tale, factual or no. He tacked conciliatory, too tired to discuss it. "I exchanged e-mails with Bateman a few times before we got here. He struck me as a straight shooter."

"Well, we have a lodge to run. Our guests are important. I'm not sure why the Kiwis were so worked up. I was concerned with their state of mind. The tree story was not something you expect from professionals."

"I agree."

"Namche is not far. You can talk to them and straighten this out. We'll require compensation for damages."

"They're not part of our team. At least not yet, officially," said James.

Gault balked. "If you expect them to stay here we'll require payment."

"You'll have to talk to the New Zealand Embassy, or whomever. Not me."

Maggie walked over.

"Call the front desk if you need something," said Gault. James noted the luster was gone from his tone, as Gault turned and walked from the room.

Chapter Seven

The chilly drizzle faded to cold mist. Maya left the lodge grounds and walked towards her home, not far from the hospital. The way was familiar but still required the minding of divots, fallen rock, and whatever else the darkness hid.

She hadn't enjoyed the dinner. Instead of an interesting give-and-take of cultural and geological insights, it had turned into a strange Western soap opera. The lodge owners, Finch and Gault, she marked as profiteers and hustlers. The woman, Finch, had given little courtesy to the Von Kamburgs' marriage, an exhibition embarrassing to all who witnessed. Maya held back urges. To kick people in their duplicitous shins. Finch and the husband, James, would have remembered her toes. Outside of the dinner, the ongoing treatment of Passang and other locally hired lodge staff colored her disenchantment.

I am quick to judge.

James's wife Maggie was a peculiarly passive woman. She had watched the show from across the table without interrupting. Why? Because their marriage was a Western marriage, maybe. Convenience and duration held together by waning conventions of Christian society.

Maya stopped and leaned on her staff. *People are good.* The Von Kamburgs were grounded in their way. They had a grasp of the needs of the Earth and the cycles of its seasons. She needed to separate them from Gault and Finch, who in Maya's mind were draped in a capitalistic gauze. Then again, what deity permitted her, Maya, the right to judge their souls? She shook her head and walked, distractedly, not paying attention to her footfalls. Through an opening in the ragged night clouds a window full of stars glimmered. "Stars show us darkness," she murmured.

Someone touched her shoulder. A sheen of red, a shadow figure.

"Abbot Gaia is returned."

She almost fainted. Red Scarf. He'd come from the monastery to find her. Heart thumping, she caught her breath and tried to calm down. The need for Gaia to see her at such an hour was disturbing.

"Forgive my sudden appearance," said Red Scarf, "but this is urgent. The abbot will speak with you, tonight."

"Now?"

"He will not sleep."

If the abbot needed to see a doctor the need might be medical. Under the dark stars on this night, it felt as though something more grave was manifesting. She would, of course, proceed.

Over the bridge and up across the rises they reached the monastery. The heavy doors swung wide and they entered the soft incandescence. Red Scarf led her through a labyrinth of turns. She lost true north, so that the interior of the monastery became a universe of its own with no compass and no hours. They walked into a keeping room, where guests might be welcomed and entertained. Full, inviting pillows were arranged around the room before the stonework of the hearth, where a low fire burned. Maya lowered herself cross-legged onto one. Red Scarf excused himself and departed.

A monk carrying a tray appeared in the doorway. He stepped into the room and, with studied grace and assuredness, set a kettle of hot tea and two empty cups on a small table next to Maya. He departed, disappearing behind a veil of gold-tasseled cloth pulled across the entryway. Maya watched as the tassels swayed, their energy dissipating to stillness. She felt the narcotic of time slowing, and resisted the drug of not heeding.

From a shadowy entrance along a different wall, Abbot Gaia emerged. He might have been standing there all along, invisible against the murals of Buddha, wrapped in his crimson robe, the polished patina of his brown skin melding with the dark colors of the embroidery.

Gaia seated himself. The kettle surrendered its vapors. The aromatic vanilla-cinnamon brew wafted deliciously into Maya's nostrils. Gaia held a hand over the kettle, wiggling his fingers in the warm steam.

"I was given the drink as a gift on a recent visit overseas. The United States of Everything," he said.

Another Western temptation, thought Maya. Yet she craved the tea.

Gaia looked over his shoulder to see that the curtain had been drawn. He lifted the kettle and poured the brown, steaming fluid, filling two cups to the brim. The scent from the cups was sweet. "You have seen the abundance of life in early winter? How growth has moved with such speed? The brothers complain they cannot keep their scalps shorn of hair." He ran a hand over his bald pate, with a frown. "Not working for me."

"I have seen children come as doubles and triples. Animal and bird. Insect and fish. An odd season of plenty," replied Maya. She lifted the cup and took a draught. The liquid rolled over her tongue, down and in, warm and pleasurable.

"A strange season," said the abbot. Gaia rubbed his hand gently along his temple. "You've met Finch."

"I have," she said. They exchanged glances, unsure if their experiences of Finch were similar or divergent.

"So you've encountered the Western bird," he said. "The kind we are schooled to beware of."

Maya didn't know the abbot well but it delighted her to see his knowing smile.

"Abbot, there is much that troubles me," said Maya. "I'm glad you have returned." She was aware the abbot had requested her presence and not the other way around. Yet it seemed he was providing an audience she required.

She paused to look at his face. His eyes looked out over the vapors, his pupils reflecting a haze of dark flame. There in the translucence of flesh drawn over bone she could see a serenity. Something truly holy about this holy man.

"The lodge vans," she said, "the vehicles that come by night to Thyzenboche monastery." The abbot showed no signs of replying. "With respect can you tell me of them?" asked Maya. "Why do they come here under the cloak of darkness?"

The abbot looked at her. He paused to pick up his tea and tip it back into his mouth. He swished the drink around before swallowing.

"The lodge is ugly," she continued. "Some in our village died to bring wood for its walls. Our people are hired, employed at low wages and released without cause. They steal our river water for money." She next said something she did not believe, to bring the issue into sharp relief. "Would the monastery join in commerce with such a place, with such profiteering?"

The abbot's unblinking eyes held her own. "This is so," he said.

"Abbot. Abbot, the lodge–" stammered Maya.

The abbot interrupted. "My shame shelters me from my dishonor." He rose and bid her follow. "Come."

They walked through long, quieted hallways, stopping before an undecorated door. "Here," he said. With strong hands he gripped two rounded handles, running like horizontal staves across the breadth of the doors. He pushed and the thick wooden panels swung open on heavy metal hinges.

Maya and Gaia entered the room, low-slung and crowded with large urns. Through unshuttered windows the low riding moon cast its somber luster. Each urn was filled to the brim with water, their open tops reflecting small pools of blue light in the lunar glow. A lid rested against the side of each.

Gaia walked to one of the urns and cupped water in his palms. He brought it to his face and touched his tongue to the liquid. His hands opened over the urn to release the remainder. He took a mug from a shelf, dipped it into the same urn, and offered it to Maya.

"Drink."

She knew the taste. "It is Everpure," she said. "The same water Passang brought to me from the lodge."

Gaia leaned against the wall and cast his eyes past her, the moon's pale wash on his face. "Three years we have contracted with Earthyield, the company that owns the lodge. They trade for water from our spring."

Maya was about to hear justifications. *Let it not be. Please, not the abbot; not the monastery.*

"You know of the order's monastery at Ranbuk. In Tibet?" he asked.

She handed back the mug. "I know of them."

"Our brothers at Ranbuk have suffered through trials; from both political excess and accidental misfortune. Their needs are grave and ongoing. We sell our water and tender the profits to them." Gaia bent over, his eyes dark. "This business we deal in brings us no contentment. Earthyield is a poor host in our land. I know this as you do." He looked down into the mug he held and shook it, watching the water oscillate into spirals.

"Abbot, the water has drawn men of science to study it. It contains an unrecognizable ingredient from deep in the earth," said Maya.

A deep, disturbingly harmonious rumble began. Gentle, concentric rings rippled from the center of each urn. Maya placed the flats of her palms against the wall to steady herself. She looked at Gaia, who showed no sign of noticing.

"I cannot see," he said.

* * *

The lodge glistened under the full moon, its roof-mounted procession of flags doing slow, silken ripples in the slack breeze. The icy rain had lifted and the skies cleared. A few lights burned in the windows of guestrooms. Softer lights glowed from the atrium, lobby, and courtyards.

Gault sat at his desk in his closet-sized office, Leslie Finch pacing before him. If she knew how indifferent he was to her executive dressing-down, she'd only amp up her spiel. The things on her mind were not the things on his. He had made inquiries about other work and received a few tepid replies. Not the kind of response he'd hoped for.

Also on the worrying side, he hadn't heard from Mr. Grace since yesterday, sometime before last night's drilling. Radio outages were making things sketchy. But he had confidence in the unit. Especially Gracey, as he called him. That man was dogged.

The drilling operation was a roll of the dice Gault felt was unnecessary. The monastery water volumes showed no sign of slowing and the monks were happy with their ransom. It was another thing he figured Griffon had botched– having a team haul a portable rig up frost-bound slopes to tap the Everpure water table. Gracey's posse was able to hide the rig fairly well, but the collapse-disguise-raise routine wore at the men and equipment. Up at dusk, work all night, tear down at dawn. He imagined even Gracey would have trouble keeping his crew from getting pissed.

Griffon had jumped the yak.

The mountain was following suit. He'd felt a small tremor a few hours ago. The geological goings-on were odd. If anything big was in the works, surely they'd get some kind of warning shot. Volcanoes didn't just blow their tops, did they? Finicky science organizations loved to beat each other with predictions that came true, right? Anyway, he had the keys to all the vehicles. He'd scramble himself to a safe place if Everest turned Krakatoa.

He shook himself; he needed to pay better attention in case Finch suffered to actually ask him something. She was nodding her head, wordlessly. Since he'd been hired, the two of them had stayed in overseas contact handling whatever business issues arose. It was manageable; base-level professional, one might say. In the few days since she'd arrived he'd found her taut and moody, less accommodating, less personable. Her avoidance of Griffon had surprised Gault. He knew Finch and Griffon were some kind of item but the company scuttlebutt tended to distort by the time it covered the miles between Nepal and Vancouver. It was a bit of a rush to see her take a stand against him.

In the end she was one more minion. Over the last few days, she'd taken pains to isolate him and pin his ears back, browbeating with action lists and (damn the word) *deliverables*. Instead of them throwing back a bottle of rum together and sharing stories from the trenches, he had to be on his game.

He did appreciate Finch in certain categories. The way her breasts moved in and out when she breathed. They must be a sight underneath the top.

"You fire Passang before you know what he did with the bottle?" Finch said, abruptly breaking the one-sided torrent.

"You signed off."

"I assumed you had asked him what he did with it."

"He said he dumped it. He ran all the way to the clinic and gave it to that Sherpa doc. He lied. What did you expect me to do?" Gault was treading haphazardly. All the premature pondering about life after Earthyield. He should be a little more cautious until he had a signed contract.

"If the Sherpa doctor has any remaining you'll have to get it. Along with any in Kathmandu. Do you understand me, Clarence? I have several urgent e-mails from Jared. He wants this done. He is not in a good way."

"Griffon already told me. When you weren't answering phone calls and knocks at your door. You're the one he wants to talk to."

Finch seemed to falter. Maybe she recognized her culpability. She'd certainly buried the lede during this so-called dialog. Gault leaned back and put his hands behind his head. "I'm sure he's told you: he wants Von Kamburg's unit disrupted. Don't help." Gault thought Griffon's dictums were absurd. Von Kamburg was at the lodge and had international authority to do what he wanted. It was a nice way to stick it to Finch, though. "You invite them to dinner. Get cozy."

Finch planted herself in front of him. "We'll be making personnel decisions. Autonomy comes from leadership and sound decision-making. Not running a little empire in your own private corner of the organization." She leaned forward. "Pray your drilling team taps the water source very soon."

Gault leaned forward and did all but spit. "I don't know where you're coming from— *little empire?* We got bigger problems here than digging wells. Did you look outside? It's a spring melt in the middle of winter. Keeps going, the bridges will all wipe out, including the one to the monastery. We can forget the water after that." He waved a thumb towards the ceiling. "Why'd you think there's a team of scientists snoring away upstairs?" He shook his head. "Something's not right."

Finch turned her back on him. He saw her fingers twitching. Gault felt a pang of guilt. Maybe he'd gone overboard. Taking out on Finch what he should be taking out on Griffon. Maybe they should open a bottle of Captain Morgan after all.

Just then, he felt another, subtle tremor. An odd sensation rolled up his back, like the onset of a neuralgia. His bleak forebodings took on a vague, tacit substance. Finch looked at him and he saw her shared alarm. A small radio receiver hanging on a hook behind his desk buzzed. Gault spun his chair to answer it. "It's after midnight." He listened for a moment, face gone ashen. He sat up and covered the receiver with his hand.

"An accident. Drill is down. Somebody got hurt."

* * *

Abbot Gaia walked haltingly down the hillside behind his monastery, where the run-off from the courtyard spring approached the river. The good doctor Maya had departed. Night was a sheltering mantle over the skyscape.

The water spluttered loud and lively in the dark silence, coursing through twisting, narrow confines, over long-polished rock, down and down, until it reached a dark tunnel into an earthen chorten, the small shrine built by his order. Each of its four outside walls was adorned with eyes: the eyes of the Buddha, ever watchful, ever awake, taking in the days and the nights with all-seeing awareness. The Buddha would recognize his bewilderment, winking– *you again?*

At the entryway, Gaia halted, his back to the chorten, his arms against the doorjambs. He raised his eyes. Rooftop prayer flags stirred silently in the hour's unseen currents. The suns and moons and planets spun above in their slow and knowing animations across the void. He allowed himself a long look, the weight of standing drained into the solidness of the wheelhouse walls.

Isn't there an answer to everything? The long life lived in faith should give one purchase. His steps felt treacherous. A fall was nigh.

He folded his arms and entered the wheelhouse. The chorten enclosed a large, perpetually spinning wheel. The insistent force of water compelled the wheel, dimly lit by oil lamps set in the walls. In this sacred place, Gaia had been shown different characters of peace. That one answer could be both right and wrong. That he would live forever. That he would perish. That he should never have become a monk. And that his choice had been correct.

This night he foundered. His past seemed perilous, the learned ways and holy remembrances on a precipitous ledge that could fail. Out through the bottom of that fractured void was the only nightmare he could not tolerate: that the human capacity for reason, and thus faith, was worthless.

Kneeling before the wheel, Gaia let his gaze meld with the imagery coursing past in endless rhyme. The colors and shapes rose and fell in long, winding patterns, figures and words scribed in hallucinogenic repetition. A gushing filled his ears, merging with the great spindle's incalculably smooth turns.

The noises grew. The wheel spun faster, oscillations that altered the visual and the aural. Gaia devoured all, now hopelessly yoked to the frenzy.

Then, though the rush of movement and noise did not cease, a clarity. A mountain. As cold vapors enveloped the great peak, it stirred, writhing and groaning. A gleaming sphere formed within it. With a culminating eruption and gushing release, the sphere broke from the summit, delivered into the blue above. White stars, in rows, lining up in welcome.

Gaia lay prostrate on the floor. It was past midnight, and the wheelhouse as a tomb.

*　*　*

The world spun and brought its new morning. It was bright, fresh, practical. Full of air, and inside that air, currents of life. Gaia stirred, half in an unremembered dream, and let his eyes flower in the light.

He heard water, flowing from the spring in the monastery courtyard, glistening in the day's dewy, fresh-minted dawn. The caragana flowers and honeysuckles at the fountain's base appeared to have grown considerably; they mounted the fount, climbing in a tousle of hectic germination. The water flowed into its basin, found the depression to the outlet channel, then poured through a culvert that led under the carved opening in the monastery's walls. Black birds hopped about the channel, sipping and singing in the day's light.

Gaia sat on a crate in his room, beside an open window. His knees were drawn up. His folded arms and lowered head rested on them. A tear trickled down his forearm, falling away to his bare foot.

He raised his eyes to the light. He saw the spring, the courtyard, and, rising beyond in white splendor, the not-so-distant mass of Mt. Everest, clearly, but unusually, higher than the peaks around it.

In the quiet of the hour, and in the streaming light from the early sun, Gaia tipped the water-filled urn and watched it spill across the floor. The water coursed out of the room, through the open doorway to the flats of the courtyard. Gaia upended another. Red Scarf appeared. Without a word, he lifted and tipped an urn.

* * *

Jared Griffon was in his office. Twin laptops were open on his crowded desk, the underlying granite shine buried by reports, folders, and a large chrome vase filled with black roses. Jill Collins came in, balancing a paper cup full of water in one hand and documents in the other. Her hands trembled as she emptied the cup into the vase.

"Put the roses by the window, Jill."

Collins moved the vase as directed. The card that had been attached to the roses' stems, signed "Heather", was gone.

"Next time set them over there, not on my desk. Make sure they're gone before Finch gets back," he said.

Collins pulled a folder out from under her arm and set it before him. She also wielded a copy of the *New York Times* and carefully set it on the folder, open to page seven. "The bank called. They want to talk about this," she said. It was an article printed in the science section. The headline read "Synthium claims challenged by M.I.T. group."

"Sooner or later," said Griffon. "Jerks."

"I forwarded an e-mail from Gault. Just came in. He sent it to you and copied me." She held the sheet up to read and took a breath. "It's not good: *Authorities have arrested three men in connection with a burglary attempt at the National Health and Science Offices in Kathmandu, Nepal.*"

Griffon stood up and took the sheet from her, reading it aloud. *"Field Worksite-D is* offline. *Details soon."*

Collins stepped back from the desk. "Maybe we can reach Leslie?"

Griffon shook his head. "She's mum. Won't answer." He sat down.

"I'll keep trying the phones," said Collins. "Static and interference are worse than I've ever heard. I talked to IT. They're telling me it's distortion happening near the lodge that they haven't seen before. Usually they figure out what to do."

"Thank you. Please leave."

She hesitated, then walked away. With a casual sweep of his hand, Griffon knocked Finch's crystal globe from his desk. The globe cracked against the marble floor, rolled to a stop, and fell to pieces.

* * *

Finch sat at Gault's desk, studying analytics and maps describing the geology near the monastery. Gault had left after a phone call informed them that an attempt to retrieve the Kathmandu water had failed. Gault, she learned, had given it a shot, despite his misgivings, using some shady locals he'd drummed up. Now they hoped the trail wouldn't lead back to them. "Got our own little Watergate stewing," he'd said to Finch.

Somehow, in light of the troubling occurrences mounting, she and Gault seemed to be in détente. She guessed it wouldn't last. She read the notice Gault had typed up and posted around the lodge.

Dear Honored Guests,

You might have noticed a significant disruption to our phone and Internet connections. This was caused by a power failure in the lodge's network server room. Unfortunately, it's likely there will be further disruptions. Until further notice please be aware that your Internet connection and phone should be considered unreliable. We apologize for this inconvenience. Our shuttle vans will update flight schedules on return trips from the airport. Flight information will be posted in the lobby area. Thanks for your patience and understanding! Sincerely, Clarence Gault, Manager, Everest Vista Lodge.

Gault opened the door and leaned his head in. "You have a visitor."

"Who?"

"The abbot. You know him, right?"

"What does he want?"

"I don't know. You'll have to take care of it. I'm up to my neck." Gault left, closing the door after Gaia entered. He stood before Finch, the shiny skin of his wrists wrinkling to furrows as he folded his hands and bowed.

"Namaste, Madame Finch."

She pivoted, avoiding eye contact, and presented a shoulder. She trusted it appeared cold.

"The monastery at Thyzenboche can no longer supply the lodge with water from our spring," he said.

Finch tapped a pen on the desk and spun the chair to face him, without looking up. "I'm sorry, Abbot, the contract runs for another two years," she said, scribbling nonsense across a piece of scrap paper. "I'm very busy and really can't talk."

"The water is no longer for sale."

She looked at him. "A legal contract can't be broken that easily. We have signed papers–"

The abbot held both hands up before him as if to say stop. He exhaled, then slowly knelt so his face was level with hers. "Memsahib Finch. The water will not be sold. What we do not use we will return to the earth that raised it."

Finch rose from her confining seat and stood, looking to loom over him, but her stance was awkward. He knelt before her, on the lodge office carpet, looking reverent, his shaved head bowed. It irked. No, it was making her furious, that he could posture as pious and waltz in expecting her to genuflect and kiss his ring.

"You make me sick," she began. She jogged her fingers as if playing notes on a discordant keyboard. "You're holy, all right. Above the law, right? This is your personal fiefdom. You make the rules till they're inconvenient, then shove them aside."

"We do you injustice." He raised his eyes. They drew her like black holes, running through and out to some other side. "There is no other way." She stared, dazed, caught in a Buddhist tractor beam. He spoke.

"The goddess mother is not pleased. She is not pleased with me, she is not pleased with you, she is not pleased with much that has gone on in this new age of the world."

She flinched, and looked away. "Get out." Finch shoved at the desk, felt a painful wrench in her wrist. She shoved again, tipping a file rack onto the floor. She wedged herself out, past Gaia, disgusted that his robe had brushed against her arm. She pushed the door open. "I'll straighten this mess out with whoever you call the police around here."

Gaia retreated the single step to stand in the doorway. His eyes met hers, brown into blue. "Gather your spirit and re-embrace the earth," he said. "It will not be long. The goddess mother—"

With an open palm, Finch slapped his face. His hands came up to touch where she had slapped. Then he was gone.

Chapter Eight

His ungloved hand dug briskly into the soft earth. "World-renowned" some had labeled him. Geophysicist of the decade. All James knew, crouched near the banks of a fast-rushing stream, was that he was playing in his favorite stuff. Rather, he was digging under the topsoil to *get* to his favorite stuff– the rocks– beneath. And there it was.

With a small Swiss army knife, he freed up a few of the rock fragments, then placed them in a lidded container. He dragged a pen from one pocket, a sticker sheet from another, scribed the name of the sample, and buffed the location on the sticker: *Latitude: 27.816667 - Longitude: 86.716667.*

Eager as he was to get his hands dirty, he'd almost missed his morning coffee date with Finch. She hadn't shown. That was that, for now. In her absence he'd attempted to reach the MEAD facilitators in Washington, with no luck. He'd give it another try with Finch on hand to clear the communications hurdles.

His team was at work outside, assembled on the maintained, sloping lodge grounds near a swift-flowing watercourse that drained from a rising valley. The waters emanated from the melting snow and ice that mantled Everest. The grass was moist, still shining with the dawn's dews. They were getting their feet wet and they were still jet-lagged. He wasn't looking to jump-start their mission with an all-day trek to the slopes below Everest, but did want the team outside. *Get some altitude, loosen up, gulp some of this amazing air.* He looked around to see what his people were up to.

Maggie, wearing sunglasses, had settled on the grassy banks, seated on a plastic ground cloth with a sketchpad in her lap. Nice to see her there. Nice to have her here.

Frew and McPhee were parked off to one side, cradling hot coffees and bantering. At their boots a twisted green juniper shoot zigzagged from the loam at its base. Frew prodded about the plant's stem. Ming and Frauz were sprawled on the grass, their faces close to the heart-shaped leaves of a red-stemmed daisy. James noted that the daisy seemed especially profuse near the lodge and had asked them to take a closer look. He walked over.

"Odd, eh, Ming?" said James.

Ming gripped the stem and bent the flower towards him. He might have nodded in response.

Frauz looked up. "Seasonally, this isn't right, even for a ban mara flower. The base soil is off," he said, riffling a bit of it through his fingertips.

Ming drew a heavily lensed camera from its bag. "Thirty megapixels with macro," he said, holding the Nikon up to James. He set the camera to his eyes and began snapping photos of the plant.

"The camera will come in handy documenting the MEAD mission, Ming," said James. "Are you okay taking some crew shots, now and then?"

"No, too blurry," he complained. "I need a tripod." James wasn't sure if Ming was refusing or just complaining. He decided to let it slide. There'd be time to assert as they proceeded.

Frauz rose and leaned over, hands on hips, looking a bit dizzy.

"Altitude gets you at first," said James.

Frauz looked up from under his grey eyebrows and nodded. "It does. I'm feeling it. At least it's not freezing."

Frauz was right. The weather was pleasantly, oddly, warm. James raised the binoculars he'd borrowed from Frauz. Everest's summit was in constant murk, a steaming froth of whiteout. It was still sub-zero up there– of that he was sure. But here, strangely balmy.

He walked over to Frew and McPhee. "Everything feels off," James said.

"This *looks* off. Take a gander," said Frew. James crouched to study the zigzaggy juniper, sprouting from a plug of what looked like silt. Frew worked the root stem out of the ground, with the plant and base intact. "Feel this loam. Like, knead it."

James pulled at a bit, which tore away like taffy. His fingers marked it, making shallow depressions.

"To begin with, it should be limestone-based or maybe pulverized granitic rock, right?" said McPhee.

"It's taken on plasticity and weird deformation," said Frew. "And it's loam." He bared his teeth in a pleased grin. "Mother Nature's messing around. Kinda neat."

Frauz wandered over. "In case you haven't been so alerted, gentlemen, our own Mr. Ming owns and operates a multi-pixel, multi-lens, multiplex-ready Nikon super camera. The thing is not sporting, though. It pinpoints our GPS coordinates. Doesn't anyone fly by the seat of their pants, in this day and age?" He pulled out his pipe.

"You might want to give your lungs a bit more breathing room," James said.

Frauz hesitated, considered the pipe, then nodded. "You're right."

"Tell these guys about the daisy."

Frauz put the pipe back inside his jacket. "The daisy is the eupatorium. The locals call it *ban mara*; 'death to the forest.' Brought over from South America in 1900 and even the goats won't eat it. A fairly obnoxious exotic, as exotics go."

"I've heard about it," said James. He looked back up at the lodge complex. "The Nepalese consider it a sign of environmental decline. Nice how it sets off the hotel. Note my sarcasm."

"Hey Doctor Von," said McPhee, rising abruptly. "The restaurant coffee isn't bad, considering. I'm going for another cuppa. You want one?"

"Stick around for a minute, Dan. Everyone's up and half-awake. I want to go over one or two mission particulars." In a loose circle, the group assembled near James, close enough that Maggie could listen without seeming to snoop. "Everyone doing okay with the altitude?"

They all nodded except Frauz, who shook his head, but smiled.

"We have Diamox. If you feel faint or funny, speak up."

"I popped one with my coffee. Yum," said McPhee.

Frauz pursed his lips, found the drug packet in a top pocket, and began looking over the ingredients.

James continued. "Most of our equipment came in this morning. On the list and hopefully in the containers are thermal sensors, seismograph, two gravimeters, one geodimeter, two correlation spectrometers, two portable ICP's, ground-penetrating radar, photometers, pirot ball, and camping stuff, the field gear. A couple things I can't remember. There's a list somewhere."

"I got it," said Frew.

"You can ask Basil what it's like to get this stuff prepped on short notice. It's all at the airport waiting for us to haul it over. A lot to carry."

"So much for my day of sightseein'," said McPhee.

"Also, there's hardware we're expecting from the New Zealand crew. Something new called a modal interferometer. The Kiwis know how to run it. I've never heard of it. Stay on top of that, Basil, please."

"Will do," said Frew.

James continued. "The radio and satellite lines usually stay pretty robust through the winter. Not this year. Thermals are messing with both. Making it difficult to operate aircraft. Report from the flights we chartered is the conditions are too dicey. Pilots had trouble with their air-to-ground and also onboard nav stuff. They were supposed to get aerial footage of the summit massive. 'No way' is what I was told. I'm holding out hope some bold pilot will grab some footage."

"What about the drones?" asked Frew.

"They should be flying this afternoon, if it clears."

"I was hoping we could get some hot blueberry muffins droned in," said Frew.

"Basil, you run down to the drive-through and bring them back."

"I intend to."

"You all know by now that transmitting information is not going well. Voice, Internet, radio. If anyone needs to contact people overseas, or has personal messages you want sent, see me. Leslie Finch should be able to help us use the lodge communications. If I can ever find her."

"But my secret blog. My legion of fans. I can't even tweet," said Frew.

"They'll wait for you, Basil," said James. "Fame like yours isn't thwarted by technicalities."

"My government is to receive a daily update," said Ming. "The mountain lies halfway into China. Do not forget that, please, Dr. Kamburg."

"*Von* Kamburg, if you don't mind." James took a moment to gather himself. He had a professorial tone that was useful early in the semester at the university. He put on his glasses for good measure. "We won't provide reports until we establish facts." Ming's mouth opened, but he remained silent. "What do you think we've got, gentlemen? Anybody care to offer an initial theoretical? You won't be held to it unless you're wrong." No one smiled. "That was a joke."

There was a noise almost out of range of their hearing. They stopped to listen. In the distance James discerned a faint, half-hissed growl.

"That can't be what it sounds like," said McPhee. They strained to hear it again.

Maggie rose and walked over to the group. "What it is?"

McPhee glanced at her. "Sounds like snow leopard. Got to be. Ever read Matthiessen? One of the rarest beasts goin'." Ears cocked again. There was a rustle in the light breeze and the soft sound of water flowing.

"They are extremely, extremely rare. I don't know how you can be sure we have heard one," said Ming.

"They have oversized cavities up around the face and nose," said McPhee. "Helps them breathe the thin air. Can't roar. Hiss and chuff is more like it. Sounds like a Scottish pub: the *Hiss & Chuff*."

"We'll keep an ear out in case it comes galloping," said James dismissively. "Back to matters at hand. Anyone want to take a stab at Everest's unorthodox behavior? McPhee, you're a volcanologist."

"Volcano makes sense, preliminarily. That said, there's quite a bit doesn't add up. I'm thinking volcano, but I'm not feelin' it, if you get what I'm sayin'," said McPhee.

"What you're feeling is probably the curry you had last night, McPhee," said Frauz. "The temperature stability is not characteristic of an igneous source. The Greater Himalayan Sequence under our feet is a core of mixed, solid rock. But the data is suggesting diffusion. Mixed signals, if I may. I won't venture a guess quite yet."

James nodded. Ming was next. "If the accumulated data is accurate the mountain is in position to fault on a cataclysmic scale. It may collapse or erupt. I believe more caution is in order. We are inside a circle that is threatened. The proportions of this event are unknowable. An evacuation plan must be drawn up. For us, for the near communities and the region within 100 kilometers."

James resisted an urge to censure Ming. "What about you, Basil?" James liked to hear Basil's take. If not informative it would be colorful.

Frew shuffled his feet. "Gotta accrue, dude. Plug in the tech."

Frew was right. Conjecture served, but controlled sampling delivered. They needed their equipment. James dug his heel into the soil and looked over to see Maggie. She was walking to the stream bank. "Wait one minute. I want to ask Maggie something." He followed her over.

The idea of asking what she thought about the mountain seemed to come from the blue. She'd been a geology major for a term, of course. It was less complicated than that. At times, in the past, she'd relate an insight that he understood later had been unusually prescient. Since their tensions at home had escalated he'd been blocking her, avoiding conflict, and side-stepping the honesty they both venerated at the center of what they were. Their lines of communication, warming from the long and exciting journey together, were re-opening.

If he was honest, Maggie's intuitions had been markedly telling on many occasions. Sometimes she'd predict who was going to win a playoff game. Or have a dream about someone who'd then show up, like she did with Griffon. Other times, she'd brought to light some aspect missed or ignored, about things great and small. The twist was, it made him feel vulnerable. As if she could access, with this unusual and at times somewhat hair-raising acumen, more about him than he knew about himself. Or wanted to know, maybe.

He hesitated. It was the Finch thing, lurking around in the background of his psyche.

Maggie took off her shades, removed her shoes and socks, then dipped a big toe into the current. "Brrrrr."

"You're brave," he said. "That's gotta be cold."

She proceeded to lower bare feet into the flow, gritting her teeth as the rush of glacier melt met the warmth of her body. "It is!" She leaned forward. "What's that?"

Maggie steadied herself with one hand and pointed to something in the water. The others joined them at the rill's bank. Beneath the surface, small silvery pellets wheeled past in the turbulence. Like a codgery prospector, McPhee waded in, sifted the water, and held up two of the pellets. They were golf-ball sized, surfaces uneven and mottled, and surprisingly spherical. To everyone's amusement and, James could tell, Maggie's slight revulsion, McPhee gave one a lick.

"Aluminum. Almost symmetrical. Looks man-made," he announced. McPhee stepped out of the stream and shook each boot to the side. He handed one of the pellets to Frew, who held it up to his nose to scrutinize.

"Weird-a-mundo," offered Frew.

"Are there more in there?" asked James, pacing along the bank. They appeared, curiously, almost identical to the ones given away at the Earthyield press conference. "I think I see more."

More of the globules could be seen, tumbling in short, stop-start spurts, down over the uneven streambed. McPhee waded in again. The pellets appeared sporadically, but McPhee was able to corral three more in the swift current. He handed one to James.

Maggie knelt at the water's edge. "Jim, look. Some kind of pipe." She pointed upstream. Set just below the water's surface and obscured by mosses and a pitched overhang of earth, James saw what appeared to be a small drain. "What is it?" she asked, standing to brush the mud from her knees. "You look perturbed."

He shook his head as he followed the apparent path of the drain along a sight line of disturbed earth. It was easy to trace up to the lodge, continuing until it ended under the pool dome complex. He headed up the slope.

* * *

The Everest Vista Lodge featured a low-lit, rosewood-paneled and bronze-railed cocktail lounge where, within spitting distance of the spectacular Sagarmatha National Park, guests could while away the precious hours.

And, noted Finch, those guests not inclined to revel in the spectacle could instead nurse an ice-filled schooner of gin and tonic or other spirit of their choice. Excellent choices, she would add, having considered thoroughly the row of bottles lining up to attention on the glass shelf over the bar.

Finch loved that Earthyield had outfitted this particular gin joint with so many lovelies. A free pass to the booze case didn't hurt either. Most fortuitously, it was open all night and day. It was mid-morning, so attendance was light. Finch, and a single hostess. A Westernized reconstitution of Nepalese music coursed from hidden speakers, slathering elevator-styled compositions into the ambiance. The music reminded her of Gault, revealing one more, albeit minor, managerial deficiency of his.

He'd been a viable prospect. He had a burly resilience which they needed for a manager so far from Vancouver. His independent thinking, back then, had been considered a plus. He comprehended the local dialect (though spoke it poorly himself). He appeared to be onboard with a clear understanding that Earthyield needed to keep the authorities mollified and largely in the dark. He also needed to administer their collusion with the Thyzenboche monks.

Once Dr. Virgil had broken through with the Synthium replication at scale, they'd needed Gault to expedite control of any remaining problematic stuff in Nepal. To be fair, the operation had moved from small industrial to hyper-tech very rapidly. Overnight it had transitioned to a large-scale, quasi-illicit water-extraction racket. His "insider" staff were tasked to retrieve the water from the monastery and get the water to Vancouver. Jared would have shuttered the lodge, except it hid the bottling operation and gave them a modernized exoskeleton in this mountain shantytown.

On this dulled morning, Finch cared more about having another gin, maybe without the tonic. The blue color of the gin bottle blurred the level of liquid inside; she poured out too much. *Damn.* Spilled. Not a thing to waste. She ran a finger over the splash of gin and rubbed it across her lips.

She sat at the bar, in the dark near the wall. Nicely tucked in. Hidden. It was stuffy, though, like lounges feel before noon. The cocktails were getting her drunk, as planned. The Nepalese bartendress (as Finch labeled her) stood some distance away, ritually wiping down every glass in the cabinet. Then she held each up, at arm's length, and shone a small light through the bottom. After the restaurant kerfuffle that got the kid fired, no glass was left behind. *Gotta be pristine, Christine.*

Finch took breathy sips of her gin, drawing just a tongue-tip. A group of tourists wandered into the lounge. They mumbled a few comments, noticed Finch, and moved on.

"Fuck you," said Finch.

She took another sip and whispered, "I'm pregnant." Finch looked over at the bartendress, who bowed her head. "I use the most advanced chemistries known to man– no, make that *woman*– to prevent this."

The hostess turned sheepishly away, set down the flashlight and took a key ring from somewhere under the bar.

"My boss, he's a close personal acquaintance, you see, he's not going to be happy when he finds out he's going to be a father. And when he hears what the nasty abbot's done. *No more stealing water from the magic well.*"

The hostess stooped out of sight, apparently fidgeting with the music. Various genres cycled up. A lovely Parisian accordion flared briefly, replaced by the Rolling Stones, and a chord or two of Dan Fogelberg, before settling on Lorde. Finch heard the keys rattling. *She's locking up the gin. Won't let me get any drunker. She's nice. A prick, but nice.*

"Meanwhile, just outside our windows at the scenic Everest Vista Lodge, the world is turning into a geological theme park." Her eyes watered into tears. She watched them gather on the surface of the bar, tiny ponds fed by her misery.

* * *

James climbed onto the lodge's deck and reached the transparent double-doors to the pool. He pulled the handles but the door barely budged. He thought of going around to try to get in from the interior. The odds of being given permission to inspect the pool complex were not good. No, he had to get through the lock.

There was a trick he'd heard about. He pulled a credit card from his wallet, held it up to the door's seam and ran it down through the center till it met the tapered locking pin. He applied slow steady pressure. The mechanism nudged, freeing the door enough for him to pull it open. He stepped inside as the door closed softly behind.

The pool water was dark. He could feel the cold emanating from it, though the room itself was warm and humid. Condensation fogged the large windows, making the space less easy to see from the outside.

He stopped. *What happened to my scruples?* Last night, doing the reprobate shuffle with another woman. Now this, a form of breaking and entering. The run-off pipe had thrown him out of his routine. He was irritated. Scruples were shunted, again.

There was no good reason the lodge should drain chemical-laden pool water into the stream that supplied the villages. The chlorine would show up in water used for drinking, cooking and washing. From what James knew, hotel swimming pools recycled their water through enclosed systems, filtering out the chemicals for safe disposal.

He didn't smell chlorine. It was a different, curious odor. He walked to the edge and crouched to study the pool's construction. The water moved in telltale ripples. They were keeping it circulated, if not chlorinated. He walked over and pressed his nose against a window to see if he could locate the spot where the pipe drained into the stream.

"Damn."

From a staff entrance at the opposite end of the dimmed complex, a door squealed softly open. It was Finch. He saw that her eyes were red and that she hadn't seen him.

He spoke. "You pipe pool runoff into the river."

She looked up. Her slight eyebrows rose, mechanically. "Is that what Gault is doing?" She moved to stand next to him, shaking her head in slow deliberation.

"There's a small outlet pipe. In the stream below the lodge," James said. "Correct me if I'm wrong: the pool water drains there. Whatever agent I'm detecting mixes with the village water supply."

Finch crouched, swishing her hands in the pool. "We've been looking to replace Gault."

"So what?"

"It's part of the reason Jared sent me here."

"A swimming pool isn't designed by the guy who manages the hotel, Leslie. This was built to spec." James wished there was a way to confirm his accusation. He spotted a hinged access panel on the floor near the wall and knelt to try to lift it. The metal rattled, but wouldn't release beyond a small, wedged opening. He let it drop with a bang.

"What's Jared thinking? Why abuse one of Earth's most revered landscapes?"

"A Tokyo firm built the lodge, including the pool. We bought it after the quake."

"What are you saying? Your organization moved in without an environmental assessment?" He remembered the pellets they'd just found in the stream. He took one out of his shirt pocket. "Ever see one of these?"

Finch stood, and pulled her arms in under her neck.

"We just fished these out of the river. Are these the same pellets you gave away at the press conference? Is Earthyield manufacturing something here? Or mining?"

Finch started, then paused. More corporate spin coming, James thought. He felt an unnerving urge to shake her.

"That pipe is not a drain. It's an intake."

James felt the lump in his throat. She was right. How else would you fill up the pool? He was an idiot. Charging into the fight without using his head because it had to do with toxins and waste run-off and carbon levels. He was responsible for running an international task force and he was picking street fights. "Leslie…"

She pulled at the belt that circled her thin waist, straightening up, her eyes blinking. "I need to tell you something."

He shook his head. "I was wrong to say what I said. I–"

She held her hand out over the pool to interrupt him. "This water comes from the monastery. We buy it from the monks."

"Monastery?"

"We have a contract with the Thyzenboche Monastery. The water in the pool is from the spring on their grounds. A van goes over every night to collect it."

"I don't understand."

Finch swallowed. "It's a cover. The monastery spring water bottled as Everpure and sold to the world. The abbot knows, though."

"Cover for what?" James said.

"The water from the monastery is chemically unique. It has a peridotite trace. Jared says it's mantle rock."

"The Kathmandu sample is from the monastery?" said James.

"The bone marrow of Synthium. No monastery spring water, no Earthyield."

James knelt on one knee, genuflecting before the shimmering aqua. "The pool's filled with the same stuff?"

Finch nodded. "The pool is always closed. Guests aren't here to swim."

James took a deep breath. Finch smelled of liquor and spoke at half volume in a strained monotone.

"Without this water there is no Synthium process," she said. "The water is a power. It regenerates universal elements from scratch. It's broken our physics."

James reeled. The water provided, Griffon exploited. He'd been unable to decipher the mystery at the nucleus. Which was why he needed James. To crack nature's code– for the benefit of Earthyield's bottom line. "You kept the discovery to yourselves to make the profit for yourselves," he said.

"We bottle a load in the lodge basement every night. Ends up at the dock in Vancouver."

"Why are you admitting this, out of the blue?" said James. She didn't seem to hear the question.

"The intake pipe was laid so we can sample the stream. Check for peridotite positives," she said.

"If you found it you could source for the mantle chemistry right from the river with no middle men. No middle monks."

"We haven't found it. Only Thyzenboche," she said.

James put a hand behind his neck and rubbed. She reached to take the pellet. "The mantle water must be leaching to the surface. Reacting with aluminum– could be the discarded oxygen tanks that end up in the glaciers below Everest. Nature's crock pot. Come and get it." She threw the pellet into the pool. "Goodbye Earthyield. We're done."

He saw her shiver, a ripple that made her shoulders heave and shake. "Leslie, okay, okay. I don't know why you're coming clean but you are. You need to tell me about Everest. Tell me about connections between Synthium and the geological expressions we're seeing."

She looked down at him, brushing blue-black tresses from her face. "We're drilling our own well up past the monastery. It's seven hundred meters deep. Still no water…" Her voice faltered. "It's leaching to the surface. Reacting with minerals. God, can't you see what might happen…"

James lowered his head to think. Finch was blowing hot and cold, yes, but her admissions had become critical data. He needed to give her space to find her equilibrium. Get her grip. This was about more than just a *mea culpa;* they might need each other, geologically speaking. "Let's take a moment. I'm not sure where we go with this. I need you to focus and help me make a sensible picture. Think intervention. Where to start. Science is calling."

That last sounded ridiculous when he said it, but it came out that way and he meant it. Finch walked to the steamed, panoramic windows. Outside, conifers moved in the wind, sliding across the panes like groping hands. With sharp fingernails Finch outlined a jagged triangle across the fogged surfaces. James rose and walked around to face her, his back to the steamed glass. Nearby was a long bench set against the wall.

"Let's sit," he said. Erect, she stood before him, slender lips and dark eyes, black hair falling across the tawny flesh of her open neck.

She took hold of his sleeves, gripping. "I'm trapped." She routed her arms around him, burrowing her hands under his jacket. In his head he resisted, but his body maneuvered to make it easier, bringing his torso forward so she could embrace him. He felt his collar go wet from the moist window. Finch tightened her hold. Through fabric he felt her fingers against his skin.

"Help." She nuzzled her head into the hard softness of his chest.

Her honesty moved him. A bridge of alluring need thumped between their beating hearts. She was lost, he was found. Her body pulsed across the thin divide. All kinds of wrong invitations sounded. She was waiting, he could tell, for the signal she could become slack in his grip, let go and be held.

She sunk her cheek into his shirt, her words halting and unsteady. "Keep you in the dark. Mess things up. Get the water. Screw the monks." Then, in a whisper, "Jared's commandments. He's going to be the worst kind of disappointed." Finch moved her arms up to his neck and with her fingers found places to roam. His head was clouded with a contradiction of tenderness, fear, shame, and arousal.

He remembered Maggie clearing her throat at the dinner last night. She and he were in their studio, fussing about procreation and offspring and the life they had built. They were sitting on the back steps. He and Maggie. That life was sliding into a pit, the escape ladder withering against a blue-hot torch.

James twisted away, removing Finch's hands from his neck. He stepped back and, his empathy kindled in deference to her plight, gently increased the space between them. "Why don't we sit down?" he said, the professor counseling the student. Finch's head dropped, her hands and arms without a place to go.

With a quiet scraping, the deck door opened. It must have not clicked shut after he'd entered. Maggie Von Kamburg entered the pool room. She walked over to stand near them and took her husband by the arm. James noticed that a distinctive smear marked the wet window, where it looked like someone had leaned against it. He felt Maggie's hand explore the dampness on the back of his jacket.

"Everything okay?" she asked.

"Leslie's upset," said James

Maggie set her gaze on Finch. "What is it, Leslie? What's wrong?" Finch stumbled away, without looking back. Maggie turned to her husband. "James?"

* * *

With Maggie, James returned down the slope to the MEAD team. He motioned for them to gather.

"Got a few more o'these, captain," said McPhee, juggling three of the silver pellets.

"Get a set of those out to Oregon, to Spa," James said.

"If we can find any flights. What's goin' on, VK?" said Frew.

James was reminded what vulnerable felt like. Really good, really bad. He spoke, hoping he'd mask the fragile state of his psyche. "We've got new data. Significant but no verification. I need to do background checks. I'll be in my room. Get over to the airport and get our equipment. The lodge rents an all-terrain thing with a tow cart for trips to the village. Get two of them. Basil, you're the man."

"Set up on the pool deck, right?" said Frew.

James nodded. "Move the tables and umbrellas to the side."

"The hotel was supposed to do that," said Frauz. "I'm noting reluctance in their so-called support role."

"They didn't, so we will," said James. "The airport's five minutes from Namche. Everything should be under my name, or yours, Basil. Also would like one of you to get over to the Zamling Guest House. The New Zealand guys are lodging there. I want to set up a meeting."

"What happened up there?" Frew asked, gesturing towards the pool.

"I thought, prematurely," James said, "that they were dumping pool chemicals into the stream. That's not the case. I have pieces of the story, only. There's a lot to find out."

"Anything about the pellets?" asked McPhee.

"Yes and no. We may learn more about what might be happening with Everest. I need to step back and gather the strands, so to speak. See what the big picture is saying. I'm also going to recruit more bodies. Get the Kiwis signed in and see who else Washington or Oregon might be able to fly over here."

"Our government is mobilizing for all eventualities," said Ming.

"You've been able to call them?" asked James.

Ming remained silent.

"I'll be in my room, 222."

Maggie and James returned to the lodge, slipping up a back staircase to their second floor room.

"See if you can get the broadband going," James said. He opened the drawer on the bedside table and brought out his iPad from where he'd stashed it, under a room service menu. He handed the iPad to Maggie and punched in numbers on his cell phone. Without his glasses, he held it close to his face. No coverage. He picked up the lodge phone and punched "O". "Hi, yes. Can I get a call out to the US?"

Maggie worked the tablet, studying the code and password card provided when they had checked in.

"When you can get a call through, buzz this room. Thanks," said James, and hung up. He went to the closet, lifted his briefcase, and set it on the bed. He pulled several file folders and arranged them across the small desk.

"The wireless is hooked up. It's slow," said Maggie. "Google still loading. Okay, wait, now dead."

"Sit down with me," said James, pushing the briefcase to the side. "Please."

She walked over to the balcony door, unlocked it and slid it open. The outside light was a white glare, a mix of the mountain's unorthodox steams and the valley's humid evaporations. She stepped out. He rose from the bed to follow.

"Maggie, I am–" he faltered. "First, I am sorry."

She kept her face turned away as she looked out into the wide expanse. He watched as she made fists around the balcony rail, let it hold her weight. The world was a grand easel in front of them, rock, ice, sky, pines walking in tall order down the inclines, tourists and trekkers dotting the swards of steep slope, and the cloudy, fretting murk of Everest, the consummate, surreal backdrop to all of it.

"It's not all you," she said. "I'm starting to lose my way. Our way. Do we still have a way?"

He placed his hand over her fisted grip. He felt her knuckles stiffen.

"You crossed some line in there. We vowed, you and I–" She trailed off.

"I did. I was really, like a teenager."

"What do we do? You have to work with her. You need to stay away." She crouched as if to do knee-bends off the rail, pulling her hand from under his, then rose back up to face him. "The way you mucked around at dinner last night in front of everyone. God, James. That was sick. It made me sick. I should've left."

"Yeah. Yes."

"So *what?*"

"I liked that she was making a play for me."

"Playing with fire. You did a lot of that, growing up."

He registered a micron of hope in her calling up of this recollection, one he'd shared with her about his boyhood gusto for risk and experimentation. She remembered he had managed to produce a small block of an extremely illicit, solid-form combustible in his parents' garage before he entered high school. That was one eventful day among more than a few. A wick was lit and something had gone *boom*.

Ah, Maggie, just stick the fork in, he thought. He wanted to be told he was a miserable, screwed-up human, do his penance and get his absolution. The realization that he could analyze the process so analytically made him feel all the more pitiful. He wanted to walk away to relieve her of the company of someone so pitiful.

"You didn't sleep with anyone, you didn't undress anyone, you didn't, but you wanted to think that the idea could be possible just for the pleasure of it."

"Maggie, I am pathetic, and sorry, and if I say 'I love you' you can laugh."

She put her hands over her face, clutching and squeezing. Her hands stilled, and slid down over her neck, and fell to her sides. Without looking at him, she reached for him. He blinked through the water in his eyes. She held him and he held her. They moved in off the balcony, closed and locked the door, and dragged the curtain across the wide picture window.

Chapter Nine

It was early afternoon when the MEAD team motored up to park beside the deck off the pool, their haul of instruments and equipment filling several wooden crates in the trailers. James stood at the window, moving the curtain enough to see them hopping out of the all-terrain buggies and unbinding the crates.

He turned to speak to Maggie. With a long sigh, she stretched under the cotton sheet, baring her shoulders and back. "The team is here. I'll go make some noise," he said. He finished buttoning his shirt. She rolled over, gathering the cotton up and around to cover herself. James put on his jacket, stepped into the hall and pulled the door to close it.

"Wait," she called, softly.

He looked in. Eyes, smiling green.

"I'll be down in a few."

* * *

Mr. Grace was steps ahead and Clarence Gault found himself breathing heavily from the exertion. "Got to cool it," he shouted. "I'm going to keel."

They were climbing a steep path to high ground overlooking the lodge.

It was a strategic spot where one could spy parts of Namche Bazar and glimpse the prayer flags adorning the roof of the monastery. Mt. Everest was not visible but in the northeast a mammoth white fume boiled, its genesis blocked by a brow of hillside. Mr. Grace, his face hidden behind sunglasses, reached a bench carved crudely into the micaschist rock. He stood and waited.

Gault puffed his way up to the spot and slumped onto the seat. "Give me a minute." He gasped. The daylight was bright but diluted. There was, oddly, almost no wind. "Listen, Gracey. We'll have to make some decisions. Finch's head is somewhere else. We aren't having much luck connecting with Vancouver."

Mr. Grace stood with his back to the sun. Gault shielded his eyes against the blinding silhouette. "Griffon made a plan. The plan is cooked. You and I have to work with what's happening here, on the ground, in the trenches," said Gault. The sun was too bright. He rubbed his eyes and looked away. Mr. Grace spoke.

"The auger tip is probably unusable. I need to retrieve it and assess. The connector assembly and the shaft's main drive are most likely damaged. I didn't get a clear look into the borehole; I don't know if we'll have to move the set-up. If there was a collapse I didn't hear it. If the auger is finished, the back-up laser, tethered, is an option. We'd have to jury-rig a drop cable and see how it performs. I don't know if it's feasible. Without the solid shaft we can't guide the digging as effectively."

Gault recognized Mr. Grace's autopilot mode: delivering an exacting sound byte of information with practically no emotional skew. It was almost spooky. Mr. Grace continued.

"There may have been a trickle of water. I wasn't sure and didn't feel it was safe to investigate. It's possible what I thought was water was blood. It's imperative to get back there, so we can review. And make some decisions. Regardless of what we find, we'll have to re-test everything. Plus, we need new personnel. I'm not going back out without a bigger team and improved logistics."

"What the hell happened?"

Mr. Grace dug the heel of his shoe into the dirt, sending a cluster of dusty pebbles over the slope. "Something reversed the spin of the auger. It came free and did a one-eighty. A one-eighty inside the borehole. From there, it shot up the shaft and hit Yates."

"God."

"I don't like fantasy. In order for what happened to have happened, various tenets of physics were pushed to a threshold nearing impossibility. The incident required a short-term electromagnetic burst, several counter-probable influences that would have to be in a position to guide the forces, and a culminating repulsion that was, again, for practical purposes beyond explainable. If you do the math. Which I do."

Gault noted how still it had become. He watched as another pebble clattered off the edge of the bank, and placed his palms against the seat. "Griffon is thinking we need to tap a different site," he said, steadying himself.

"Considering what's happened the initial plan is no longer viable," said Mr. Grace. "There are other mitigating factors. The deeper we drill, the more it appears that the rock at the bottom of the shaft is soft, like a putty. The auger was fighting to get through that, which contributed to our difficulties. I have no idea what was down there because it wouldn't stick to the bit. We had no way to analyze. When we brought the bit up it was marred, but clean. One additional point I will mention. The snow and ice kept the yaks and zopkios from attempting to graze near the current location, but we are getting an early melt, an unexpected thaw. Berries and fruits are sprouting out of ground where they shouldn't be germinating."

Gault remembered the Kiwi tree escapade. "What do you recommend? I'll pass it to Finch and let her handle Griffon's flak."

"I'll take a buggy out tonight to inspect the borehole. If it's not collapsed, we can go forward without a location change. The next step will be to haul up the main drive and check the auger. As I stated, if the auger is damaged, we can try the tethered laser. The laser may be more effective cutting a path through the pliable substrate. I'll also inspect the shaft and confirm whether or not the water table has been tapped."

"That's a lot of work," said Gault.

"There's also a body to retrieve."

Gault remembered Yate's face, not much more. *Poor rat.*

"The physics, the science, is intriguing. If I wasn't under contract, I'd consider offering my services elsewhere."

That was a thing to hear. If Gault interpreted it correctly, Mr. Grace was suggesting he'd switch allegiance to the MEAD team, just for the chance to play with Von Kamburg's toys. *Whoa. And wow.* It was time he and Gracey hiked down the hill.

"I suggest you and Finch consider alternate sites," said Mr. Grace. "I won't guarantee we can continue. If the weather continues to warm, the monks expand their pastures, the tech is no longer operational, and or the abnormalities escalate, you can let Griffon know we will stand down."

"That's typically long-winded of you, Gracey. In this case I agree." With a heave, Gault hauled himself off the seat, and stood. He the tall and soft-bellied next to the slight and formidably wiry. "One more thing I need to tell you. The abbot showed up yesterday. Finch met with him. He intends to stop the sale of the water."

Mr. Grace set two fingers to his mouth, as if to say "hush." Any expression was rare from this guy. Truth to tell, Gault didn't really know the man standing next to him. Mr. Grace had come over last year to scout and implement the drilling. He was a contract player. Unlike the sluggish IT people, with Mr. Grace they had won the lottery. He was tenacious, cool-headed, and surgical. Yeah, that was it; *surgical.* Through his previous dealings with the man, Gault would already have wagered that Mr. Grace's loyalties were unanchored. Now he'd heard it with his own ears. Another meeting with him, at a less circumspect moment, would be good. Might be work they could do together.

"Did you see that last pebble go over the hillside?" said Mr. Grace.

Gault nodded.

"It moved off the face due to vibration. Yet we felt nothing. There's more here than meets the eye."

Surgical and enigmatic Grace.

"Go do your recon," said Gault. "We can talk tomorrow. My gut is telling me this is not the place to be. I'm beginning to think we should shut down. Think about getting out." He looked at Mr. Grace, whose face remained blank. "Thanks for the updates, Mr. Grace. I'll let Finch tell Griffon the good news."

* * *

Jared Griffon strode towards Virgil's office. The Everest water was displaying unexplainable aberrations, a change from the relatively steady patterns they had seen. Virgil said the water was transmuting. He couldn't predict where it was heading. He re-read Virgil's scrawled note, which he'd found tacked to his office door.

Water trouble. Stop by. We need a chat.

When Virgil worked long hours, his overtaxed seams started to perforate. Griffon had witnessed the phenomenon enough times and considering all on their corporate plate, he didn't need Virgil's alarmist fuss. Much had been ticking along to good effect. There were issues in Nepal, but distinction and prosperity were taking root in Vancouver. No iceberg for this Titanic.

Still. There was an iceberg, a big one, most of it below the waterline: the fertility enhancer that had shown up in the water. It undercut Griffon's ability to think as straight as he wanted, or even sleep well. Over-population had always gnawed at him. Virgil thought he was overreacting. Griffon understood how powerful the water was, in the chemical realm. It was easy for him to see how powerful it might be as a biological catalyst. Water evaporated, traveled in clouds, could easily make its way into the bloodstreams of humans across the world. If the Everpure was truly enabled as a super-proto-fertility enhancer, he'd have to kill it at the source. At the spring, at Everest.

Virgil had been tasked to execute the formula that would *cure* the water. Griffon trusted this scribbled request to meet meant he had an update on the cure, and not just some additional exasperating distraction.

The door to Virgil's office was open, the overhead lights their standard dim. The scatter of the man's working debris spread over the floor, overflowing from cabinets and dangling from hooks. Hums hummed, beeps beeped, pings pinged. *I wonder what I pay the electric company to keep these plugs juiced.* He fought the urge to get side-tracked.

Virgil was leaning in, face close to the sickly green light emanating from his display.

"Virgil."

Virgil did a one-eighty in his seven-hundred-dollar ergonomic chair. A mocha wafer poked from his jaws. He looked at Griffon, brushing off crumbs, face slack, hair a bowl of dark fudge.

"Greets," said Virgil, one-eighty-ing back to face his monitor. Griffon watched as he closed several browser windows. MIT chat room. Bill Nye. Three Stooges. Griffon had all of it tracked and knew every employee's web habits. But. *Petty stuff. Remember why you're here.*

"Something in the newest water, Jared. Synthium going haywire. We need to shut down the forges. Take a breather and see what's shakin'. Forge workers might need to start wearing radiation exposure badges and I know you don't want that."

Griffon pulled up a chair and sat. Virgil was crazy but not a fool. The water was the weak link; always had been. For a hideous moment Griffon thought of calling Von Kamburg. Virgil continued.

"The latest batch is not synthesizing in the usual manner. Our production pipeline is designed to handle a degree of inexactitude. You built that in and it works. But today, last few hours, unrecognizable elemental compounds. More disturbing is a suggestion of possible radioactivity. We may need to shut down our shiny furnaces. Forge workers could be exposed."

"Slow down, Virgil. We have legacy water from previous shipments. Use the surplus legacy for now, till we figure this out."

"It's gone. Research gobbled it."

"Christ, Virgil." He shoved his chair away. "You knew this was going on? Who tapped it? Was it Jules?"

Virgil popped another wafer into his mouth, and bit. It splintered, crumbs sailing out in damp trajectories. He held the bag out for Griffon. "You want any?"

Griffon wiped his face and sat up. He could either laugh or cry. The man was guileless. A court jester with the aptitude of Stephen Hawkings. Griffon would find out what happened to the legacy water eventually. More important things loomed. "Let's nail this, Virgil."

Virgil bobbed his head in a less-than-affirming nod. "I'll humor your request." He began flying through links to internal-access-only data and pulling up cross-referenced code. Water reactivity charts manifested, along with indicators explaining why radioactivity might arise. This is better, thought Griffon. Virgil crackled at savant speeds when he put his mind to it.

"Something is happening in Nepal," said Griffon. "The US Geological Survey won't say. It's possible the Everest area is starting to react to the Thyzenboche water."

"What's the use of knowing that? It doesn't help us. If we can't figure out the core reaction for ourselves, if we remain dependent on a water source that's supplied in earthenware by bald monks, do you expect we have long-term viability?"

"Okay. Just get to the stuff on the note you wrote."

Virgil tapped the mouse with a single finger. The screen filled with a close-up photograph of a moth.

"The water is no longer stable. I don't see how we can continue. It does what it wants. A moth got into Chamber Five yesterday. Don't ask me how. That's a production chamber we've been using since day one, with no recorded deviations." He tapped the mouse again. The same photo was repeated, sharing two halves of the display. Those two split into four. Then eight. Sixteen. And so forth.

"When the new shift came on, there were 327 moths replicated in the chamber along with the freshly synthesized mineral. Lithium, in this case. The Lithium might also– get this, it's wild– might also have been imprinted with a chemical translation of the moth DNA. The moth getting inside the chamber in the first place, that's a separate problem. But I do need to reiterate: it's the water, not the chamber."

"Can you isolate the rogues in the water? Maybe we can't reproduce the reaction, but if we identify the differences from the legacy water, can we strip out the reactives?" asked Griffon.

"No."

"Why?"

"Are you kidding? The whole process, in fact the whole organization, is dependent on solutions and reactions that are impossible to reproduce without a supply of Thyzenboche kool-aid. We've never figured out what the water does at a nuclear level. That unknown known is now unknown. Rumsfeld would be tickled. The water's constitution worked and was largely stable. No more. It's transitioning. Something else is happening."

Griffon felt his patience waning. Virgil needed to fix the problem, not make excuses. "Should we shut down Earthyield?"

Virgil rose to his feet and buttoned his lab coat. "Jared, pardon me. I eat junk and don't sleep and watch too much crap on YouTube." He stood in his doorway as if to shoo Griffon out. "Give me a week and another box of Godiva meltaways. I will fix. But cure before fix."

"Yes. Progress on the cure, Virgil. Tell me where you're at."

"98%. Almost done. The moth accident is, ironically, going to serve as the template for our next test."

"Good. Do not allow any other task to take precedence. Cure before fix. You got that?" Griffon stepped through the door into the hall and paused. "If I need to I will drop the cure into the Thyzenboche spring myself."

Griffon was alone on the elevator. He leaned against the wall to take the pressure off his feet, staring blankly at the elevator's illuminated floor indicators. A comforting scene formed. A warm remembrance of his head cradled in the lap of a female, long fingers tenderly stroking his brow. Auburn hair. Soft voice. Maggie. It was *Maggie.* Their trajectories were heading into the same strange void. The ease with which she reappeared disturbed him. Un-had lives not worth the bother.

Still.

The immovable asterisk of Maggie had blighted James Von Kamburg as a candidate for Earthyield's team. Griffon had had a dour evening when the reconciliation of his corporate need for Von Kamburg's acumen came up against the certainty of seeing her in the flesh if her husband was hired. Nearly the deal-breaker, that.

His recall chilled; the warmth of their days together dialed back to a sullen purgatory. They were never soul mates. In those scant months they'd found little in common. She never gave her body unreservedly or completely. He experimented with the idea of love. Never found it easy to identify the components. The divide went postal when he informed her he thought she'd be a good candidate to bear his offspring. There was over-population and there was Griffon, after all.

She left. It was no disaster. A failure of appreciation on her side. Still, it marked him, this particular failure. Nothing in Jared Griffon's cache of practical decency or calculated coercion had been enough to make her stay. He pushed his fist into the elevator's wall.

* * *

It was late afternoon in the high Himalayas. The ache in Leslie Finch's head had subsided with the oblivion of some much-needed sleep. She was awake, with nowhere to go. She needed to put space between her and Gault and Von Kamburg and the slate blue Lycra vassals of Griffon. She wanted nothing and no one. She laced up her hiking boots and put on a lightweight grey windbreaker. Hood up and sunglasses on, she found a back stairwell and climbed down to an exit door.

She walked to the rear of the lodge grounds and slipped out, stepping onto a less-traveled pathway that led down into Namche Bazar. She'd hope for isolation in the crowded thoroughfares there, in the stew of mad colors, noises and dirty elbows. She passed under the eaves of dark firs and came to the top of a spur. In the distance, below, she spied the gate to the village. It stood out, a garish red trellis. From there, the trail switchbacked down and across a terraced flat. Beyond the village, she could see a vast, sweeping gulf. So deep and wide was the gorge which Namche adjoined that, viewed from across it, the slopes on the other side appeared washed and indistinct. Clambering over its brink, tiny figures emerged, moving like drugged ants, liberated from the abyss. Immensity and spectacle, all around. She paused to look back at Everest. It was hidden behind its distinguished forecourt, the great shoulders of Lhotse and Makalu.

She took a deep breath and coughed, starved of oxygen. Altitude sickness was no joke; the elevation, outside the lodge, made itself known. Her head felt light and her boots heavy. She would, hopefully, be able to cash in on the workouts and daily morning run she'd made a ritual of in Vancouver. More breaths, then a careful stretch and her body felt better.

A different sickness was looming. A disquieting recognition of how little she cared about where she was. At one point in her young adulthood the idea of a trip to the Himalayas would have put her on cloud nine. This was where she and Jared had walked such an awesome path forward, together. Now it was the staging area for her lowest low. Her lowest low at the highest high. She sighed, vacantly bitter, pulled her jacket tighter around her, and continued down the hill.

Small lanes, cramped shops, dirt alleys, spillways muddied with multitudes. This was Namche. She studied the faces. Tricked-out trekkers, unshaven street denizens, slicked-up lodgers, the odd muddle of un-designate-ables, and the locals, in the jumbled hanging cloth they called garb. She tallied expressions: beaming, fretting, oblivious, undone, composed. Masks with souls behind. Paradise was sludgy with people.

In the crush there were men and maybe a few women looking for a casual score, a night under sheets with female anatomy. Not all of them, but enough. You could see it in the eyes. She welcomed the glances, abhorred the expectation, couldn't avoid indulging in the imagined gratifications.

But among the Nepalese locals, there was not a recreant. Stalwarts, to the woman, man and child. Grinding, hewing, carrying, sweating: there was no easy way out of doing your part to get through the next few hours of life. Find and cart the firewood to boil the meat for the evening meal. Heat more water for bathing and laundering. Keep the animals in good stead. Stay warm in the rain and cold and thin air. They were stolid, hardy and hearty. Even the damned abbot was a stalwart, a redoubtable example held up for Finch's indiscriminate scruples to mull over.

Anyway. None were here to share their secrets of survival.

She slipped out of the main thoroughfares and moved off to a side path, slanting up towards a nowhere fringe above the village. She found a broad boulder to sit on. Namche Bazar stretched like a postcard below her, in the faded daylight of the high valley. She took off her boots and shook out the crud. The Earth, the spinning sphere with two melting polar caps and an equator around its belly, at her feet. She took off her socks and dug her bare toes in.

This was good terra firma, purest dirt, and she could register its connection to living.

She'd been raised on a farm in upstate New York. Growing up, *Pilgrim at Tinker Creek* had been one of her favorite reads. Way before it was fashionable, her parents were zealous activists for the planet. Nature stood forth without a coded agenda, revealing a path to goodness and things that counted. If she performed to their expectations, young Leslie would be an instrument to help course-correct humankind's screwed-up stewardship of the world. Finch knew her mission early, and keenly. Her parents had, Finch believed, included it in her DNA– Save The Earth.

That shiny future was a casualty to the alchemy of the Synthium grail. Never really sound science, the marvel of Synthium was dependent on Thyzenboche water for vitality. She and Griffon had built their planet-saving castle on sand. The Buddha-laced H_2O was no longer isolated at the monastery. It was frothing up from somewhere below, its properties outbound in the meltwaters from the glaciers, where James found the silver spheres, instilling its agents of mutation into everything it touched. And the monks were bailing anyway. Earthyield was dead in the water. Maybe Earth was next.

She had things to say to Jared. She'd get more than she'd give and more than she wanted. He'd carve her concerns into a funk of remorse, like he had when she'd finally gotten close enough to see into his heart. He hadn't fashioned an ever-after story nor pretended he would court her to keep her. What they had in front of them was plenty, he waxed. She could stay or not. She'd be a fool to leave. She wasn't that dumb, was she?

Her proposal of matrimony probably started their current long slide into disunion. She wanted to marry, hoping a formal binding would lock down their speculative stock. Jared never said no, directly. She had broached it a single morning, a few months ago. His reply was succinct, something like, "Did you log off securely?" The "m" word was ignored, the idea dispersed into the ether. Heart in dogged pursuit she had soldiered on, the blinding draw of Earthyield's firmament enough to dope the stupidity of staying with him.

This man James Von Kamburg. Why the strange attraction, now? A complicated opening act for her and him. Not to mention the lurking spouse. A missed opportunity, maybe. Further botched by her drunken tears and ruinous confessions by the pool. She'd disclosed Earthyield's secret recipe. Pandora's box was open.

Lastly and mostly, there was the mountain, spitting up silver pellets, shoving something tectonic around below them, pushing pines through its crust like pins through Styrofoam. The world was as unstable as the stuff going on in the human lives it supported.

Jared's directives had stuck with her. As a duo, his shrewd operating sense and her SWAT-team responsiveness had been a brilliant one-two punch. His orders were to disrupt the MEAD mission, block communications, steal back the Kathmandu water, pacify the authorities. She refused to act on any of it. What difference did it make? Gaia was shutting off the water. She could picture Griffon's panic when he found out. She wouldn't be the one dressed down at the other end of *that* phone conversation. Not this time. He could go screw *himself,* for a change.

A breeze rose, wafting up the slope and blowing her hair over her eyes. She took a deep breath of good air. In her mind, she set her thumb to the crystal globe she had given Jared. She imagined it was his head. With concentrated pressure, she pushed her thumb down and flattened it.

She stood up. Got to get to work. Which way was north? She started walking. Getting out of Nepal alive. She would concentrate on that.

* * *

James Von Kamburg had handed out assignments and then

disappeared with his wife. Frew had noticed something different about James since his march up the hill to browbeat whoever had been messing with the clean mountain stream. He was holding cards close to the vest. Not like him, but, to be fair, James was a stickler for not doling out faulty data. Whatever it was would come out, the bigger the sooner.

Frew was just back from checking in on Frauz, who seemed the worst-for-wear as far as the altitude. McPhee and Ming were still unpacking the crates which had been carried to the outside deck. McPhee looked up.

"You're back, Frew. I hope Von Kamburg doesn't expect us to sit out here all night and keep watch over the stuff."

"I will go and see if Gault can supply a night security guard," said Ming.

"Good idea," said McPhee. Ming marched off.

"Frauz is okay," Frew said. "Says a good night's sleep will do him. He's using the oxygen. Pulls the mask off to take a puff of his pipe."

"We'll hear if he blows up," said McPhee.

Frew laughed. "The lodge still can't get through with phone or web service. The guests are ticked off. Five-star rating in jeopardy, I'd say. Anyway, I'm heading out. Gotta find those Kiwis. The people who put up the moola to send us here will get snarky if we don't fetch the modal thingamabob from the down-under lads."

"What the blazes does that thing do, anyway?" asked McPhee.

"You should never mock equipment you don't understand. It only reveals your menial upbringing," said Frew, imitating Frauz's Swiss formality. "I'm going since I'm walking. See you guys tomorrow a.m.," he finished.

"Don't roll off a cliff because I'm not climbin' down to fetch your cadaver," said McPhee.

Frew hitched up his green army surplus coat, shoved his hands into its deep pockets, and headed out. He was looking forward to the excursion. He would find the New Zealand gents and then sashay into the town proper for some local character. A useful break from the hullabaloo.

He appreciated his boss but needed space from the "Von Man." They'd seldom traveled together and certainly never with the missus in tow. With everything going on there was no way he'd convince VK to throw back a bit of local grub and quaff some crafty brews.

Frew liked the team. Ming was a bonehead but the bone in his head was smart. He annoyed James, also, which was entertaining to observe; as long as it didn't drive his boss to distraction. The rest of the gang was certainly cool by him, especially that live wire, McPhee. McPhee had wanted to climb (*take out* as he put it) at least one "minor" slope before the MEAD expedition moved into high gear. After they'd hauled the crates to the deck they took a break to eat. McPhee had stuffed a fish sandwich in his mouth and bolted. He was back in an hour, ruddy-cheeked, and pleased with his quick scouting jag. A good potential carouser, that one.

The geological happenings provoked a certain thrill. Frew had a basic trust that reality's willingness to deliver tedium was directly proportional to the histrionics humans infused it with. If the media went crazy, with fearmongering and the imminence of disaster, the anticipated event would flop. The big Eastern snowstorm that never hit New York, after they'd shuttered the buses and subways. Perfect example. And the reverse: the drought out West no one paid attention to ten years running. Ten years of water doled out for mostly agribusinesses, a tap left to run and run dry. Lake Mead was showing its white bottom, the Sierra Nevada snowpack was a brownfield, and big cities pondered afterlife as ghost towns.

His team was summoned to explain why Mt. Everest was 72 feet (21.85416 meters to be exact) higher and rumbling, now and then. And why someone had found speckles from the earth's mantle in their morning tea. He and James had pocketed big dollars for the geophysics department and an all-expenses-paid trek to this world-heritage status region. Frew figured it would all turn into yesterday's news soon enough.

It was true the big quakes of a few years ago had brought hard times to Nepal. He felt for them. But like Christchurch in New Zealand, you can't locate a city on a tectonic fault and expect lazy days in the sun. Kathmandu was rebuilding with that in mind and seemed to be getting back on its feet. The rural peoples took the geology in stride. Mother Nature would do what she would do. Whatever data the MEAD team drummed up would get fifteen minutes of fame before the next celebrity twerk took its place.

It was good to breathe the mountain air.

As the light faded, the stars began winking hullo. Frew took out his flashlight and sent a beam along the well-worn trail he was following into the village. Then he sent a hullo back upstairs, pinning the beam to the middle star of Orion's Belt. A shooting star flashed through the beam. "Whoa. Nice."

He saw others trekking back towards the lodge including a lone male, hooded and moving furtively. A black rider, unhorsed, thought Frew. Where were the other eight? Carousing in Mordor, no doubt.

He stopped at the village gate. The Zamling Guesthouse was his target. He took out a scrawled sketch of its location and shone his flashlight at it. Should be close, through the gate, on the right, Marg Street.

Man, what a city. Frew had done his homework and buzzed with anticipation; he was stepping into an ancient, venerable conurbation. Namche was not large by any Western standard. But compressed in its borders, sinewy atop its terraced, rock-slashed flats, was abundance. You were in Nepal, but what could you want for?

The several dozen lanes crisscrossed a bowl filled with canted, erratically fashioned structures. Lights bloomed from round, square and rectangular windows. Hydropower had obviously been tapped to good effect. The terraces stepped down in broad uneven strips, a long-ago practical grading done to establish level terrain. *Imagine the effort. You have to love when the land says this and the people do that and it works.*

He passed under the gate and down uneven stone steps. No rail and fairly steep. At its southern edges, nearer the great gorge, Namche had a penchant for dispatching visitors who didn't tread attentively. First thing on the agenda was to avoid getting too knackered. *Be wary when merry or things may get hairy.*

There it was, the Zamling Guesthouse, its foundation carved into the slopes behind. Frew opened the wood door and made his way inside. It was warm, noisy and cramped. Two young ladies stood at the check-in counter. One smiled at Frew as he squeezed past to get to the commons room.

A crush of people mingled near the long bar. Others filled most of the tables. The soul-warming sound of animated voices melded with a background pulse of flute, bell and singing bowl. Warm yellow light shone from oil burning in fat lamps. The wood beam ceiling was festooned with pots and pans. A tranquilizing ambrosial vibe, thought Frew. Could be Happy Valley near Portland.

By the New Zealand-accented sound of it, two Kiwis were ensconced at the bar, nursing flagons of Nepalese mead. Frew approached. "Excuse me. Are you by chance John Bateman?"

"I am."

"I'm Basil Frew, from James Von Kamburg's Everest team."

"Hi. Ed Edwards. You a Yank?" Edwards arm was in a sling.

"Massachusetts, US of A," said Frew.

"Grab a stool if you can find one," said Bateman, looking around. Frew dragged one from the far end of the bar and sat down.

"Doc Von Kamburg sends his greetings."

"Good to catch up with you fellows at last. Basil, you said?"

"Basil."

"Something to wet your whistle?"

"Sure. What're you having?"

Edwards motioned for the bartender to pour another flagon of a dark-looking vintage. "They ferment this up the hill behind here." Edwards took a sip and hissed through his teeth. "Smooth."

"Gotta sample the local character," said Frew. The drink came sliding across the bar and skidded to a stop in front of him, Old West style. Or so he imagined. It was tart and kind of raw. Local stuff. Good. "We heard you lost your lodge rooms," he said. "We're hoping to bring you back up there."

"Not necessarily necessary," said Bateman. "This place is okay by us. Don't feel like you have to take your shoes off to walk on the carpet." Edwards laughed.

"James would like you up there. We'll get the rooms squared and let you know."

"Are we officially in?" asked Bateman.

"On the payroll, you mean? James would know but it's my understanding, yes, you are. There's also a fuss being made about the modal interferometer. If I got that pronunciation correct. If you opt out we're supposed to fetch it. Before you scram outta Dodge City."

Edwards and Bateman looked at each other. Frew'd have to tone down his Americanisms.

"Can you bring your team to the lodge tomorrow? We'll go over what we're planning. James wants to get your report first-hand. We're hearing varied accounts..." Frew stuttered to a halt.

"Tree popped out of a birthday cake is what you probably heard," said Edwards. Frew laughed. Edwards continued. "There was a disagreement involving potato chips and unusual plant growth." Edwards and Bateman's expressions changed. Frew could see it had been no joke.

"What happened to your arm?" asked Frew, gesturing at Edward's sling.

Edwards set his drink down. "A tree came up out of the snow and shoved me over the hill."

"Can you describe a bit more– scientifically– what happened on the slope?" asked Frew.

Bateman tapped his knuckles on the bar. "We're concerned," he said.

"We've been in touch with the joint commission in Kathmandu. Phone coverage has been dodgy, but we got through. The rub is the Everest readings are being doubted. Which is understandable. We're doubting them also. We reported our tree story and the legitimacy of our credentials took another hit. We want to get witnesses up there."

Edwards stared into his draught. Bateman drew a small red camera from his shirt pocket, powered it on and tapped the touch screen. He handed the camera to Frew. Frew saw a photo of a tree in snow. He pulled the camera up to his face. "Mind if I copy this over?" he asked.

"Do it, mate," said Bateman. "I was right there. The tree muscled up through the snow crust and knocked Eddie down the slope. It looked like… like…"

"Like that snake sparkler we used to light as a kid," said Edwards. "That black ash thing, looks like a finger, grows out of the pellet when you put a match to it. Ever see those? That's what the bloody tree did."

Frew nodded. He had a handful back in his desk in Oregon. Black Snakes. He launched Bluetooth and downloaded a series of the photos to his phone. "What are you thinking?" asked Frew.

"The mountain is in an unprecedented aspect," said Bateman. "I'm unsure of my ability to judge what's going on despite having seen it with my own eyes. Eddie and I have been talking about it. We don't know if we should stay."

Frew could see the situation had disturbed the New Zealanders. In his brief experience being around any of them, he'd found Kiwis to be stouthearted, sturdy types. The fact that they were bothered at all, bothered Frew.

"What are you guessing?" asked Frew.

Bateman shook his head. "I'm not, mate. I'm not."

"I think the best thing to do is come to the lodge. We can sort everything out. James will want to know what you have on Everest. I'm sure he'd like you to stay on."

"You think the lodge will have us back?" said Bateman.

"Did you bust up the rooms?" asked Frew.

Bateman sighed. "Up on the mountain Dawa and I worked on Eddie's shoulder and got it back in line. The dislocation. It hurts but you can do it in the field and I've done it so I did it."

"It did hurt, you bastard," said Edwards.

"So we could hike down without Eddie looking like Lon Chaney. You know; Igor, from the old Frankenstein movies," said Bateman. "Anyway. We got Eddie back to the lodge. We were wired. Fresh off the mountain, Eddie hurt, the tree. We wanted to relax and brought brews up to the rooms. Ike Muldoon and our Sherpa Dawa Tensing were in one room, Ed and I in the other. Everybody got a little soused. Dawa spends a lot of time spooking us about violating the sacred. Ike went and killed off a box of chips Dawa had stashed. Dawa's a little guy with Gurkha blood. Found out about his warrior lineage after the skirmish. Anyway. I guess he felt those chips were sacred. They ended up wrestling out into the hall."

"Mates lettin' off steam," said Edwards.

"The Sherpa practically broke Ike's arm over his bloody potato chips. Petty stuff, stupid stuff," said Bateman. "They cracked a lamp in the hall and pretty much trashed their room. We've split them up. The lodge manager, Gault was his name, right, he shows up and says we are being thrown out. I don't blame him."

"Do you have a flight out?" Frew asked.

"We have seats, we think," said Bateman. "The guy at the airport won't confirm. The hotel parent company– is it Earthyield?– has space reserved on every flight for their commercial spring water. And there's the iffy weather. He told us to come up early afternoon and see."

"Stay another day. Talk to James."

"I like that we've been activated, don't get me wrong," said Bateman. "I'm getting a bad vibe from the mountain."

"We've been listening to Dawa too much," said Edwards. "He conjures up bad karma. He's a great guide and a helluva porter. Just won't give up his thing about offending the great mother."

That was enough. Best to wait till VK could hear them out tomorrow. Frew took a moment to scope the commons room. It was getting late and probably better to get back to the lodge. If there was action to be had on Namche's main street it would have to wait.

"Can you be up in the hotel lobby around 10:00 a.m.?" asked Frew.

"Yeah, we can do that. It'll give us time to stop at the airport," said Bateman. "We can haul the modal unit up so you'll have it either way."

"All right. Thanks for the mead, gents. Hope your shoulder feels better soon, Ed. Nice meeting both of you." Bateman and Edwards raised their flagons as Frew drained the last of his. He saluted with a final hoist and pushed his way towards the door.

Chapter Ten

It was early evening in Khumjung, and James needed a moment to rationalize what he was about to do. At least *slightly* crazy– he could admit that.

Leslie Finch was nowhere to be found. Clarence Gault had a litany of excuses for the lack of broadband, absence of cell coverage, and inability to supply almost anything they had requested. James knew his team was fortunate to have secured use of the all-terrain buggies before Griffon's edicts had taken root. Finch's confession had changed his perspective. He felt more data was needed, though, before he could himself come clean with a revised strategy for both the MEAD mission and a course of action that would expose Earthyield.

He was reluctant, also, because Finch had confided in him. She'd come undone before his eyes. The black-haired corporate VP on fire in Vancouver was now an unnerved young woman out of her element.

The stakes were shifting for both of them, the situation morphing from an ill-conceived corporate malfeasance to a potentially globe-altering eventuality. Griffon was playing obstructionist like it was a game. James believed that Griffon would cease the ridiculous counter-measures if he knew the totality of what was transpiring but James couldn't get the word to him.

So. Deliberate. The threads in front of him were tangled, the scope of factors he needed to address expanding very rapidly. *Take a smaller bite. Work to get something useful happening.* Which is why he was crouched next to the lodge garbage.

In the fading light, James and Maggie had tucked themselves into a recessed corner of the lodge façade, near the loading dock. They huddled in the shadows behind a dumpster, and the row of thick bushes grown to conceal it. The retaining wall behind adjoined the garage, where, according to Finch, a van would soon exit en route to its nightly monastic sojourn. Through a small crack, James could watch it being loaded with what must have been empty urns. It was hard to make out clearly, but he could see there was an overhang, and that the van was parked halfway under it, and that a person should be able to step from the overhang to the vehicle's roof.

At least slightly rational, anyway.

Whoever was loading was working in dim lighting, and as noiselessly as possible. It seemed a slow process and neither James nor Maggie could guess how long they'd be in this holding pattern.

James, in a hooded jacket and sweatpants he had brought along for the workout room, looked about warily. The gathering dark was small reassurance. Maggie refused to negotiate her firm grasp on his waist. She hadn't been able to abandon the drama they'd just come through. It was his fault. He'd wounded her, further jeopardizing the already shaky chapter they were going through. Thwarted her reemerging ease. They were fragile again. She squeezed his arm. He tried to explain, once more.

"I don't know, Mag. She's got problems. She was drinking, I know that." He zipped up his jacket, unintentionally forcing her arm away. "We talked this out, I thought."

"She was coming for you."

"Don't put it that way. Please," he said. Maggie pinched the skin under his shirt, eliciting a muffled *ouch*. "Don't. Do that." He looked at her.

"The transaction– the *deal* Leslie told me about, between the monastery and Earthyield– I need to see it happen. I'll tell Jared I know the whole story. This madness of hassling our Everest team, along with holding back all the research his company has about the water's properties. Got to stop. He'll respond. Don't you think?"

She leaned to look through the retaining wall crack. "James. I have to tell you something."

James pulled his sleeve up and looked at his watch. "Maggie, what?"

She let go of his waist and slumped against the wall. "He wanted me to bear his children."

Not the best time to take this on. He lowered himself to sit beside her. "Jared." She nodded. "Tell me."

"He thought we'd breed– God, how did he put it– *efficaciously*. Actually said that once. Strategized five, at least. Five fertilizations was his target. He called them that. Fertilizations." She paused. "Romantic opening salvo. Motherhood was the last thing on my mind. I thought having kids was a great way to ruin your body, kill any chance of getting into the Freer Gallery. And also, why? You're happy with your partner; why?"

She isn't making this up.

"When you came along I wanted the whole issue to go away. Didn't want to think about kids, pro or con."

He tried to slow his breathing, already ratcheted by the prospect of his impending roof ride. The air was thin enough without this dialog. Sweat rolled down his spine, and his hands had gone cold.

"When I told him he could get his offspring produced elsewhere he took it hard. Couldn't get a handle on it, really. He would never marry and never have kids unless it was me. So he swore us off. We would never reconcile. I could go screw myself. I was gone. I remember he called a day later and told me to come back. Didn't ask. Told me to. He was irrational about it, after a point. I loved him. For that." She looked down. "The last thing I said to him was 'stuff it'."

This is past, James thought. Don't drag it through your psyche again for me. Not right now. He needed to climb– and get to the overhang.

She looked up, her voice taking on a timbre of mortification. "I wanted him. I wanted to paint. That's all. We went from workable to completely screwed in one semester. *Fail*– with a capital *F*." She put her hands over her eyes and held them there. "It sounds like an awful movie, especially now that I want those kids…" She squeezed his arm.

"You would know a bad movie," said James. He grasped her hands. They were warm against his cold palms. "You should have told me. It wouldn't change what we're good at." He brushed back her hair. The van doors rattled. "I have to roll."

"Who's writing this script?" she said.

James poked her in the ribs, to kid them out of this extemporaneous spiral. "Don't be so optimistic."

Maggie made a face, a combination of unspooled vulnerability and received grace. James saw it there, a coruscate flare, hadn't comprehended of such a thing until this moment. If not their progeny, she was expectant with some intuition.

"White stars," she said.

James had to catch at his oxygen-starved breath. He put one hand on his chest and one on hers. "White stars?"

His wife's face was luminous, her eyes misty. "Not sure," she murmured. Out of nowhere a butterfly flittered into view. It hesitated, treading air, then it was silently off, like the muted nothing-colors swimming in the cornea after a bulb flash.

"You better go." She peered at his face, smiling. "What if the van drivers see you? They might hear you, you might slip off the roof. God, James, you're not the Governator." He almost laughed, and they both covered their mouths. Then kissed.

"I love you," he said. He hopped onto the dumpster and clambered to the top of the wall, finding footholds in the uneven stone ledges cantilevered there. He crouched, pulled the hood over his head and moved to the brink of the overhang. The van's engine coughed to ignition.

He placed a foot on the hemp bag bungee-corded to the roof rack and stepped down as quietly as he could. The van gunned into gear, motoring forward, propelling James onto the bag. The vehicle pulled away from the garage. He managed a cursory thumbs-up from the van roof, hoping Maggie would spy him from the shadow of the bushes.

What are white stars?

Maggie waited until the vehicle had traveled some distance, then straightened herself up. She stepped from behind the bushes, brushed off her vest, and walked to the lodge's front entrance, as casual-looking as she could manage, whistling to herself. She saw Maya, staff in hand, with a cloth loosely bandaged around her right forearm.

"Maya. What happened?"

"Leeches. Common in the lowlands. Not at these altitudes, usually."

"Will you be okay?"

"Yes, yes. Like mosquitoes to you."

She began undoing the wrap, revealing an arm healing, though still blistered in red. "Ointment has taken the poisons out. The wound needs air." Maya stuffed the cloth into her pack. "Let us go inside. I have learned much."

* * *

James got a better grip on the bag with each turn. The ride was not particularly rough, but it was dark, and the slopes beyond the road edge varied from friendly drops to end-of-life escarpments. If he concentrated and the van's noisy racket cooperated, he could hear snippets of banter between the driver, Max, and his cohort, Flick. James slid carefully toward the edge of the roof. The next section of road, over and beyond the bridge, required the driver to ease off and more guardedly navigate the rock-strewn, gully-ridden way. The engine quieted, steady and slow.

"Finch said we had to get the water. Stay on schedule. She's a pain, but she's a honey," Max said.

"But the monks said forget it. What are we supposed to do?" said Flick.

"You know those monks. They won't raise a finger to stop us. They're not allowed to harm a flea."

"I don't like barreling in there like this. It's jive."

"Jive. You crack me up. Hey. I do what Finch wants."

Crumbling rocks briefly hid the conversation as the van reached the end of the bridge. James cupped an ear.

"Gault told us to follow the yellow-brick Finch." The two workers guffawed mightily. The van crawled, slowing down again. James rolled onto his back. The stars took on an unusual green-yellow cast and looked as though they were swimming. Galactic clusters appeared to lose their centered gravity and, more unnervingly, began falling from the heavens. *God, please. Am I having a stroke?*

One of the green-yellow beads landed on James's arm, a gentle alighting akin to the touch of a fallen feather. It was a lightning bug. Suddenly they were everywhere, vast undulating swaths. Far from their normal home in America, this genus, *Photuris,* was flashing warm weather pheromones. The van stopped. James lay with his face to the sky, entranced.

"Check it out! It's beautiful!" Max said.

"Freaked," said Flick.

"I heard they're poisonous in Nepal."

"You're full of it."

"They touch you, you go green, get warts, then croak. Didn't you get the memo?"

"What!?"

"We gotta roll up the windows." James heard the window motors engage. "Kidding, Flick. Just kidding."

The window motors stopped. Max continued. "I have never, ever, seen anything like this. I have to write Missy when we get back. Incredible. You remember them growing up? Stuck 'em in jars. Never saw this many."

James was taken back, to another time.

He was nine, and chasing fireflies across his yard in Maryland. Mesmerizing, they never failed to elicit wonder. Now there were hundreds of thousands, borne on the stir of air, aloft in multitude. They tended to greens or yellows, with the occasional rogue turquoise or violet navigating this luminous sea. Swarm was all James could conjure to describe it.

He was taken back again, to a different time and a different memory.

He was just out of college, at the bachelor party of a close buddy. Twenty or so good friends, gathered to celebrate an upcoming nuptial, were ensconced at a tranquil backyard patio in a friendly neighborhood block of Swissvale. Sub sandwiches, chocolate meltaways, beer and whiskey. The Doors blaring from the speakers, coolers full of ice, lawn chairs and black plastic garbage bags. James didn't imbibe (then) and often ended up as designated driver. When the boys were in full party mode, not offering much in the way of sobriety, he'd drift to a spot away from the revelry. He didn't mind, good guys, these. Without immediate company, he had glanced up at the sky. There they were.

White dots.

Essentially, stars in the daytime azure atmosphere above him. As he watched, more slowly emerged out of the blue. Someone had yelled "look!" and they all did. James the scientist was transfixed. The dots were lining up in rows and spaced equidistant. One-two-three-four-five in that row. Another row, perpendicular, one-two-three, then another. Seven-five-three. As far as he could surmise, based on the bit of clouds drifting past below and around them, they were immobile. He was flummoxed. The scientist said no. The semi-incurable somewhat-romantic realized an ironic and keen joy. Objectively, they couldn't be witnessing this.

Ken, the party's host, had come over to James. Side by side, they gawked. "That. Man. That is scary," he said. "Area 51. Some big flying thing escaped from Area 51. What do you think?"

"The only thing I've ever seen that I can't take a decent guess at," said James. "I'm going to call my brother. Can I use the house phone?"

"Yeah, yeah, go in. I'll stand watch."

James went in and dialed up his cosmologist brother George. If you wanted scientific corroboration, George was the man. George wasn't home, and by the time James got back outside there was only one row of white dots still visible, and it soon faded into the blue. No one could say what it had been. Pre-Internet, pre-camera phones, pre-Twitter, nothing reported or recorded, officially or otherwise.

The van rattled onward.

He was far from Maryland, in a territory of baffling contradiction once again. Like the white dots lining up in the daytime sky, his experiences during this Everest mission were exhibiting more and more clues that bucked established tenets of science. Such as this sky, multi-colored with fireflies from another continent. Somewhere out there in the vast black, filling up its dark space like an immense invisible groan, a venerable summit of rock and ice was insinuating that it was more than inert matter.

White stars.

Wait…

A single firefly snagged in the hemp. James raised the cloth and shook it gently until he saw the bug unceremoniously wing away. Like the grand finale of a fireworks show, the band of coalescing colors intensified into a final glowing flare. They shimmered down the road, a phosphorescent living gleam winking out behind a bend near the bridge.

White stars in the daytime sky.

Is that what Maggie meant? I must have told her the story.

The van continued, trough to rut, along the moonlight-daubed lane, and at last approached the monastery. James looked ahead. A group of sandaled monks stood as a barrier just inside the courtyard arbor entrance. Their stance was not militant, but firm. Turning to face the entry gates, the van's headlights played on their robes, casting long shadows that trailed out to the walls behind. The van pulled forward and braked to a stop, its high beams blinding, its engine idling loudly. The monks shielded their eyes but did not budge. James gripped at the hemp. He saw one monk near the front begin fishing inside his robe, as though he was about to reveal a pearl-handled revolver. Out came a pair of sunglasses which the monk put on.

"That guy's funny," James heard Max say.

"They do not want visitors," said Flick, in a slow monotone.

"That pistol still in the glove compartment?"

James couldn't believe what he was hearing. In a slow burn, he made two fists. The monks tightened their cluster, moving up near the van's hood. The sound of the engine ceased.

Max leaned his head out his window. "Yo. Is Red Scarf around?"

A monk answered in Nepalese.

"What's this? Pig-Latin? Can we come in? Can you move out of the way?"

The monks did not.

"Get out of the way," Max commanded, with a loud, cranky yell.

Flick chimed in. "Please move. We need to pick up our water."

Red Scarf appeared, walking through the assemblage and standing at the front. "Urns are empty. There is no water," he announced.

Max stood inside the cab and leaned his upper body out through the window. He waved his hand, gesturing for the monks to scatter. "We're coming in to fill them up. You owe us water. Get out of the way."

The monks crowded in tighter.

"Move! You'll get hurt if you don't," Max repeated. The van's engines revved. A few of the monks were alarmed and looked to their brethren for protocol. The group held.

"Get out of the way!" Max howled. He laid on the horn. The monks crowded under the arbor, some nearly touching the van's hood. The rear tires spun, brakes barely holding, the van kicking up dirt as it momentarily revved without motion. The monks will scatter, James prayed. He clambered to look in the driver's side window. Max's sweaty fist fidgeted at the handbrake, thumbing the release knob. If he let off the brakes, the van would knife into the monks.

Gotta do something. With his right hand, James clenched the hemp bag in a white-knuckled grip. He flung his upper body over the side and reached in through the driver's window, just as the van lurched forward. With desperate force, he grasped the steering wheel and yanked it, forcing the wheel down and over. The van pitched left, careening through the gates, the monks scattering. James glimpsed the unbelted Flick slide into Max, who lost his own grip on the wheel.

James thought he felt a rib crack as he wrenched with his arm to spin the wheel the other way. The vehicle skidded into a sharp right and tipped, sliding upturned wheels first into the courtyard wall. James heard the muffled crunch from mid-air as he bounced off the vehicle's hood, landing with an emphatic splash in the water channel that ran along the inside wall, its bed of silt and mud cushioning his fall. Grimacing, he rolled to get out of the wet muck.

Three monks came to attend as he sat up. He was gently helped to his feet, his clothes glistening and muddied. He felt a crimp in his left elbow, the one he had stretched to reach the steering wheel, to go with the bruised rib cage.

"Did you bang your head?" asked one monk, wearing a distinctive red scarf. "You fell on your posterior."

James ran his palm over the back of his skull. A tender knob rose there. "I'm okay. Maybe a towel?" Legs spastic with adrenaline, he sat back down. Red Scarf spoke to another monk, who hurried inside the monastery.

The van had crumpled part of the wall. Loosed stonework rattled down as the wheels spun to a stop. The engine smoked and sputtered, sizzling and dripping oil. Several monks hurried over. One reached in through the broken front windshield to turn the key and kill the motor. Max and Flick lay dazed under the powder and plastic of deflated yellow air bags. James wiped mud from his eyes. He saw Flick attempt to clamber out of the passenger door window, slip, and fall in a heap, onto Max.

"Arrghhh...!!"

Several of the monks pulled open the van's rear cargo doors. The empty urns tumbled out, and were removed and carried off. As James watched, Max and Flick were assisted out onto the grass. Nicked, scratched, and woozy, they both sat against the flipped-over roof, the hemp bag a cushion for their backs. The monks brought bowls of water, flashlights and towels. Max was tapping at his cell phone when it was lifted from his hand. He reached out as if to stop the theft, then flopped back against the van.

James shook some of the water from his hands and wiggled his wrists. They still worked. A towel was being proffered, dangling in front of him. He looked up into the earnest face of a Buddhist religious who, after what could have been a very serious accident, represented his first responder. It was too much.

James felt his face break into a cheesy grin. "My wife's gonna kill me."

"Stand," said Red Scarf without a smile. "The Abbot Gaia will see you."

James ran the towel over his face. He rose slowly and straightened out his spine, half-expecting a pop. No. He was okay. Bones solid, muscles more or less intact, he could stand up– even walk. *The Governator after all.*

A second towel was brought, along with a cloak he could drape over his wet form. He dried his head, again feeling the tender lump at the back of his skull. Escorted by Red Scarf, he was led through the courtyard doors into the lamp-lit monastery's main hallway. A floating haze wafted through the corridors, the air hinting a different incense at every turn. Woozy air, James thought, and found himself reaching for the hem of Red Scarf's robe, never actually touching it. Abruptly, he was in front of large wooden doors. The doors swung open.

His back to the entryway, Abbot Gaia sat cross-legged before an altar distinguished by a shining crimson Buddha. A warm fire murmured its song of quiet crackling and muffled pops. Candles graced every surface, and their flickering light played faintly throughout the sanctuary.

Red Scarf motioned for James to enter, then pulled the great doors shut, leaving James alone with the abbot. A cloud of incense billowed before him. James, his eyes still finding their way in the fluted light and shadows, moved to a floor pillow near Gaia and, with a groan, lowered himself. He made an attempt to cross his legs. *Not likely.* He stretched them out, cultural faux pas be danged. He was stiff and wet. And Buddha's nose was cracked.

James began to isolate more details: a plug of cotton filling a hole in the ceiling, a metal bucket cradling wood kindling, and worn copies of *National Geographic* stacked in a corner. He felt an increased visual acuity. Since he'd bumped his head? He wished there was clearer air.

"Can somebody open the window?" He wasn't sure if he had said it or thought it. Gaia had yet to speak.

The fire warmed him. He unwrapped the cloak and set it beside him. He wondered if the situation, atmosphere, fragrances– this suffusion in the sensate– was tantamount to *tripping.* Not a few of his students had urged him to go for it, insisting the experience would take him places he might never otherwise get to. He'd always deferred. Didn't even take aspirin. Tripping; maybe he was. For a fleeting moment James thought the abbot was garbed as a member of Sgt. Pepper's famous band.

James settled on the pillow and ran his roughened hands over his face.

He slapped himself lightly across the cheek.

"Namaste." The abbot was standing, bowing.

"Hi, hello, Abbot?" asked James. He reached under his torn jacket into his muddied shirt pocket and pulled out his wire-rims, now slightly bent. They might help clear his fogged head. He wiped them with a sleeve, put them on and turned to the abbot.

"Sorry for the commotion." James extended his hand. "I'm Dr. Von Kamburg– Jim."

"I am Gaia, abbot of Thyzenboche Monastery." Gaia bowed again but did not take or shake James's proffered hand.

"Abbot." James crossed his arms. "I'm a scientist, invited by your government to make a geological assessment of certain anomalies occurring on, near and beneath Mt. Everest."

"I had news you were coming to Khumjung," said the abbot with a genial grin. "I understand you studied in Maryland, USA?"

"I did my undergraduate at the University of Maryland. You know it?"

"My masters degree is from the University of Maryland. Political science and environmental policy. I think of it as a dualistic major."

"Maryland? You?"

The abbot bowed and slowly set himself down on the floor pillow.

"What years did you study?"

"The middle 1980's."

"I was there in 1990. Just missed each other. That is kind of hard to believe, Abbot."

"Yes. I didn't join the fraternities." The abbot uncovered well-taken-care-of teeth with what James took to be another smile. "What is it you hope to learn?" he asked. "About the great mountain?"

The doorway opened and a large bowl of hot chocolate was brought in on a tray by a young monk, who immediately departed.

"Please drink, Doctor. The monks thought perhaps you'd prefer the cocoa."

James gathered the bowl in his hands. It was insulated with a woolen coverlet, the drink hot and steaming. He took a small sip to test the temperature, then set it down to cool.

"The mountain is going through some extremely unusual geological phenomenon. Part of the evidence is a water sample we have. The water is, um, the water may come from your spring."

Gaia's seated profile, silhouetted in the glow of the sanctuary's candles, looked like the Buddha statue. James rolled his head on his neck. *Does it always grind like that?* He thought he saw a mouse trot past the front of the fireplace.

"The water is of the soul of the Mother Earth. It is blessed," said the abbot.

"Have you been selling this water?"

"For three years almost."

"The company, Earthyield, that buys the water. Did you know they're using the water for purposes other than to sell it for drinking? That they use it to replicate minerals?"

"We have discontinued the agreement."

"They're making a mint," James added. His thoughts took to an odd roaming mash-up: the employment offer from Jared, Maggie's bare back, and, briefly, Leslie Finch, with merlot spilled on her thigh. *I have to focus. Focus, focus, focus.*

Gaia rose to walk towards the altar. He took a candle and began to light incense burners recessed into the altar's sides. Freshened smoke tendrils curled into the room, like a long-fingered masseuse with supernatural reach.

James picked up his cocoa and swallowed a draught. "What's in this, Abbot?" he asked, licking the glace from his lips.

The abbot remained near the altar, standing utterly still. "Do you believe in things greater than the things of man?"

"What's going on here, you mean? The laws of science are bent. Not broken." James felt bewildered and was finding it difficult to manage any notions worthy of an abbot's attention. "Not yet, anyway."

"The Sherpas named the mountain long before you called it Everest," said Gaia.

"A name?"

"*Chomolungma*. Translated, to your English, *Goddess Mother of the Earth*."

"Appropriate."

"More than you know." Gaia walked over to James and crouched directly in front of him. This is most unlike an abbot, thought James. He abruptly seemed to James a poseur, who knew far too much about far too much. James felt a stress fracture in the fulcrum of his intellect, a rising pressure that worked against his ability to know truth from un-truth, in whatever manner he had been able to in his short life on earth, and he feared he'd be compelled to believe what the abbot was about to instill.

The abbot spoke. "The goddess mother is with child."

James sat frozen, staring straight ahead. His clothes felt dry. The fire had gone out. The abbot was gone. James grasped the hood on his jacket, pulled it over his head, and rolled himself over onto all fours. I'll crawl home, he thought.

* * *

Maggie lay in her bed, unable to sleep.

The room was dark except for the minute blue light indicating her cell phone battery was recharging. She flipped the phone onto its face. She had closed the curtains and unplugged the alarm clock. Pitch black, she wanted, though dawn couldn't be far off.

Her mind hadn't stopped racing. Her husband and their marriage, their studio in Oregon, the airport in Delhi, this bed in Nepal. Maya, with her intimations that a metaphysical occurrence might be at hand. And *white stars,* suggested at the edges of a dream or memory she couldn't remember, no matter how hard she tried.

The night hours had dragged. What if James had been discovered and beaten or arrested? It was hardly a crime, what he was doing, but he could easily end up in some official, embarrassing, legal mess. What if he had fallen from the van, over a cliff? What if he was bleeding to death?

In ten more minutes she would get up and tell Basil everything.

There was a click. The door to her room eased open, a shaft of washed light struck the far wall. A cast shadow took the form of her husband. She watched him in, his steps slow, pants muddied and hair tousled. He moved to the opposite side of the bed, took a moment to smooth his matted hair, and dropped to sit. She could see he was exhausted. At least he was safe, and here.

"Everest," he said, in between easing breaths. Bending with a creak, he undid his boots.

"What happened?"

He threw each grimy boot towards the balcony wall, gently brushed off his pant legs, then lowered himself flat on the bed. With a groan, he tucked his legs up, lifted the linen sheet and slid in next to his wife.

"You're covered with mud," Maggie said. "Are you hurt?"

"Sorry about the mud. Sorry I didn't show up sooner. Got a bruise or two. I took a break and must have fallen asleep." He felt at the back of his head.

"What happened at the monastery?" she asked.

James blessed himself. The sign of the cross, she hadn't seen him use since their wedding.

"Everest."

"Tell me what happened."

"Everest is expecting."

"What does that mean?"

"I met the abbot at the monastery. He said the world is pregnant. Expecting a baby– *a baby Earth*– soon. Loony, crackpot, nuts. But it's a great idea. You have to admit. Nicely aligns with what we're seeing." He looked at her. "Don't you think?"

"Did you hit your head?" she asked.

"Need some daylight without incense blowing up my nose."

"Sweet Mary," said Maggie. She pulled the covers up around her bare shoulders.

"I'm not sure what to do," he said. "Sorry about this mud. Should get undressed. So beat..." He moved to find the crook of her neck. She pulled him closer. A strange scent emanated from the dank of his clothes. She heard his breathing lengthen, slowing, into sleep.

The room's curtains moved in the breeze from the slightly open balcony door. A faint impression of the moon came through the cloth. A glint of grey-white luminescence fell across her husband's profile.

Abruptly, her strange dream moved from the shadows into the half-light.

Chapter Eleven

In the steaming sunshine, a mother lode of the latest in portable geologic technology preened like a quiescent dynamo on the floorboards of the pool deck. Geodimeter, seismograph, correlation spectrometer, petrophysics implementer, ground penetrating radar unit, gravimeter, thermal sensors, gradient field magnetometer, electron beam supplementor, and pirot ball. In addition, uncrated and under the fastidious regard of Ming & Frew (Limited), several cased laptops, three field generators, and a slick composite map dispenser that looked like an espresso machine.

Maybe it does serve a cuppa, thought Frew. Various duffle bags of camping gear were set against the deck rails. Ming tallied materials and checked for shipping damages while Frew penciled the inspection results on the ledger.

"We have this down," said Ming. "As you people say."

Frew chuckled to himself. He was playing yang to Ming's yin and there was mojo. He'd never seen a dude apply such laser-like focus to the dutiful unpacking of crates. Ming & Frew, Ltd. indeed.

Frauz and McPhee had hauled the radar unit from its packaging out into the light. A long orange extension cord ran from the unit to an exterior electrical outlet. McPhee had powered up the unit, coupled it to the gravimeter, and was crouched near its base reading voltages.

"I'll do the calibration set-ups," said Frauz. He spun a handful of dials then tapped the back of his pipe against the main sensor access panel.

"Stop wackin' at it," barked McPhee.

"These things need a little wake-up call, Daniel. I wouldn't fret," said Frauz as he went ahead with another tap.

Frew thought they'd done a pretty danged decent job of getting this stuff uncorked for the adventures ahead. Where was the good doctor, so he could show off?

The doorway from the inside pool dome swung open. James stepped out, blinking in the strong light. "Good morning," he said, blowing on the hot coffee he cradled. Maggie and Maya followed. Maggie nodded hello to the team and led Maya across the deck to the ramped steps, where they seated themselves.

"You came out from the inside. How'd you manage that? We're supposed to stay out here, right?" said Frew.

"I'm commandeering space," said James.

"You radical," said Frew.

"I talked to a staffer, the lobby guy Charlie. Showed him our mission permissions doc. He unlocked it."

Frew smiled smugly. "I like that. And hey, guess what?" He held up the shipping manifesto and shook it at James. "We got all the stuff checked in." Frew covered his pointer finger and aimed it at Ming. James was doubtful. He ran his knuckles under bloodshot eyes.

"You look like you had a fun night out, Dr. Von Kamburg," said McPhee. McPhee gestured at Frauz. "*He* had a good night, at least. Got some kind of dopamine hit from sleeping with the air mask. Can't slow the chap down."

Frauz held an ear against the housing of the gravimeter unit. The meter's calipers were twitching.

"How you feeling, Xavier?" asked James.

"Bodacious, thank you for asking. A night with oxygen and Arthur Conan Doyle brought me up to snuff." Frauz patted at his chest, indicating his renewed solidity, then returned to tinkering with the gravimeter. McPhee shrugged his shoulders. James took a careful sip from his cup.

"Found the Kiwis last night," said Frew.

"When can we meet?" asked James.

"They said they'd come up around ten this morning. They were shell-shocked, VK."

"Welcome to the club."

"Bateman says they did get drunk. I have photos of the tree. Crazed."

"They should be up here, part of the team."

"We might see them waving goodbye when they fly over. They have tickets out of here. Afternoon flight. Weather should be good enough if it holds," said Frew.

"I'll see if I can patch a call through to Bateman. They need to leave the modal interferometer with us," said James.

"Ah, I should have emphasized that. They may yet show," said Frew.

James felt at the bump on back of his head. Shrinking but still tender. He found a makeshift seat on one of the smaller crates. "Anybody have anything to report?"

Ming stepped forward. "I have new directives. These are concerning our operations and planning. They came in by electronic courier from the north last night."

"Electronic courier?" asked Frew.

Ming continued. "There are significant concerns about safety and border violations. In the coming week, a contingent of research and military personnel will be deployed along the border between China and Nepal, in the vicinity of Everest. This contingent will initiate an independent investigation of the phenomena. There will also be a government liaison expecting to meet with the lodge concerning the water draw. This is to insure the subterranean water table that is being tapped for commercial purposes does not in any way bleed water resources underneath Chinese territories. The liaison will be expecting to see documentation to that effect."

Frew opened his arms as wide as he could. "Ming. We're twenty miles from China."

"This calamity continues to be underestimated. My field research is not being ignored by Peking."

"Peking? What happened to Beijing?" Frew bobbed his head. "You've been here one whole day, dude. You call it field research?" Frew wagged a long finger at Ming, shaking his head in slow motion.

"It's not a calamity, Ming," said McPhee. "You never read *Chicken Little?*"

In the moment, James didn't have the mental energy to deal with Ming's latest screed. Even so, and despite his gifted science acumen, it might be worth finagling a way to send him packing. And do an end-around on Earthyield's blockade. An idea quickly percolated.

He'd ask McPhee to undertake some covert work inside the lodge. If anybody on his team could hack the hotel's communications hardware, it'd be Dan. James would prep a terse message for Charles Bennington. Bennington was a US Senator, and the United States' representative at the urgently assembled consortium that had commissioned the MEAD team. Somebody with enough clout to get Ming officially booted, and Griffon under control. James could also kick-start the idea that a UN outfit might have to be mobilized to deal with certain extracurricular activities. Not least the Red Army lining up to march in from the North.

There was a sudden squawk from the ground penetrating radar, and from Frauz. "That is it," he said. They turned to see him peering at the gravimeter's display, smoke from his pipe curling near his ears. They gathered round the unit.

"What have you got?" asked James.

"Well, we've only just powered up but I thought why not and sent a number of calibration pings down and under, in the direction of Everest. Consider this an appetizer. That said, the gravimeter doesn't make data out of circumstantial evidence. It reads what's there." Frauz did a little bounce on his heels. "There's a *batholith* below Everest. The gravitational center of the batholith is climbing."

"What's a batholith?" asked McPhee.

"A batholith. You really don't know," said Frauz. "A volcanologist. Lord, what do they teach at university these years…"

James and Frew studied the read-outs, trying to decipher the unusual data spooling into view. Frauz rummaged an inside pocket, retrieved a leather-bound geology field guide, and stuck the found page in front of McPhee's nose.

"To wit, Mr. McPhee." He pulled the book from McPhee and proceeded to read. "*Batholith:* a great mass of intruded igneous rock that rises from a considerable distance below the surface of the earth."

McPhee snatched the book from Frauz's hand. "It's called a pluton aggregate, Frauz. Come into the twenty-first century."

"Aggregate or batholith, it's rising," said James, his eyes locked on the meter. "The process typically takes 20 million years. The gravimeter is suggesting a three-meter vertical ascension at every ping."

"Quite evenly distanced. A geospatial match to the break in the Mohorovicic," said Frauz. "I'm trying to calculate how soon, if it continues rising at this rate, it might rupture the crust. Drat! There goes the electric."

The radar unit's display flickered and went black. It flickered back on and included a text message: *The delete command is not undoable. This message courtesy of your onboard e-battery. Evaluate power requirements and reboot.*

"Yes, computer, we know you are flawed. We'll have to stand down till Mr. McPhee provides electricity," said Frauz.

"We'll dig out the generator," said McPhee. "Bloody hotel electrician nowhere to be found." He moved to lift the lid on one of the crates.

"Dan, wait," said James. "I've learned some things. Listen in, everyone."

James had been trying to decide the best way to inform his team about the backwash of new facts threatening to swamp their undertaking. He needed a crew willing to continue even as the evidence was mounting that what they'd signed on for had gone off the tracks. There were risks outside of everyone's expectations.

He looked over at Maggie. She'd been strangely quiet this morning, after his slow wake-up from sleeping in. She wasn't saying much about his exploits at the monastery, nor about what the abbot had said. It was time to bring the crew up to date. He'd start with the small stuff.

"The management of the lodge has been instructed to impede our mission," James said.

Frew's eyebrows rose. "Come again."

"Earthyield is the sci-tech company that owns the Everest Vista Lodge. Based out of Vancouver. You know about the Everpure water; the Kathmandu sample. The water's source, claimed on its label, is near Everest. The specific source is not listed. Inquiries were made into the source and the permit disclosed, indicating the water was taken from the river headwaters above the lodge. The river is in fact not the true source. The water is from a spring at the Thyzenboche Monastery, two or so miles from where you are standing. The retail water sales are a cover. The water is collected as part of an industrial production process. It's a critical ingredient for Earthyield, the centerpiece of their ability to synthesize minerals. Let's just say their skyrocketing stocks are tied to control of the water and its source."

James paused to sip his coffee. He looked discreetly over the cup's lip to study his team's reactions. He would have to work up slowly to the lead story. "I was at the monastery last night. To make it short, the monks will no longer sell the water. Earthyield's got a problem, as you can imagine."

"Bizarre," said Frew. "This adventure is taking some weird turns."

James continued. "I don't know how much of the communications crash is real and how much is the lodge jerking us around at the switchboard. The point is we can't count on messages getting through. Nor do we know if incoming messages are being blocked. The mountain's current instability is a contributor, but there's no way to be sure."

Ming got out his smart phone and tapped at it. James continued. "There's no kind of legal enforcement up here, at least that I can locate, to help us with this. Earthyield is more or less running the local show. Basil, after the meeting, I want you to go and see if any of the hotel staff can help, under the table, so to speak. Stay away from Gault and Finch. Start with Charlie, maybe poke around the IT room. Don't spend more than an hour. We have a lot to do."

"There's a constable barracks near Namche," said Maya. "They might assist us, if we show them our permissions letter. And Passang may be able to help you find more friends inside the lodge."

"Good, thanks, Maya. Maybe you can check with the constables. We could try sending messages out by plane. Pretty iffy, really slow, but an option." James looked at Ming. "If you'd care to share the secret of electronic courier routing, we'd love to hear about it, Me."

"It would not be permitted. It is a protocol of our armed forces."

James blew out a long, stewing exhale, then continued. "There are critical challenges in front of us. We are cut off. The mission to deliver substantive data on Everest is threatened. The US government and its partners in the endeavor, China, Nepal, India, and New Zealand, are prepared to deploy help. I can't get through to green light anything. That's where we stand. Let me know if anyone is able to get online or use their cells."

James stood up, hands on the small of his back. "We have the short wave. Dan, if you can get the batteries recharging somewhere, please."

"Will do."

"We are going into the field, tomorrow," James said.

Frauz blew a long smoke ring off to the side. The crew looked at each other.

"I'm expecting a few nights out with possible exposure," said James. "Everybody bring their warm stuff. Don't be fooled by these springtime temps. I expected to commandeer the lodge all-terrain buggies, but it looks like that won't be happening. Maya has reserved us some local transit, yaks, and Sherpas to help us carry the gear."

Maya stood up. "I must go soon. The tower. You wish to know its location."

"Sorry, Maya, yes. Maya has to get into town. She's leading a session on midwifery and will probably be delivering newborns too. She's found out the location of Earthyield's drilling tower."

"Drilling tower?" asked Ming. "Our government–"

"Ming," James interrupted. "This is not a discussion."

"Our government will want a mission abstract before we start. I expect they will make a move if it is not forthcoming. You do understand 'make a move', Dr. Von Kamburg?"

James ignored Ming, looked at McPhee. "Dan, pull out the map, take it inside with Maya and get the coordinates." He looked over at Maggie. "Maggie, you might want to join them. It might come in handy to know where we're headed."

She nodded and rose. After a quick rummage through the map dispenser, McPhee located the tube labeled "Khumjung 1-1200" and they headed inside.

"What does Finch say? You two have been connecting, haven't you?" asked Frew.

James didn't prefer the way Frew had phrased the question, and was glad Maggie was out of earshot. "I took a ride out to the monastery last night. Talked to the abbot. Maya also found some things out. And, yes, Finch," said James. "Earthyield is drilling a borehole a few kilometers northeast of Thyzenboche. They're using a portable drilling derrick, trying to tap the water table that feeds the monks' spring. Based on the rock and topography, there should not be a significant water table where they're drilling. That said, I'm expecting they did due diligence before committing to the spot they picked. Their borehole has reached a depth of 700 meters, according to the information I was given. Very deep. Very illegal. In this case we're fortunate: we'll drop sensors into the shaft and be able to measure for a number of parameters with that much less surface distortion. Do you agree, Xavier?"

Frauz took a long drag on his pipe. "It's always an advantage to get your sensors as close to the proceedings as possible. Especially true in this case, considering the erratic composition of rock we're dealing with."

McPhee came out carrying the map. "I got it, Doc. A nice hike. Stone's throw from Tibet." McPhee unfolded the map out across one of the crate surfaces. Tibet was close, but not a stone's throw. James was sure McPhee was trying to get a rise out of Ming. Ming walked over to look at the map. He snapped a photo with his smart phone, murmured something, and walked off the deck, tapping and swiping his phone with appreciable intensity.

"He's not worth having around, Doc," said McPhee.

"He's without peer in his field. Not sure what to do with him."

"He can go back to his field."

Maya appeared in the doorway, backpack on and staff in hand. "I must go, Dr. James," she said. "There are many mothers-to-be at the airport village. Passang will arrive this afternoon to assist you. He knows the mountains and the paths you will need to take."

Maggie appeared, carrying a loaded-up backpack. McPhee led her to one of the crates, where she extracted a shortwave radio handset. Maggie opened the top of her pack and set the shortwave inside. She closed the flap, pulled at the bungee cords to secure it shut, and shouldered the pack.

"I'll check that off the ledger," said Frew, wielding a pencil. "Where's Maggie off to?"

"Maya's got her hands full and Maggie's offered to help," said James. "They'll stay in touch by shortwave, keep us updated on the situation in the village and at the airport." Maggie came over and kissed James lightly.

"You have enough food and water?" he asked.

"Maya has us well-stocked." She shifted the weighty pack. "Be careful," she said, then whispered in his ear. "I'm working something out. In my dream, the one with Jared, there were white stars in a blue sky." She reached for his hand, squeezed it, and turned away.

James wanted to stop her. What did she mean? The two women strode down the steps and onto the path towards Namche. James closed his eyes, casting about for a note of optimism to set against this separation. Green and alive, Maggie's eyes.

Frew jostled him into the moment. "VK, this is increasingly fuzzy. I like vague as much as anybody, but is there a point we might get to?"

James walked to the edge of the deck. "Ming. This is important."

Ming slid his phone into a jacket pocket, and walked to the bottom of the deck stairs, where he stood leaning against the rail. James took out his glasses and wiped them against a shirtsleeve, an old habit that sometimes smeared them more than cleaned them. *Time to let the ridiculous cat out of the ridiculous bag.*

"To go with the geological anomalies we are witnessing, Maya has been tracking other metrics. She handed me an updated report this morning." James pulled a folded sheet out of his jacket pocket. "Maya was herself startled by the indicators. She'd been noticing changes over the last few months. An increase in pregnancies. Unusual warmth. Atypical plant growth and species propagation. Her staff began to report the same things. She pulled cross-checks on averages for the Khumbu region. Births, temperature, plant and animal diversity, a number of others. In the last year or two, the numbers started to skew. In the last month or so, startling: growth, diversity and fertility rates are off the charts."

He returned the page to his pocket. "Bugs, plants, and humans proliferating at accelerated rates. This stuff needs a separate, dedicated bio team to deal with it. I'm providing it as ancillary evidence."

James noted Ming walking up onto the deck. "Based on what Earthyield has done with Synthium, we can state with reasonable certainty that the earth is releasing powerful chemical catalysts into the water beneath Everest. Rocks are reacting in ways that seem to defy physics. We've held the stuff in our hands. Solids gone to putty."

McPhee produced a can of tobacco chew and shoved a plug inside his lower lip. Frauz tilted his head, as if preparing to look properly askance.

"We have unexplainable climate increases going on. Thermal aberrations. Oddities in just about every category of physical science."

"This is beginning to sound like a religious experience," said Frew, wariness creeping into his tone.

"Beneath it we've got an enormous *something*. Whatever it is, it's rising towards the earth's crust."

"And it adds up to…?" asked Frew.

"The earth is pregnant." James blinked. "Expecting. With child."

Someone cleared his throat, twice. Frauz and McPhee glanced at each other. McPhee sent a wad of soggy chaw over the rail. Ming folded his hands together, formally, as if he were about to bow. Frew put both hands in his pockets, which James knew to be a Frewian omen of disdain.

"You did have a long night," said Frew.

"The earth is softening up to deliver a brand new world. In effect a planetary baby," James said.

"An interesting premise," offered Frauz. "A bit on the side of– how might I put this congenially– absurd."

McPhee looked around at the others, perhaps wanting to assure himself it was some joke he was not in on. "Give me a bloody break, Doctor," he said. "You *are* joking."

James shook his head.

"Are you joking? That you're not joking?" said McPhee.

"Seriously– seriously serious?" said Frew.

Me Ming lowered his hands and spoke. "The evidence as paralleled to a human pregnancy is compelling. The physics we would need to verify."

That was an unexpected vote of confidence. If not confidence, at least not outright contempt. James drew a long finishing sip of his coffee, crumpled the cup, and tossed it into one of the crates. "I spent a long night with the abbot. He is convinced."

"It's quite imaginative but, really, professor," said Frauz. "How would we confirm this astonishing condition? And, might I add– who is the father?"

"I went to the monastery, last night, as I said. Short story; I was thrown from a moving vehicle. The monks got me inside, a little woozy but okay. Took me to the abbot. He put up the idea. I can still taste the cocoa and smell the incense. Whole thing feels like a dream, this morning. It sounded as stupid to me as it does to you. I can't get past it."

"Shame you didn't bring a stick of smoky stuff back to share," said Frew. He started pulling lint out of his pockets and watching it drift to the deck. "Yeti dropped in for tea, while you were there, I hope?"

James grimaced. Continuing with gritted teeth was the only way through. "We've got to drop a probe down that borehole. Combine our sensors, link them to our field computer, and send it as deep as it'll go. We should get hard data on properties. Heat, composition, animation. Maybe more."

"Yes," said Ming. "Perhaps an inkling of life."

Frew looked at Ming, then James. "Count me out when you publish," he said, gyrating away from his mentor.

"Take Occam's Razor to it, Basil," James called after him.

"Will someone put me in touch with a bona fide scientist?" Frew stepped off the deck and walked towards the hills behind the lodge.

"What does Occam say?" asked Ming.

"When you have two competing theories that make exactly the same predictions, the simpler one is the better."

"We don't have two competing theories," said Frauz. "We have an isolated ill-considered impossibility."

"We have a theory that the Earth is doing something else besides giving birth, and the theory that it is," said James.

"I think your plan to retrieve the data from the hole is sound," said Ming. "From there, we can go forward." Ming had unexpectedly become an advocate.

McPhee was rifling through the camping gear. "Looking forward to the hike, Doc," he said.

* * *

Clarence Gault was propped in the doorway of Leslie Finch's lodge suite. Finch had her back to him, looking out her balcony window.

"You better get on the move, Leslie," he said, savoring the reverse dressing-down. She looked beat, thought Gault. Battered and bettered. Too bad. He let out a satisfied breath, sneering at his own folly. The place was going to hell in a handbasket. The note he had written describing phone and network breakdowns had morphed from fictional to factual. His attempts to contact Griffon had come up blank. The networks, phone and web, cycled in and out unpredictably. His IT crew was flummoxed. "The mountain's sweat is influencing electromagnetic waves," one of them had said. Gault had wanted to cuff him.

Finch remained silent and unmoving. She appeared oddly unkempt, her pants scuffed with dirt and her hair lustreless. This was not the Finch he'd come to despise.

"I've got a man dead. I've got a van missing. I've got monks in revolt. If you don't get on the horn to Griffon, we're going to have to—"

Finch turned to face him, eyes bloodshot and her usual sultry sheen a seeping façade. "The phones don't work."

"Look, do *something,*" said Gault. "Keep dialing, stay on the line, you might get a window." There was a jot of soothe in his tone. The girl was breaking. Gault exited, pulling the door shut so it might register somewhere between a hard close and disturbing slam.

Finch felt her shoulders jerk. She slumped back and exhaled a sanguine sigh. "After Jared and I are back in the saddle, Gault can kiss his job and corpulent self goodbye." She went to the room phone, picked up the receiver, and punched a button.

* * *

Dr. Virgil had forsaken the Earthyield monkey suit and come to work at this ungodly hour wearing Hawaiian cotton sweat pants and a loud reggae shirt. Security had been loath to let him enter. 'What do you think this is, Google?' one of the guards had moaned. It was 3:13 a.m. He punched the clock, entered the empire, and bumped into Griffon coming to find him in the hallway near his office.

"I need a carb hit, boss," said Virgil, striding past Griffon to the vending kiosk. Griffon followed. Virgil pulled a crumpled dollar out of his crumpled wallet and gently tendered it into the vending machine. It promptly spat the dollar back out. "Gawd," Virgil said, voice squeaking as he yawned wide. "I don't need this."

Griffon sat down at a table in the small alcove, pushing a greasy box of half-eaten fried chicken away from him.

"You have a dollar bill on you? Unwrinkled?" asked Virgil.

"No."

Virgil rummaged into his pockets fishing for coins. He spoke over his shoulder, knowing Griffon would be pleased at what he had to say. If he could manage to say it without keeling over after 36 hours sans sleep.

"A fluke, Jared. That's what this is," said Virgil. "Somebody remembered the Synthium was slightly less potent before we switched to stainless steel chambers. Early on, the chamber inflow linings, our Everpure water conduits, contained plastic derivatives. Polyethylene and some others. You sure you don't have a dollar? Has to be a smooth one. No wrinkles."

Virgil stood on tiptoes, reached up over the top of the vending machine and felt around for coins that were occasionally tossed there. He brought his hands down and brushed them together, shedding cobwebs, dust and chewing gum particulate.

"We might need to head out to McDonald's before–"

Griffon closed his eyes, shook his head and rose. He walked over to the machine, waved a plastic card in front of it, and the transparent front, with a click and hum, unlocked and sprang wide open. Virgil drooped his shoulders in quiet amazement.

"Oh. Wow. Nice." He clicked his teeth together, then reached in and extracted a bag of Martin's potato chips.

Griffon waved the card again and the machine shut. They proceeded down the hall to Virgil's lab and entered. Virgil bashed his palm against the space bar on his keyboard and seven screens lit up. "Rats. It didn't prompt for the password. I blew that." He twisted around to tell Griffon. "All-nighters do this to your mind."

"Okay, Virgil. Tell me," said Griffon.

Virgil sat down and key-tapped. Animated graphs popped up on three different displays.

"Forget the screen. Just tell me."

Virgil spun in his chair, ripped open the bag of chips and, between crunching bites, spoke. "What happens is a small amount of the polyethylene liner in the intake flow conduit leaches in with the source mineral. The plastic is incorporated into the mix. The water is acting on the source element and anything in the containers. We never realized it. The polyethylene neutralizes a key catalyst inside the base synthesizing mechanism, diluting and thereby blocking the replication of the natural elements in the formula. Kind of like plastic and dirt don't like each other. Never the twain shall meet."

He held the chips up to his mouth, tapping at the upturned bag. "These are really good. Made near Lancaster, PA. Cooked in soybean oil. No lard. A fair amount of the chips made in Amish country use lard." He folded the bag flat and stacked it on a pile of empties. "Chocolate as a chaser. On deck."

"What's the end result, Virgil?" asked Griffon.

"I had the team introduce a micro-laminate. Microscopic plastic wrap, in a manner of speaking. It's attacking the peridotite's replicating abilities quite dramatically. The fertility reaction is not only locally thwarted, it falls off exponentially. I think a small amount would probably kill off a major chunk of the water's potency. At least as far as organic yields. Kind of a micro-mega-condom, as crude as that sounds."

"Good, Virgil. This is good." Griffon leaned to rest his forehead in his open hand.

For the first time in their careers together, Virgil thought Griffon might be yielding to the forces beating on him. Virgil had never seen it happen, so couldn't be sure. It struck him as a good thing. A learning moment for the man: Griffon had no balance, no tipping point he might spring back from. A lesson in weariness and loss might be a stepping stone. He'd discover grit, backbone and pluck. Virgil pointed a long finger in the general direction of the vending kiosk. "Can we get chocolate? You want one?"

Griffon looked at him, nodded, rose, and the two walked the short way to the kiosk. Griffon once again opened it with a wave of his card. Virgil secured two Milky Way bars and a Mallo Cup. "Snacks in these things, Jared. Gotta get some variety going."

Griffon card-waved the machine and it closed. The overhead fluorescents threw a pale off-green wash over his face. He looked ill.

"Ironic, eh," said Virgil. "A man-made synthetic plastic– we are calling this particular iteration c-456– blocks the powerful, naturally occurring synthesis of the Thyzenboche water. Science reverses course and lights up the way. You gotta love that."

Griffon's eyes widened, the look of someone trying to be more alert than his body was able. "Look good across your calculus?"

"A lock."

"You will need to stick around. I'm going to need c-456 in canisters we can air-ship. Call the team in. Now. Twenty tanks, ten liters each. As soon as possible. If you need something to keep you awake, let me know." A spacey ringtone sounded and Griffon pulled his cell phone to his ear. Virgil knew the ringtone: it was Jill Collins's auto-messaging, used when she was off-duty.

Griffon looked at Virgil. "I have to take this call. Get on it." He turned and walked towards the elevator bay.

Virgil called out after him. "One of those vending cards, Jared. Next time you pencil in an overnighter, that's what I'm looking for."

Virgil studied him as Griffon walked away. The man had no faith. In all their years working with the incredible water and playing eyewitness to uncanny, preternatural happenings, Griffon had never offered a plaintive 'Amazing universe, eh?' or 'Thank God we found the stuff.'

Virgil had a simple blueprint for faith. The "invention" of popcorn, in nature, meant that a cool mind was behind it all. He defied anyone to deny that popcorn could not have happened by accident. It was delicious, nutritious, and expeditious. Kids and adults loved it. Even his aardvark loved it. It grew readily, abundantly, a hearty crop. Freshly generated, it could fill a house with its heavenly aroma. And, for heaven's sake, it popped when you heated it. There was no reason for a universe devoid of a sentient, engaged consciousness to create such a brilliantly conceived novelty, such a rambunctious ingredient, such a joyous thang, if it were one big crapshoot.

He could taste it already. Time to grab a bag. He'd slid a piece of cardboard behind the vending glass, precisely where the lock engaged when Griffon had waved his magic card to secure it. If things had gone as he planned, it should be easy to lift, grab and go.

* * *

Griffon reached the bay and punched the up button. He hit another button halting the elevator between floors. Privacy. Leslie Finch, finally. He tapped a key on his phone and held it to his ear.

"Hello, Jared Griffon."

"Jared."

"It's you." The connection was far from perfect, with plentiful static and clipped gaps in the voice transmission. But he could hear her.

"Jared. I have to get out of here."

"You don't sound happy."

"Bring me home. It's all coming undone."

"Calm down a minute, Leslie, calm down–"

Finch began sobbing. "Jared, I need you."

"Tell me what's going on."

"I talked to James. I told him–"

"You told him."

"I told James. About the water, the Synthium, the monks." Silence. "You will hate me," she said.

"What are you doing over there?"

"I'm alone."

"You're not making sense."

"I'm pregnant."

"You're not pregnant. If you are, you won't be."

Griffon ran his fingernails across the elevator wall, tracing the small dent he'd made with his fist, after his last visit to Virgil. "Tell Gault I'm coming over. Everything we've accomplished is on the line, thanks to you, baby. I hope you're happy."

Chapter Twelve

At the summit of Everest, a low rumble began again. The terrain lurched upward and expanded, hissing and crackling as it folded out like putty into formed solids. Where flags and oxygen tanks had lain, an open rupture, spreading methodically outward, its edges undulating like no earthly rock, writhed into being. The surrounding slope rippled, pliable, reacting more and more like soft clay in the ongoing shuffle of geological improbabilities.

* * *

Gault was not in a good state. The drilling had stopped. The ground tremors were increasing. His guests were raising hell and he couldn't blame them. A number were pledging to initiate legal action. Others were grateful to be heading south, expressing very strongly that the lodge had failed to diffuse the confusion and that misinformation was being disseminated as to the gravity of the crisis.

Gault didn't see any way to stem the PR damage: it was obvious things were no longer running as expected. The weather was clammy, the mountain (the 5-star reason for booking here) was invisible, masked by a permanent fog of fumes. The lodge had shuddered a few times. These weren't the almost-imperceptible vibrations that had left a few tourists questioning whether they had 'felt something.' A window had cracked, a bottle of red wine had left its perch and landed unbroken on the carpet of the lounge. Not like any earthquake any of them had experienced. Akin, but something else.

Lodge guests wandered with their luggage from the lobby into the waiting van shuttles, departing in bunches as space in each vehicle allowed. The lodge staff was busy escorting the guests, moving luggage, and processing the checkouts of those departing. Gault saw the tourist who had drunk the 'bad' water, who'd been moved with his family to one of the lodge's premium summit suites, pacing agitatedly near a front window. His family sat on a lobby couch, gawking in awe at his decidedly fuller head of curling hair.

I'll be glad when that idiot's gone, thought Gault. I'll be glad to get the hell out of here myself, the sooner the better. Now for the latest pain. He took a breath. It was time to corral some heavies and confront Von Kamburg.

* * *

James stood at the front lobby desk, Frew beside him, waiting for the attendant to pay them some attention. Charlie was missing, the New Zealanders had never shown up, and the drones never appeared, to take photos or deliver beer, which seem to incense Frew more than anything.

"We could have droned a hand-written note back to the States," he said. "At least they've managed to get the guests on their way out of here, mostly. Hope someone's remembering to feed the fish." Frew did a few knee bends, then straightened. "What do you think Bennington's up to? You'd think someone would have the smarts to call missing persons, at least."

"I don't know what *they* know, but one thing *we* know is they're not hearing anything from us," said James. "We might still get a message out on one of the flights, if they're flying in this muck. If Dan gets the shortwave going, I'll call Maggie and ask her to connect with the airport, try to find something out."

There was a rumor that a newspaper brought in yesterday carried a wire story about the communications outages near Everest. James was hoping Bennington would get pro-active and find a way to get word to them and step up a response. Get some choppers in from Kathmandu. Hike some assistance in if they couldn't fly it in. It hadn't been a week yet since they'd been in Nepal but he had to believe the MEAD team's administrators were vigilant enough to know there was trouble. It was starting to border on ludicrous. Bennington would get an earful if James ever got through.

Frew had had no luck with the IT staff at the lodge. They were either dismissive or too busy trying to fix the mess to bother with him. Charlie was gone; he might have been caught for collusion, after he'd let James into the pool area, but there was a rumor he'd quit. James had asked McPhee to 'permanently' disable the locks on both the inside and outside pool entryways and McPhee had agreeably done so. Unfortunately, he also had had no luck finding any viable networks he could tap connecting the MEAD team to Bennington and co.

The strange transformation of the science mission into a para-military operation was particularly galling. James had no idea if the lodge staffers were slate-bluebloods ready to go to war for Griffon's causes or just employees who didn't want to lose jobs. His team hadn't been cast for an action movie. The two contingents circled each other suspiciously, when they weren't gawking in the direction of the highest point on earth. Everest was clearly undergoing something other than business as usual.

Getting out of town had become the principal activity and in fairness, James thought the lodge was on the ball there. The vans moved the guests to Namche, where they could negotiate flights out or start an escorted trek down the valley.

Frauz and McPhee strolled past, heading for the front door. McPhee shouldered a knapsack and carried a large duffel bag. Frauz carried a leather suitcase and wardrobe portmanteau. Me Ming was not in sight.

"I knocked on Ming's door a couple times. Not sure what's up with him," said James.

"Maybe he's been electronically couriered outta here," said Frew.

James laughed. "We'll miss his expertise if he's really gone over the wall."

"I have a feeling he'll show up. Far hike to Peking."

"Sir!" James hailed the attendant, who finally turned to face them. "We are staying overnight, with our equipment, using the pool complex. That's both inside the dome and outside on the deck. We will check-out of the lodge tomorrow morning."

"I will need the manager's approval. Please wait."

"We don't have time to wait. Ask Mr. Gault to meet us at the pool." The attendant pulled a face, but didn't reply. James looked at Frew, his eyebrow cocked. He addressed the attendant again.

"*Tell* Gault to meet us at the pool." The attendant nodded, forgoing the usual grin, and hurried off.

James and Frew walked the inner corridor to the pool, through the domed complex and out onto the deck, where Frauz and McPhee were consolidating the equipment they would take into the field. McPhee had lined up pouches, rucksacks, slings, bungee cords, rope and a collection of his sadly unused mountaineering carabiners.

"Probably need more rope. How many yaks did you rent?" ask McPhee.

"I can see we'll need plenty," said James, propping the doors wide. "Maya knew what we wanted to carry and said she'd take care of getting enough porters and animals to haul it. Has a local named Passang lined up. Says he's the boy for the job."

"*Boy for the job,* that's reassuring," said Frew.

"The big expensive stuff bumping against the side of a yak for six clicks. It's gonna be tricky," said McPhee.

James motioned Frew to one side. "We can't wait for the New Zealanders. Modal interferometer or no. I asked Maggie to let them know our plans, if they cross paths."

"I'm still hoping they show. Especially with the slightly unconventional theories being floated around here," said Frew. "Be good for you to see their reaction when you deliver the Earth mama line."

James had no time to reply; they looked up at the sound of doors swinging open from inside the pool complex. Gault walked out onto the deck, followed by two men, one who wore sunglasses.

"I want these doors and the inside doors to the pool dome padlocked," said Gault. "Dr. Von Kamburg, I brought you some help. This is Mr. Grace and Mr. Spencer. They'll join your team and make sure you are able to follow the customs and obligations we agreed to as tenants of the region."

James eyed Mr. Grace and Spencer. They wore variations on the odd ostentatious garb he had seen in Vancouver, where he'd glimpsed Earthyield employees during the lab tour. "I don't need your men. I need the all-terrain buggies, if you can spare those," he said.

"Sorry. We have to get the tourists cleared."

"You're not using the *buggies* for guests, are you?"

"Sorry," said Gault.

"Where's Leslie?" asked James.

"Leslie's away, busy."

McPhee and Frauz walked over. McPhee pulled up his shirtsleeves a hair and cracked his neck, just a tweak. Frauz ran his knuckles under his bearded jaw. If he's going for John Wayne, it ain't working, thought James.

"Put me on the phone to Jared Griffon. I can straighten everything out," said James.

"Satellite, cells, broadband, all down. I can tell you that Mr. Griffon is coming over from Vancouver."

"That's useful. When's he due?"

"Twenty-four hours, give or take."

"He'll have to reach us by shortwave," said James. "We're gone at first light."

"Where to?"

"The drilling site."

"Drilling site?" asked Gault.

"You know," said McPhee. "Deep hole. No permit. That site."

"No one asked for your two cents, squib," said Spencer.

"Tell me something, gents," McPhee continued, "how'd you get word on Griffon showing his mug over here if you can't get those phones to work? Isn't he in Canada?"

Mr. Grace turned his black lenses in the direction of McPhee. "Can I ask your name?"

"Daniel Mortimer McPhee."

"That's Irish or Scottish," said Mr. Grace. "Do you climb?"

"I climb. I'm from Wales. Who are you, Mr. Foster-Grant? Take off your shades and show your face."

"I'll take him out," said Spencer.

Mr. Grace shook his head. James felt his pulse ratcheting up. Was he actually about to use his fists to punch another human? More likely he'd be using his legs to get the hell away.

"Tell bonehead to chill," said McPhee, addressing Mr. Grace. "Take off your glasses."

"Dan, don't–" James was interrupted. Someone hustling up the steps. Passang bound onto the deck and halted, ruddy cheekbones shining above a fixed grin. He set his slight body between Gault and James.

"Doctor James?" asked Passang.

"I think that's me."

"I am to carry gear. Maya says look for the red beard!" Passang bowed, then stood up tall and grinned broadly at Gault.

"Just you?" asked James.

"No, cousins. Around the corner, having smoke. Plus yaks. Good yaks."

Gault made an attempt to hide his scowl.

"Mr. Gault, how are you?" said Passang, with what James thought was a beautifully ingratiating grin.

Spencer stepped back, looking less inclined to play thug. Mr. Grace stood in his place.

"Look, Gault, we're not trespassing. We've paid for our rooms here. And somewhere you have a document from the Nepalese government that says we should expect cooperation. Not a crew of bouncers," said James. "We'll sleep on the deck tonight. We're out of your hair first thing a.m."

"Griffon prefers that you're already gone," said Gault. "So do I." He addressed Mr. Grace. "Move this equipment off the lodge grounds. Get more hands if you need them."

Another commotion, more shuffling and banter, as five Nepalese marched up onto the deck. Each had a long-blade *kukri* knife sheathed at his belt; they were Nepalese Gurkha warriors.

"Passang," bellowed the lead Gurkha, "is the tea brewing?"

"Come. Greet Doctor Von Kamburg," said Passang. The Gurkhas wandered up in a circle around James, all broad smiles, shaking the hands of everyone, including Gault, Spencer and the MEAD team. Mr. Grace stepped back.

"Please meet Gaje, Kulbir, and Sher. And this is Ganju, and that's Thaman," said Passang. The Gurkhas settled on the deck, leaning against the crates, barking for tea, or chang, or whatever could be had.

Mr. Grace had disappeared. Gault and Spencer stood for a moment, back to back.

James looked at them. "Don't mess with the locks. Don't mess with the doors."

* * *

Griffon lowered his head to mask the SUV's motor as it sped down Granville Street towards the Vancouver International Airport, and held the phone to his ear.

He had dialed up the most powerful and proactive politician he knew, a US Senator: Charles Bennington, Chair of the Senate Subcommittee on Energy and Commerce. Bennington's committee had their circumspect digits in everything from foreign trade to environmental policy. Bennington had invested in Earthyield, through channels, and was a staunch guardian of the environment. He appreciated that Synthium might simultaneously make him money and save the planet.

Griffon had just learned, to his deepening consternation, that Bennington had sanctioned the Von Kamburg mission. Mt. Everest and the surrounding area were indicating– how had Bennington put it– *anomalies*. Von Kamburg was on site to investigate. Bennington had only managed sporadic contact with them.

Griffon felt ill at ease. He had a snowballing list of things to tackle, and not much time to get them under control.

Every snippet of news he got was feeding a great, black bloodsucking engine of ruin. A silver spike was being nailed into the heart of his company's most indispensable operation. But, he also felt compelled. Which was good. He knew his own powers waxed in proportion to the challenges he faced. His lover's pregnancy should not have happened. The situation with the monks was unraveling. And the geological permutations were startling, even with his inside knowledge of Everest's…how to phrase it…*condition*. Whatever was going on in the deeps under *Chomolungma*, he was tethered to all of it.

As was often the case, a move to the front lines was necessary. He knew his involvement would move the pieces on the board, to useful effect. "Senator, listen to me. Declare the area an international emergency zone. I've got a team ready–"

"We are dealing with the situation prudently, Jared," said Bennington.

"Senator. I've got facilities in Kathmandu and an operation right there, two clicks from Namche, at the mountain. I've got aircraft, personnel–"

"You've got a hotel there. You bottle spring water. It's not a forward command base, unless I'm mistaken."

Griffon didn't have time nor an inclination to delve into Synthium secrets. He was walking a high wire. Maybe he and the senator were both walking high wires. Neither of them was coming clean with everything he knew. The senator continued.

"We're mobilizing units to deploy if Von Kamburg indicates there is an emergency. We're waiting to hear. What we thought was a short-term communications blockage has become ongoing. The trouble doesn't end with radio and phones and the web. Satellite imagery has been disrupted. Airlift status, even a drone fly-by disrupted. If it isn't the weather it's distortion in the instrumentation and in the case of the drones, long-range operational control. In five days this has gone from a science excursion to a possible rescue scenario."

"Senator. The Von Kamburg team is a crew of research geologists. They are in a potentially dangerous zone. You said it yourself. Give me the authority to replace them, get them out of there, and let my team take over." His driver sped toward the airport entrance, its green sign flashing overhead as Griffon looked out his gun-seat window.

"You can play an important support role. I appreciate that," said Bennington.

"The investment is at risk, Senator. People are at risk."

"The investment means nothing if there is a potentially catastrophic geological event pending. That's the only issue, and Von Kamburg has the best unit, a very capable team, on the ground there now, to find that out. What I can do is offer your assets to assist his team. Don't mention investments to me again."

"Okay, Okay." Griffon had said all he could. The senator wasn't going to budge.

"I've got to run," said Bennington. "Let me know if you learn anything from your side as far as updates from the MEAD team. As I said, we're prepping a unit to go in for evacuation purposes if they need that. Based on the most recent reports that kind of crisis is not pending."

"I will share what I get. Please do the same from your end."

"I will. Goodbye."

Griffon shoved the phone into an inside pocket and spoke to his driver. "Everest is rising, do you believe it? They have solid data the mountain is rising. And it's not being called a geological crisis." The driver raised his eyebrows and tilted his head a bit. Griffon pulled the phone back out and tapped in another number.

"Virgil! Virgil, it's me. I need a shipment of the c-456 sent off to Kathmandu. Virgil, stop. I want twenty canisters in Nepal when I get there. Send them out tonight." The SUV pulled up to the airport departure terminal.

"Yes, Virgil, the cure. *The cure.*"

* * *

Unrecognizable night noises played in the eerie atmosphere of the Khumbu, a metamorphosis underway.

Steam and fog cloaked the region's great rivers, the Dudh Kosi, Imja Khola, and Bhote Kosi, these three the headwaters of the most sacred Ganges. An onlooker might have noted the succulent abundance of sweet fruits emerging like pupae, an unorthodox and quickened bumper crop from the flourishing trees. They would have seen the odd drove of red pandas ranging the upland woods en masse in search of barberries, snowcress, and milk-vetches. When that fruit was eaten, for there were many mouths in need of it, the pandas would be reaching for the leaves of bamboo, cinquefoil, and poppy.

Keelback lizards peered from rocky boltholes, scrabbling for familiar insects to go with never-before-seen prey, some given away by their glow of green flame. Skinks pounced on the keelbacks. There was plenty to eat and many were eaten.

The jungle crows soared like falcons, mounting the strange updrafts to scout for every sort of edible and being rewarded with abundance and never-before-tasted dainties. Then— no warning— bats descended on the crows, attack squadrons of beating leathery wings, bearing down on plumage with moon or sun behind, a ballet of torn bodies and falling feathers.

Most notable of all, *Panthera unica.* So rare were sightings that myth had abraded reality. The snow leopard had emerged out of need from its hidden labyrinth of caves, overhangs, hollows and dens, to find sustenance. Bumper litters of cubs had grown quickly on the flesh of wild goats, boars, weasels and foxes. More was needed. Bears, jackals, and yaks were out and about in numbers, crawling and stepping and running, confused and overrun in the hunt for the normal they had known, in this new uncontrolled confusion of life.

The snow leopard, the crown prince of the recluse, now hunted in packs.

* * *

Passang had done a covert recon, checking in with his hotel co-worker pals to see if he could get any useful news. Exhausted, James had stayed awake to listen, then sent Passang off to quiet his Gurkhas. Passang didn't have much to tell; all but a small number of tourists had departed. The staff had been informed they were to stay overnight before a building-wide cleanup and lodge lockdown the next day, as ordered by the hotel manager Clarence Gault. Finch was nowhere to be seen. Passang had avoided Gault.

The MEAD team, save Frew, slept inside under the pool dome, on the cold tiles. Outside, just visible to James on the deck, Frew, Passang, and the Gurkhas slept with their feet up against the equipment.

At one point in the stillness and chill of the pre-dawn hours, James stirred from a troubled dream, awakened by the sound of liquids in motion. Valves and pumps below the surface of the pool were moving the water. He could hear it running, gurgling and fretting down and away into some catchment in the lodge's sub-basement where Earthyield's machines would bottle it and package the boxes that would carry it on its way across Nepal to an Indian port and from there by freighter across the ocean to Vancouver. At least he so surmised in his half-awake state.

He dragged himself and his sleeping bag the few feet to the pool's edge and dipped his hand in the water. Ever pure. These droplets on his palm might be Earth's amniotic fluid.

Soft splashes marked the end of the water's porting. Must be automated, thought James. Even with everything that was happening, Griffon's systems stayed on task.

* * *

James cracked an eye open. Morning had crawled over the horizon, pale and diluted. James, and if his tossing and turning was any indication, McPhee also, had slept fitfully in their bags on the pool's hard tiled floor, which had done a slow cooling down through the night hours. Frauz had made his bed on the bench near the wall, where smoke rings floated gently roofward. Frew had slept outside, to keep an extra eye on the equipment. James rolled over. Through the window, he spied Passang and the Gurkhas, huddling under cloaks, quietly sipping tea.

McPhee raised his head, took a bleary-eyed peek, and burrowed back into his bag. James sat up, groggy. First thought: get McPhee to test the radio. Last night, he had tried to call Maggie. The short wave had buzzed uselessly and shut down. He'd kept it on the recharger all night. So far, Gault hadn't cut off their electricity. Which was sporting of him, as Frauz might say. If daffy, as McPhee might add.

Frew made his way inside, balancing a steaming cup of tea, sliced lemon and spoon on the small plate that held it. "Sleep soundly?" he asked, setting it carefully on the tiles. "I didn't. Too many knives glinting in the dark."

Frew sat down next to James, who had pulled the sleeping bag up around his shoulders to ward off the chill.

"Must have slept on that damned bump," James said, rubbing at the top of his head. "God, it feels like an icebox. Gault didn't switch off the electricity but he cut the heat in here. The prick."

"Did you just say what I think you said?"

"No."

"This is a new Von Kamburgian mark for degree of ticked off," said Frew.

James smiled and shoved his palms into his eye sockets.

"You want this tea?" asked Frew. "It's hot. I was afraid to say no. It's all they drink. Don't ask me where Passang dug up the lemon and china. Maybe the staff is sticking it to Gault. Which leads me to wondering if the lodge is still serving coffee. Especially to Rogues R Us. An espresso, actually, is what I'd like."

"I'm not taking you on any more trips," said James, lifting the tea to his mouth for a cautious sip. Frew was Frew, and that was a good thing. The tea, tepid, green, not so exciting.

"It wouldn't be bad if I knew what they were saying," Frew continued, thumb out in the direction of the deck. "You know who they are? What they are? They're *Gurkhas.* The Green Berets of Nepal. Did you see those knives? Holy heart failure, Batman."

James set the teacup down and wriggled himself out of his bag.

"You should be happy, though. I think Passang succeeded in selling them your goddess mother story," Frew said.

James looked at Frew and didn't quite smirk. "I'm not claiming it yet, Basil."

Frew plucked the lemon slice from the plate and rubbed it across his front teeth. "Packed my toothbrush somewhere in the bottom of my duffel." He slumped flat on the tiles, spread his arms wide, and swept them forth and back, as if making a snow angel. "Ming's nowhere to be found. I think he boogied for Tibet."

"Maybe the hotel will tell us if he checked out. Did Charlie manifest?"

Frew sat up. "You know what? Passang told me that Charlie is his uncle. Helped get him the hotel job. Passang said Charlie warned him it was a lousy place to work. When Passang got fired I think it pissed Charlie off, which is maybe why he let you into the pool complex. Then he quit. Or was fired. No one is sure around here. Good people, but slightly wacked as far as trying to get to the bottom of things."

"Fate so fickle." It was McPhee, rousing one sleeping bag over.

"Rise and shine, Dan. I want to radio Maggie."

McPhee slumped back. "Room service. Scrambled eggs, bangers, and a hunk of laverbread, please." He raised himself on an elbow. "Let me get some cold water on me face."

McPhee shuffled off to the pool's restrooms. Frew stood and walked to the window, where he looked out into the white murk. James groaned, rose, and followed. The Gurkhas were just visible where they'd gathered on the lawn, doing a combination stretch-and-act-regimented routine. One had his shirt off. Small in stature, the man's muscles rippled like steel coils beneath his skin.

Frew wiped at the condensation. "I hope Ming's okay. I can't figure him out, really. He was starting to come around when we were unpacking."

"He was the right man and the wrong man," said James. "His reading of the borehole data would be particularly valuable. But I was close to snapping. Tell you the truth, China's overseers might be surprised at how poorly he cooperated. Someone over there must have got him cranked up, some relic who's missing the good old days of the cold war."

"Good morning, gentlemen." It was Frauz, who looked perfectly coiffed, despite having just emerged from his plaid sleeping bag.

"Hey Xavier. How was the bench?" asked Frew.

"Fonky."

James and Frew both laughed. McPhee reappeared and headed out to the deck. James, Frauz and Frew followed. The fog had thickened overnight, but was somehow brighter.

"Odd light," said James.

"Water vapors, I'd say," said Frauz. "Bending the spectrum, probably carbolic distortion through the helix curve."

"I was just gonna say that exact thing," said Frew.

"No you weren't," said Frauz, blowing smoke at Frew.

Abruptly, from inside the dome, they heard a door squeal open. Gault stalked onto the deck and stood in front of James. James noticed the Gurkhas, with a quiet nonchalance, form up out of the white and gather near the deck steps.

"You've got a call. You should hop to it. There's no guarantee the connection will hold."

James followed Gault back through the pool complex. They turned several quick corners to reach Gault's office, where air-to-ground radio static was crackling loudly. Gault picked up the transmitter and handed it to James.

"Hello?" said James.

Jared Griffon was co-pilot of one of two twin-engine Otters, in the air roaring over the southern flanks of the Himalayas en route to the airport at Syangboche, the same field that Von Kamburg's team had used less than a week prior. The planes bucked and pitched in the turbulent gusts. Through the windscreen, Griffon watched the second plane dissolve and reappear in the frenzy of white and wind. It flew some distance above, but too close.

He turned to the pilot. "Move that aircraft back another 300 yards." Von Kamburg's *hello* crackled through the headset. "Hello. Can you hear me? James?" Sharp bursts of static cut into the transmissions, further gutted by the throb of the Otter's powerful radial engines.

"Jared. How is it up there?"

"We're rockin' and rollin'."

"Don't land at Syangboche. Land at Lukla."

"Lukla is out. Too far."

The plane jerked violently. The pilot hauled at the yoke as the second plane flashed overhead.

"You there?"

Griffon yelled over the noise. "Yes, listen–"

"It's not just wind up there, Jared. Erratic thermals, bouncing air pressure, static charges in the clouds. You should turn around."

Abrasive screeches and zaps fused into clamor. Griffon barked through it. "We hit a pocket."

"Jared. I know about the water. About Synthium. And the monastery. Leslie's told me everything."

"Leslie's unstable."

"I need to use your borehole."

The static intruded again, loudly. "I've talked to Washington," said Griffon. "We think it will be safer if you cleared out– whoa!" Griffon's aircraft pitched forward, thrown again by a sharp wind shear.

"Are you okay?"

"Wait–"

Griffon tightened his seat belt and leaned into the glass. Below, a dense murk swirled, blanketing the villages of Khumbu. Briefly, two ribbons of water gleamed through the haze. In an instant before the fog packed in, Griffon noted the watercourses merging. Pilots used the confluence to confirm their final approach up the valley.

"Did you see that, Tim?" The pilot nodded. James's voice crackled through.

"I need to use the hole, Jared."

"Stay put and we can talk at the lodge. We're on the ground in thirty."

"You know what the water does to rocks. It's doing it to plants, animals, people. Everything's gone fertile. It's crazy down here."

"Maybe you're out of your league on this one, Doctor."

"We're reading a massive, metamorphosing batholith. It's rising."

"Evacuate. You're not safe."

"The water— your Synthium water— it's a byproduct of whatever's going on under Everest. It's reaching some sort of critical mass. We could use your help."

"You're out of your league."

"Jared. Wake up. This is not your penthouse conference room. There's a mountain getting ready to shove us out of our stupor."

"You sound like Finch."

"I'll see you at the drilling station."

"If you show up there, you're responsible for what happens." There was a final, piercing burst of static, as Griffon bellowed over the racket. "Jackass."

* * *

Finch pushed the unwashed hair back from her eyes. She reached into her jeans pocket and felt for the van keys. God, her jeans were disgusting. *Must have brushed past something greasy in the kitchen.* She'd grabbed the extra set of van keys from Gault's office. That part wasn't hard. Losing Gault had been trickier. He'd been hunkering around after her, like some slope-backed Neanderthal. Luckily he'd been pulled away by the call from Jared's aircraft.

He was out of sight, so now was the time. She got into the driver's door of the van and pulled a lever beneath the seat to tuck it closer to the wheel and pedals. She looked behind. Several cartons of Everpure water were stashed in the back. *I won't get thirsty.* Never drove one of these, she mused. *Good it's an automatic.* She fumbled, trying to insert the key into the ignition.

Gault burst through the door from the lodge kitchen. "Where're you going?"

With a flick of her finger, Finch locked the van doors. Gault rapped on her window. *Bang, bang, bang.* Finch rolled the window halfway down and leaned away from him, staring with cold eyes.

"You can't take the van. Jared is royally pissed. Von Kamburg is heading to the drill site."

"You don't need the van."

"We need it. You can't take it. What about the mess we're in? You helping or cutting out?"

"I'm going to meet Jared. We're getting married. I'm thinking shotgun." She paused, so her heart could beat. "Nah. Too old-fashioned."

"Screw us, huh?"

"Screw you."

"You blew our cover with Von Kamburg, now you're blowing us off to run back to your boyfriend. Get out of the van–" Gault reached in, groping for the window switch. The upper surface of his hand was covered with coarse hairs, she observed. She wanted to slap it. Instead, with an urgent twist of the key, she started the engine. She hit the switch to begin winding the window up; but couldn't overcome the pressure of Gault's grasping arm. She hit a button on the sun visor. The garage door clattered upward. Gault's face seemed to enlarge as he set his eyes upon her, cheeks puffing pink.

"No promotion this year, Clarence."

She grasped his arm and sunk her teeth in. He pulled away, grimacing, stricken. She spat in his face and pressed her foot to the gas pedal. The van lurched, and she hit the brake. She took a moment to lock in her seat belt, as Gault, spinning in pain, sucked on his wrist, looking like a kid ready to sob. She regretted the mess. It wasn't like her. With a more deliberate touch on the pedal, she gassed the van out of the garage and onward.

"You mother," Gault hissed.

Chapter Thirteen

Von Kamburg's Mount Everest Allied Discovery team, minus the representative from China, Me Ming, and accompanied by Passang and the warrior Gurkhas, led five heavily laden yaks across the lodge courtyard, which had undergone a metamorphosis. A week ago it had been patchy with snowy mush. Now the mush had melted to reveal slick mottled grasses, unkempt and blotchy with bleached tans. What looked like churned earth scarred the fringes.

James appreciated the team's mettle. With Griffon arriving, they had hustled even more urgently to get away from the lodge. The evening prior, the equipment had been painstakingly wrapped and fastened to ensure it would endure a long day's yak journey across unpredictable terrain. Most of the larger pieces had not yet been assembled, making them easier to pack but creating a potential bottleneck once they had to unload and get everything up and running in the field. They'd had to leave more than a few of the units crated on the deck. There was simply too much. Although fieldwork had been anticipated, this SWAT-team sortie had come out of the blue.

Frauz had fussed especially over the gravimeter, supplementing the padding with his now unnecessary overcoat. With a fair amount of perturbation, scrupulously described to James, Frauz had visualized the gauges, heat sinks and calibrators jounced and bounced and smelling of yak when he finally got the machine set up. He'd taken a spoonful of Pepto for the indigestion.

Now they were on the move. Many on the team hoisted backpacks, brimming with gear. The altitude-acclimatized Gurkhas and Passang bore the heaviest loads and guided the yaks on leads. Along with their primary cargo, two of the yaks carried extensive lengths of cable, secured in loops at their flanks. McPhee had "borrowed" a bit of extra cable from the lodge's storage shed, along with a few wrenches and a crowbar, just for good measure.

The day was warm, not yet hot, though edging that way. Frew told James it was *un-reasonable* weather. The air moved, animated by hidden currents, a slow swirling vapor that muted sound and color. Through a stroke of good fortune, the steam didn't curtail their ability to see the route forward. The looming bulk of Everest was faintly visible, though a hazy mantle continued to mask the summit.

Ahead, vines crawled the lodge sign, choking the silver blue characters that spelled out the name. The team moved under the formal stone bulwark of the front entrance, itself now an arbor of silverstripe and rhododendron, trestling skyward over the grey marble. Three substantial toads hopped for cover as the lead yak clopped past.

Before they had headed out, James had made another attempt to reach Maggie and Maya. No answer. The uncertainty began to gnaw at him. Was she all right? When would they get a chance to hear each other's voices? The rising fog, breathed into one's lungs, brought a strange refreshment. James thought it a curious form of nourishment. He stopped to inhale a deep draught of air.

"Be safe, Maggie." He reached inside his vest to take his glasses out and felt a piece of paper. It was a note from his wife.

Jim, not sure what this all means as it's been coming back in bits and pieces. In case we don't get to talk again, soon enough, I wrote this note.

I saw the white stars, in the dream I had, just before you got the letter from Jared. He and I were pushing a baby carriage down the sidewalk. I could hear the baby, cooing. In the sky, I told Jared, look up. White dots aligned in parallel and perpendicular, to form the shape of a tree. It's not a tree, he said, it's the mountain. I looked into the carriage and there was no baby.

I believe the Earth's going to do its thing.

Wish you and I were together. I love you.

Maggie.

James couldn't help but look up into the blue. Clouds, steam, sky.

With an abrupt squeal of rubber, a lodge van came barreling around from the rear driveway. The yaks shied, the Gurkhas heaved at the leads. One duffel bag was thrown and nearly stomped. The van veered, flying past in a pall of dust and thrown gravel.

"That was Finch," said Frew. He jogged out to watch her off.

"She's not herself," said McPhee, dusting off his pants. "Whatever that is."

James saw the van as it disappeared over a second rise. Followed, in the distance, by the harrowing cry of some unnamed animal. Whatever it was, left him unnerved. Where was Finch going, nearly wrecking into them in her half-cocked haste?

The note was confusing. And disturbing. *Stars, earth, baby.* A recipe at odds with its ingredients. He had to bear down again. Concentrate on one useful action. He ran his hands over his face.

"Let's move, please!"

* * *

Finch continued down the pocked road heading in the general direction of the airport. She remembered the road to the airport was rutted and often muddied. Bad as it was the day she flew in, it had been clear of trees, shrubs, and vines. This new growth had erupted into a riot of tangle; weeds, brush and limb. The tire-furrowed middle of the track was clear enough; the road's flanks were a throbbing leafy wall.

She wanted to see Jared, watch him come running to her, see him fall on his knees. She'd tell him a few things he'd need to change. If he couldn't be a different man, from that moment, she'd have to let him know this was the final fail.

A weird fog poured up, escaping from holes in the earth, venting vapors from an inexplicable underground furnace. She ran her palm over the window, smearing open a space through the condensation in front of her face. Leaning forward, she could see better. The van lurched and wobbled. She began to sweat, the salt from her forehead drizzling into her eyes, stinging and distracting.

She rounded a bend and slammed on the brake. A large dead thing lay straddled across the road. A beast. Not a yak; the fur was red brown with white under the neck. Some kind of feral mountain elk? Elk in the Himalayas. That might not be right. She jammed the stick shift into reverse, spitting grit over the fleshy bulk. She yanked down on the wheel and steered the van past.

* * *

A loud roar split the MEAD team's ears as Griffon's planes thrummed into view, flying low, flaps down. The aircraft bucked and side-slipped. The yaks, startled, reared their heads and stamped. One broke from its tether and headed off down an incline, two Gurkhas in pursuit. Passang gave James a succinct *here we go again* look. The aircraft disappeared into the foggy white, headed for Syangboche Airport. The errant yak was corralled, and the team took a moment to regroup.

"Why does Griffon need two?" said Frew. "Bringin' a blue army? Nut."

"I hope they can land in this muck," said James. "He's a fool for flying in this– a fool for coming."

Frew nodded.

Von Kamburg's expedition marched northeast, for a short while following the dirt road away from the lodge. Heeding Passang's directions, they bore left from the road and entered a gully, which presently opened out into a wide, thick-tussocked landscape. As verified by McPhee, they were following a path in the general direction of the monastery and its yak pastures beyond. From there, the Earthyield drilling location should not be much further. McPhee had calculated a six-kilometer hike one way.

The yaks trudged unheeding, flanked by the troupe of hikers and their gear. The way was littered with gray rock and bounded by high-stemmed stitchwort stalks. Several times, James thought he heard a curious crunching noise, as if a tree were grinding up out of the soil. He looked around and saw only the wide, foliage-brimming landforms. One time out of the corner of his eye, a freshened shoot, shuddering, then stopping. Maybe.

Ahead, what they could see of Everest's lower flanks struck them. The familiar couloirs of its storied history were gone, their veneer, especially at the higher elevations, replaced by soaring, striated seams of color, grey-greens and mustard-tans, set off by needles of grim red. Cobalt-tinged vapors, alive with flashes of static, danced its upper reaches, veiling whatever might be going on at the summit.

McPhee stared up at the blankness where the peak was hidden. He whistled. "If this was climbing season, you'd have a gaggle of cooked geese up there."

Frew concurred. "Looks godawful."

"On the mark, Basil," said Frauz, squinting at the tableau. "The word monstrosity comes to mind."

"Not a monster, sir," corrected Passang. "She is the goddess mother."

"The goddess mother-*f-u-c-k-e-r,* don't you mean," said Frauz. Passang's face went blank. Frauz continued. "Although I'm not accustomed to using the full-on profanities I think the sentiment resonates. I also so honor

Chaucer, who at times thought it necessary. Somehow I don't imagine the royal mother has maternal instincts for the peons crawling up her flanks." Passang wandered away towards the back of the marchers.

"Better pipe down, Mr. Frauz." McPhee dipped his head towards the Gurkhas. Frauz crimped his shoulder and turned away, some version of plussed and non. Frew jogged to catch up with James near the front.

As Frew reached him, James lost his footing. "Whoa–" Frew caught him under the elbow and he stumbled back to his feet. They stopped to study the imprint of his boot. Not in mud or dirt. The molded impression, complete with brand logo, was sunk into a flat, sulfur-colored rock. "Thanks," James said. "Here and there, where it's yellowed-up, ground has gone pliant. Pass the word."

"Insane." Frew moved back through the entourage spreading the news, then returned. "They got the word. Everyone is game."

"Good crew," said James. "Considering it's gone from a generic scientific incursion to something like *Forbidden Planet*."

"You mean the *Rocky Horror Picture Show*," said Frew. He paused. "James."

"You *never* call me 'James'."

"I'm interested in your professional opinion."

"Shoot."

"What happens if the bath-o-baby reaches the crust?" Frew asked.

James shaped his palms around an invisible sphere. "How big is it? Have to start there once we get readings."

"No way it can reach escape velocity."

"That should be true."

"It's impossible physics to suggest otherwise," said Frew.

"You are spot on," James offered. He gestured at the mountain. "Look, at that."

Frew didn't.

"I'll try to get at the heart of what the abbot thought," said James.

"These won't be his words, which I can't for the life of me remember; it's my paraphrased version. We've screwed around long enough, we being humankind. The mechanisms of life are not insentient. We've triggered something–"

"We've heard every end-time spiel. We both care or we wouldn't pay attention. This one belongs in the *Enquirer*. How can you not know that?"

"If I hadn't seen the abbot I'd be on your side. I'm in the middle."

"We should be heading the other way. It's looking, possibly– and I've talked to McPhee– like it could be a Yellowstone or Taupo scale caldera blow-out. Or worse. Though that's hard to believe even for me."

"The abbot suggested that the Earth, to survive, is designed to protect itself."

Frew sneered out loud.

"Producing offspring, staking a future, like we do," said James.

Frew shook his head. "You should've boogied with Ming." Frew quickened his stride, zigzagging away, then back. "How can we pretend this bunk is legitimate? We have nothing. We need facts. Then warn people. Then, if this keeps going the way it is, we brainstorm radical surgery."

"Radical surgery? Such as nuking a volcano? Now you sound as crazy as me," said James. "We're going for data, Basil, as you and I tactfully agreed years ago is the only way. That's the mission."

Frew stopped, took out his water bottle, and tipped it back into his mouth. After a few swishes he spat it out. "Water tastes like… something."

"Where'd you fill it?" asked James.

"Hotel tap. I'm not pregnant."

"Basil. We have a chance to know something about this. If I didn't think so I'd turn around and tell everyone to get the hell out. If we can tease something from the borehole, we can deliver. It won't be our call after that, but at least decisions will be based on what's actually down there, under Mt. Everest." James put a hand on Frew's shoulder. "The world is unlikely to buy into the abbot's... fairy tale, as you'd probably call it."

"You got that."

"We are here, we are on site, I don't know if there's time to find out what I want to know. I think we gotta try."

"You know what you are risking. Do you think this team, and these Nepalese, do you think they know?"

"There's no way to do this without them," said James

"You need to spell out the threat," said Frew. "This is not going to be a picnic. Let whoever wants to head back. Don't sell it like it's some elixir that's going to save your screwed-up planet."

"You're right." He looked out. Not far ahead, the slope stepped up in ledges. There, to the left of the trail, water melting from the upper slopes splashed off a low cliff, cascading into overflowing gulleys below. James pointed. "Stop at that rise. Top of the waterfall. I'll make the case, you monitor. Make sure what I tell everybody is clear, so they understand what we're up against. We can find out who's in and who's out."

"What about you? You going solo if everyone runs?" asked Frew.

"They're not going to run. Not everybody. Me– yeah. Have to keep on. The abbot was right, I think. Right enough. Everything done to the planet, every way humans have screwed with it, I can see how justified this eventuality is and how logical it could be. Hard to turn a blind eye to justified and logical."

"I'm managing," said Frew. He moved ahead of James, sprinting off towards the ledges.

James put a hand in his pocket and felt for the note Maggie had written. He looked up. His own willingness to buy the Earth as mother-to-be was still conditional. Something had to give.

* * *

Finch pushed her heel into the gas pedal. With a lurch, the van clumsily spurted. The road twisted and she careened, following it downhill. Somewhere ahead, there should be a fork where the road split, heading to Namche or the airport. Should be soon.

A gryphon, wingspread wide and talons unsheathed, swooped low, a blur in front of her windshield. She remembered seeing this Himalayan vulture once before, its great shadow falling on she and Jared on their visit to Nepal long ago. Or maybe it wasn't so long ago— *but that time was gone forever.*

She felt a liberating recklessness. The trailing hopes for herself and her life were spiraling away, like the baited end of a fishing line, cast with vigor and weighted to sink into the faraway deeps. Was she still on the right road? Torn vegetation was sticking to the windshield. She might drive off a cliff. Or end up doubling back and motoring through the lodge's lobby, straight into the fish tank.

The disturbed, steamy airs reached Finch, refreshing her face and lungs. She gripped the wheel with one white-knuckled hand. The other hand lifted a bottle of Everpure water to her lips and guzzled a long draught. She wiped her lips with her tongue. Jared had always coveted her tongue. A lovely man, *that bastard.*

Things had gone wrong. She wasn't sure if finding Jared was the answer, really. Did anything matter now? If the mountain exploded, or imploded, or its psycho waters cauterized the world's elements into jelly, they would all die. Her life, her work, her ebbing energy to save the world had shrunk to a stark, singular motive. Make Jared suffer. Then they could love again. She could salvage *something.*

From above, a sudden roar, aircraft engines heaving, bright and powerful. Jesus, it was Jared. She looked up.

A tree exploded up through the ground. She slammed the brake with her foot. The van splintered the tree, pitched over and skidded, spitting up rocks and dirt. It smacked with a grinding shudder into a dense bulkhead of foliage, settling with a hiss on its side, framed by overhanging branches and great dripping fronds. The engine went dead. The van's wheels spun down. Back at the road, the tree trunk wrestled upward, unfurling its fractured branches.

Finch felt the front tire gyrating on its axle. A carnival midway amusement, the wheel spinning down, the player's fate ticking past, slowing; win, lose, draw. The wheel ticked over, paying out its final inertia. Redemption. Or goodbye. She couldn't see.

She looked down at her clothing. No blood. She pulled the visor down to study her face in the small mirror. Blood trickling there, over an eyebrow and down the cheek. The red of blood was dark. She smeared it with her hand.

She shoved the visor back and pulled herself slowly up, aches calling for attention all over her body. The airbags hadn't deployed. The shattered driver's side window, now at the top of the tipped-over van, was the way out. She found a flashlight in the glove compartment and used it to smash at the glass that had not broken away. She wriggled up and through the opening, panting.

She lay down flat on the tipped-over van's side and took slow breaths. Bit by bit she calmed, more able to deliberate. Insects buzzed and gasoline dripped, under a canopy of stimulated foliage. The carnival wheel had stopped, the arrow resting under the words: *You might be okay.* She had the feeling that she was allowed to hope. Hope that always came with an asterisk.

There was another sound. A shuffling, scuffling of movement in the brush. She looked down, between her boots, framing the scene with her toes. *Conserve strength. Not ready to test muscle and ligaments.* She was fast on her feet and limber. *Observe. Decide.*

Two grey forepaws at the edge of the van. Unsheathed silver-white scalpels. *Asterisk.*

The animal jumped, supple, deft, poised, up and onto the van. It moved cautiously, muscles rippling beneath fur, a margin kept for its safety, to a position behind Finch's head. It studied her, the meal it knew it would have to compete for with other cats on the prowl below. In a fleeting awareness, Finch saw her eyes reflected in the pupils of the big cat. She froze, her body abandoning her.

"I've had enough of this screwed-up place."

Finch grimaced, squeezed her eyes shut, and rolled, falling over the van's side, hoping to scramble somewhere, anywhere, nowhere. The leopard leapt from the van, and with two other animals already on the ground, moved in to vie for prey, and sustenance.

* * *

James heard them again. Animals baying in the distance, baffling screeches, howls, and yelps.

The Von Kamburg entourage had reached the ledges and James had gathered the team to lay out his intentions. He wanted to be doubly certain they understood the risk. Before he could begin, there was movement in the brush. Passang motioned for the Gurkhas to be at the ready. The crunch of feet sounded.

John Bateman, Ed Edwards, and Dawa the Sherpa crashed through a thick hedge. They wore full backpacks and each carried a metal walking staff. A single yak, loaded with a single container, accompanied.

"Yanks!" said Bateman.

"Kiwis!" said Frew.

The Gurkhas sheathed their kukris. James held out his hand in greeting. Dawa came to shake it first.

"I found you," he said, pointing at one of the sporadically embedded footprints. "Not too hard!"

"Ike Muldoon trekked out," said Bateman. "We never got a flight. The airport's a mess."

"Did you happen to see an American woman assisting a Nepalese doctor? In town or at the airport?"

"Absolutely. We met your wife, Maggie," said Bateman. He looked at James, who had his palms up, waiting for more words. "She told us what you were planning. She and the doctor are okay. Dealing with the newborns, mostly."

"Ah. Good news. Thanks," said James, shaking clenched fists.

"Lots of crowds and a fair amount of nasty pushing and shoving for yaks, porters, and gear," said Edwards. "Namche's locals don't seem worked up. The village is business as usual except for too many damn pigs and dogs."

"How's your shoulder?" asked McPhee.

"Sore, but I'm mobile."

"We figured you didn't need surveying equipment, so I only brought along the modal interferometer," said Bateman.

Frauz smiled.

"What the heck is it?" asked McPhee.

"We were supposed to be trialing the prototype. It's some new-old hybrid for getting good reads from way, way down," said Bateman. "Could be useful, was my thinking."

"We're glad you showed," said James. "Have a seat. I want to make sure we're all on the same page."

Bateman and Edwards lowered themselves to sit.

"There's not any good way to say this. Anyone who continues forward may be risking their life," said James. His audience showed no special concern. One of the Gurkhas polished his blade. Dawa tore open a small bag of potato chips to share with Passang. "Mount Everest may remain stable. It's also possible our next reads will tell us bad news. A caldera-level eruption or similar event. Usually this kind of thing builds over several weeks. Everything about Everest's current metamorphosis is unprecedented."

A smoke ring from Frauz's pipe drifted down and impacted near his boot.

"To conclude, I'm vetting a theory most of you know about already: that the earth is on the verge of giving birth." Bateman and Edwards looked at the other members of the team, understandably, to gauge their take. Frew pursed his lips, but otherwise held steady. "If the birth takes place," said James, "it may be on a scale that obliterates the entire region."

He gave them a moment to ponder. "I appreciate your willingness to continue. If you want to turn around do it now, with my gratitude for the distance you've come."

The Gurkhas began standing, eager to get the show on the road.

"Shall we continue?" said Frauz. They all stood. James saw Bateman and Edwards head over to talk with Frauz.

James felt a hand on his shoulder.

"You are leading a crew of masochists." It was Frew.

"Scientists," said James.

"Leading us to the promised land. Watch this, Moses," said Frew. He held his canteen up, and tipped it, allowing a thread of water to spill. Instead of falling perpendicular to the ground, the stream angled.

"It's generating its own gravity. It's that big," said James.

"We need to reach Washington," Frew said. "I take back all the funky things I ever said about nukes."

James called Bateman and Edwards over. "You might want to see this. Basil, would you mind?" Frew tipped the canteen and they watched as the filament of water angled five or so degrees off center.

"I was stumbling a lot on the way up," said Bateman. "The soft rocks, I thought."

"Can't believe I'm seeing this," said Edwards, running a finger through the water.

James pulled a compass from his vest pocket. The needle bounced, unsettled. He hailed McPhee, who trotted over.

"Compass is being affected by twin gravities," said James. "Reading for magnetic north is probably useless, and will get worse. Can you and Passang navigate without?"

"Of course. Maya penciled everything on the map. We're not that far. I'll double check with Passang, but no worries in that department, captain."

"Good, thank you," said James. He stood, and called to the crew. "Let's go."

They continued, the ever-present mist morphing from thick to thin and back.

As they trudged upward, James wondered where his passion for some kind of bad human-vs.-good Earth justice might take him. Would a caldera-type eruption even compare to a planetary nativity? The birth of a new Earth might compromise the crust, degrade our orbit, end life as we know it. If I had the power to stop it, would I? Should I? After the way humans have sickened the planet, doesn't Mother Earth have the right to defend herself?

James pulled up to walk shoulder to shoulder with Frew. "Basil, I want to ask you something. I want you to answer in the spirit of collegiality." Frew's generally amiable countenance receded to a furrowed stare.

"What if this really is the way the Earth reproduces?" asked James. "Would you consider destroying the Earth's own offspring?"

"Who do you represent?" asked Frew.

"I'm asking the question. I don't know how big this will be. I don't know what it'll mean for life here, or on a new world if that's what's happening. But the Earth… the Earth is saying something."

"You're sick."

"Who represents Earth?" asked James.

"First of all," said Frew, "we probably don't have an option, other than nuking the shitfire out of the Himalayas. That'll go over well. But maybe it'll help. So here's my question to you: if we have an option to possibly prevent the end of the human race, should we chuck that option for a fresh, clean, baby planet, untainted by people?"

"I'm not deciding anything," said James. "Just asking; if humans continue to make the planet sick, what should the planet do, in defense?"

"The planet shouldn't do anything. Humans should do everything."

"If they don't? If we don't?" said James.

"The planet will shut down and that will be that. We're a long way from that."

"You and I know how bad we've screwed mother Earth, Basil."

"Signing up to support Armageddon is not my idea of sustaining the existence of humans on the planet. We should turn around, get the freak away from the rabbit hole."

James wished Ming was still around. He was alone with his mad theory, approaching a mountain that might loom over a valley of death. Maggie's premonition or vision or whatever it was felt like nothing more than a dream. Right now, so did she.

Chapter Fourteen

Maya and Maggie sat on a splintery pine bench, outside, in the cooling shadows below the air traffic control tower of the Syangboche airport. Maya, her eyes closed and staff resting across her knees, rocked a newborn. They had both worked into last evening and were already into another busy morning. This was a short, needed break.

Maggie thought about the note she had written to James. She should have copied it, word for word, to be able to re-read it. Her dream had been succinct and felt so sincere. Weighted, to be meaningful. A counter to doubting, that he might exercise.

But now, since she had put distance between herself and the mountain, she had taken on the doubt. The dream and its meaning had begun to feel suspect. Or maybe the immediate circumstances were eroding her psychic energies.

A dog barked and she woke up. What was in front of her eyes was no dream. The airport, in fact, was from some sort of nightmare. She'd watched yesterday as a few incoming flights had managed to land. Each landing was an event, the dark shapes of the planes forming out of the white fog. Some bounced to a stop and one did a low pass and never came back. Those that successfully landed were swarmed. The grounds crew, such as they were, had taken shovels to several plants that had somehow shoved up through the soil overnight. A few of the bigger growths had caused what looked like stress fractures in the already patchy runway.

Maggie noticed that a shipment of Everpure water had been loaded and airlifted out, despite a general sense that the evacuation of people should take precedence. With communications broken across the board, it was hard to know what the official stance was. The mayor of Namche had written and posted a notice that there would be a recess in some of the town's services and anyone could stop by his office to say hello.

The New Zealand team had shown up at the airport. John Bateman, their leader, was an amiable sort. As James had asked, Maggie relayed the MEAD team's plan to hike to the drilling station. Bateman had been somewhat startled by the revelation. He'd said he would talk to his men and discuss their options. She heard concern in his voice and guessed that maybe they had seen enough of this premonitory place. One of them had ended up trekking off then and there. Bateman had departed with his Kiwi mate Edwards and Sherpa Dawa, along the path that led down the valley and out of the Khumbu.

The short-wave radio so far had refused to function. There was no way to reach James, even if she had something useful to tell him.

The airport lobby now served as a makeshift birthing center. It had more space than the health clinic and was just as close to the village. It had running water, heat, and enough room for several cots to be laid out. Maggie knew she would need a better night's sleep tonight than they'd managed last night. Assisting in births, diagnosing and treating a few injuries and illnesses, finding scant moments for rest, tested her stamina. She couldn't speak for Maya, who seemed inexhaustible.

Two Everest Vista Lodge vans were parked near the strip, drivers and staffers inside. They were probably carrying more water to be shipped out. Sad that Jared didn't see fit to put human safety in front of his raw materials, thought Maggie. To be fair, though, he may not know.

A shout came from somewhere. They looked up to see a Twin Otter on final approach. A second aircraft circled higher, a grey silhouette in the low ceiling, waiting its turn. Both aircraft wobbled in the deviant updrafts. Maggie watched, mesmerized that she might witness a crash. Who knew what unorthodox forces were at work on their aerodynamics? She found herself muttering– *come on.*

The Otter grew in size and dropped in altitude, wings see-sawing. Its fixed wheels scraped the runway, throwing up debris. A bounce, airborne again. Another touch, and a spittle of dirt and rock. Finally, the aircraft's wheels settled, the prop reversed, the speed ebbed. Maggie couldn't draw breath.

Thank you, God.

The second aircraft came in, repeating the drama of waggling wings and airborne uncertainty. It managed a shorter bounce and quicker stop.

Thank you again. That's all for right now.

As their twin engines spun down, the planes taxied to a point some distance from the tower, near a corrugated-roof hangar where the vans were parked. From each plane emerged three men. All wore Earthyield slate blue outer gear except for one, who wore black jeans and a dark brown rag wool sweater. The sweater, thought Maggie. Looks like a Harley, made in Scotland. Kind of thing Jared would wear.

The lodge vans motored forward and parked near each fuselage. Other Earthyield employees appeared from some hidden alcove, apparently sent to wait for these arrivals. Side cargo hatches were opened and personnel got busy off-loading a number of black crates.

Maya rose and went back inside the building, cradling the infant. Maggie stood to follow and recognized, with certainty, that it was him. Jared. She went to find Maya, who rested on a bench, her legs stretched out, rocking the infant. A contingent of Nepalese helpers attended to several newborns and their mothers, all congregated across the rug-strewn floor.

"Maya. Come out," Maggie said.

Maya looked up and nodded her head, but her eyes seemed reluctant.

She rose and carried the newborn to the mother, who was nursing one of her other two new offspring. "I will be back. The babies will cry. We will get more formula from the hospital reserve. Soon."

The mother leaned over and began to whimper. Maya touched her shoulder, squeezing it lightly, then followed Maggie outside.

"See that man? The one pointing near the front of the plane?" said Maggie, indicating.

"Yes."

"That's Jared Griffon. He's an old friend, someone I know... someone I knew very well. He'll help. Come on." Maggie began walking towards Griffon.

Maya stood. "Are you sure of this *bideshi?*"

"Maya. He's guilty of things, yes, but the situation's changed, hasn't it? He's brilliant. He and James, if they tackle this together, might work out what's happening. They're scientists, for God's sake." Maggie paused. Invoking science felt odd. As did serving as apologist for Griffon and his corporate excess. She dared not think of their brief time as intimates. If she could help it.

"He was a friend. Maya." Maggie continued towards the aircraft. Maya put on her daypack, grabbed her walking staff, and followed. They reached the Earthyield contingent, still busy off-loading and mobilizing for the trip to the lodge. Jared had his back turned, barking instructions to the crew.

"Burns, call Virgil and tell him we made it. We got the c-456. In case he missed that," Griffon shouted. "Thank him. I'll check in when I can."

"We are not showing any networks," said Burns, one of the Earthyield crew. "I'll see what I can do."

Maggie hesitated, then reached to touch Griffon lightly on the shoulder. He turned. "Jared. Welcome to Nepal."

Griffon opened his mouth slightly, in a smile started but never finished. "Maggie," he said. "God. You." He extended his hand.

Maggie took it and leaned to hug him. She intended it as an embrace meant to recognize both the significance of their past and the *past*-ness of it. She felt his forearms beneath the sweater. Arms that had wrapped around her, long ago. He would honor what they'd had. They'd be associates with the vague promise of a friendship rebuilt in some future. She pulled back and extended her arm to introduce Maya. "This is Maya Danheela. She's a doctor with the local hospital. Maya, Jared Griffon."

Griffon extended his hand to Maya.

Maya folded her hands in the traditional Nepalese greeting and bowed. "Namaste."

Griffon drew his arm away, running his hand along his shirt sleeve. He straightened up and, Maggie thought, segued. "Where's James?" he asked, looking beyond her.

"Heading towards Everest. I haven't talked to him since yesterday morning."

"No radio?" asked Griffon.

"The radios are in and out. Have you gotten word about what's going on?"

"I've heard. Everest is rising." Griffon mounted the ramp to the aircraft. With a heave from the shadows inside the cargo door, he retrieved a flare pistol, and laden utility belt.

"The mountain will give birth."

Maggie didn't recognize the voice. *Maya.* Wielding a tongue that sounded as if a different person were speaking through her. A preternatural shiver ran up Maggie's back.

Griffon was silent. Maggie noted the crew had opened one of the crates. Inside were red cylinders, decaled with blue skull-and-crossbones. The gloss of aluminum flashed in the gauzy sunlight with each cylinder's offload, an ethereal adding up of the potion's volume. She wondered if this Jared Griffon had any resemblance to the one she had shared a couch with, plying calculus, drinking ciders, sleeping on balconies to watch red moons.

"I need to know as much as I can. Can you ride with me to the lodge?" he said.

Maggie turned to Maya. "The mothers? Babies?"

"As safe and comfortable as we can make them," said Maya. "If I can be taken to a drop-off point near the clinic, where there is food, and formula for the newborns, please."

Griffon nodded, slowly. He led them to one of the vans and opened the passenger side door, then got in to drive. Maya sat in the middle, Maggie in the passenger seat. She took a look behind her. The ominous red cylinders were slung from a metal carriage in the back. Two of the Earthyield crew squeezed themselves in, unable to pull the cargo doors shut. The two vans headed out, past a sign that read *Everest Vista Lodge - 2 kilometers.* The cargo doors swung wildly with the turns and clattered at the bumps. It was hard to talk over the din.

"Mr. Griffon, if you stop we can bungee these doors," shouted one of the crew.

"It's a couple miles, we can make it," Griffon hollered back.

Maya turned to Griffon, piercing the clamor with her voice. "Will you help us? We might use your transport to bring food and supplies from our clinics to the airport and village. Many new mouths to feed and mothers to nourish."

"You have yaks for that," Griffon rattled back. He glanced at Maggie and seemed to momentarily soften. "We'll see once I get the cargo to the lodge."

The vans bounced up the dirt road over a chaos of pebbles, under bizarre tongs of greenery, and through a tunnel of smothering steam. It was as though some minor god had tipped a gigantic vat of dry ice over the land, the strange vapors blanketing surfaces and hissing like an albino snake.

Maggie raised her voice. "James will use the drilling site to drop probes. He wants to gather data. Take something back that will allow us to call the right shots. He's not sure how wide an evacuation should be, if it's even necessary." She was negotiating a thinner and thinner high wire that would keep her emotionally connected to a certain *Jared* but still able to parley objectively with a certain *Griffon*.

"A probe won't work. Nothing like this has ever happened," said Griffon.

With the detached voice Maggie found both compelling and disturbing, Maya spoke again. "The land and water show us what we need to know."

Maggie didn't really know Maya, but had found affinity with her in the compressed time and space. Without James, Maya had become her confidante. This Maya was channeling dogma. Navigating practicalities with her would be tricky, if she kept at it.

Griffon buffed the windshield in front of him. "Hard to see through the muck."

"You should speak with the abbot," said Maggie. "James talked to him. You know him, right?"

"The reincarnate Lama Gaia. This is science, Maggie, not chanting and religion."

Maggie looked to Maya, who spoke. "Your water supply was taken from the earth's fertile fluids. You covet the supply, though it is not yours. You would protect your stake at any cost."

"I've come to salvage a legally contracted operation. Not your concern," he said.

"Perhaps you can now see the water is part of the gestation."

"You have a business certificate to go with your shaman degree, do you, Doctor?"

"Your industry will fail when the gestation is complete," said Maya.

"I see that everyone within a hundred miles is in danger. Or maybe a thousand miles. Maybe the whole planet."

"Does the mother die when the baby is delivered?"

"Maggie, this friend of yours is a bit carried away," said Griffon

Maggie noticed that his nostrils were flaring, his breathing was labored, and his hands were sweating. "Stop the van and let us out."

Griffon gestured to the rear of the van. "We brought along a treatment for the Earth's unfortunate condition that we hope will do some good."

Maggie noted signage she hadn't seen when the cylinders were loading, a word stenciled along the crossbeam that held the carriage in place. *TOXIC.*

"You are proud or naive to think you can prevent the goddess mother from giving birth," said Maya, her voice now completely alien to Maggie.

Maggie entreated again. "Stop the van and let us out."

A flock of crow-like goraks winged over, black shadows slashing the fogged sky. Griffon's van motored along the road followed by the second vehicle. It was a confused, muddied track, with greenery encroaching everywhere. Occasionally they maneuvered past a bush growing in the middle of the route.

The van rumbled past skid marks that led off to the right and disappeared beneath thick bush. The growth formed a dense wall, thick trunks grown astride where the tires had skidded. A shorn trunk of green wood lay splintered along the road's edge.

Griffon had a lot on his mind. His business, at the apex of its success, was in great jeopardy. Possible criminal charges in the offing. Leslie a worthless traitor– and stupidly pregnant. Maggie Von Kamburg across the seat from him. Like their road trips in college. The recollection of times past, spent with this woman, had rushed back the instant he'd seen her face. Her body was alive and he knew all of it, every fine inch. The sultry blink of her green eyes resurrected from grey ashes. That alone so evocative. Recollections meant to remain on the other side of a door he had long since locked.

So it had opened. Slam it shut and lock it again.

Slam. Click. Locked.

Now. Back to business.

The thing with Everest made sense. How the water, the Synthium-catalyzed water, fertilized, replicated, and generated cloned minerals into being. If the Earth was pregnant, standard physics couldn't be counted on to constrain its properties. Griffon didn't yet, or couldn't yet, believe the Earth was pregnant, though he could see that it followed logically from what had occurred and what continued to manifest. He would work inside that construct until the truth suppurated forth.

Interrupting the phenomenon would not be easy. There were no guarantees. If by some mad unthinkable twist the Earth was pregnant, the course of action he was planning was a karma-destroying dash across a no man's land of ethical ramifications. His great discovery and shocking breakthrough with Synthium, the one that would have rocketed him to both fame and long-standing fortune, was in jeopardy. Despite that, two notions drove him: first, that the unleashed organic fertility had to be stemmed, for the good of the over-populated world, even if it meant the artificial fertility he had tapped and wielded in his labs disappeared forever. The second– the one that made his palms sweat– that the birth of a new Earth had to be halted, because if it took place, this overpopulated world might be gone.

He'd need to think as the moment to act drew nearer. Actually, no he wouldn't. He knew precisely what to do.

* * *

The team had taken a break at the top of a rocky outcrop so McPhee could try the shortwave again. The anomalous fog thinned. James caught a fleeting glimpse behind, at the land they'd traveled over. The lodge appeared small but distinct, looking remote and isolated. He could just make out two vans moving on the overgrown road that led to it.

"Sir!" Passang announced. "Friends coming to the lodge!" The team stood to watch.

"Got to be Griffon," said James. "I wonder if Maggie saw him come in. Dan, did you get that shortwave to work?"

McPhee looked up at James, spat out a small wad of tobacco, and shook his head. The fog began to close again.

"What is it? Moving, near the lodge. Can you make it out?" asked James.

"I see it," said Frew. "Animals. White. Some grey. Numbers."

Frauz set down his pack, retrieved his binoculars and looked. "They're in a herd." Frauz offered the binoculars to James. "Snow leopards," Frauz observed. "Well-nigh mythical and here witnessed as threat."

Frauz was right. They were beautiful, solitary, elegant creatures he had always admired. These leopards, thrust into this bizarre bio-convulsion, were only doing what any species would continue to instinctively do; find food, feed young, survive.

James took the binocs as it struck him: Maggie might be there. If the leopards were massing to hunt she was caught. He drew a deep breath and pulled the binocs up to look: ten or more snow leopards were making their way stealthily down a low ridge behind the lodge.

* * *

Griffon wiped his palm over the windshield again, clearing a swath through the smear of condensation. The mist swirled in front of the moving van. Maggie and Maya had not said a word since Griffon had power-locked the doors. The lodge sign loomed up out of the fog. Behind, they could see vague outlines of the building.

The van slowed up the front driveway and pulled to a stop. Griffon cut the engine. The second van pulled up behind. The Earthyield crews trundled out, undoing the cables that secured the cylinders. The lodge doors hissed open. Gault stepped outside to stand in front of them, hands on hips. The doors closed behind, trapping the pressurized air inside.

Still inside the van, Griffon faced the women. "Once I find out what I need to know, you can go." He placed a hand on his chest, lowered his head and took a few deep breaths. Two of Griffon's crew positioned themselves on either side of the van. Griffon unlocked the driver's side door and stepped out.

"Gault, escort the women in the van to your office. You two," he said, addressing the crewmembers, "accompany them."

Griffon unlocked the passenger side door. Maggie stepped out, then Maya. Maya lifted her staff and tapped at her palm. Griffon unholstered the flare pistol and held it out to one of the crew, who seemed hesitant to take it.

"It's a 12-gauge Verey," said Griffon. "Five shells capable of passing through a wooden door at close range. Don't be afraid to use it." The crewmember glanced over at his cohort.

Maya's eyes narrowed. *"Hera!"* she cried.

Twisting to see, Griffon caught his heel against the curb. He fell and instinctively rolled. The snow leopard hurtled over him, leading with unsheathed claws, lacerating the next human in its path. The crewmember and animal crumpled in a fusion of guttural screams and ripping flesh. More snow leopards pounced into the scene, growling and spitting.

Griffon triggered the flare pistol, aiming it at the rippling spine of the leopard mauling his crewmember. The hot flare impacted, igniting the leopard's skin. It shrieked and fell, spastic with pain, chemical powders blazing in bright yellows from the perforation. The crewmember fell, bone exposed in his torn right arm, dark blood coursing from his neck. Fragments from the flare glowed like hot coal on skin, clothing and driveway.

Griffon glanced behind: a second leopard was poised on its haunches, readying a leap. Griffon ducked as the animal sprung, tearing his sweater in another near-miss. He rolled, somersaulting to bring the full weight of his body down on the beast. The stunned leopard squealed, as flare smoke billowed into its face. Choking and whining, it vaulted the twitching corpse of the wounded leopard, then pivoted, hissing loudly.

Griffon fired another flare. It missed its target and bounced off the van, spewing smoke as it catapulted across the courtyard.

Through the reek, Maya looked up to see a leopard poised on top of a van, Maggie just below. It leapt. Maya lunged forward and swung her staff, a cracking blow to the leopard's head. It landed, turned and bared its white teeth. A third flare phosphored into its forelegs, splattering the animal's hindquarters. It raced off crying, tail spitting fire.

Maggie stumbled, looked up at Maya, and pointed to the hedge that followed a line around the corner of the lodge. Maya nodded. They raced for cover. In a moment they had scrambled up and into the dumpster behind the lodge, safe for the moment. In the darkness, their heels crushed through layers of loud plastic. Maggie lifted the lid slightly to let in light. Empty water bottles.

Gault staggered inside and hit a switch pad, manually overriding the automatic doors. Some of the crew leapt inside the vans. Two made a break for the lodge. Gault toggled the doors in desperation, trying to make room for them to get through before any leopards followed. One man fell across the threshold, his torso preventing the closure. Gault hit the switch, but as he watched the man was caught by the ankle. There was screaming, and there was blood.

He watched through the windows as another hapless crewmember was overwhelmed by leopards. More flares were fired into the herd, marking phosphorescent trails through the fog. A shot cracked into the floor-to-ceiling panoramic window. It fell in a shower of glittering shards, with a forceful hiss of venting pressure.

"What the hell," said Gault. This was heading south.

Wounded and bleeding, one of the crew crawled towards the broken window. His hands reached up to the serrated edge of glass. A leopard pounced, plunging teeth into his upper thigh. The man fell through the serrated opening, falling in a thrashing heap before Gault. The leopard clamped down with its jaws and the man's leg snapped. The animal paused, crouching to leap. Gault retreated, tripped, and fell on his back.

Above him, Charlie was suddenly there, blasting white foam into the animal's face. Charlie— the clerk who had quit. The white foam blistered forth, coating the leopard's eyes, filling its mouth. The animal gagged, snarled and leapt out through the window. Two staffers moved in to help the victim.

"Get tables. Try to cover the hole," shouted Gault. He pulled himself up and wiped his scalp of someone's blood. Tables were upended and dragged against the shattered opening. Outside, in the fume-blanketed courtyard, Gault could see leopards on the run. Flares whizzed past their flanks and sizzled in their white grey pelts. Charlie was there, wielding the extinguisher against a wounded leopard cornered near the second van. It snarled viciously, jaws foaming in panic. Its flare-eviscerated leg was an ugly tangle of fur and blood. A flare hit the cat in the ribs, killing it. Gault saw that Griffon had fired the shot.

Pressurized air. Can't be all gone. He hit the switch again, opening the front door. A blast of clear air vented out through the haze of smoke. The air roiled, the white murk curling to the sidelines. Crewmembers cautiously stuck their heads out of the vans. The snow leopards were gone. Two figures were on the ground. Another was bent over, retching.

"Get the first aid kits," shouted Charlie.

Lodge staffers rushed out to begin the triage.

"Get some people positioned to keep an eye out for any more animals until we're sure this is over," shouted Griffon, as he helped a wounded crewmember limp inside. The man's foot was smoking; a simmering flare had melted his heel. The uninjured formed a cordon while the remaining wounded and dead were helped or carried inside.

Three dead animals lay near the front doorway, sparks and smoke chewing at their torsos in grisly cauldrons. Another shivered, back broken, beside a pillar of the lodge's stone archway. In a sudden last act, two leopards pounced on the wounded animal and dragged it away.

Gault felt sick; not least for the leopards.

Maggie and Maya lifted the lid of the dumpster. A film of yellow smoke was scuttled in the grassy verges. Neither people nor leopards were in sight. A disquieting background of rustling remained, some strange vitality in the stillness.

"We have to get away from here," Maggie whispered. Maya nodded. They climbed out of the dumpster and ran across a short open stretch to reach a gully on the back end of the lodge grounds. They vaulted a short fence into the coniferous woods, then ran until they felt they were a safe distance from the lodge, and Griffon. They threw themselves down, panting.

Maggie waved her hand in front of her mouth, an instinctive attempt to draw oxygen. Her sleeve was wet with a dark stain. "It must have clawed me." With care, Maya rolled up Maggie's sleeve to expose the wound. The arm was bleeding slightly. They hadn't noticed it in the darkness of the dumpster.

"I may have whacked you with my staff," Maya grinned. Maggie returned the smile. Maya reached into her pack and pulled out a satchel of bandages and antiseptic. She cleaned and bound the wound.

"Can we find my husband?" Maggie asked.

"We will make our way to the drilling site. I believe we are only short hours behind."

"Plenty of adrenaline to go around," Maggie said.

"Yes. We'll need to be fast, and keep a wary eye out for leopards."

"And Griffons," said Maggie.

Maya nodded. They rose to a crouch, looked around, and headed away through the mist.

Chapter Fifteen

Where am I?

Griffon woke up. He'd dozed off, exhausted. He ran a hand through his black hair and down the back of his neck, wrestling himself into the present. *Nepal, after an overnight flight from Vancouver. Then a prop to the airport near Namche. A ride to the lodge with Maggie and the petulant doctor. Then, snow leopards.*

He flexed his shoulder blades and sat up. He was on a couch in front of a dark, oversized fish tank, which had cracked in the melee. There were towels on the floor to gather the water. Behind the leaking tank, in a shadowed corner, two human forms lay enfolded in white.

This is brutal.

He looked at his clothes. One trouser leg was slightly torn, and splats of yellow flare dye marred his sweater. He coughed in the depressurized air, and stood up. Lodge employees were securing slats of timber to straddle the shattered window.

He heard moaning. In a meeting room off the lobby, he glimpsed three of his crew lying on makeshift stretchers. He called to a young helper as she came from the room. Most likely one of the Nepalese medical technicians he paid to have on site at the lodge in case of a guest emergency. "How are they?"

She shifted the laundry bag slung over her shoulder. "Their bleeding has been staved and painkillers dispensed. They are fortunate, considering. It's possible the leopards were weakened. They do not hunt in packs and must be starving if they are. Ordinarily they would prove more lethal."

The technician knew her stuff. She continued.

"Messengers were sent to the clinic asking for doctors or skilled nurses, and warning of the herd. Runners sent, though we have vehicles here. It is shameful." She turned and hurried down the hall. Whatever was in the laundry bag was coming through the bottom, staining it red.

Then his directives hadn't gone unheeded. If the clinic was unable to assist, the messengers were to continue to the airport and Namche and find any available medical assistance. All on foot, though– he would need the vans. Messengers would get there sooner sprinting anyway, with the roads so overgrown. It wasn't a time for easy decisions.

Gault arrived with a tray of paper cups. "I have water." Griffon nodded and took a cup. He was thirsty, and took small sips.

God. An hour ago, he'd been looking forward to a shower, something special from the restaurant menu, and a few hours shut-eye in the lodge's executive suite. Maybe even with Finch. A dress-down then a make-up. Who knows– they'd had crazier episodes. He'd get a short breather before mounting the mission to the drilling site.

But the world wasn't cooperating. Reason was losing its footing. The lodge looked like a war zone, thanks to a freak show of crazed animals. Everest was incubating a colossal eventuality only a few mountain ridges away. The Nepalese doctor had bent the story further. Time felt damaged, and the Mountain, impatient, calculating its own schemes.

He shook his head, widened his eyes.

"Where's Leslie?" he said.

"You didn't see her at the airport? She took a van to meet you." Gault rubbed a hand over the bandage on his forearm, where Finch had used her teeth.

"No," said Griffon.

"Then I don't know where she is."

There was a strange crackling. He and Gault turned to watch a leafy tendril writhe through an opening between the boards. One of the crew pinned it with a length of wood and hammered it as if it were a rabid python.

"Got no words for this," said Gault.

Griffon stared through the fogged murk. Every now and again a branch rattled the panes. Dirt churned up in small mudded vents outside the entryway. "We lost two people," he said. "A glorious moment for the Earth. That's what I was told was happening over here. A birthday party." He brushed debris from his sweater and hair. "Mrs. Von Kamburg and her buddy better be fast on their feet. Send out a posse. Get the Nepalese doctor. We had wounded here and she ran. Earth mother. More like Earth bitch."

"A posse? We're running out of people," said Gault. "These are desk attendants and teenagers who clean rooms."

"What about Charlie? The front desk guy."

"He quit. Not sure why he was here. Off the payroll. Maybe he was lunching in the back with his pals. But he took it to the leopards. Saved my skin."

Griffon lowered his head and began pacing near the boarded-up glass. "So, Gault. The monks are in breach of contract. The water is ours to take. Here's what we do. Prep two vans. Gas them up and load the urns. We'll send a team over and take one last load. The Everpure's potent enough at this point to keep me in business for a useful duration."

"We're not prepared for leopards," said Gault. "We have flare guns, a couple machetes. Somebody dug up a few .22 caliber pistols. It won't be safe. Who knows what the hell else is out there?"

"You have to step up here, Gault. High stakes. You get it?" Griffon paused. "You lead the monastery run. Get the water, get back, get to the airport and ship it out on the Otters we chartered. The pilots will be ready. Then get back here as fast as you can. We have things to accomplish."

Gault took a long breath.

"You either man up, Gault, or get me someone who will," said Griffon.

"Okay, okay. What about the monks? Am I supposed to storm the monastery?"

"Look, they are holding two employees, right? Max and Flick never came back. It's a rescue mission. Call it just war if you want."

Gault wrung his palms. "What about you?"

"I'm heading out to the borehole."

"To do what?"

"Von Kamburg's right, to a point. Everest is priming for a big show."

"A volcano?" asked Gault.

"I don't know." Griffon stopped to wave a finger in the air. "The local shaman, she knows. It's a baby planet."

Gault sat down on the armrest of one of the lobby's plush vermillion couches, its cushions dank with spent extinguisher foam. "This all sounds crazy. You really want to go out there? Shouldn't we evacuate?"

"Not until I drop seven kilos of cure down the borehole," said Griffon. "I'll need the all-terrain buggies. I want Finch. Rustle a crew and locate her. Where's Mr. Grace?"

"I'm not sure. But he knows you're here. He likes to plan and might be working on that."

"Find him. Get Spencer, too. They should know the fastest way to the drill site."

"What's the cure do?"

"We'll find out."

"There's a chance to stop it?"

"A long shot. Our lead guy in Vancouver thinks it's a decent shot. A loose analogy would be removing the amniotic fluid from a gestating embryo. If it works, that's the *how*." Griffon winced, taken aback by his own words. He walked to the fish tank and looked down, where a fish still twitched on the carpet. With the heel of his boot, he crushed it.

The front doors slid open, their bent runners squealing. A man briefly studied the room, then walked over to Griffon. "Mr. Griffon?"

Griffon nodded.

"We've located the body of a woman."

Griffon nodded at the messenger. "Who are you?"

"Mr. Grace. I lead the drill crew."

Griffon looked past Mr. Grace, focusing his eyes on the fish tank, noticing the drip of its slow leak.

"We believe it's Leslie Finch."

Griffon turned away. In the shadows he saw the white sheets covering the dead. "How did she die?"

"Probably one of the leopards. She was not intact." Mr. Grace made a slight, respectful bow and stepped back.

Griffon rubbed his palm into his brow. *Leslie.* The torments were stacking up for attention. He didn't have time for them right now. *Even for her.*

"Gault," he said, "get the all-terrain buggies fueled. We'll need food and water and whatever weapons you can dig up. Get the c-456 carriages mounted in the sleds. In two hours I want to be moving."

Gault spread his hands in supplication. "With respect. Leslie is dead. And two of the crew. We should evacuate."

Griffon looked up. "Gault. Gault. This is complicated. I'm not in the mood to get democratic–" With a crack, the fish tank side slipped and, in a kind of slow motion, dropped onto the hardwood floor. Fractured glass, bright blue water, writhing fish, the Statue of Liberty, and Charlton Heston exploded out in a broad swath at the feet of Gault, Griffon and Grace.

The ground angled up, lifting the floor, splitting wood and toppling lamps, showering loose items in a wide cascade. Staffers cringed and ducked, covering ears and diving behind couches. Griffon braced himself against a support column, Mr. Grace bounded towards the window barricade, Gault went to his knees against a couch. Dust crumbled from the ceiling, as a juniper sapling punched its way up through the center of the detonated tank.

The movement ceased. Moans from the injured could be heard again. Griffon stooped near Gault, who had burrowed between two of the couch's pillows. "Gault!" Gault rolled over and tried to sit up.

"Gault," said Griffon. "I don't blame you for wanting to get out of here. But we have a chance to stop this thing. If we can't, it could get far worse than this taste we just had. You think about that."

Griffon set his gaze in the direction of Everest. "For Leslie, there's nothing we can do."

* * *

The low rumble rippled down the valley, underneath and past James and his team. He crouched to hold his balance as the ground swelled, then swept under them, rising and falling in a wave. Plants ruptured the earth, twisting and angling in a crowd of others, pitching the humans and sending the yaks into near-hysteria. The wave continued down and away, a scouring heave.

James lifted his hand from the pliant ground. "That had to be a contraction."

"Don't start," said Frew.

Bateman crawled over. "Gentlemen. That was no fun to ride out, but it's good for our credibility. Crazy Kiwis are not out of their heads, after all."

"Let's hope the world gets the news from us *personally*," said Frew. "As in we *survive* this."

The three of them rose. Passang and the Gurkhas soothed the yaks, stroking their great manes. The beasts were jostled back into line, their freight retightened. Calmed again, the animals stretched their long necks to reach the new growth of berries and fruit shining about them.

James wiped putty across his pants. They had watched in horror as the leopards stormed the lodge. Maggie could be wounded. The earth was shifting beneath them. Get going and get back.

"We should move!" he called.

The Gurkhas smacked the snacking yaks on their flanks. They bellowed, and moved forward.

* * *

Gault, with Griffon behind him, warily slid open the lodge's front door. The air had changed again, warming, though not quite balmy.

"We're not going to need any thermal jackets, that's for sure," said Gault.

Two vans and two all-terrain buggies were parked in the front driveway. The Earthyield crew was on task. The vans were already loaded with the empty urns, and the sleds were connected by strong hooks to the buggies. The sleds had been fitted with the cylinder carriages, which now each held ten canisters of the c-456 cure. A tarp was thrown over each sled and bungeed down. Packs were shouldered, small sidearms and flare guns were holstered. A few of the crew had scrounged wooden poles and sharpened their tips to fashion makeshift spears.

After the leopard attack, many of the lodge workers had left. Gault didn't blame them. Claws and teeth were more than their meager paychecks compensated for. An added incentive was to bolt further from Everest. Gault considered joining them. The goddess mother was showing displeasure. And Griffon was off his rocker. Gault held the keys to one of the vans, though, so he could make that decision later, with or without the so-damned-precious Everpure water.

Gault looked to see if Griffon was watching him. He never had the sense that belief in a higher power did any good. But this might be an appropriate time to check in with a possible afterlife-residing Big Daddy. He offered up a brief prayer, the best he could manage. "You, up there, please consider saving my sorry butt." He couldn't help thinking of Finch. She was many things: a pain, a distraction, a coworker, and a goddamned stunning woman. What a waste.

"Rest in peace, Leslie."

He cleared his head and looked over to see Griffon and Mr. Grace, seated in their buggy. Mr. Grace was in the driver's seat.

"Let's get this show moving," shouted Griffon.

Griffon motioned over to him. "Gault. Come back with the water. We had a contract. When this is over, the monks are going to get a rude introduction to international law."

Gault nodded. *Go stuff yourself,* he wanted to say. Not out loud, not just yet.

Griffon's buggy, with sled in tow, pulled out, looping around the lodge's main driveway, its fat, deep-treaded tires bouncing on supple shock absorbers. The buggy and sled with weighted carriage moved at a speed not much faster than walking. Two crewmembers with spears bustled alongside. The second buggy followed. Several more men moved out behind, all wearing the organization's slate blue Lycra. God, thought Gault, they look like they're heading off to storm Shangri-La.

* * *

James and his team had ascended a long slope, then lost altitude, dropping into a gullied streambed. Aged stoneworks suggested part of the area was used for seasonal livestock grazing, though it seemed quite a distance for herders from the villages. Perhaps the monastery's herd browsed here in the summers. They followed the watercourse upstream through knee-high grass, then started a wide traverse that, if the location Maya had provided was accurate, should reveal the drilling site.

Passang, eyes bright, scoped the landscape for creatures. There were many, though none he saw as an immediate threat. What appeared to be dark-furred bears stalked on a wooded escarpment far off to their left, several hundred meters distant. Vultures stirred out of the forested canopy, spiraling up in pursuit of gulls, pigeons, and thrushes. An enormous bat flapped noisily overhead, shrieking, soon joined by others swarming from hidden recesses.

A flash of blue caught Frauz's eye, just ahead, growing in a lee of juniper roots. He stepped closer and bent down. It was a blue pinkgill mushroom, and vivid– a radiant, stunning cyan. Here was the holy grail of mushroom-hunting club members worldwide. This find would catapult Frauz into the inner circle of mushroom-hunting royalty. A pity he didn't belong to such a club.

Edwards nursed his sore shoulder. He probably should have skipped this expedition. Too much physical exertion for a guy trying to heal. Instinctively, he stooped and dipped his hand in the stream. He shoved his wet fingers under his shirt to massage the bruised clavicle. "Feels good." A curious warmth spread through the muscle, and more alarmingly, down into his bones. He swooned, feeling faint, and looked around for Bateman or Dawa. They were trooping off ahead. He rose unsteadily and made his way forward.

Something crunched under McPhee's heel. A huge, ugly bug. "You see this? Think it's a weta? Supposed to be in New Zealand."

"Ask Bateman. He's a Kiwi," said Frew. "Check the map. We have to be close to the borehole."

McPhee pulled the map from his shirt pocket and unfolded it across a hard rock surface.

Passang noticed McPhee studying the map. But Passang was their guide and wanted to fulfill his role well. He also hoped to bring balance for the suffering he had caused by stealing the Everpure water. Perhaps he had drawn the mountain's ire by causing the events that had brought this foreign team to the altar of the great peak. He didn't know, but he would do what he could to see it through. The sacrilege of the lodge owners might then be undone.

He wanted to be first to see the drilling station. Following the trail was hard. Not from rocks, climbs or seracs that might crush bones, but from the reshaping that the *Goddess Mother* was causing. Certain landmarks led to the drill tower. These landmarks were altered or missing. He was better off using his inner compass. His *gut,* as his Western acquaintances would say. He looked up. The murk of white thinned, revealing a kaleidoscopic landscape. Everest's towering flanks were every color but grey.

"Sirs! The drilling site!"

James saw it. Man-made forms amid the rocks, and a tarp-covered shape that rose above the rest, set on a flat shelf ahead of them. He brought Frauz's binoculars up to his eyes. There it was, unmistakably, a half-hour's march still to go: a confusion of piping, containers, and whatever was under the tarp. It looked, oddly, like tacky lawn ornaments in an uncared-for garden in Oregon. The rocky flats should have been desolate but they brimmed with gentians, poppies, and rhododendrons. As James watched, a growth sprung from a small bluff above, spilling debris into the site.

The tarp-covered assembly must be the retracted tower. Something wet was trickling out of a small tube at the lip of the drill casing, creating puddles about the base. He could also see butterflies: swallowtails, blue apollos, goldenforks, and a great satyr, darting about, concentrated near what might be the bore shaft. The water was drawing creatures. It had some magnetic aspect that made itself known to living things, he surmised. *Life to life.*

McPhee hollered over towards Passang. "You nailed it, brother. Let's move."

Again, the mountain rumbled deeply, though this time there was no detectable motion. The rumbling faded over a long minute, then disappeared. A foreboding silence settled in. James noticed the air had stopped moving and the plants had ceased spewing from the earth. He had a vague sense of– what– energy consolidating? Maybe. Though it was quiet, something was still churning below the register of his ability to hear or feel.

They cut across the traverse towards the flat. Once or twice they lost sight of the drilling station, slogging beneath a huge overhanging boulder and marching into and out of a fold of hillside. In less than an hour they had covered the distance.

The broken staging area for Griffon's illegal borehole was an ugly place, blighted by its human trespassers. That said, nature was pushing back. Green, growing, right out of the rock, no less. The Gurkhas led the yaks to a spot towards the rear of the flat, where the slope angled up sharply. Nourishment for the animals, from fresh grasses to low-hanging fruit, was plentiful. They began to graze contently, tethered to the trunks of the trees they fed from.

The Gurkhas undid the equipment bindings. Dawa and Passang lowered each container to the ground. Bateman and Frew opened the containers and began spreading associated pieces of equipment out on plastic tarps, readying it for assembly. Frauz and Edwards poked around with their boots, flagging softer spots and marking solid terrain, where the equipment might be set up without sinking.

James noted that Frauz seemed to be transferring his heretofore unimpeachable affection for the gravimeter to the handling of the modal interferometer. The man carefully managed the Gurkhas un-yak-ing of the unit. As if it were his precious pipe, James thought.

He motioned for McPhee to come and help him inspect the borehole. "Dan, let's take a look." The drilling tower lay in repose, stretched several meters horizontally, its hinged base adjacent to the open shaft. McPhee undid what appeared to be anchoring pins and gripped the tarp in two fists. With a forceful snap, he pulled it off the assembly.

He wrapped his hand around one of the tower struts and tugged. "Sturdy stuff. Aluminum, or a steel hybrid, maybe. Some hydraulic gizmo to raise and lower, by my reckoning."

James stooped to study the water trickling from the borehole shaft. The vividly hued assortment of butterflies he had seen with the binoculars flitted about, occasionally alighting to slake thirst in the puddles. "Water coming up here." He pointed to a solar panel set on a stand, cabled to a pump near the base of the shaft. "There's the pump. Solar power. Fuel cells. Lithium-fission, I'm thinking. Anyway, Earthyield forgot to pull the plug."

Frew crouched before a blue metal box the size of a milk carton. A buried cable ran from the box to the tower. "I think this contraption controls everything," he said. The lid was festooned with weedy stems. He wiggled the top open and peered inside. "Check it out, VK."

They studied a set of labeled controls. "Clear and basic," said James. "Somebody did some tidy engineering."

Frew placed his thumb on the switch labeled *Power* and clicked it to *On*. The unit cycled up, accompanied by the steady hum of energy. Lights came on in the lithium-fission battery bank. "Stand back a ways," said Frew. "I'm going to try to raise this. Might help us center the cable drop."

James and McPhee looked at each other and stepped back. Frew hit the button labeled *Raise*. The hydraulics kicked into gear. The tower rose, motors driving the hydraulic hinge, angling the assembly up from its base. They watched as the tower, hissing and clicking, climbed to a considerable height. It slowed to a stop, perpendicular to the earth, locking into place with a final clack.

"Shut it off," James said. "There may be stored battery power we can use."

Frew flicked the switch to off.

"You gotta admire the tech," said McPhee. "But we didn't need it raised to drop the bloody cable over the side, Mr. Frew."

Frew grinned, as unsheepishly as he could manage.

"Should be getting photographs of all this. Evidence and posterity," said Frauz. "Now that we need his camera, the fellow's gone missing. I can't say I miss Mr. Ming. But I'm wondering where he's got to."

* * *

Gault raised a foot and tested his stance. Ugh. Then did the same with the other. It was progress, only just. He and selected other *Earthyieldians* (a worthy sobriquet for our pathetic gang, he mused) advanced along what had been the road from the lodge to the monastery. It was soft, unpredictable, and unnerving. A month ago, this had been covered with ice.

Two vans followed, creeping along as slowly as Gault walked. He'd been driving, but deferred when he realized how precarious the route was. Two Yieldians, wielding machetes, chopped away at the suffocating foliage. New growth lurched up constantly, glistening with fresh green fronds, spitting brown earth, and startling rats and rabbits from the already overgrown brush. The roar of whitewater blanketed the proceedings, as melt water surged in the river culvert ahead.

Gault stopped to run a towel across his wet brow. The towel's slate blue embroidery read Everest Vista. He unbuttoned his shirt and wished he hadn't worn a long-sleeved undershirt beneath. The vans behind him slowed. Two Yieldians, scouts, on foot, disappeared around a bend in the road that led to the bridge. After, the lane ascended to the monastery. High rock walls hid the scouts, and the bridge, from view. With their machetes dropped to their sides the two returned and motioned to Gault.

"Take a look," one of them said.

"We got a problem," the second one offered.

Gault tucked in his sopping shirttail. They walked around the bend and saw it. In front, two bent abutments and some twisted wreckage were all that remained of the metal bridge. Washed out by the rushing torrent, its anchoring support struts had been wrenched from the softened substrate. The water boiled past under the tangle of steel and cable, a chasm of fume and torrent.

On the opposite bank four monks sat in the grass, nonchalantly observing the water. Next to the monks, dozing on makeshift stretchers, lay Max and Flick. Another figure was stretched out in a sitting position, one elbow in the grass, the other holding the 35mm camera that covered his face. He appeared to be in deep concentration, immersed in capturing the strange permutations all around him. He wore his black jacket, emblazoned loudly with the color orange.

Gault bellowed over the clamor. "Hey!"

Me Ming lifted his head. He tucked his camera into a kit bag and rose. He raised an arm and waved. The water crashed loudly between them, an impassable divide that only their voices could bridge.

"Say your most devout prayers," Ming shouted. "That the monks may bless you. The end is at hand!"

Chapter Sixteen

Griffon's buggy lurched, buckled, and pitched over the uneven, sporadically pliable, vegetation-surging terrain. It was as though he were back in the aircraft over the turbulent airs of Syangboche. Griffon knew his adrenaline was flat-lining. He hadn't slept much since leaving Vancouver. The long haul and no rest were getting to him, mind and body.

The Earthyield entourage generally followed the path used by Von Kamburg's team, easily tracked in the mud and rock. Mr. Grace knew various routes up to the drilling station, and Griffon assumed he'd selected the most efficient for their vehicles. He was a silent, composed driver, but provided no companionship, leaving Griffon to observe and think.

Griffon wondered if the rest of the world had heard anything about the situation at Everest. In the short time since he had landed, it had gone from irregular to irrational. He hoped that Bennington was mobilizing back in DC. He second-guessed his directives to Gault. Flying out in these conditions was reckless. But all communications were blocked.

Leslie was gone. He would never see her again. She had turned on him in the end. Now that he was here, he understood how her breakdown could have come about. Still, he wouldn't forgive. *Trust is precious. You can't synthesize it.* She'd stuck it to him, giving the game away to Von Kamburg, abandoning everything they'd built. It shocked him, though, that she wasn't around to be properly chastised, and he knew the thin air wasn't the only reason he'd gasped for breath before they started out.

Better for her, anyway to be gone. Hellish to live through… all this.

Other images stirred in his mind. Trees, bursting. Leopards, baring their fangs. Flares, hot like death. Death, cold like white. The unexplainable, implausible, and unreal, melded with facts. For Griffon, fact-based decisions had always triggered empowerment. He'd seen it work and made it his mantra. But what were facts when physical laws were not bound by physics?

Still. He might be able to hold this thing together. He'd have to get the cure to the borehole and into the mountain, then see if the mountain's strange labor would stop. Whatever chemical or nuclear event was bubbling down there, his cure might have a chance to slow it or kill it. Getting to the borehole was the key. Someday, he would sleep.

The convoy moved forward, the lead walkers' navigation hampered by the new plants bursting out of the ground, which hid the hoof impressions and boot imprints. One of the spear-carriers stumbled. Griffon watched as the man fell headfirst into a sinkhole of grey slop.

"Hey, whoa, help me!"

Spencer scrambled to reach the man, but Griffon could see Spencer's knees buckle. He tripped and wallowed, frantically, now equally caught in the mire. Several men linked arms to drag Spencer and the spear-carrier from the sinkhole. Coughing and gagging, the man who'd dropped the spear saw it disappear under thick brown suds.

Mr. Grace stepped out of the buggy and spoke to Griffon. "Get out."

Griffon stepped out as the wheels on the left side of their buggy sunk in a hiss. The buggy settled, trapped in the sticky soil. The other driver jammed his buggy into reverse, hoping to avoid the bog. The wheels of his towed sled sunk in a froth of muck, also pinned.

"Disconnect the sleds," said Griffon.

Mr. Grace called out directives, and everyone reacted rapidly, but the Earthyield team was stymied. As they worked, the ground seemed to harden around the vehicles' wheels, setting like cement. In the end, they were only able to retrieve one sled and one buggy.

"We won't be able to ride much further," said Mr. Grace. "The trail is overgrown, the soil unpredictable. We'll hitch the remaining sled until we reach the ridge up there. I'd estimate it's about half a kilometer from here."

Griffon looked at him. Whoever he was, he knew what he was doing. Gault, in this instance at least, had hired a shrewd operator.

Mr. Grace pointed. "See that? The ledge with the waterfall? We'll need to be on foot to climb that."

The freed sled was reconnected to the remaining buggy. The ten c-456 cylinders from the partially sunken sled were dispersed to ten of the crew, including Spencer, who lowered them into their backpacks. "These ain't heavy, but they ain't light," he said. Grunts and curses could be heard as the team proceeded, carefully picking their steps.

"Keep your eyes open. It's slippery and sticky," said Mr. Grace.

* * *

Maggie and Maya stood next to a rushing watercourse. They had made their way upstream, following the banks of the same tributary that flowed under the bridge to the monastery. Below, an insane jigsaw of liquid tumbled past, a broth of shrubbery, branches, rocks, and (sad to see) drowned beasts. A fallen tree was wedged between the two vertical walls of rock bordering the torrent, forming a makeshift bridge. Chunks of ice cracked and splattered against the log. Wood and leaves splashed by in the froth, chewed up and bulleted away in the current.

"We have to cross to get to your husband and his team. They are on the other side. I am not sure of another way," said Maya. "If there is another way, it is much further up and may be impossible."

"You mean *impassable,* I think."

Maya smiled. "The meanings are close enough, yes?" Maggie watched as Maya studied the current, and the seething energy within. "The Earth is alive, is it not?" she said. "We will cross." She flashed her teeth in another grin.

Maggie responded with a churlish shake of the head. This was not good. This was trouble, more like a body blow. She might not survive the next few minutes. One slip, she'd be gone, crushed and drowned, both at the same time. With her own death suddenly imminent, two clichés came disturbingly to bear: her knees lost their strength, and her lived years flashed by in a montage of jumbled scenes. The montage ended on a dark note: a freeze frame of the empty baby carriage from her dream.

With a powerful, grating *thwuuump,* another tree barreled down into the first. Branches splintered, heartwood ruptured, bark was shed. It was as if a scaffold had come sailing in across the divide, trapeze-like, and with great precision, wedged itself perfectly to complete the platform. The freshly created "dual-log" passage over the water appeared to be more safe than the single log. A hollowed inversion between the two brawny trunks created a scooped middle. It was far from perfect, but less worrying. Maya smiled at Maggie again. Maggie grinned back, posing, the best she could do in the moment.

The two women stepped down and began their traverse, dropping to a straddle-crawl across the wet wood. Maggie went first. When she looked down despite herself she glimpsed the frantic, unstoppable motion between the trunks. The clamor kept them from talking. She didn't want to see Maya's grin. Her Nepalese companion seemed to be enjoying this.

Maggie reached the end of the logs. She warily snuck her knees onto the matted soil beyond and scrambled off the bridge. With one hand anchored to a shiny overhung fir root, she held out the other to Maya. The root started to unravel, its tubers popping from the dirt in tiny flowering bursts. But it held. Maya took Maggie's hand and jumped up, safe.

* * *

"Xavier's not exactly a fan of binary," said James. "Not the best time to be tinkering with the modal interferometer. I'll trust, for the moment, he knows what he's doing."

Frew laughed– nervously, James thought– as James watched him attach the various probes to the end of the cable they would lower into the borehole. James hoped they had enough length to reach the bottom. The sensors were extracted from various pieces of equipment they'd cannibalized. There was no existing machine designed to gather the type of data they were hoping to amass. The MEAD brain trust of Von Kamburg, Frauz, and Bateman had drawn up the blueprint Frew was following. Frauz had been especially insistent about rigging a sensor for the modal interferometer, which took considerable finagling as it required an analog-to-binary field converter. To the surprise of everyone, Frauz had one in his kit bag.

Passang and the Gurkhas had set up their "instant village" (as Frew called it) off to the side. They had rustled up a stove to make tea (what else, observed Frew). For the yaks, more fruit and berries. All they wanted, in fact. James wondered if the beasts could overindulge and end up needing antacids.

The rumblings had ceased. The wild eruptions of trees and bush paused. James didn't like it. It was something akin to the eye of a hurricane. He focused, and helped tighten screws at the business end of the tech that would interpret the data when the probe dropped.

He *did* feel good that they'd contrived a capable unit. Most of their field equipment had been designed to work as a discrete unit. They'd engineered these singular capabilities into a theoretically multi-faceted cross-functioning gem, and ended up with some hybrid of rock-analyzer, seismic scanner, bio-arbiter, and super-sized ultrasound. The smaller, tube-infused modal interferometer–*mf*–was positioned next to the box-cabinet bulk of the Von Kamburg Unit–*VKu*–and would provide a supplemental feed, courtesy of Bateman and Frauz. A workstation platform for the laptop completed the unit. All together, they vaguely resembled a refrigerator and a vacuum cleaner, without their housings, in a buddy movie. It'd be funny if the situation wasn't as sobering, thought James.

He thought again of Maggie. *White stars.* The riddle wasn't budging and he didn't have a load of spare time.

Again, and all too soon, the sound of ground fissuring. An ugly, deformed, plant-like shape hatched its way out of the broken earth, dripping with slime. James stifled a gag– the thing was vile, and oily, like viscera. Like a malformed appendage it writhed up, slumping and decaying as it grew, a seething mutation come to life. As they watched, it hardened and fractured. One of the yaks nosed in for a sniff, only to rear back in disgust.

Dawa and Edwards used hooked sticks to drag the freakish canker to the edge of the escarpment, where they kicked it over. "I don't want to think what that's about," said Edwards.

The clock was running. James looked over to see that Frew had finished mounting the sensors. "Good to go?" asked James. Frew nodded. They heard the thrum of McPhee's generator powering up.

McPhee called over to James. "I'm going to wind the cable onto the capstan. When that's done, I'll bring you the probe end. We have our generator, spare batteries, solar, and stored power in the tower unit. We shouldn't have to page the hotel electrician."

"John and I have a connector ready for our modal link." It was Frauz, though at first James couldn't see him. He and Bateman were crouched, working on the other side of the cabinet stack. Frauz stood and held out the connector. "I should mention that the modal interferometer we're about to operate is the only one in the world."

"How do you know that?" asked Frew.

"I built it."

Frew and James exchanged the same look they had exchanged when Tensing Spa was pontificating about the curious events occurring in Nepal. Wonders had a way of never ceasing.

McPhee approached, electric power cable in hand, casting a sidelong glance at the cobbled-together stack. He spat out a plug of chew. "I don't know exactly what this Vonkamfugger you built is supposed to do, but I got the power to juice it."

* * *

Maggie and Maya reached a rock ledge. To avoid Griffon, whose caravan they had glimpsed in the distance, they had followed a route that would bring them around to the far side of the drilling site.

For the first time in many days, the skies seemed to be clearing. They looked up to catch a glimpse of Everest's summit. Maggie gasped. This was a mountain profile different from the one documented in countless photographs taken by countless cameras. Everest's peak had become a broad, inexplicable rim.

"The mountain is changed," said Maya and she bowed.

Maggie nodded, the word *understatement* caught in her throat. *One had to get past the firewall of one's own incredulity to embrace that the incomprehensible was taking form before you.* Was that in her note to James? Too late.

As their view of the summit dissolved into haze, she looked again. *Wait. Something else…*

"Maya!"

* * *

"Let's go, you weasels! The probes are ready to drop. Nice and easy— we've got a long way to go. I don't want to bash stuff into the bottom." McPhee sounded like a line boss. James and Frew assisted as he played out the cable, lowering it into the borehole, delicately managing its controlled descent into the depths. The Gurkhas gathered to watch. James could hear Passang attempting an explanation.

"Who told you this thing was 700 meters?" McPhee asked James.

"Leslie Finch."

"Think we could get her on the shortwave?"

"Did you get it to work?"

"Good point. Damn thing never woke up. Sorry— I know you'd like to talk to your wife." McPhee shook his head and looked up with apologetic eyes.

"Don't fret over it, Danny. Got enough on our hands," said James, throwing him a grin. "The borehole data is critical. I want to be able to lock down some facts, for an outside world that's in for a shock, regardless of what we find. And I want to have something to tell him when Griffon gets here. He seems to be under the impression this is some hiccup that'll mess with his business workflow. If he knows more, he didn't tell me. One thing I do know. He won't be far behind us."

One of the Gurkhas began to speak loudly, pointing towards the top of Everest, which suddenly appeared from behind the dissipating overcast. A convulsion shuddered under them. The motion roiled past, down the valley. They looked up, half-expecting to see hot flares of lava shooting from the peak. Something was airborne. But not molten rock. James saw the beads as they began to impact, pelting into the earth around him.

* * *

Griffon was impressed. Mr. Grace had kept the caravan going, despite the heat, erupting foliage, unstable soil and threat from wildlife. Griffon would talk to him about joining the company, once this was over.

Griffon, recognizing but refusing to own the mercenary nature of his own thinking, couldn't resist mulling the logistical fact that Finch would need to be replaced. Right now, time to think tactical. Von Kamburg was a hill or two away.

James was not a common fool. But like too many fools he seemed to embrace the illusion that the universe, at base, was founded in benevolence, that problems happened when man *messed with Eden.* That was wrong. Griffon understood that the rarer, more enlightened man, set his heel to the throat of that notion, and witnessed the world bend. Sometimes awkwardly, sometimes poorly, but to the committed and tenacious, always, in the end, the world was pliant.

Everest might undo his industry, it might spread the contagion of unchecked fertility in its biologically active fluids, or it might– although this still seemed very unlikely to him– lob a ball of dead rock into the atmosphere. You could fall on your knees and venerate the ways Mother Nature reveals her glory. Abject acceptance. Surrender, more accurately. *Or you could act.*

His cure was a potent chemical compound. Instead of buckling to the events occurring here, his team would direct them. *He* would act, and Mother Nature could go back to her cave, fever-stoked legends, and evolutionary dullness.

If there was time, he might try to explain to Von Kamburg what he was planning, and why it had to be. Von Kamburg would certainly understand that the world couldn't afford unchecked fertility. And why Von Kamburg would want to stand by without trying to halt a mass ejecta that might collapse the mantle, throw the equator offline, and send up an ash cloud to end ash clouds, Griffon couldn't guess. *Nectar of Maggie?* Perhaps. Maybe the professor had lost the plot listening to the provocations of his woman, who seemed in cahoots with the mojo of her Sherpa doppelganger. Mother Earth's little helpers, gone off the deep end. Ironic for a female once so set against procreating.

Maybe once Von Kamburg got his probe readings the man would beg off and not disrupt the injection of the c-456. Then again, he didn't sound sensible when they'd talked through the ground-to-air static. Griffon felt the holster tucked against his chest, and tightened the shoulder strap for the umpteenth time. He hadn't had time to unholster the pistol during the leopard attack– and the flares guns had been effective.

Though he'd been licensed to carry a concealed weapon for decades, he never thought he'd need to pull the trigger. But if the dialog broke down, and events were at a critical stage, and someone was *stuck,* he figured the barrel would help them see his point of view.

Then, a strange *fwhoomp,* echoing out from Mt. Everest.

One of his crew saw it first: the sky over the mountain's crown seemed to puff, like air blown through an exit portal. Was this the eruption? They were caught, too late to run, too close to escape.

A convulsion rippled beneath them, almost tipping the sled. It wasn't an eruption. At least not volcanic. No magma, lava, or pyroclastic flow ensued. Nevertheless, something was about to hit them.

The first ejecta whorled down, a missile that glanced off Griffon's shoulder. He covered his head, got low, and crawled out of the buggy to see what had hit him. It had splintered into fragments against the sled. It looked like sapphire.

* * *

"Straight above us. Something is falling," said Maya. They hurried to an overhang and ducked beneath. Splatting and crackling, a plethora of glitter pelted down on them. The pieces settled, some blackened and smoking like shards of a strange lava. A few flowered into daubs, like putty thrown against a brick. Brightest were the crystals: blue topaz, ice diamonds, and flashing emeralds.

* * *

James was struck dumb. Again, no precedent for what he was witnessing– gems falling like hail. Many he could name: pyrite, fuchsite, amethyst, tourmaline, zircon, cobalt. He picked up a dark fragment. It was his birthstone, black obsidian. Others were unrecognizable, mutations of known geology. He looked around as the deluge slowed. His teammates were smitten, and he watched them scramble. There was plenty of dross to go with the plunder.

As a few last pellets caromed in around them, James cautiously stood, hoping for a clear view of Everest. The vast fume of white had returned, as opaque as it had been before the ejecta.

Frew dusted himself off, brushing away bits of diamond. "Not. Volcanic."

"You believe this?" said James. His team had pocketed a tidy share of gemstones. He wondered if any were tempted to bolt. Especially the Nepalese, who all had suddenly appropriated a lifetime of wages. "No one's running back to hire a hedge fund manager. Yet, anyway. Let's get to it." James was glad to see McPhee, his shirt pockets bulging with crystals, again on task feeding the cable into the borehole.

"Speed it up, everyone. Let's get our data and get out."

* * *

Griffon was less than pleased with the behavior of his subordinates. All but Mr. Grace had acted like starved rats, rooting wildly at the manna of jewels. Mt. Everest had vomited plenitude for the besotted. Two of his crew had spent short minutes scooping gems, then bolted, with a departing salvo of shouts. Griffon heard one distinctly: "Up yours, Griffon."

He turned to Mr. Grace. "Imagine. Some of my employees are now worth more than me." Mr. Grace had lost his sunglasses, knocked from his face by a jade pellet. He reached to put them back on, took a look at Griffon, and put the buggy back in gear.

Griffon rubbed his palms together. Cold, useful reason flooded back in. This magical interlude was meaningless. "Everyone! Get moving."

* * *

Blue and red light pulsed across muddied faces as the Gurkhas packed in for a closer look at the contrivances going on before them. James thought they looked like banshees, war painted in moving color.

Passang turned up at his shoulder. "I will tell my cousins to make room," he said. Then added, in a soft voice, "The *bideshi* with Griffon will soon know: the goddess mother is with us." James wanted to nod, but something stopped him. Motioned to move by Passang, the Gurkhas stepped back. Edwards and Bateman stood nearby.

The cable had bottomed out with only meters to spare. The batholith's gravity had influenced its perpendicularity, and the sensors had made contact with the housing near the bottom of the shaft. They'd winced at the slow, scraping echo trilling up the borehole. James hoped the sensors hadn't been damaged.

McPhee cranked the generators. The laptop was plugged in and cycled up. With Frew beside him, James logged in. From behind, a finger tapped him on his shoulder.

"Excuse me, my good man." It was Frauz. James and Frew parted to give him room. James knew that Frauz's distaste for technology didn't offset his brilliance with analytics. He was best equipped to interpret the read and provide objectivity. *A useful thing, objectivity, if it was still possible in this strange epoch.*

Frauz took a moment to tuck down the back of his jacket and roll up his sleeves. "It's quite warm," he said.

Frew fanned his palms behind Frauz. "Get on with it!"

"One does one's best work when one is relaxed. Not when one is pressured," said Frauz. He turned and winked at Frew, whose eyeballs rolled into his skull. Frauz worked the laptop like an old hand, first priming the sensors, then launching the analytics. So much for his Luddite reputation.

"Sensors green so far," said Frew. The screen displayed a graphic identifying each sensor, with empty boxes waiting to be filled via each unit's data-gathering.

"Let's see what we get." Frauz clicked at the mouse. The computer whirred and the Vonkamfugger stack (McPhee's name had stuck) hummed. "Probe sensors online. We have data incoming. It'll take a bit to process into visible infomatics." Frauz looked back over his shoulder. "Ducky, one might say." Frauz aimed his bearded chin at the generator. "Keep that thing humming, Mr. McPhee."

"You coming out of the dark ages?" said Frew.

Frauz smiled back at him. "I acknowledge the new-fangled usefulness of this computational invention." Electronic bleeps ticked forth over the steady thrum of the generator.

"What're we expecting to see here?" asked Frew.

James spoke up. "The software gives us a graphic interpretation. Estimates what it doesn't know. It'll show plus-minus probabilities along with variant threads to mitigate randoms. Based on what we decide is significant." He ran his fingers against his forehead, pushing back red hair. "We should get mass, movement, magnetism. Really, I don't know what all we might get. This machine is a hybrid. Hard to predict what it can predict."

"I think you'll also appreciate the analog contribution," said Frauz, dipping a shoulder in the direction of his modal baby.

"Will it tell us the sex of the thing, that's what I'm curious about," chimed McPhee.

Frauz grinned, Frew bowed his head. James covered his eyes. Frauz tapped more keys on the laptop, then took an annoyingly longish moment to drag his pipe out of his pocket, into his mouth and light it.

"Should be something on screen any minute now," he said.

Passang and the Gurkhas crowded in. Bateman and Edwards came over. The screen refreshed into a new interface, the sensor indicators now shifted to a corner. Slowly, the software rendered a geometrical wireframe sphere. It resolved against dimmed background colors approximating the earth's crust. It rendered further and began identifying, with text call-outs, the sectors beneath and above Everest. Smoke from Frauz's pipe wafted in front of the screen. One of the Gurkhas coughed.

Numerals began to appear, generating in red against the graphics. Data was flowing forth. Mostly, it was bewildering, an amalgam of numbers, summaries, flags, and mean standards.

Frauz spoke. "The batholith is ten kilometers in diameter, approximately. Wait, wait, wait– hold. Apologies. It's twenty. Twenty kilometers diameter. Scaling instruction bug there; code thing. I'm mortified."

James saw McPhee make a quick glance back towards the mountain. "We're about twenty-three kilometers from the summit. The batholith isn't necessarily going to rise up exactly through the center of Everest. We're too close."

Frauz punched more keys. The batholith wireframe, animated in two dimensions, moved in segmented steps up towards the indicated surface of the earth. An outline of Everest provided a reference comparison for scale. "Looks like 850, maybe 900 million metric tons. Goodness."

James placed a finger on the screen and ran it from bottom to top.

"Can you estimate how much time we have before the thing reaches apogee?" asked Frew.

Frauz looked at him. "Apogee is the highest point reached. The earth's surface is a marker, but the batholith could well continue beyond. *You* want to know when it will breach the summit." James saw that Frew was too disturbed by the sensors' findings to be irritated by Frauz's nettlesome manner.

Frauz was dealing with trepidation in his own way, as they all were. James found himself caught, wanting to believe and not believe. As a team, they were walking a slender line, scientifically, all being coerced by scientific evidence to certify the impossible. Radical material. Who knew what an objective response should be? But what he did not want, was insurrection. They were still a team on a mission.

"Xavier. Based on trajectory and speed, when will the batholith reach the top of Everest?" asked James.

Frauz tapped at more keys. The screen scrolled, more figures manifested. "Gracious," said Frauz. He took the pipe from his mouth and faced them. "Gentlemen, whew." He wiped his forehead. "We are due."

"*Exactly* when?" asked James.

"It's a projection, remember. But it should be accurate, give or take. Projecting an acceleration, exponential, calculating in a list of x variables and estimating." Frauz put a finger on the screen. "Seven to thirteen. Hours."

Passang spread his arms to motion the Gurkhas away again. "Gaje, Kulbir, give room."

"Frauz, let me in here," said James. He stepped to the laptop and began to key in prompts. He wanted a look at plus-minus bias, something that would add rigor to Frauz's opening muster. Anxious, he keyed in faulty instructions. His programs overlapped, and the computer's *busy* timer began spinning.

"*Ahh*— I can't believe I did this. We have to reboot," said James.

Frauz stepped forward. "Let it go. You'll want to see this, anyway." He flicked a switch on the stack and activated the modal interferometer's feed. The switching exercise temporarily disabled the digital sensors; the screen blinked black and refreshed, the display background now a beautiful landscape somewhere in Switzerland. "Insights into molecular activities, courtesy of the modal interferometer."

They waited a beat as the analog translated. James stared into the screen, amazement and fear benumbing his ability to voice anything. The modal unit was presenting artifacts of biological data, a stream of base parameters that spoke of something far from lifeless. He found his voice and, with it, lost his thin veil of objectivity.

"Look at this. A breakdown of composition based on gravitational densities. 40% water, 28% carbon, 14% oxygen. DNA of a new planet."

Frauz hit more keys.

James gawked. "It's spinning on an axis. *It's kicking!"*

There was a lurch, followed by a low, portentous rumble. Behind them, a cudgel of rock overhang caromed down in a shower of dust and earth. James stabilized the workstation as it vibrated against his grip. The ground steadied. The air fell silent.

"Transmuting hydrocarbons," said Frauz. "I thought it might be something like this."

James looked at him. "You mean what I think you mean?"

"It follows that human interference in such crass and insidious volume would eventually seep down and affect something at the atomic level. The introduction of so many artificial qualifiers overwhelmed nature. The evidence in front of me suggests a dormant quantum catalyst was triggered. Some fundamental survival equation, dwelling at the Earth's core since the beginning."

"Our climate fiasco set it off," said James.

"Spontaneous transuranic– what should we say here– generation. The physics had to be in place. *Have* to be in place. Wouldn't happen otherwise," said Frauz. "But, yes. We managed to inundate the Earth's ability to continue its quantum-level life-sustaining processes. A signifier was provoked which activated something engineered five billion years ago."

"Then Griffon's water– or rather the Thyzenboche Monastery's water– is a provisional adjustment to accommodate planetary scale incubation," said James. "The planet was designed to hatch a separated organism– *baby,* as it were– if the hosted organisms managed to corrupt the Eden they were asked to steward."

"I think so," said Frauz. "Extraordinary. Although I'll allow your metaphysical inferences to go unrefuted for now."

James shook his head for the umpteenth time. He tapped the keyboard and watched as the wire-framed sphere regenerated. The *busy* icon was gone. He zoomed out to get perspective on the batholith's position relative to the surface. It continued to travel. Up.

"It has everything but a heartbeat," said James. He looked around. His enthusiastic affirmation of the abbot's "truth" had muzzled the tongues of his associates. Maybe someone could offer an alternate summation. McPhee, Edwards and Bateman stood still.

Basil. Like a black adder calming to spring on its prey. "Can't be," said Frew.

James looked him square in the eye.

"Is."

As impossible as the white stars, James realized. And as real. The unexplained, beyond the rules. In that Maryland yard, many years ago, he'd been led to an open window, that looked not only out, but *through.* In a long life, his experience of seeing those stars– lining up in their rows, white in the blue sky– had gathered dust. Every so often, toted out as a humoring memory. Now, the apprehension flowed like a king tide: *the white stars. The fireflies. The batholith.* The great paradox. Seeking to understand, you did when you understood you'd never. Maggie, blessed and blessing, had set out the clues, inklings that shone of possibilities never traversed. And impossibilities that never were.

It was so dreadfully new-age sounding, played out across his own psyche, both a torment and a release. He'd broken the spell of needing to know. He only needed to *accept.*

Then, he heard the sound of a man yelling.

Chapter Seventeen

Through the white swirl of mist Griffon could see the drilling tower. One of his crew had spotted it on the rise ahead.

"There it is! Move up the hill," Griffon shouted. They had discarded the second sled and buggy below the waterfall. The men carrying the cylinders staggered forward to scale the wall before them.

Griffon saw that Von Kamburg and his team were at the site. Gault had warned him about the Gurkhas. Outfitted in khaki and grey camouflage, they moved about near the tethered yaks. Gurkhas might be an obstacle to imposing his will. Still, he held the advantage. He had the numbers, and weapons. Even a Gurkha falls with a bullet in him.

Some back chamber of his head began pounding.

* * *

One of the Gurkhas sidled over to Passang, who then wandered over to James. "They want to know if you wish the visitors to be stopped or sliced," said Passang.

James looked over at the Gurkhas. He hadn't fully appreciated their lethal potential.

"Making joke. No sliced," grinned Passang.

"Passang. Don't do that." James wiped a hand over his brow. "Wait for orders from me, Passang. Please make sure they sit tight, till I do. No slicing. Got that?"

"Okay, Doctor."

Passang made his way back to instruct the "tight sitting." James motioned the MEAD team of Bateman, Edwards, Frauz, McPhee and Frew, into a circle. "I don't know what Griffon will do. We'll let him see the evidence. It's also copied to this." James held up a USB stick, then dropped it into his shirt pocket. "Something to show the world." He buttoned the pocket closed.

"Once we're done with Griffon, we'll move out as fast as we can tear down." Another subdued rumble rolled beneath them.

"Leave the computers," suggested Frauz. "In fact, leave all of it."

"Whoa. It's a lot of stuff to just throw out," said Frew.

A second rumble sounded, deeper and longer. Bateman looked at Frew, raising an eyebrow. "You're gonna have to carry it by yourself, mate," he said.

Dawa trotted over to the group. "Sir. They're coming from below, up the hill."

James heard scrambling and grunts as suddenly, the first of the Earthyield crew appeared. Several men clawed themselves up over the lip, lugging weighty backpacks. He saw the man who had confronted them at the pool, Spencer, dragging a large duffel. His cohort, Mr. Grace, next scrambled onto the top of the flat. Lastly, Griffon, who looked across at James and halted. He uncapped his canteen and took a long swig.

The Gurkhas rose as one, brown hands out at their sides, palms itchy. A few gripped their knife handles as if they were sword hilts. In the hands of the Gurkhas perhaps they were. For now, they stood in a semi-circle surrounding the Vonkamfugger stack.

Sweat streaming down their faces, the Earthyield crew pulled off their heavy packs. "Stack the c-456 near the borehole," said Mr. Grace.

"There." The red cylinders were removed from the rucksacks and carried to a spot near the shaft, where they were laid out in rows.

"Don't like the look a' those," said McPhee, in a subdued aside to everyone.

Griffon, accompanied by Mr. Grace, walked up to James.

"James."

"Jared."

"Ended up in your own little Earthyield-funded lab after all, didn't you?" said Griffon.

James stared at Griffon. "You're running out of things to control, Jared."

"I don't give up as easily as some people."

"There's not a lot of time. Do you want to know what we've found?" asked James.

Griffon straightened his back and looked around. A hush and a beat. Both factions halted, watching. James knew they were all on edge, keen to observe their lead players mounting this last-ditch summit.

"What have you got?" Griffon asked.

"It'll open your eyes. Come and take a look," said James. The two walked to the laptop display.

Mr. Grace stationed himself next to the borehole, directing the uncoupling of the c-456 canisters' safety-locks. Once unlocked each cylinder could be armed by pulling out the firing pin.

Griffon studied the screen. "Quite amazing," he said. Griffon tapped at the keyboard, accessing more of the data. That's a bit brazen, thought James. "Heat. Gravity. Rising. Spinning," said Griffon, more like a marketing whiz-kid than someone who should be astounded. James still believed he might get it.

"Seems to be," said James. "Something transuranic kickstarted the process. A catalyst engineered to salvage life at an atomic level if that ability is threatened by unnatural interference. Gave you your water. Gave us a new earth." James felt an urge to put his hand on the kid's shoulder. "Don't overthink it, Jared. Occam's Razor. With multiple theoreticals, the simpler one is usually correct."

A held-breath pause of time and space. James prayed that Griffon would recognize something he himself wouldn't have countenanced, until everything had dovetailed, transforming him into a believer. *The Earth was speaking.*

It was Griffon who spoke. "What do you think?"

"Earth's progeny," said James. "I know it sounds ludicrous. I don't expect you can realize it, know it, at first. Until you let yourself– feel it."

Griffon smiled with his eyes. James thought he might be stifling a laugh. "No, I mean, what do you think will happen?"

"Our preliminary data says it should have inertia for escape velocity. It could take out a big area. Impossible to predict specifics. But widespread geophysical abnormalities, yes. That's a given."

"End of life on Earth?"

"Mother dies, baby lives. Possible. Not what I–"

Griffon interrupted. "A cleansed world. Utterly new. Organics in genesis. Recombinant DNA. Life uncorrupted."

This was hopeful, thought James. The man was naming the kind of highlights that a reborn Earth could engender. He had to play devil's advocate, so Jared would see that James understood the stakes. "There's risk for everyone in the Everest region, at least. It's possible the world will suffer on a cataclysmic scale."

Griffon made no answer.

"But there's this, also. An intuition that the Earth is not a malevolent monarch. She will enable a separate, undefiled entity, but not in order to eliminate the species she has carried this far. Mother Earth will survive this birth."

James accepted that Griffon would not do well with the last. There were no guarantees as to what might happen. Yet, now that he knew– accepted– the great secret propelling the events at hand, an inclination that hope made more sense than despair keyed into him. They would live. Of course he couldn't know it. *But.*

Another reverberation beneath them: a deep, disquieting *boom.* No more time for ethereal musings. He was a scientist after all, not a mystic. He'd leave the heavy lifting to the holy triad of the abbot, the doctor, and the wife. For the present, the mission was to survive.

"We've run out of buffer time," said James. "We have the data. We have to move. Evacuate the Khumbu region and get everyone as far away as we can. Get the word out to the world. Explain what we've learned here."

"I was sure before seeing," said Griffon.

James knew what was coming next.

"We kill it."

Griffon turned abruptly, nodding to Mr. Grace. "Move the cylinders into position."

The Earthyield crew moved in, hoisting the cylinders to the borehole, and setting each one against the casing that encircled it. Soon, twenty red canisters, neatly stacked in a circle, surrounded the hole, twenty firing pins at the ready.

The Gurkhas looked like marathon runners just ahead of the start gun. James guessed that action, not observation, was in their blood. Their eyes shifted between the cylinder deployment and Passang, who looked to James for some signal. His own team also seemed unsure. *I can relate.*

McPhee, ever unflustered, had squatted to observe the proceedings, one hand resting on the Vonkamfugger stack. He spat out his Copenhagen and rose. In quick succession, he pulled up four stakes that had anchored the cable in the soil, gripped the cable at its junction with the stack, and pulled. The connectors flashed blue, the cable uncoupled. He backed away as the cable snaked in a whiplash of dust and flung stones, twisting wildly up and around. With a last slashing strike, it tore at the forearm of one of Griffon's men, then whistled down the hole into the dark.

James was glad; feelings of helplessness and outrage were mixing in his gut. He guessed McPhee was reacting to the same thing. The sensors at the bottom of the shaft would all be crushed anyway, if Earthyield did what it appeared they were planning to do: drop the cylinders into the borehole.

The Earthyield crew rose in unison, brandishing arms. "Stay back from the shaft!" one of them shouted. The stricken man cradled his arm, where the Lycra was stained with blood. Flare pistols were unholstered. Two men drew revolvers. The Gurkhas made ugly faces. Passang held his hand up to stay them.

James could see the Gurkhas, champing like thoroughbreds, or maybe bulls, at the gate. He had to make a last attempt to curtail this madness. "Griffon!"

Griffon looked at him.

"Do you have it in you to rethink this? What you're about to do? I'm telling you as your mentor, as a peer, as a co-inhabitant of the planet. Jared, as a friend, for God's sake. *It's wrong.*"

"Not at all," answered Griffon. "It's c-456. A synthetic chemical. If it works— and we expect it will— it should arrest the event." Griffon lifted one of the cylinders, cradling it like an infant. "The *cure,* as I call c-456, is based on data from the Vancouver labs. Where you could have ended up, with the world's finest research capability at your fingertips." Griffon ran his hands over the skull-and-crossbones and looked up at James. "Think of it this way. The chemistries in these red cylinders will cause a reaction. What you label *amniotic fluids* will transition to inert. *Dead,* in a word." Griffon smiled. "I suspect I'd have the majority opinion on this one, Dr. Von Kamburg. Say, seven billion humans, give or take. You get that when you save the planet."

He turned to Mr. Grace. "Keep everyone away while we complete this." With a cursory glance over his shoulder at the Gurkhas, he added:

"Especially them." Mr. Grace deployed the Earthyield crew in a ring about the borehole.

"Boggin," said McPhee. He licked his tobacco-speckled fingers, then looked up at James. "What do you think, captain?"

James watched as the cylinders were primed. Each appeared to have a small explosive cap that would trigger when it hit the rock at the bottom of the shaft, releasing the mixture inside.

"We either stop them or get the hell out of these parts," said McPhee.

Frew stepped up to James, who could see his hands were trembling. "If Everest delivers we are going to die. If that stuff can prevent it we might live."

One of Griffon's crew poised the first cylinder over the borehole shaft. Griffon took the cylinder from the crewmember's grasp and tilted it towards the hole. He pulled the firing pin, shouting. "This is it, Doctor. The end of the Synthium water. The end of your big Earth baby. We both lose." He released the cylinder into the shaft. They heard the long scraping, a despairing, receding, echo as the c-456 plunged into the belly of the earth. "But I still win."

James looked behind him. His team waited for him to say the word. "There's a new Earth rising. If we don't act, it may die." He walked forward. "Come on."

The Gurkhas released the leather catches holding their sheathed steel and raised the blades skyward, and then promptly re-sheathed them. Passang had asked for *no slicing*. They moved forward, along with McPhee, Bateman, and Edwards.

"I don't know, Eddie," said Bateman.

"More than we bargained for," said Edwards.

"What are we supposed to believe? Or do?"

Frauz retreated to the green thickets behind. John Wayne be darned, he would skip the war. He dropped on his belly behind a boulder. Branches snapped and the brush was elbowed back. A sandaled heel landed, along with a colorful staff, next to his nose.

At the shaft the Earthyield crew stood ready, taking aim with flare guns. Two of them cocked revolvers. Spears and machetes twitched in the gauzy light.

James stopped, a spear tip brandished not far from his forehead. *Does one push it to the side, or go around, or under?* Female voices, from behind. Maggie– calling to him. Then, another female, strong, fervent, deliberate.

"O mani padre."

Like a lioness riding the wind, Maya charged. Her staff cocked above her shoulder, she plowed into the Earthyielders. The Gurkhas stormed in behind. James saw the Gurkhas land first blows, then he waded in. He felt incapable– and a fool– pacifist, academic, husband, poised to strike with intent to harm. In a sobering flash, the stupidity and logic of bloodshed blended. *Fight to live, live to die, die to live.*

Griffon was crouched at the borehole, his back turned as he prepped the next cylinder. James lowered his head and, leading with his shoulder, rammed straight into him. Griffon sprawled, the cylinder flying. He gaped at James, stunned, then coiled, groping for his holster. The gun came out, his arm swung up to aim. Maya's staff cracked. The revolver fell, hit the rim, and bounced into the shaft.

James rose and stood over him, hesitating. A moment too long. A blow across the back and he was on his knees. Someone with a spear behind him, wielding it like a baseball bat, swinging wildly. A bright flash, and a burst. A marking flare hit the tower's metal cross-bracing, splattering hot paint into the spear-wielder's eyes. He screamed and stumbled backwards, following Griffon's gun into the shaft.

Good God.

James crawled away from the smoke, gasping. Tracers lit up the steamy air; some maniac was trigger happy. He heard a sizzle, and a groan.

The Gurkha Kulbir, molten heat cooking in his chest, fell. More flares, trailing wakes of smoke, rocketed into the melee, electric torpedoes gone berserk. He felt a shudder and turned. The lithium-fission battery pack had been hit and exploded, spewing fragments and venting a lurid pink smoke. Had to be a strontium nitrate cartridge, James guessed. A highly compressed emergency flare that would burn long. The thick cloud boiled down over them, boring into eyes, searing lungs, and blotting friend from foe.

Christ.

James saw Maya, gagging, the reek invading her lungs. He saw Griffon hoist two more cylinders to the shaft's rim, a hand on each firing pin. The pins came free in Griffon's hands and both cylinders slipped into the borehole.

I have to stop him.

The pink cloud swirled. Griffon was retching, holding an arm over his face. A moment later, James saw him hoist two more cartridges, pull out the firing pins, and slip them into the borehole. James could hear Bateman, calling through the murk. "We gotta get back, Eddie. The bastards are using live ammo. Get down, man!"

Live ammo. Can't breathe.

If James didn't get fresh air, he would collapse. He crawled, gasping for breath, to the escarpment. A current of unsullied air wafted up from below. He gulped, trying to purge the nausea from his corpuscles.

"Jim!"

It was Maggie. He looked back, trying to see through the colored fog. There she was, crouched near the interferometer. Frew, also. Frew must have begged off. A pacifist first. Like James had been, a few minutes prior. Frew didn't want to stop Griffon from dropping the cure. Frew wanted to save the world. This world. *Can't blame him. Can't call him a traitor. Don't know what to call anybody.* A bullet whizzed by. James cringed again, flattening. He had to get to his wife.

Another appalling shudder– *boom*– followed by a yawning, horrible gag. A caustic reek rose from the shaft. A tearing screech followed. One–two–three–red cylinders scorched their way up and out of the shaft. They rocketed skyward, ricocheting out through the tower superstructure, leaving contrails of mist, water and mud. Griffon, stricken, stumbled back.

Maggie.

James took a deep breath, stood up, lowered his head, and ran as fast as he could towards the interferometer. *Can't see, can't breathe, can't leave Maggie in the middle of this by herself.* He saw her. And was suddenly down again, his mouth mashed against rock. Spencer had cuffed him across the face. "Asshole. You caused this mess." James looked up at the revolver in Spencer's hand. Spencer tottered, then steadied. "You can join my buddy Yates in hell."

A shuddering *boom*. The *pop* of the gun discharging. A gurgling *spludge* of sound. Spencer was up to his waist in a slosh of grey, the mud pooling around him. He lunged, and slipped further, the thick drool sliming up to his neck. James's hands felt like rubber, nerves not speaking to muscle, trying to unfasten his belt, to save the man who had just tried to kill him. The bullet must have missed. Spencer's face went white. He raised one arm and opened his palm, as if in supplication, and then he, and his arm, were gone.

In the swirl of fog and confusion, Maggie heard shots, cries, the thud of knuckles and the mountain's declarations, churning in the deep. Still acrid, the pink gauze was thinning.

Maggie looked at Frew. "We have to help."

Frew shook his head. "Bad dream."

She covered her mouth and darted into the haze. She found Maya, breathing hard, lying against the shaft casing. She pulled her up to sit. Maya coughed and spat, then rubbed at a welt on her cheek.

"Were you hit by the cylinders? When they came out of the shaft?" asked Maggie.

Maya shook her head.

"Can you stand?"

Maya grinned her grin. "I'm okay." Groggy, she stood, flexing her shoulders. They couldn't see Griffon. Maybe he'd fallen. Lying about the shaft base, several of the c-456 cylinders remained, untouched, their firing pins intact. Maya set her staff across them.

"Help me. Do this." She lifted a cylinder and bore it through the thinned smoke towards the escarpment lip. Maggie heard the echoing clang of metal, then the spittle of pressure released as it hit somewhere below.

James heard the cylinder fall, along with another sharper, rock-fracturing sound: fissures were opening. *God, you are making this tricky.* He stumbled forward, holding his bruised mouth, calling out. "Maggie!" There she was, near the shaft, hoisting a cylinder, ungainly with the load. "Maggie!"

James saw her body wrenched, jerked into the casing, head striking cement. Someone had pulled her down. Hot with rage, he leapt forward, and skidded to a halt. A gaping fissure now yawned between him and the shaft. There was Maya. He saw her staff rise and fall. He saw a man, doubled over, fending off her blows as he cowered against the shaft. *Griffon.*

Griffon lurched for one of the cylinders, yanked out the firing pin, and slammed it against the casing. The tank erupted, spitting into Maya's face. She dropped to her knees, slathered in the toxic spew.

"I'll kill you," said Griffon.

A rippling shudder knocked everyone to their knees. Maya, blinded, fell into Griffon's grasp. He clenched her wrists in a death grip. Convulsing, she thrashed against him, trying to break free.

A rising scrape, metal against cement, preceded the *whoosh* as another cylinder careered out of the shaft opening. It ricocheted off the tower's bracing and shot in a mad spiral into the knot of tethered yaks. The cylinder skittered past, fizzling as it tore out the slope's undergrowth.

Griffon hated the Nepalese creature he held in his grip. A hidden violence, the long-capped vessel of his pent-up pain, was cracking open. A demanding cruelty plunged like a sharp needle into his reason.

He forced Maya's head over the shaft, pinning it against the rim.

The rumbles, again. Deeper, *boom,* longer, *booom,* slower, *boooom,* from the foundations beneath. A cylinder, please, begged Griffon. Come on up and rip the head off this witch.

Booooooooom-kkkrack!

Accompanied by an ear-splitting, ground-shuddering heave, Griffon felt a profound physical displacement– as though his own body weight were suddenly annulled, as if the core solidity of mass underneath Mount Everest had broken, as if the very Earth would no longer hold them.

He covered his head, a din of destruction erupting all about him. Foliage fractured through the ground, rocketing, roots and all, up and over the mountain cliff. Geysers of water and steam vented. Those able to flattened and tucked, a last, desperate protection against the maelstrom at hand.

The tower platform sundered, the supporting slabs cracked, the assembly foundered. The cylinders near the shaft rolled away from the pit. The tower's superstructure moaned, bending and crumpling. Hydraulics and gears spilled forth in a shower of debris that pummeled and cut him. With a jarring hiss the tower collapsed. Metal twisted, snapped, and wound down in a chaotic drowning, he and Maya beneath.

Chapter Eighteen

Griffon opened his eyes. He grimaced, then made a token attempt to push away the tangle of twisted struts. Cut by shards, bleeding, his body was pinned beneath the bulky lattice of the collapsed tower wreckage. With a shallow breath, he faded back to unconsciousness.

James stumbled to the middle of the flat, where the smoking hulk of shattered steel formed a monument to their senseless clash. The borehole was barely visible, the landmass around it shunted into broken chunks and overturned earth.

"Please…" someone moaned.

Maggie lay near the wreckage, a dark smear matted inside the shine of her hair. James slid his arms under his wife and gently raised her. She opened her eyes and squeezed his forearm. "I'm all right," she whispered.

He gently set her head against his folded knee and pulled out his Swiss army knife. With it, he was able to cut a strip from his shirt sleeve. Brushing aside her hair to locate the wound, he wrapped the cloth around her head and tied it off. A lot of blood, and a blue bruise, but he couldn't see bone.

He took a moment to look around. Those able to, rose cautiously, stunned and shaken, testing limbs to confirm they were whole.

The ground under them trace-faulted. James knew the signs; the supporting bedrock was losing density. He heard no rumble. It was rather a bottoming out, like the last dip of a good roller coaster. It made his stomach flutter.

McPhee crouched beside them, nursing his own split lip with a finger massage. "We gotta be gone soon, Doctor," he said. "You felt that." He pointed. "You see these?"

More fissures had opened in the earth. And something else was happening. Steam vapor and flare smoke were crawling across the ground in long sinuous strands. The fumes drained, threaded by some impossible suction into the deeps. The Earth was inhaling.

Griffon stirred again. *I must be drifting in and out. Have to buck up.* With scant space to maneuver, he forced himself up on his elbows to look at the human lying nearby. It was a female. But her face was appalling, as if she'd been sprayed with acid. Through the bent, broken struts surrounding him he could see a thin man, standing nearby.

"Dr. Maya. Can you hear me?" asked the man. He was one of Von Kamburg's team. Looked like a hippie.

Maya stirred. Griffon moaned, then reached out feebly to touch the bars. And remembered where he was and what he had done. Where was Mr. Grace? *Mr. Grace needs to get busy. Get me the hell out of here.*

Without getting killed, Frew was trying to get a bead on the situation. He stood at the wreckage, wary of not keeping an eye on his own back. Another man, from the Earthyield side, walked to the wreckage, leaned over, and pulled at one of the black tower struts.

"The struts seem adhered to the soil," said the man. "We'll need manpower and any tools available to get these people out."

Frew nodded. "I'm Basil. Can we do this without getting shot?"

"I don't know. I'm Mr. Grace. I'll be back."

Frew watched as Mr. Grace approached members of the Earthyield contingent, who seemed as shell-shocked as he was. There were wounded on the ground, being treated. Standing, a small group gathered to hear what Mr. Grace had to say. Frew could also see the Gurkhas, and they didn't look ready for any truce. At least one of them was down, and Frew thought he heard a snarl from that direction. As he watched, though, Passang and Dawa moved among them. Hopefully, they'd at least move the confrontation back from the brink.

Mr. Grace returned, along with two others. All of them began tugging at the wreckage. Before long, more of those not injured joined in, from both Earthyield and the MEAD contingent. Grunts and moans, and frustrated cursing, replaced the sounds of a skirmish. There were humans trapped here, one from each team. *One minute we're animals, the next we're chums.* Not likely. Frew kept up his guard.

Maggie raised her head gingerly and ran her hands over the bandage around her scalp. She looked up at James. "Where's Maya?"

"She's under the collapsed tower. Jared too. It fell," he said.

She clutched at James's shirt. "Help her," she said, her voice faltering. "Help them…"

He stood. "Everyone," he shouted, "be careful. There are sinkholes forming. Watch your step." A few of the Earthyield crew sneered at his words. But at least there were no longer weapons being brandished.

James saw Mr. Grace and others working with Frew. McPhee was there now, also, with his crowbar. The stupidity of their confrontation remained. He hoped the harrowing tension could be dialed back. Damage done, though.

Frauz had stolen over to tell him there were fatalities, including– this a numbing shock– Ed Edwards, struck by a bullet. The Gurkha, Kulbir, also. Griffon's team had also lost men, Spencer among them. The uninjured Gurkhas brooded, hovering over their dead and wounded cousins. One of them tore open the front of his shirt and let out an ominous Nepalese roar. A second set his arm to the man's shoulder. James felt the ground rumble again.

Slapping its flanks to rouse some haste, Dawa and Passang maneuvered a reluctant yak towards the wreckage, then roped it to the imprisoning bars. As James watched, the yak strained and grunted, hooves sliding in the mire. The debris refused to budge.

From across the flat, a voice; Maya calling for Maggie. "Are you all right, memsahib?" James could see her, lying flat on her back, her head framed by a confusion of black metal.

"Maya," called Maggie, struggling to sit up. "Don't move. We'll get you out."

James rose and clambered to the wreckage. He joined those grabbing and pulling at the metal struts. His boots sank, his feet slipped, and he tried again. They were all doing the same thing with the same results. The crossbars creaked and warped. The strange pyramid of buckled metal seemed, if anything, to be doubling-down into a more strangulating cell.

James could see a dark red stain seeping through Maya's clothing, from her torso. A support brace might have impaled her. Her face was awash with a chemical burn. If she wasn't blind, it was a miracle. Frauz came over again, bringing a few meager medical supplies.

He spoke quietly. "All we have is this first aid kit."

James had no solace to offer. He looked around. Kulbir's body rested near the rear slope. As James watched, Passang reverently pulled a cloth over the deceased, then knelt to offer a Sherpa blessing. Three Earthyield bodies were nearby. James noted one of the Gurkhas bowing before the three bodies, honoring them in like fashion. *That's a thing to witness, considering.*

James looked around to see if he could find Bateman. He was slumped against the hill, cradling Edwards. James took a deep breath, and walked over. Bateman looked up, tears marking his red face.

"Came to see Mount Everest. Have a drink. Hike a peak. Now he's dead."

James knelt, and placed his hand softly on Edward's forehead. "Peace, Edward."

Bateman collapsed, sobbing, his shudders shaking the corpse of his friend. James backed away. Dawa appeared, and sat down next to Bateman. James saw the Sherpa gently place a hand on Edward's vest.

James hurried back to the wreckage, a cold dread spreading through his psyche. People had died– *Frew had been right about the risk*– and those still alive were in mortal danger. They had to get further away from Everest.

He saw Griffon shove with his shoulders, writhing vigorously. Some of the bars relented, and he had a little more space. He bent back a piece that had pinned his chest, and managed to free his upper body. He sat up. James clambered carefully over the tangle, able to get close.

"Jared, are you hurt?"

Griffon looked at him, then pushed against the wreckage with his heels.

"Can you reach Maya?" James asked. Griffon might be able to get direct pressure on Maya's wound.

"NO."

James began an awkward crawl, feeling like an uncoordinated kid on monkey bars. He called back to Frew. "Throw me something that will work as a compress!" James could see him hustling to find a dressing.

He strained desperately at the wreckage, and wondered again why it was so damned difficult to move. The soil had set up like fast-drying glue. The tower was big, but not gigantic; the cage around Griffon and Maya had dropped over them in a ragged heap. One moment the ground had been porous and spongy. The next, after the shockwave, it had solidified back into rock. But selectively, James would swear.

"Get a saw," Griffon ordered. "You need to saw through these bars."

Griffon was right, but no one had brought a saw. There was a softer murmur under them, the Earth once again recalibrating in the deeps. A strange, gradual ripple, emanating warmth, ceded from below, drifted across the drilling flat. The bars surrounding Griffon leaned; the trap was loosening. The rock immobilizing the struts was transitioning, again.

Balmy air wafted against his neck. *Wind.* The smoke of battle cleared, the fog scattered, and for the first time in many days, James could see daylight blue in the sky.

But then it happened again. A much more guttural rumble. The unnerving bellying-out that accompanies a trace fault. The ground they were standing on was not going to be any form of stable for much longer. To survive, they had to get the hell out of there. *Thruump.* Several thick-fronded boles burst from the fissures, glistening with moisture, flowering with blossoms, laden with fruits. The yaks had had enough. As one, they pulled the now weakly rooted trees loose, clearing their tethers, and stomped off over the slope. With a surprisingly soft splat, and pitiful last grunt, one of the yaks disappeared into a pool of rock-colored silt. James saw Dawa put both hands on top of his head.

Maya, in a voice now fragile and broken, rasped, "The Goddess Mother will wait no longer."

Somehow, Maggie heard, and called to Maya from where she rested. "We won't leave you, Maya."

Maya turned at the sound of Maggie's voice, and James saw her smile, through the burns and the pain.

"I will be honored as midwife to Chomolungma," she said.

James heard Griffon curse. He'd finally managed to get himself upright, standing. The bars were loosening, the ground giving way, but as he pushed, James saw how his feet slipped, unable to get any traction in the softened earth.

"God. Christ. Jesus." Griffon stopped. His body went slack, and he fell to his knees.

From the bluff overhang, a mix of stone, pulp, and uprooted plants fell, splattering across the flat. A light fixture and solar battery unhinged from the wreckage and fell in a shower of sparks.

"We can't wait any longer," said James. He clambered back to Maggie. Tears streamed down her face.

They heard Maya pray. *Oh revered Universe, grace them. Bless the children. Bring us peace.*

James wished he could at least have placed a cooling cloth over Maya's face. As he watched, she lowered her head. Her smile faded, and her breathing softened, her life energies winding down.

Again, the overhang slipped, sending forth a clay and putty slop that pelted the flat. A treacle of brown muck spread to reach Maya's legs. Griffon spat sludge from his mouth. The crew at work attempting to move the bars stepped back. It was futile.

James helped Maggie up, and they moved towards the lip of the flat, where Frauz joined him. "Everest is commencing into a final stage," said Frauz. "Leaving would be prudent."

James looked about him. Mr. Grace was mobilizing to get his own wounded moving. The Gurkhas were coming over, led by Passang. A hastily built rock gravesite served as a cairn for Edwards and Kulbir. Bateman knelt before it on one knee, rising when Frew and McPhee each placed a hand on his shoulder. The three moved across the flat to James.

Passang hurried to the wreckage. His heart fluttered. Here was Maya. He lowered his head. "Memsahib. I bow to the divine in you." He could see her briefly struggle to open her ruined eyelids. The creases of happiness and toil that had marked her skin were scars. *So beautiful a soul.* He turned away.

Mr. Grace approached the wreckage. He positioned himself so Griffon could see him.

"There's nothing we can do without additional help," he said.

Griffon's face was blank. "Get it."

"I will." Mr. Grace turned to his remaining crew. "Go."

* * *

Senator Charles Bennington didn't waste time worrying. He'd spend his emotional energy where it would serve. He went back to the thread that connected the current events in one telling conduit.

Some years prior to Nepal's recent, devastating earthquake, Xavier Frauz of the Bourn Institute had alerted them to what he termed "interesting" disturbances under the Himalayas. Frauz had labeled the disturbances *twitches*. And suggested that a more discerning eye might be kept on the area.

Monitoring of the Everest vector was taken up a level. Not long after, the twitches had translated into the earthquake. After the earthquake, the alert level was raised again. Bennington recalled the ensuing phone conversation with Frauz.

"Good morning, Charles. The twitches are twitching again. But in a different way," said Frauz.

Something more than tectonics was at work under the mountains. A suggestion by Frauz, supported by the Nepalese academic Tensing Spa, theorized that, beneath the planet's crust, climate change might be transmuting hydrocarbons. Interfering with the primary systems that supported life: there was evidence of a possible mutation of organic compounds.

Bennington knew Frauz was no alarmist. By the same token, he didn't want to instigate a worldwide panic– nor be party to a career-ending embarrassment if the new red-flagged *twitches* resolved as benign. Bennington and Spa would work under the radar. Under the guise of the joint New Zealand-Nepalese survey mission, led by John Bateman, the geological forces at work under Everest would get a more exacting examination. Even Bateman wasn't told the full scope of what his surveying, enhanced by Frauz's enigmatic modal interferometer, might yield.

In the last weeks, the situation had transformed. The strange water from the Khumbu. The Mohorovicic displacement. The Everest elevation anomaly. All lines converged at the summit of Everest. The Von Kamburg team was sent in to accelerate the mission, assist Bateman, and expose what the world might be facing. Von Kamburg had landed, and his team had reached the hotel, Bennington knew that much. From there communications had gone blank.

He had just hung up from a phone call with the USGS concerning an alarming confluence of fluctuating, erratic telemetry reads from the Khumbu region. Satellites, oceanic monitors, seismographs, and other sensors were flashing a cold red. Something big was, perhaps, about to breach the earth's crust.

He'd waited too long. It was time to call in the SWAT team. And past time to call the Secretary of State.

* * *

The surviving members of the Mount Everest Allied Discovery team, along with Dawa, Passang and their Gurkha companions, made their way down the mountain track. The injured limped, supported by those who could help. One of the Gurkhas, Thaman, had taken a blow and fallen unconscious near a smoking flare cartridge. Now he was breathing hard, rasping and faltering on his feet.

"Doctor!" Passang ran up to James. "Can we stop to make stretcher?"

James nodded and they halted. They'd come down from the drilling station flat the way Griffon's crew had come up. Through the thinned reedy haze they recognized the wide fields below, from where they should be able to spot the lodge, soon. Some of the terrain had shifted in the upheaval of buckling faults, but most was still recognizable. The watercourse they had passed in the morning still streamed off to their right, but it was muddied, and– James nudged Maggie so she would see– carried silvery pellets along in its brown froth. The climb down over the rock steps should be just ahead.

Passang and the Gurkhas tore up strips of their clothing and created a makeshift sling. Thaman would be seated in it and carried by two of his companions.

The Earthyield remnant was minutes behind. Mr. Grace stayed in the rear, urging the wounded stragglers forward. He didn't personally know any of the men who had survived. Yates and Spencer were dead. Griffon was near what would be the epicenter. In trouble. The odds of any of the rest of them reaching safety were negligible. There was nowhere practical he could consider. They'd make for the lodge. If Gault had returned with the vans and the roads were passable, they could shuttle to the airport. If the runway was still intact, it's possible some getaway might be mounted. By now, every seismograph in the world would be indicating.

He had told Jared Griffon they would return with help. He meant to honor the promise. The caveat was– and he hadn't had the inclination to tell a man in such a state– help would have to come from Kathmandu. He'd have to mobilize an effort with the Nepalese emergency rescue services. The Earthyield survivors had no working radios, no way to get the rescue effort underway until they could make direct contact. There was no guarantee helicopters could fly in and land near the borehole flats.

The Earth was heaving, and Jared Griffon was very close to the action. Time did not weigh to his advantage.

He looked behind to view the mountain. The high slopes of Everest were transforming before his eyes. It would be interesting to see. But not worth dying for.

The Gurkhas bore Thaman. To James, he looked like a tribal chieftain being carried on his throne, except his head was slumped on his chest. Fortunately, his breathing seemed less labored.

James led them down the rocky steps, the waterfall surging close by. The silver pellets glimmered in the cascade, knocking together in a cacophony that sounded like the bells of a muted wind chime. A strange soundtrack to a strange now, thought James.

Frew was just behind him and Maggie. James was grateful for his watchfulness; several times he'd assisted in catching Maggie as she stumbled or slipped. She wasn't weak, he thought, but neither was she strong. Mostly, she was silent.

The path traveled into a muddle of treacherous bogs that hadn't been here a few hours ago. More of the– *what did they call it in New Zealand after the earthquakes there–* liquefaction. *Soil liquefaction was a phenomenon where saturated soil substantially lost its strength, and stiffness, in response to an applied stress, usually earthquake shaking or some other, causing it to behave like a liquid.* Maybe his ability to think like a scientist was returning. He remembered most of the wiki description by heart. With a cold laugh, he wondered how long it would be until the wiki was updated to include "planet giving birth."

"Watch your step here," he called out.

They spread out, dividing and searching for the fastest way through.

"You hearing this?" asked McPhee, trotting up near James. James nodded. Not long after they had come off the drilling flats, the ground, or maybe the foliage, or both, had been trilling in a low-octave *thrum*, something like the Otter engines that had brought them in. Those aircraft, James was reminded, if they were still at Syangboche, could fly them to safety. Maybe not safety but at least *somewhere not here.*

"It's spooky," said McPhee. "In the bog it's louder, and getting louder by the minute."

Hearing McPhee, Maggie looked back at James. "We'll be okay."

McPhee glanced at her, looking as if he thought she'd clonked her head. She had, after all. But any intuition from his wife meant more, now, and James guessed it wasn't just an expression of hope. He took it, ironically, as a hopeful sign.

A small blessing that he'd noticed: the curiously rich-feeling air around Everest was easier on the throat. It seemed to nourish, hydrate and energize. When they'd paused, he noted how surprisingly un-winded everyone looked. In place of panting were deep expansive inhalations. He would swear the color in everyone's face improved with each breath.

Plus, the weather held clearer. That said, the sun's light seemed filtered. Something in the color was different. Most intriguing, there were– how to describe it– new colors for which the human eye had no prior experience as a receptor. At least James thought so. The scientist, James Von Kamburg, was waxing, despite all.

He helped Maggie out from what appeared to be the last stretch of bog. They moved forward over the rolling lea that would lead them back to the lodge, downhill. Because the terrain was no longer a trustworthy indicator of landmarks, they calibrated on the late afternoon sun for bearings. Heading south and west. The Everest Vista complex was still not in sight. James wondered if it had collapsed. Not likely, but what was on this day? Hopefully, the lodge had not succumbed to one of the seismic undulations that had rolled down off the mountain. Not that the lodge offered protection. Distance was vital. They needed to get as far away from Everest as possible.

Another loud rumble boomed from the depths, masking the buzzing thrum, and shaking their already rattled nerves.

"Keep moving, blokes. Bloke-esses. Keep moving," McPhee said, encouraging.

James looked back at Frew, behind his wife, keeping close watch on Maggie in her unsteady state. "Been a day," said James. Frew was solemn.

"If we didn't block what they were trying to do," said Frew, "the chemicals might have reached the batholith. Or the batholith risen into the chemicals– been cauterized by the *cure*. The reaction might have stopped the rising. Halted this cataclysm. How does it feel to know you may have signed Earth's death sentence?"

As suddenly as it had bloomed, James's brief spell of optimism dissolved. The down slope trek continued. With trepidation, James ventured a glance behind him. Everest filled the sky. She was white, along with a mélange of those new, never-before-seen colors, and gleaming like an upstart.

* * *

Griffon had taken a moment to iterate. That had been good policy in business. And life. Short list his options. He studied the woman who lay placidly nearby. Her eyelids were swelled and sealed. Her face a hideous vestige of what it had been. Somehow, despite the bleak set piece they shared, and the odd thrum vibrating up from below, her voice soothed him. He'd heard one or two subdued phrases. There was a peace in her he couldn't equate with her plight.

"Jared-ji. I pray for you."

So, she still breathed. He was sorry he'd had to do what he'd done. To be fair, after her feral onslaught he'd be surprised if his ribs were intact. Maybe he didn't regret it. What had pissed her off so much anyway? He was only trying to save the world.

Just then, Griffon noticed a different sound, a *twitchy* sound.

It got inside his head and reverberated. *Got to calm.* He concentrated, but couldn't wield a thought or memory to distract. The future was where he had to be. As always. *Live through this, get out, stay alive. Muster the energy to break the trap. I should at least say goodbye. She's a human being.* He worked to get closer to Maya. The black bars were so frustratingly inconsistent; now they seemed to give way, as if permitting him to reach her. He stretched out a hand and, with agonizing exertion, was able to touch her fingertips. Her eyelids unglued, flickered open. Milk-white retinas. Acid-blistered. Griffon swallowed.

She took a long, deep, last breath. Then went silent. The horrifying retinas pulsed, preying, prying. Looking through him. Griffon pulled his hand from her dead flesh and ran it across his jacket.

Another low rumble. And *twitches.* The noises had moved into his gut. The bore shaft was an echo chamber, sending up its plaintive truth serum from the deep. *You, Jared Griffon, are not long for this world.*

Have to get moving. The earth lurched. Two tree trunks burrowed up, pressuring the sunken base of the struts, forcing them from where they had been seated. Several sprang free, jimmied from the doughy soil, twanging away from him. The trap was weakened.

Rumble.

Excitedly, he pushed with renewed purpose, then screamed in pain. *Damn.* He must have broken ribs, or just snapped one.

Keep trying. Whatever energy remained in his body had to be poured into one final attempt. Gritting his teeth, he clawed his way out from under another brace. *Twitch.* Failure not an option. *Rumble.* Future needed him. Another strut came free. He contorted his frame to slide under what looked like the way out. Pain shuddered up his torso. Where she had cracked him with her staff. He felt a wave of nausea, spat, then pulled himself through the rectangular opening, shedding the steel. No more struts. Free.

He knelt and inspected himself, running his hands over his chest and head. And felt a tug. Something still held him. A torn edge of jagged metal snagged on his jacket. He slid his arms from his sleeves and pulled the jacket from his shoulders, then rolled away from the wreckage.

Twitch. CRACK.

His eardrums shattered. The ground beneath gave way. He saw Maya's body slip into the disintegrating borehole. He was lifted and catapulted.

Face first, he slammed into the churning ground, skin tearing and bones detaching. He lay still, a scourging static coursing through his system. He could barely move his head. But from where he lay, on unstable shifting soil, he could see Everest's summit. Steam poured out in great bulbous flourishes. From Everest's crown something materialized. His viewing perspective, from thousands of feet below, prevented him from getting an accurate sense of what was taking place. But geologically, Griffon knew, it was *wrong*.

Chapter Nineteen

US Senator Charles Bennington was on the phone with the Secretary of State when his assistant raced into the office.

"Hot phone from China, Senator," she said. "It's live. The Ambassador." The assistant lifted a hinged panel on his desk, revealing a white phone. She punched in a code and set the receiver on the desk.

"Mr. Secretary? I have an incoming White," said Bennington. He gestured for the assistant to leave his office. "Yes. Yes, certainly, Mr. Secretary." He hung up the black phone, and raised the white one to his ear.

"Senator Charles Bennington of the United States of America. Please state your name."

He listened as the Chinese Ambassador's voice was translated by a diplomat. The Chinese Air Force had scrambled a surveillance aircraft to fly over Mt. Everest.

"The Everest region is undergoing a geological event of unparalleled nature," the translator continued, after a pause, when the Ambassador had completed a sentence in Mandarin. "You have been contacted because of your special relationship with Beijing. Also because you are part of the office administering the MEAD mission, which is on-site in Nepal."

"Have you had communications with Me Ming? Have you spoken

with him, directly?" asked Bennington.

"We may have." There was some sort of stumbling hesitation at the other end. "Our flight crews will return from the flyover in the next fifteen minutes. We expect to receive a visual report from the crew, along with telemetry. These we will share. This does not appear to be a volcano."

"What does it appear to be?"

"We have not an idea. Its shockwaves are reverberating into the ground, water and air in a one thousand-kilometer radius."

Bennington reached for the bottle of Rescue Remedy he kept behind his copy of Jules Verne's *Lost World*. He opened the bottle and took a small swig. "What can we do?"

"Have you heard from Me Ming?"

"We have not heard from any member of the team since a day after they deployed," said Bennington. "However, we have been made aware through various agencies that the area is showing increased geological activity. A secondary team is being activated that will fly into Syangboche and assist. They deploy tomorrow." Bennington again heard some sort of group chatter. A different voice came over the line; a voice speaking English with a Chinese accent.

"Senator Bennington. My name is Zhang Jei Me. Me Ming, the Chinese member of the MEAD expedition, was able to relay reports to us from the Khumjung. He had been equipped with special technology. I regret he became somewhat un-diplomatic in sharing this ability, as events unfolded there. Not long after it became apparent that communications had become sporadic, we provided him the permission to let Dr. Von Kamburg send and receive messages, as long as the nature of the technology was not compromised. Me Ming insisted against that idea, for which we apologize."

Bennington knew the Chinese had been working on a smart, medium-range optical radio tech, code-named *Fangworm*. The Chinese would have been able to trial it with the Nepal-China borders in such proximity. *Von Kamburg will be more than ticked,* he thought.

"Unfortunately, our last transmission from Me Ming suggested he, himself, was perhaps under mental stress. We hope to question Dr. Von Kamburg in this matter, to be sure he was not singled out."

"We had background on Ming's professional predisposition," Bennington replied. "That said, I'm sure Ming's scientific credentials made him a worthy and welcome member of the team. I believe Dr. Von Kamburg had a veto to include or not include the candidates. He would not select individuals who might have compromised the mission." Bennington paused. "If Ming has had difficulties, I will ask you to reserve judgment till we get some hard data as to what is happening near Everest. I would want to talk to Dr. Von Kamburg."

"We stand by the selection of Dr. Von Kamburg as the appropriate person to lead the MEAD team. To get to the point, as there is urgency; Me Ming proclaimed the following. Allow me to read the transcript. *The world, through the womb of the mountain the West has crowned as Everest, will deliver a child.*"

Bennington had a flash. That it made a terrible kind of perfect sense.

"I wanted to forward the notion," said Zhang.

Bennington stared at the curtains in his office. He couldn't think what to say. But had to get off the line. Things were going to get hot in the world's situation rooms.

* * *

"I think I see it."

James stood on his toes, trying to verify he was looking at the lodge's banners, still fluttering like ship's masts above Griffon's shattered fiefdom. The low-riding sun was in his eyes. The thrum played in his skull. What looked like lodge flags might be, for all he knew at this point, flying eels.

The maddening thrum hiccupped. Probably not good.

The blast hit them.

A pounding, palpable wave blasted down the scarp, sending them keeling to the ground. Then unnervingly, up. They were partially weightless; gravity had lost its dependable grip. Feet rose above shoulders. Hands clutched at roots, plant tendrils, boulder's divots– anything that might anchor.

Great masses of grey slathered overhead, flung off the spindle of creation. The gale tore at them, flinging water, soil, and animals in a monstrous conflagration. It was a cauldron, a chopping, coursing, savage tunnel of wind, made up of all form of loosened matter.

"James…" Maggie cried out. James stretched over her, shielding and weighing her down, as well as he was able.

In horror, they watched as Frauz was lifted and carried off. The wounded Gurkha followed, spinning inside a wheel of detritus. He cracked against a boulder, bones and body a rag doll.

A greater blast struck. Behind, back the way they had come, they could see parking lot-sized pieces of glacier go airborne and burrow like great scythes into the landscape, striking just beyond where the drilling station must be. Behind and above that– even more inconceivable.

The roof of Everest had opened. The new planet born.

Mount Everest and the surrounding summits had undergone a tectonic reconstitution. They were now a single gargantuan mass. The soaring slopes that had made up several peaks of more than eight thousand meters had fused into a single, unfathomably monstrous tower of rock. Incalculably huge crushing agents, glaciers that had moved for eons under the great summits, were lifted and capsized. They spilled their contents in great roaring sheets, the frozen equivalent of pyroclastic eruptions, powering both air and boxcar-sized ice jags ahead of them in an unstoppable destructive swath.

Snow and ice flash-heated, melted, and followed the glaciers as liquid, an epochal flood to sweep clean the ruined world. But rather than submerge the land, the water was redirected, and sent another way, falling into dark, bottomless fractures that circled the vast stage of Everest's ongoing parturition.

Raising his shattered arms, Griffon covered his face, cowering under the shower of debris, burning in the steam and gasping against the blast of liquid air that pummeled and tore at him. Somehow, he had to watch, and twisted, wanting to know the face of the goddess mother. And found himself balanced between the curious, amazed scientist he'd been and the inconsolable, inflexible, money-power-fame operative whose ego had brought him here. How trite, he thought. Pay attention, said the scientist– putting a choke hold on the other fucker– I'm a one-man audience for the greatest show on Earth.

At the top, a portion of the hidden sphere showed, revolving in ponderous movement. Slowly– he saw with certainty– it was rising. In an exquisite abandonment that Griffon could not deny was miraculous, the uppermost portion of the sphere began shearing from the grey residue of its cocoon. Prodigious mounds of dough-like material were flung like shot put, missiles of gob launched in every direction and splattering as bombs where they fell.

Griffon considered.

It was siphoning something unseen out of the air. A conversion was occurring at the point of transition. Like a Petri dish photographed in stop-motion, the sphere's surface bloomed with streaks and splotches, then widening patches of a new color. How would he document it, if he were able? Like a bright pale black, shot through with green fire.

Dark matter. Had to be, thought Griffon. The sphere was drawing dark matter like a cosmic sponge. Layers were adhering. He could see it gaining mass. Getting bigger. As if some unseen giant were tossing transparent mud at a ball and, upon impact, the mud became opaque.

The new planet would grow in the same way, devouring dark matter, expanding exponentially, consuming this fundamental building block that coalesced over it and into it, generating mass from the space between the stars.

Griffon made a fist. And cried out. Even moving his fingers hurt. *Such a shame to die.* The Synthium market paled before the commercialization potential of dark matter.

A great *whomp-whomp-whomp* oscillated through Griffon's bleeding ears, breaking his muse. The sphere's rotation accelerated. The thing was serious. It was heading for the sky.

The New Earth reached an apogee, poised at a midpoint on its journey out of the mountain womb. The massive surface of the sphere was a sea, seething, incoming, incomprehensible, twenty kilometers across, ten kilometers of it towering above Everest's unrecognizable summit. The land swelled and lifted, an obliterating wall that crushed into the flats where Griffon lay. The tangled heap of the drilling tower was seized. A jagged strut hooked under Griffon's leg, as the hand of a parent might reach for their child's. He was dragged into the maelstrom and pulled upward into the great rising. A silent cry escaped him, the final awe-struck expression of Jared Griffon, as he was obliterated, lifeless, into the heavens.

The sphere disencumbered itself of mother Earth, its mass an unwavering bulk that gravity was powerless to staunch. It revolved and churned, a thundering cataclysmic engine that levitated through roiling steam and vapors. From its underbelly fell tonnage of rock, earth, and water, splashing down into the great, receding maw beneath.

The towering cone began to contract. There was a slackening and a solidifying as the prodigious opening receded. The land moaned and wailed in an agony of cross-purposed forces. Red-hot lava frothed, late to the party, spurting in spasms like monstrous strings of hot confetti.

The fresh, gleaming sphere, crackling and alive with the steady static of dark matter infusions, hung a thousand feet above Everest, balanced over the world. Separately, on the opposite side of the sky, the rising moon, stillborn child from some other eon, shimmered as a pale globe in the east.

* * *

James had a hand over his head and another across Maggie's back. Several miles in the direction they had come from, the sky was a new age version of the London blitz. Flaming spires of molten rock shot up into the fume of boiling vapors. The debris of up-ended glaciers cascaded down the immense bulk of the contracting prominence. Boulders and ice blocks spiraled end over end, colossal rolling pins that hit the Earth in shuddering thuds.

"Maya," Maggie said with pain in her voice. "Jared."

Yes, both somewhere back there. Where no one could survive. James held her.

His team had barely made it out. The danger from everything that had rocketed skyward, rocks, ice, lava, had been tempered by the conflicting forces. The mammoth "birthing" energy had suddenly been reconfigured by the pull of twin gravities, saving them from an immense, one-way wave of destruction. The flood of melt water he expected had not come. Something– luck, fate, the abbot's boss– was conferring a margin for survival. Very small, but very there. He hoped Mr. Grace's crew was not far behind.

The shock of the initial expulsion diminished. Long, steaming vapor trails bloomed upwards, the local atmosphere drawn to the rising sphere. Earth, rock, plants, and ice strained against the pull of the two gravities. Some were wrenched from the surface and drawn up to merge with the bright, coalescing body. A yak ascended belly up, docile as a lamb set for shearing. A butterfly, vainly fighting the pull, seemed to accept its fate and winged gracefully in a vanishing spiral towards its new home.

The team had thrashed for deep-rooted plants and, gripping them, managed to stay earthbound, a furious initial effort that had kept them from being pulled into the rising, reversed gravity. Both gravities tugged at them, even as the new planet's ascension was diminishing its effect. Still, James knew, unpredictable physics were in play.

"Stay alert!" he yelled, trying to be heard over the swirls, crackles, and crashes.

"Sir." It was Dawa, pointing at several ominous-looking shapes flip-flopping through the air, end over end. They were vehicles. As they watched, one of the shapes fluttered madly towards them: a troop carrier vehicle. James noted the Chinese military markings, red on green star, as it whirled wildly overhead, crashing into the brush beyond.

"Got to be kidding me," said Frew. "Look at them. Poor bastards are being sucked up like bugs in a vacuum cleaner." They watched as the remaining flotilla accelerated towards the sphere.

"Whew," said McPhee. "I don't think Ming had time to get to the north side of Everest. But he was spot on, anyway. The Red Army did show. Trucked them right to the mountain. They have an unsealed road all the way up to the base of the north ridge there, exactly opposite from where we're standing." McPhee managed a small grin. "Okay, *not* standing right now."

To James's reckoning, his team was at the edge of the pulling forces. Everest's summit was twenty-three or so kilometers from the drilling flat. They had put maybe three kilometers between them and the shaft. He prayed Frauz had landed somewhere soft, but didn't hold much hope for Thaman. The three Gurkhas had crawled forward to where he had hit the boulder with such force. More airborne detritus shuddered over them, or looped in great arches towards the ascending body.

"We're not out of this yet. Stay down!" hollered McPhee.

James crawled to Frew, root by root, yelling over the scree of noise.

"You believe this?"

Frew nodded. "Primal ooze, certified fresh."

"What?"

"If we get sucked up into that thing, that's what all of us will be," said Frew, turning away.

James blinked.

What if he'd got it all wrong? What if this was nothing but a scaled-up freak show, sanctioned in his dreams of an Eden-like new beginning for the polluted mother world? Maybe the thing would drop back down and crush. An extinction-level event and no History Channel left to fetch advertising revenue for recreating it. *God, what have I done?* Griffon had tried to prevent it. James had chosen to help secure it.

Accept. He wiped his eyes, smudging the wetness across his cheeks. Whatever else it was, the new planet was beautiful, and appeared to be growing as it ascended.

"It is as Maya foretold," said Passang, staring. More than Maya, James thought to himself. We are lush with soothsayers, all things considered.

The sphere rose inexorably. The forces at ground level were lessening. James thought he noticed a specific diminishment of the gravitational pull. Chunks of earth and wood fell in slowing arcs, plowing into the landscape and leaving in their wake great cloven furrows.

James reached inside Maggie's pack and withdrew a half-full bottle of water. *Everpure.* Where'd she steal this? He held it to Maggie's lips. She drank a great, gasping gulp. James took a sip, recapped the bottle, put it away, and whispered into her ear. "I think it's a girl."

She smiled weakly at him. A single teardrop rolled from her eye, slipped off her face, and spiraled upwards. He motioned to McPhee. "If we can get over this slope, we can get out of this open field; maybe a little more protection."

"Can't say anything will make much difference, considering. But misewell try," said McPhee.

"I'll tell Gaje, Sher, and Ganju," said Passang. He and Dawa headed forward. They could see the Gurkhas gathered a short way ahead, all looking skyward. Thaman's body must have come loose. It was drifting up, over their heads.

"Good God, this has got to end." James turned to McPhee. "Lodge can't be far. Gotta get somewhere that has a roof." James looked back at Maggie, Frew and Bateman. "Let's go find Frauz."

Particulate continued to skim the air like paintball pellets. Crouching low, with a cordon of hands supporting Maggie, they scurried forward.

"Xavier!"

Their cries echoed out, breaking against the surrounding foothills.

"Frauz!"

They rounded a bend and heard a voice.

"Seems unfair." It was Frauz, puffing on his lit pipe, his back to a grey, sludgy wall of rock. Frauz took the pipe from his mouth and pointed it at the sphere. "It's turned its back on major aspects of our physical laws. Do you realize how many printed manuals are going to be obsolete? As if we need more trees felled for books. Though I prefer books over computers."

"Xavier. You are quite alive," said James, patting him on the shoulder.

"And imagine the tides, with the moon and a new planet competing to influence the oceans. Good gracious me," said Frauz.

With an untoward gust, more debris blew by them, both harmless fragments and one or two potentially lethal tree branches. Based on the amount and speed of the material coming their way, though, things seemed to be calming. At least James hoped.

"Are you sure you're okay?" asked James. "You looked like the flying nun."

"I'm rather sore," Frauz said. "I believe I can move at speed, considering." He again held his pipe up towards the sphere, suspended as an impossible bauble in the heavens. "A dense core with reverse polarity, is my guess."

"An opposing polarity to repel Earth's gravity. There's no such physics, Xavier," said Frew.

"There is up there."

"What about dark matter?" said Bateman. "I've been shaking my head and dark matter, dark energies are filling in some of the blank."

"What you might be saying is we don't know what the bleep is going on, so why not dark matter?" said McPhee.

Bateman grinned. "I might be, mate. I might be."

McPhee put a hand on Bateman's shoulder. "Then again, Bateman's Bodacious Theorem might be your legacy."

A small boar sailed overhead and crashed into a boggy pit on the far side of them. The boar rose, shook itself like a wet dog, and proceeded to clamber out of the slough and shuffle off. The Gurkhas, along with Dawa and Passang, were coming up the trail behind.

"Let's go," said James.

"One more thing," said Frauz, not yet standing. "I'm stuck to this rock."

Frew and McPhee managed to laugh. They reached behind Frauz and, with a combination of tearing and separating, detached Frauz's jacket from the grey slab. Frauz brushed himself off. "The rock was like a pillow, soft on impact, and then solidified as I sat, recovering. Used to be plate tectonics took several generations to effect this kind of adhesion. Now it takes minutes. My jacket remnants will become a most precious specimen, I suppose."

At last, they spotted the Everest Vista. It appeared intact, at least from this distance. They reached a shallow gully that Passang insisted would intersect the lodge access road. The Gurkhas and Sherpas headed with vigor down the gully. James hoped some of the Gurkhas' rage had dissipated by now. He didn't know what to say to them, how to honor their deeds and sacrifice. Another thing to do later, if later still came.

Frew looked over at James. "It's been a trip. Thanks for inviting me."

"You still want to work with the guy?" said Maggie. She had improved, James was glad to see. The less volatile environment. The rejuvenating air. The water. The damned, beautiful water.

"At least we're alive, for now. And you got your baby," said Frew. They looked back towards Everest.

"Still pulling at things. Gathering up the flotsam and jetsam of the universe," James said. The gravity of the new sphere was definitely scaling down. Finer, loose material around them swirled, more like a light breeze. They could feel the weight of their own mass reestablishing.

"It's crying and it's hungry," said McPhee.

"This is going to sound somewhat inappropriate and I don't mean disrespect," said Frauz. "But I want to make an observation. It's got human DNA to work with. Foliage and fauna from mother Earth. Certainly will have mechanisms we can't guess, such as John's suggestion that dark matter is involved."

"What are you saying?" asked Bateman.

"I'm not exactly sure. Perhaps that this strange new world will combine the ancient with the novel and move us along the evolutionary ladder, so to speak."

"You're a bit ahead of schedule, Xavier. There are little things we might do first, such as survive," said Frew.

"That's a salient point," said Frauz.

"Looks like the stuff they dropped in the shaft had no effect," said McPhee. "Either the reaction was too slow, or there wasn't enough, or it didn't work."

"That's a hard one," said James. "May be repercussions below, or up there. I hope not."

"We'll have to trust Mother Nature will figure it out," said Maggie. She put a hand on James's sleeve and lowered herself to lean against the gully wall. "Let me sit for one minute."

"Sure." For the first time in a long time, James was able to notice the time. It was late afternoon, the long day waning. He had a sense that the unnatural warmth of the past weeks was already retreating. Clouds that looked like clouds scudded over them. Maybe there could be a normal somewhere still, yet. He leaned against the dirt wall next to his wife and closed his eyes. From his jacket pocket he brought out the now-crumpled note she had written, and nudged her. "Thanks for this."

She smiled. He squeezed her hand and leaned his head back against the turf.

The New Earth, the great marvelous sphere rising up and away from them in the northeast, was not a place the entire world's population could reach if mother earth continued its decline. He didn't know if anything could be claimed as a gain. The advance of science, maybe. Insight into dark matter.

He was sure there were casualties. The Chinese detachment on the north side. Whoever had been there would have been caught up or crushed inside the collapsing valleys. Surviving that, they'd have been gutted inside those glacier detonations.

Mr. Grace and the rest of Griffon's team hadn't been far behind them. James hoped, and would bet based on his short experience around the enigmatic subordinate, that Mr. Grace had survived, along with those he led.

Less comforting was the thought of the nearby indigenous Nepalese. There were villages up and down the canyons in every direction. It was possible Namche was rubble, or buried. And it might be even worse. The seminal tectonic reverberations would have sent shock waves into the Earth's existing fault lines. The ring of fire become a ring of doom.

Something told him to keep his cool. Does the mother die when the baby is born? She suffers and she heals. It's not actually healing, to be technical. It's a return to the health that enabled the reproduction, gestation and birth. He'd have to trust that model would be proven here.

If the human model held. No reason it should. No reason it shouldn't.

Maybe he'd never left the abbot and was about to wake from an incense-induced fever dream, with a nasty bump on the head. But, he thought, *this* counted: there was a sentience in the universe beyond what he had guessed. If this was the Earth's child, if it was a renewed, pure beginning of life that could evolve beyond the missteps made by its current guests, and if the code that triggered this gestation had been in place through time, there was a hope beyond hope. *Accept,* Professor.

Frauz and Bateman were moving down the gully towards the lodge road. James helped Maggie to her feet. Her green eyes sparkled in reflection, as if each jade iris and each black cornea were glimpsing– *white stars.*

James turned into the wind and faced west, where the skies still shimmered in blue. Nothing. He looked back into Maggie's eyes, holding her face tenderly.

"What…?" she said.

They were there. Reflected. White dots, stationary, aligning in rows, symmetrically spaced, perpendicular and parallel, three, five, seven. Another heartbeat. With each blink of her beautiful eyes, they faded, and were gone. She smiled luminously.

"I'll tell you later," he said, and kissed her. The lightest of rains began to fall.

* * *

Abbot Gaia and his monks assembled in the courtyard. They had watched the events on the horizon and in the sky. The air had stirred in concert with the epochal proceedings. Many of the monastery's prayer flags had been torn loose. They fluttered down into the courtyard like a twilight snowfall, confetti of the loosed spirit. One or two came to rest in the pool beneath the fountain, where the spring water flowed in sputters, from trickle to gush, by turns opaque with mud or translucent aqua.

A few of the monks remained on the ground, prostrate, hands covering their heads. Red Scarf knelt. Gaia stood, his eyes serene. From underneath a fold of his robe, he retrieved a medium-size cigar. He struck a match and lit it, inhaling a long sumptuous drag.

"Happy birthday," he murmured.

Eugene, Oregon
11 months later

The painting, an abstract, rested on the easel. It was a colorful acrylic that vaguely resembled a rabbit leaping over snow-capped mountains with two moons in the sky behind. One moon, actually. The other wasn't a moon.

James Von Kamburg sat at his desk, talking on the phone to his associate and research partner, the newly installed Dean of the Geophysics and Earth Sciences Department, Basil Frew. A single aluminum pellet rested on the desktop. James studied it as he conversed.

"The water in the monastery is normal," said James. "The Earthyield reserves in Vancouver are almost gone. They can't nail the chemistry. Looks like that's not going to happen 'ever', according to their lead guy, Crispin Virgil. He's got a funny bone like you."

"Funny, I don't have a funny bone," said Frew.

"When do you leave again for Nepal?" James spun the pellet like a top, catching it before it spiraled off the edge of his desk.

"Three weeks. Stopping in New Zealand to see the Kiwi Bateman. See if I can talk him into another modal adventure."

"Have a safe trip, Basil."

"I will. Best to the triad and Maggie. How are they?"

"They're all doing fine, thanks. I'll be in touch. So long."

"Be well. Namaste."

James hung up the phone. He put the pellet down and walked out of the room. The pellet swayed, settled, and ceased moving.

He entered the nursery. A soft, early morning light streamed in through thin, breezy curtains. Maggie lay asleep in her nightgown, on the soft couch they had purchased for middle-of-the-night feedings. In three separate cribs were the sleeping triplets. Girl, boy, girl. A stuffed rabbit guarded each crib. The boy began to stir. James lifted the baby, brought him to his shoulder, and walked gently to the window.

The fine glow of dawn lit his face. He drew the curtain back and looked out.

The horizon was splashed with purple, orange and pink. A cold full moon shone in the sky to the north. In the southeast, smaller to the naked eye, rose a golden blue-green sphere, a faint trail of celestial vapor still evident in the multi-colored skies beneath.

*

* * *

* * * * *

* * * * * * *

Acknowledgments

Many thanks are due to many people, not all of whom will appear
here by name, but who show up in my work as they have shown up
in my life. My gratitude to each of you, along with those noted below;
an extended, exceptional, idiosyncratic cadre of friends and family
whose lives I've been blessed to fortuitously share.

For encouraging me on the creative road, down through time,
Mom and Dad, brothers and sisters. For bringing the untameable
imagination of children into the living room, Luke and Rebecca.

For several decades of spousal-inflicted involvement in a plethora
of her husband's 'works of art', Louetta Heindl Kambic. You are missed.

For your own inspiring creativity, as part of a mutual project or
otherwise: Jeff Lucas, Dan Mulholland, Ken Gormley, Matt Kennedy,
Don Maue, Jim McCool, Brian Parker, Dan Yazvac, Pete Niederberger,
Kevin Kambic, Mary Ellen Snyder, and Lizzy Cunnane.

For ongoing appreciation and shared enjoyment of the realms,
Sam Rossi and Tim Joyce. For scientific advisement, George Kambic,
and Jim (von) Kilburg. For reviewing early drafts, Ray Diroll, Bernie Kulifay,
Bev (von) Kilburg, Bob Smith, and Erin Friez.

For an expeditious review of the legalities of publishing,
Mike Grayson. For timely feedback over the home stretch, Murray Annals,
Clare Corban-Banks, Anne Kingsbury, and John Harper.

For sharing a wealth of proficiencies and transforming my writer's
journey– my initial publisher, Amy Rogers.

For your intuitive, steadfast endurance of many drafts and uncountable
amendments enroute to something the rest of the world might enjoy, and
with love and appreciation for your companionship and grace through
the tumult and wonder of any given day, Alison.

Matt Kambic

Matt Kambic hails originally from Pittsburgh, Pennsylvania.
He currently resides in the seaside town of Raglan, New Zealand.

Matt has served as a writer, art director, content developer and producer for a
portfolio of commercial and academic clients. His work has been featured on television,
in Disney games, and inside museums. He has done work for Duquesne University,
The National Robotics Engineering Center, Kennywood Amusement Park,
The National Scenic Visitors Center, Pittsburgh Filmmakers, and many more.

Along with his writing, he is an accomplished illustrator, ardent filmmaker,
aspiring playwright and occasional musician.

Everest Rising is Matt's first book. He has since helped illustrate or
write several more, and is currently working on a stage play and short film.
Matt is Co-Founder of Chalk Hill Publishing, along with his spouse, Alison Annals.

Find out more about Matt at **www.mdkambic.com**.

Everest Rising

Designed and engineered by
kambicreative & Unified Field Productions
www.mdkambic.com

Also written by Matt Kambic
The Sherpa & the Beekeeper ~ Summit on Everest
Last Voyage of the S.S. Panglossian
(with Matthew Kennedy)

Also illustrated by Matt Kambic
The Walking Stick's Story
(written by Alison Annals)
Letter to a Weta
(written by Lee Kimber)